To Hayley

JASPER

(For the love of Jane book 2)

GRACE WILLIAMS

The smut continues

With love

x Grace Williams

x x x

Jasper

ISBN: 9798680205884

Copyright 2019

Cover design Grace Williams

First Edition

Disclaimer

This is a work of fiction. Names characters, places and incidents either are the product of the author's imagination or are used fictitiously, and are no resemblance to actual persons, living or dead business establishments, events or locales is entirely coincidental.

Please be aware there are upsetting parts to this book.

Contents

Dedication

Acknowledgements

Play list

Chapter 1   Taken

Chapter 2   Searching for you

Chapter 3   The past comes back to haunt you

Chapter 4   I failed you

Chapter 5   You won't break me

Chapter 6   All coming together

Chapter 7   Say goodbye

Chapter 8   Holding back

Chapter 9   I knew it

Chapter 10   Take me to my happy place

Chapter 11   I will find you for her

Chapter 12   I cant do this anymore

Chapter 13   Got you

Chapter 14   Revenge is sweet

Chapter 15   Belle

Chapter 16   Don't take my hand darling

Chapter 17   Its up to her now

Chapter 18   The long wait

Chapter 19   Come back to me

Chapter 20   Healing Time

Chapter 21   21 homecoming preparations

Chapter 22   Coming together

Chapter 23   Time to let your hair down

Chapter 24   Girls night

Chapter 25   Getting ready

Chapter 26   Going home

Chapter 27   Settling back in

Chapter 28   A new beginning

Chapter 29   Time to relax

Chapter 30   Time for fun

Chapter 31   Planning a new beginning

Chapter 32   The kindness of new friends

Chapter 33   My best friend

About

Links

THANK YOU

Dedication

For my wonderful Mum and Dad, you made me who I am.
Miss you both so very much. Always your little girl x

Acknowledgements

To my wonderful beta readers, your support and suggestions make these books special.

To my readers, thank you for wanting more, for your feedback and ongoing support. I hope you enjoy this as much as Jane and continue on the journey with Moses too.

To my beautiful Sister, Thank you, for letting me bounce ideas off you, for listening to me waffle and putting up with me.

Thank you to that special person who helped to make it work, for your ongoing support and help.

Love you all. G.xxx

Play list

I'd come for you – Nickleback

Dance with my Father – Luther Vandross

Music to my eyes – Lady Ga Ga

Let's get it on – Marvin Gaye

Heaven – Kane Brown

All to myself – Dan and Shay

Chapter 1

Taken

Listen to I'd come for you by Nickleback

Jasper woke with a pounding headache, he was holding the side of his head, he was confused as hell. He squinted opening his eyes, trying to focus and work out what time it was and what the hell had happened.

The last thing he remembered was kissing Jane and seeing her face change from love to fear. He rubbed his head as he sat up groaning, he was stiff as hell probably due to the way he had landed.

He moved his hand away from his head and looked at it, his hand was covered in dry blood, he looked at the floor, more blood, he got up feeling like his head was going to explode and went to the bathroom, he pulled the light on, looked in the mirror, the side of his face was covered in blood, his hair was matted against his head.

He started coming round properly and then realised he hadn't seen Jane. He rushed back into the bedroom.

"Belle, Belle, where are you? Fuck that hurts." He held his head the pain ripping through him.

He dashed around the house in and out of the rooms looking in cupboards and behind doors. He shouted again.

"Belle, Belle, please darling, where are you?"

He started feeling sick, he was growing more concerned and very confused. He sat down on the bed, trying to calm his breathing and think properly. He started talking to himself.

"Breath Jasper, come on, slow your breathing down, deep breath in, slowly out……. you're no good to anyone if you panic." His breathing came back under control.

"Okay think, lets retrace our steps."

His memory began to clear, he went back to the door that led to the garage, he pulled it open, her trike was still there.

"Hang on" he dashes over to the garage door.

"It wasn't locked." He held his head with both hands trying to remember.

"Fuck, fuck, fuck, come on head clear for fucks sake I need to think straight."

He started to think back to the early hours when they got home. "Belle reversed in, I picked her up and carried her over the threshold, I was about to close the garage door, I didn't lock it, Shit!, I didn't fucking lock it!!, I came in with Belle in my arms and kicked the door closed, he looked around at the door, it didn't shut! I carried her into the bedroom. Did I kick the door hard enough for it to close?"

He remembered her face again, that fear in her eyes like she was about to say something.

"I didn't turn why the fuck didn't I turn?"

He fell to his knees in the bedroom holding his head with both hands. He screamed, a deep, painful scream it came from deep in his heart.

"Beeeelleeee……."

He screamed her name as loud as he could and hung onto the end of it like he couldn't stop saying it. He sat there for a moment holding his head.

"I need to find her, Belle I'm coming for you, I will find you Belle, tell me where you are baby, I'm listening. I promised you I would protect you, I said I'd come for you Belle not matter what. Don't give up baby please."

He got up off the floor, fishing into his jeans to find his phone. No missed calls, he rang Jane's phone, it began to ring in the bedroom, he searched around for it, it was on the floor just under the bed.

It had fallen out of her bag.

"I need help", he put Jane's phone down and scrolled through his to find Moses, he dialled and waited. He didn't even know what time it was, but he didn't care, Belle was gone.

Chapter 2

Searching for you

The phone was ringing. He was trying to hold himself together. It rang twice. Jasper didn't even know what time it was.

"Jay, brother what's up. Is it Jane?"

Jasper took a deep breath trying to control himself. He ran his fingers through his hair and down over his face.

"She's gone Moses. She's been taken." His voice broke into a choke.

"What the fuck are you talking about Brother?" Moses shouted, slowly throwing the bed clothes off and jumping out of bed.

"Jasper, fucking tell me man." He ran into the next room. "G wake up its Jane, wake the others." He ran back to his room, dragging his Jean's on and pushing his feet into his boots.

"We got home, I carried her to the bedroom, I saw fear on her face next thing I'm waking up with a head injury and she's gone." He held his head again.

"Fuck, fuck, fuck. Don't do anything don't touch a fucking thing. We're on our way." He shouted hanging up.

He threw his phone onto the bed put his head in his hands screaming at the top of his voice.

"Noooooooo, you were supposed to be fucking safe here Jane. Where the fuck are you?" He covered his face. "No, no this is just a bad dream. Please someone wake me up. Not my girl."

G came running in pushing his arms through his t-shirt.

"What the fuck is going on Brother?"

Moses took his hands from his face. "Are the others up? Get ready were going to Jaspers. Jane has gone she's been taken. He's hurt, knows nothing."

G ran out of the bedroom shouting at the others to get their boots on. He hammered on the other apartment door. "Hurry up were moving in 2."

They grabbed their keys, jackets and helmets and ran out of the door. They were on their bikes and away in minutes. It was 4am so no traffic to worry about. 10 minutes later they arrived at Jaspers, they pulled into the drive and ran to the door. Jasper pulled the door open when he heard them arrive. He was ashen, he stood back to let them in.

"Start from the beginning Brother." Moses asked, putting his hand on Jaspers shoulder.

Jasper took a deep breath, ran his hand through his hair and began talking, he explained everything he remembered and what he had found when he woke up. Gwen stepped forward and hugged him.

"We will find her Jasper."

He held onto her tight. Looking down at her "She's my world Gwen. I was supposed to keep her safe. I should have locked the door instead of carrying her to the bedroom."

"This is not your fault love. Come on, show me to the kitchen I need to clean your head up."

"It's fine Gwen honest." He said putting his hand up to the blood-soaked wound on the back of his head."

"Don't argue with her Brother." Matt said putting his hand on his back "That's a pretty big cut you have there."

Jasper nodded "Okay. I haven't called the Police yet. But I suppose we better."

"No." Moses growled. "We will sort this ourselves."

Gwen followed Jasper to the kitchen everyone followed, he grabbed the first aid kit out of the cupboard and passed it to Gwen, she started to clean Jaspers head, every time she touched him he winced and pulled away.

"I'm sorry Jasper, there is a lot of dry blood, we might need to get you seen by a Doctor. I'm not sure how deep this goes."

Jasper sat quiet, just nodding. "It's okay Gwen, just patch me up, I'm not going anywhere unless it's to find Belle."
Gwen smiled sadly. She put her hand on his shoulder. "We will find her love."

Moses was walking around the kitchen on the phone. "Shadow it's me, yeah I know it's early, we have a problem, Jane has been taken, yeah we think it's him. We need your help Brother, anyone you can call on, we need CCTV checking on site, at your place and any homes around Jaspers, we're looking for any vehicle that has stopped for a long period, yeah he would have played the waiting game. No, I am sure it's him. He wouldn't let anyone else do it for him and nobody else has a reason to take her. Okay, see you soon, thanks Brother." he hung up, wiped his hand down his face and sighed deeply. He looked over at Jasper. "How's the head J?"

"It's fine, what can I do? we have to find her Moses, tell me about this arse, what is he really capable of?"
Moses sat at the island on one of the high stools and put his head in his hands.
"I won't lie to you, the guy is pure evil. He wants her dead. He has been biding his time, he will play the long game, he will make her suffer, she is stronger now than she was back then, G worked with her for a long time, she can defend herself if she has the chance, but he's a big arse motherfucker."
Jasper felt his heart sink, "So what do we do now?"
"Shadow is on his way, he is going to make a few calls and get a few of the guys together that could help us. Do you know if any of your neighbours have CCTV?"
"I don't, but I am prepared to knock on every door and ask, he looked around at the clock on the wall, it's was now just after 6am. Too early at the moment I suppose?."

Gwen cleared up the last of Jaspers head putting some steristrips on it to hold it together until they could get him seen to. Jasper got off the chair, kissed Gwen on the cheek and walked to the bedroom. He pulled his t-shirt off, it was covered in blood, he screwed it up into a ball pulling into his nose inhaling Jane's scent, he choked on his tears again, looking up to the ceiling.

"Hang on Belle please baby." he whispered.

He threw the t-shirt into the washing basket and grabbed a clean one out of the drawer, he pulled it on and headed back to the kitchen. He heard more bikes pulling up on the driveway. He went to the front door as G opened it. Shadow, James and Animal walked in. They hugged him and G and followed them into the kitchen. Gwen and Linda were busy making drinks and finding their way around the kitchen. Moses got up as the guys came in and they hugged each other.

James spoke first "Jasper, I need you to tell me everything you remember. Every detail is important, can you show me where you think she was taken and how?"

Jasper wiped his face with both hands, sighing heavily, he moved towards the garage, everyone followed.

"We got home, Belle parked the trike." he said pointing at it, as she went to walk into the house, I stopped her, I was in the process of locking the garage door down. I told her to wait, scooped her into my arms to carry her over the threshold. I remember kicking the door with my foot to close it, but I don't think I did it hard enough. I took her to the bedroom laid her on the bed, I bent over her, about to kiss her, then I saw her face change from happy to fear, she didn't have a chance to say anything, all I remember then is waking up."

James stood looking around as they walked back into the house looking at the floor and walls in case anything showed up or he found a trace of anything.

"Thanks Brother. Can I set up my laptop somewhere?"

"Sure, anywhere you like, there are electric points next to the table or my office?" Jasper pointed to the door.

"I will use your office; I need to make some calls and could do with quiet while I am looking."

"Whatever you say James, just tell me what you need."

"Thanks J, coffee and plenty of it." He said walking towards the office.

"Coming up." Gwen shouted

James made some calls to friends, he couldn't do it while others were listening, he could only tell them so much. He got into the city cameras and knew what time they had got home and that gave him a good idea of when Jane was taken. That time of the morning there wasn't much around on the road either. He scanned the cameras, nothing jumped out at him, so he went back a bit further to see if anyone had followed them.

He sighed and ran his hand through his hair, Gwen came in with another coffee, he looked up.

"Thanks Gwen, that's really kind."

"You're welcome, anything yet?"

He shook his head, "nothing, it's early days. I'm viewing cameras at the moment so changing the times slightly, I'm sure something will come up."

"If you need anything James please shout."

"Thanks Gwen I will."

Jasper was waiting for Gwen when she got back to the kitchen. "Hey Gwen, I know the guys must be getting hungry, would you mind giving me a hand, we have all the food anyway for today I don't want it to go to waste and Belle would go nuts if we didn't eat."

Gwen nodded, touching him on the arm. "Of course, I will, you know her well don't you?"

He nodded, "does it sound stupid to say I feel like I have known her for years? It's like my heart has always been waiting for her?"

Gwen smiled properly, "No, love it doesn't at all, it shows how much you love her and you both deserve to have found each other." She touched Jasper on the back as she moved around the kitchen. "She's stronger now, she wouldn't have told us all the truth if she wasn't, I think she was expecting this for the last

10 years, mentally she is prepared and she had been training with G for a long time. She will fight for her life now, she has you to fight for. She had nothing before. Or so she thought."

Jasper put his arm on Gwen's shoulder and hugged her into him kissing her head.

"Thank you Gwen, I needed to hear that. You really all think it's him, don't you?"

"Yes, we do, who else would take her? She has only ever helped others and apart from the guys on site and those she has met from the Skulls here she doesn't know anyone else."

"That's true, I better call Graham and Chicca they will want to know too."

"I'm sure Chicca knows by now and she will be here soon, go and call Graham the more of us that know the better, someone may know something they don't even know is important. In fact, I will see if G has called home. I will grab Jax she can help me prepare the food, go and see the guys, you are more help to them than to me."

Jasper laughed, "thanks Gwen, you know how to make a man feel useless." She laughed.

"Point taken though, I will call Graham." they both walked back to the lounge.

"Jax can I borrow you please?"

She looked up. "Sure Gwen, I could use the distraction." They walked into the kitchen.

"Jasper has all the food they brought yesterday and wants us to feed everyone."

"Great, tell me what you need me to do."

"Well there are steaks here so we could grill them off slice them and put them into the brioche rolls with salad leaves?"

"Good idea, I will start the steaks."

"Thank you Jax."

"Do you think it his him Gwen?"

She nodded. "Now I know the truth yes, I am certain. I never liked the guy he gave me the creeps, but how did he find out she was here. He doesn't come to the club and nobody would talk to him if he did anyway?"

"All very strange." Jax replied getting the steaks ready to cook.

"You okay their Lin?" Gwen asked. Linda was washing up and making coffee for the guys.

"I'm good, just keep telling me what you want."

"Will do."

Chapter 3

The past comes back to haunt you

Jane woke up and tried to talk, she could taste blood in her mouth, she needed a drink. She went to move her hand to wipe her mouth, but it was stuck, she looked down and saw she was taped to a chair. She put her tongue out to lick her lips, she was gagged too. She tried to move her hands again trying to get the tape to move, nothing, she looked down in the dark she could make out her legs she pushed hard again but nothing, she bent forward her heart pounding hard, trying to reach her face but her hands were too far away to reach. She screamed as hard as she could but all that came out was a mumble, her mouth was taped to well. She started to move frantically in her chair, screaming and pulling she was like a crazed animal that had been caught. The chair was moving slightly she needed to be careful or she would topple backwards. She tried to focus and look around the room. It looked like a bedroom; it didn't smell so great either. She could make out the bed and a cupboard. The curtains were heavy and blocked out any light. Next to her was a bucket. Her heart was pounding, he wasn't here, he must be around somewhere, she knew he wouldn't be far away.

"Jasper." she screamed, "Please baby, I love you so much, please look for me, tell Moses. Please, please, please if you love me please don't let him win."
All that was heard was a mumble. She started to sob hard. She knew what Mark was capable of, when he was mad, she would really suffer. He must have been watching her, but for how long? Why hadn't she sensed him?
"Did he see Jasper propose? Oh god, what if he did, that will just anger him more. I have to get out of here." Jane became frantic again, "I won't let you do this to me again, you won't win, I'm

stronger now, you will see!" She grew angry. Just how G had showed her to do in the gym.

She heard noises coming from behind her. She felt her body prickle, her head became hot, she began to tremble, her mouth was so dry, she couldn't breath, the fear was raging inside her, he had sat in the room all that time watching her...

He got up and walked around the chair, he didn't speak. He stood with his arms folded looking at her. Jane was trying to control her breathing, she closed her eyes, "Breath, breath." she repeated.

The room lit up, Jane squinted trying to see it was so bright. She opened her eyes slowly trying to focus in the brightness.

"Hello Jane. It's been how long? Did you really think you were safe.......? Moses did a good job, I will give him that, but, here we are again, he's not as good as he thought is he?"

Jane didn't speak, not that she could anyway, it was safer to stay quiet until he told her to speak, she remembered that much. She sat still and silent waiting for the first punch.

Jane's head flew backwards as the first punch landed on her left cheek, it jarred her neck, she felt her eye swell straight away. He didn't speak just smiled. The muffled sound of Janes pain making him happy. But it wasn't loud enough, he walked towards her expecting her to flinch but she didn't, that annoyed him, he picked at the side of her face where the tape was stuck down and ripped it off without any thought, the tears sprang into Jane's eyes and slipped down her face, now he was happy, he had that evil smile back.

"Hurt did it? That's nothing Jane, get used to it, I said you would regret this, and you will. Your life is mine and I will do with it as I wish."

He laughed deeply and walked out of the room, slamming the door behind him.

Jane held onto her sobs until the door shut behind him and she let go of it, trying not to let him hear her, she sobbed quietly her throat hurting from holding it in. If he heard her he would enjoy it. Jane was desperate to feel her face, she could feel the swelling and blood running down her cheek, it wasn't much this time. If it stayed this way, she could get through it and hopefully be found in time. She wasn't giving up, she couldn't let him win.

Mark went back into the kitchen area, he had the hydrofluoric acid on the side, he was sure he had enough to get rid of her, he would need to do it in the bath, he went into the bathroom and checked the deepness, he stood looking, rubbing his chin.
"Well luckily you're short and with a few broken bones I will be able to fit you in here and still fill the bath. I cant wait, they will be looking for you forever, they will never settle. That's payback. Poor Moses, oh and Jasper, pretty boy Jasper. Fucking wankers, I have what you both want and you are note getting her back"

The acid was readily available so ordering it wasn't questioned. The place he was staying wasn't interested either, nobody took any notice. He went back to the kitchen happy with himself, he wouldn't need to try and move her body now, if any of her bones were left, he would bag them up and put them in the refuse shoot. He unscrewed the bottle of bourbon and poured a few fingers worth, he knocked it back in one and breathed out loudly, as it hit the back of his throat. He went over to the chair grabbed the remote and sat down, he searched through the channels looking for something to watch but nothing interested him, he threw the remote onto the settee.
"Crock of shit, all these channels and nothing to watch, let's go and have some fun instead."

He pushed himself up out of the chair and walked back towards the bedroom, picking up his Glock as he went, he couldn't believe how easy it was to buy guns out here too. He shoved it into the back of his jeans and opened the door. Jane jumped, she wasn't expecting him so soon. He walked over to her and released one wrist ripping the tape fast showing no care or compassion. But then why would he, he had never cared for anyone or anything anyway.

Jane felt relief and wiggled her wrist twisting it around to bring the life back into it, she looked at him questioningly, he nodded allowing her to take the other off, she did it gently, her legs were still tied so he knew she wouldn't go anywhere, he wanted to watch her squirm when he hit her, having her tied up completely was no fun. Jane touched her face and around her eye, she winced but didn't speak. Her head swung back suddenly as she felt the contact of his fist on the right side of her face. Her head jerking back again, like she had been in an accident, she instantly held her face in her hands and sobbed quietly, she couldn't hold it back this time, he had hit her far harder, she felt dizzy like she would pass out, this wasn't his full strength either or should would be out cold.

"Stand up!" he demanded screaming at her, his spit landing on her hands.
Jane pushed herself up trying to stand but the tape holding her to the chair was cutting into her ankles, she was holding onto the arms trying to stand straight, he grabbed her elbow squeezing her arm and pulled her up, the tape ripping into her skin, she winced again. Mark slapped her face, her head flying to the side, her lip popped, she felt the blood running down onto her chin, she wiped it away with the back of her hand, she wanted to stare at him but knew he would get too mad, at this pace she could cope so she chose not too.

 "Look at me" he bellowed.
Mark was staring down at Jane. His knuckles white with rage as he made fists with both hands. Jane looked up at him saying nothing.
"You're pathetic" he spat, "You think keeping quiet is going to make everything okay? you fucking tramp?"

Jane shook her head, he was mad, she didn't know what to do for the best. She buckled holding her stomach, the wind knocked out of her, as his fist connected with her stomach she was desperately trying to breath, gasping to get air into her lungs, the pain taking over, her scream muffled. The tears rolling down her face. She sobbed quietly. Her knees going weak. The only thing keeping her on her feet was the tape round her ankles, the pain ripped through her body.

"I said fucking stand up, I see I need to knock some manners into you while you are here, so you do as you are fucking told."

Jane was in pain, she couldn't straighten herself up. He yanked her up again, spitting at her. He was sweating, she could feel the rage in him building she knew it well. She could smell his sweat, it was a hot day, the adrenaline pumping round his body wasn't helping, she could see through one eye and saw how his t-shirt clung to his sweaty body, she was repulsed by his smell.

He pushed her down into the chair and walked away.

"I've had enough of you for now." He growled as he walked away pulling his t-shirt away from his sticky body.

Jane slumped back. Sighing with relief. Her pain from his punches hitting her hard as her body began to relax. She closed her eyes and tried to block it out, trying to think of something else. The light in the room went out, she was happier in the dark she could dream about nice things.

Jasper came to her mind straight away, she tried to talk but her jaw wouldn't move properly, she lifted her hand to cup it, he had dislocated her jaw she was dribbling a mixture of blood and spit. She closed her eyes letting more tears flow and began talking to herself.

"You can do this Jane, you have to, Moses didn't keep you safe all this time to let you die now. Don't let him win, you have a life now with Jasper, Ohh, Jasper." she sobbed holding her jaw.

She wasn't sure if the tears were for him or the pain.

"Please don't let me die here, I don't want to die, please baby, find me."

she screamed in her own mind trying to believe if she said it somehow Jasper would hear her.

She drifted off to sleep for a while lost in her thoughts of Jasper.

Chapter 4

I failed you

Moses needed some air, he had been pacing around between the lounge and kitchen, ripping into everyone.

"J, can I get outside through here?"

"Yeah sure let me unlock the door."

Jasper unlocked the doors and pushed them open, Moses squeezed his shoulder as he walked out

"Thanks Brother." he said and went onto the patio.

He walked down the garden, feeling sick, he rubbed his hands over his face, exhausted from the news and not being able to do anything, he didn't know this place which made it harder. He rounded the corner and saw the roses, he walked to the end where Jane's laminated sheet was laying near by. He knelt down to read the poem. The memories of that night came flooding back, seeing her lose the only thing she ever wanted, he couldn't hold the tears any longer.

"Janeeeee." He screamed at the top of his voice

He started to pound the ground with his fists. The anger and frustration raging through his body, the tears kept coming, turning to a sob.

His fists were covered in moisture, green stains and dirt from the ground. He wiped his eyes pushing his fingers hard into them trying to stop the tears.

He sat back on his ankles looking up to the sky. "I let you down Jane, this is the second time. I don't deserve you or your love. How could I let this happen twice? I made you a promise I would never let this happen and now you are gone, I don't know where, we are assuming it's Mark, but we don't know for sure."

He sighed heavily and sat with his head in his hands.

"Jane I love you, I always have, you are my girl and always will be, I just wish I had the courage to tell you how I really felt, I have been in love with you for years. I didn't have the courage to tell you as I knew you would run, your friendship has always been more important. But now I wish I had."

Jasper heard everything Moses had said, he just placed his hand on his shoulder, he was surprised he hadn't heard him come up behind him. Moses looked around. As Jasper knelt next to him.
"You heard me didn't you J?" he asked feeling sick.
"Yes, I did, it's okay. I understand, honestly, how can she not steal your heart? I would have been concerned if you didn't admit it. But between us we have to stop blaming ourselves and put our heads together. You know her better than anyone, Gwen tells me she has been working on her strength and how to defend herself with G before she left?"
"Yes she had, she is much stronger than she used to be, he belittled her for yours, it started off as a joke, then it got worse, the first time he hit her we were there. But she wouldn't listen, you couldn't talk to her, she thought she had deserved it." He sighed heavily.
"Okay so that's good, she knows what he is capable of too, she knows when to be quiet, but she has grown so much, she doesn't take any shit on site. Even if it affects her, she never shows it. Come on Moses, let's get back inside and see what James has come up with. Let's get our heads together, we are no use to her feeling sorry for ourselves."
You're right, I'm sorry J." he sighed standing and brushing down his knees. "Let's get our girl back."
Jasper smiled. "That's better, this is what she would expect from us."

They walked back into the house together. The girls had just finished cooking and placed the brioche rolls in the centre of the table.
"You are just in time. Gwen said looking up. "Come on everyone tuck in, we need the strength and brain power."

James came out of the study. They all looked at him.

"Eat James, then we can talk." Moses said looking at him.

The others joined them and the kitchen fell quiet as they all ate. Jax and Linda went to grab more drinks for everyone as they finished eating.

Once they had finished James spoke first.

"Okay we need to get our heads together guys. Girls clear the table. Jasper do you have paper, pens and post it notes?"

"Yes of course, let me get them."

Jasper came back with a white board he had stored, it was a tabletop he used in meetings, he put it up.

"Perfect." James thanked him. "That will do nicely, okay we need every bit of information we can get our hands on, the cameras are not showing much at all, we need to be more specific. So, we all need to go away and get some information."

Jasper, I think it's late enough now we can knock on some doors, will you go with the guys and see the neighbours?, but before you go, can you call your security team and see if anything was picked up on your cameras."

"Of course." the guys followed him, they grabbed paper off the table and a pen.

Okay I will do the other side of the road. If you guys can do this side Jasper directed. It might be wise to take your phone, let me send you a picture from the day you arrived, show her face."

"Great idea" the men agreed, they swapped numbers and Jasper sent Jane's picture to them, they split up and Jasper rang the site whilst he walked out the door.

"Guys leave your cuts behind, we don't want the neighbours getting the wrong impression." James shouted as they headed for the door. They dropped their cuts on the chairs as they walked out.

"Shadow, get back to the dealership, check out the cameras, he could have been watching."

"Sure thing James."

"G, can you call home, see if anyone has any idea, someone must have seen him, none of this was by chance, someone has information."

"On it Brother." he said as he pulled his phone out of his pocket.

The girls cleared up and wiped down the kitchen.

"What can we do Graham? Gwen asked.

Give me a hand let's get things written on the board that we know already.

 "Sure, Jax said, grabbing a pen and heading to the board.

G returned a few minutes later, everyone looked up at him.

"Okay I skyped everyone, nobody has seen him. He has been off the grid for a while."

James punched the table.

"Fuck sake, someone there is holding back."

Jasper walked back in. "Okay they are working on it, they will call me back in a while, I have asked them to go back a week. I will head out with the guys, girls you coming, we will get through the houses much quicker?"

"Great well done, good thinking!"

Jax, Gwen and Linda followed him out, they split up into twos and headed to the first door.

Chapter 5

You won't break me

Jane was woken by a slap across the face. As she opened her eyes the pain of every punch and slap ripped through her. She was stiff and hurting all over. She looked up at Mark.

He stood grinning at her. In a silly babyish voice he spoke to her. "Oh dear, does that hurt Jane, pushing his bottom lip out for affect, then he turned back into the snarling animal he was. He spat out his words.
"Well get used to it bitch, it's only going to get worse from here on in. I have seen enough of you already, you are that pathetic bitch you always were. He took his gun out of his jeans waistband.
He pushed it into her cleavage, that was covered by her t-shirt.
"So where do you want me to shoot you first?" he snarled pushing the gun harder into her breast bone.
Jane stayed quiet. Her heart was pounding he had never had a gun before, if she said the wrong thing he could just shoot her. She was scared now. He was too volatile, she had to try and keep calm and not piss him off even more by doing the wrong thing.

"Speak to me you ignorant fucking little hoar." he spat
"What do you want me to say Mark?" Jane replied, which didn't really make sense as she was still dribbling.
"Oh, it has a fucking voice then."
He put the gun under her chin and pushed her head up. He pushed the barrel into her throat. She could feel her heart pounding, she was about to cry out and beg him not too, but he didn't like tears, that wouldn't work. She had to stop herself from crying.
"Tell me what you want me to say?" she spoke again.

He got close to her almost touching noses, he glared into her eyes.

"Drop that fucking attitude little lady!" He snapped and hit her at the back of her head with the gun, he put it back into the waist of his jeans and grabbed her hair at the back, dragging her head back.

"Look at me hoar, she could feel his spit hit her face. I don't know why I wasted so much money on you. I should have finished you that night in hospital, what a fool I was, this time I will do it properly."

He let go of her head and pushed it back, as he went to walk away he spun around and punched her again in the stomach, Jane folded in half, he knocked the wind out of her again. She was gasping to breath, panicking wasn't helping her either or the fact she couldn't open her mouth properly, her spit and dribble covering her clothes.

He stormed out of the room and slammed the door, Jane was trying to regulate her breathing and catch her breath. She needed to calm down.

Jane closed her eyes, she was trying to take deep breaths to bring her breathing back under control.

She started to feel better and sat quietly. She imagined Jasper was sat in front of her. She let herself be transported to him. She lifted her hand to touch his face, she smiled at his hair, so perfectly combed all the time, the sides shorter than the longer bit on the top, she felt her fingers run through his hair, it was so soft, he smiled at her. Her fingers travelled down to the crinkles at his eyes, tracing all the little lines, she stared into his kind eyes. She felt them talking to her.

"I love you Belle, don't give up baby, I will find you."

She let her hand continue down his face, she loved his round nose and chubby cheeks, she imagined what his children would look like and it made her smile. She had never liked men with beards but his she loved. She ran her fingers across his nose and down to his lips, they were so soft, he smiled as it tickled him. He kissed her fingertips softly smiling. She moved across to the dimples in his face, she loved kissing those, his smile lit up his face, his eyes twinkled that's how she had fallen for him, it was perfect. Her fingers trailed down his neck and onto his Adam's apple, he swallowed and it moved which made her jump. She giggled as did he. Her fingertip continued to the place she loved to kiss, the deep V of his throat. She loved tracing his face while he slept, he would wrinkle his face up which made her smile. She moved her fingers across his shoulder, he was wearing his trademark white V neck t-shirt, she loved him in it. The fabric taught across his muscles, as she traced the bulges on his arms. She never understood why people called them bangs.

"Wait for me Belle." she heard him say, "We will find you darling, please don't give up."

She felt herself drift off to sleep with memories of Jasper on her mind. She needed to sleep as much as she could to build her strength up, she wasn't going without a fight, she had something to fight for now.

Chapter 6

All coming together

It was mid afternoon and everyone came back to the house. James came out of Jaspers study, carrying his laptop. He had made some calls now he had Marks full name he had made headway.

"Okay guys, first up we have conformation that Mark got a flight out of Southampton and landed here almost 10 days ago. I have traced through the cameras and found this."
He turned the laptop around and everyone crowded in. They saw Mark walk through the airport and into baggage. He didn't have much with him but enough to look like he was on holiday, everyone shouted when they saw him. James looked up at Jasper. He could see the anguish in his face and his fists ball up. His knuckles going white.
"You piece of fucking shit." G shouted at the screen, Jax put her hand on his shoulder.
"I am going to rip your fucking head off when I find you, make no mistake, you will now pay for everything you have done to the Doc. I won't listen to anyone this time."

Moses came up behind him and also put his hand on his back. James looked around the room at everyone.
"Well there is no mistake that's him then? Okay now we need to trace him from there. He left the airport without a ride. So, tracing the town car he took would not be easy, so we need some help. Anyone got anything else?"

Shadow walked in as they were talking, his big voice boomed out.
"We have the motherfucker on the cameras at the dealer. He sat outside for almost a week watching. He was there J when

you came for your ride out, he also followed you back the day you guys arrived with Jane, he was there the night of the BBQ too, he must have followed you back."

"Did you bring the footage Shadow?" Moses asked.

He produced a memory stick, they placed it into the laptop and watched what had been captured.

With that Jaspers phone rang, it was the security team at the site. He answered quickly.

"Jasper here. What have you got for me? Okay, sure, yes work email is good, thank you buddy, we all really appreciate your efforts, yes of course we will keep you in the loop."

He hung up and everyone was looking at him. He logged into his email on his phone and turned it round so everyone could see the video before he emailed it to James. They could see him clearly sat across from the entrance in a 7 seater car. This time they had a clear picture of the registration plate.

"okay now we are getting somewhere, we need to find out who has rented this car to him and what address he has given, to try and trace him on street cameras will be hard, there are too many dodgy hotels around here to call on.

Everyone was feeling more positive. Matt cleared his throat, he had knocked on the house right opposite Jasper and the owners had been fantastic at helping them, he had seen the footage and knew it was going to upset everyone.

"Guys I have more for you." Everyone looked around at him. "Okay I spoke to the neighbours opposite, they heard you both come home on the trike and saw another car stop outside their house, nobody got out straight away which they thought odd. Anyway they watched the garage door close but could still see light under it, they thought maybe the person who was in the car would be following you in, anyway they went off to bed and it was only this morning when they saw all of our bikes they knew something must have happened. They viewed the footage from their CCTV and didn't know what to do, when I knocked and asked they happily gave it to me."

He gave the memory stick to James and he loaded the video. They watched as Jane and Jasper pulled into the driveway and Jasper got off the trike to open the door. The other car pulled up and shut its lights off. The garage door closed but not fully and yes you could see the light under the door. The next thing Mark got out of the car, he looked up and down the street and dashed across the road, he lifted the garage door and crept in. All went quiet, they watched him come dashing out of the garage with Jane over his shoulder, he threw her into the back of the car and drove off.

The girls gasped and held their breath when they saw it and breaking into sobs seeing her being taken away was as much as her friends could bare. The room fell silent for a second, everyone left with their own thoughts, the girls walked towards the men hugging tightly. The last images ripping at their hearts.

Jasper squeezed his finger and thumb at his nose trying to get rid of the tears. He couldn't cope, seeing Jane being taken away. He turned to look at Moses. He reacted the way G had done earlier and got angry. He smashed his hand into the table. Letting out a scream like and animal caught in a trap.

"Arghhhhh." His scream went on and on. Jasper walked up behind him and put his hand on his shoulder again, Moses turned to Jasper. The tears spilling down his face. They hugged each other.

"Brother I am sorry, I should never have listened to Jane all those years ago, I should have finished him. G is right. I'm sorry."

Jasper broke the hug, he put both his hands onto Moses shoulders.

"We will find her Moses, we will get her back and this time you can do what you like to him. I won't stop you; I just want our girl back and safe."

James spoke, "Guys please focus now, I know that hurt to watch but we need to get our heads back in the right place."
Everyone turned standing together, arms across shoulders and holding onto each other. Shadow was at the back with his arms outstretched across all of them.

"Okay we have more than we could have wished for. We know the vehicle, we know he sat at the dealership, outside here and on site. So now we need to find the cameras to trace him backwards, I will speak to some people and get them to help me. Hopefully they will all lead us back to the same place. We then need to come up with a plan once we know where she is. We have to assume he has a gun. How does he think he can get Jane out of wherever she is, a body is not easy to move when it is asleep or dead." He put his hands up as Gwen gasped. "I'm sorry, but we have to be honest about all the eventualities." The men nodded.

Shadow spoke, "I will speak to a few of the outlaws, they carry guns and will be happy to help us, we need to keep you guys clean we don't want you getting arrested and not getting back home. Jasper, we will not involve you with a weapon either. The outlaws don't give a fuck they will take his life and deal with the body after. There is a pig farm out at Waterford so no issues getting rid of the body I am sure they will be happy to break in and feed him to the pigs."
The men laughed. The girls just looked at each other feeling queasy.

"Guys I think we should all get something to eat and rest for the night, we need to keep our heads in the right place, we are going to be no good to Jane if we are tired."
They all nodded agreeing knowing they wouldn't sleep much but they at least needed to try.
Gwen spoke. "There is still plenty of food in the fridge Jax, Linda and I will get it out and lay up the counter you can take it from there.

Jasper smiled, "Thank you girls, you are keeping us going today." he grabbed them all as they walked away kissing their heads, they all cuddled into him.

"Anytime Jasper." they replied in unison.

Shadow rang one of the outlaws, Dark Angels they were nicknamed, he knew they would do anything for a bit of trouble and he would drop everything to help them.

"Well fuck me, I didn't think I would hear from you Shadow, how's it hanging Brother, what can I do for you, it must be fucking serious for you to be calling me?"

"Axel, we need your help. In short one of the girls from the club in the UK Jane has been taken by her ex, she is in danger, he vowed to kill her and has waited 10 years to get this opportunity, Moses and G are here they have been visiting."

"I'm listening."

"He beat her bad when they were married, she escaped, Moses took care of her and kept her off the grid for 10 years, now someone has told him where she is, he has been here almost 10 days watching her every move. We believe the catalyst is when Jasper here proposed at the BBQ and he followed them back last night. We have videos of him at every point James is now on the case tracing it backwards to where he is staying, we have to assume that's where he is keeping her."

"Motherfucker! Axel yelled. Where you at Shadow, give me a day and we will be there. I will bring some fire power and some boys. Get as much information as you can and find out who the fucking prick was that told him where she was, I want to rip the bastards head off."

Sure thing Brother, I will text the address for you now. Thank you Axel."

"No need for thanks, you can wait until we have her back then we can celebrate. See you tomorrow night."

Shadow went back into the kitchen, everyone was stood eating, they turned to look at him.

"I spoke to Axel."

James nodded, Moses and G smiled, they knew his history, he was a good guy who took out the bad guys and got a great deal of pleasure out of it. Especially when it was a woman who was affected.

"He will be here tomorrow night with a few of the boys, he wants us to get as much information as possible for him. I told him you and G were here Moses. He's in the know, so will be planning his attack on route.

Jasper was frowning and looked at Moses. "Is he good Moses?"

"One of the best Brother, he will have no issues taking him out and if he brings who I think he will then there is no question about him being taken care of. He's a good guy to have on your side. I wouldn't want to be his enemy. He has boiled a body before in a fryer, just for the hell of it, he takes no shit from anyone. We will not need to go in guns blazing, these guys will do it for us, we can just get Jane and get the hell out so he can deal with Mark, we just need to get James to sort the cameras out, we will take a vehicle that isn't registered to any of us in case anything comes back on us."

Jasper nodded, not sure what he was listening to.

"Okay, will he need paying? I am happy to pay if that's what it takes?"

"Don't insult the man, he doesn't do it for the money not for club members and family, just think of him as a Dark angel."

Jasper nodded. He was exhausted from the day and all he was trying to take in.

The girls made coffee and Jasper went to get bedding for everyone, he had plenty, he offered his bed to anyone who wanted it, they all refused. Linda Jax and Gwen took the spare room. The rest of them took the sofas and the sun beds which the guys brought in and bedded down on for the night.

They all laid awake in the dark waiting for sleep to take them.

Jasper laid down on his bed. He could smell Jane on her pillow, he grabbed it and cuddled into it, inhaling her smell. He could feel the tears again, the day had been exhausting, seeing the video of her being taken was ripping his heart out. He cried himself to sleep holding her pillow. He sank into a deep sleep and began to dream.

It was Sunday morning, their favorite day of the week. They had no plans to go anywhere it was a day to chill out and have some fun. Jasper got up to make tea for them both, leaving Jane spread across the bed. Just the sheet covering her, he could see her nipples were hard they were showing through it , he stood in the doorway watching her, she made a beautiful moan and opened her legs slowly, the sheet falling between them outlining her body. Jasper smiled thinking she must be having a naughty dream. He went to the kitchen and made the tea. As he got back to the bedroom, he saw Jane was up already in the bathroom. He put the tea down on the bedside cupboard and walked in. She was sat with tousled hair on the toilet leaning on her hand. He smiled down at her finding his cock getting hard already, she looked so beautiful in the morning with her hair a mess and the sweet look on her face. Jane beckoned him with her finger, she sat up straight and pulled him closer, his cock hardening more, she opened her mouth, his cock slipping nicely in. He held onto her head and hissed through his teeth as he felt her tongue tease the end, he would never tire of this, every time he felt her lips around his cock was like the first time, pure magic.

Jane sank her nails into his bottom which made him jump and push deep into her mouth, she smiled, "success" she whispered. "Fuck Belle, that is so good" he moaned, "hurry up, I want to taste your pussy."
Jane stopped sucking and looked up at him. "I'm done."
She stood wiped herself, then washed her hands, taking his she walked back into the bedroom. Jasper was desperate to taste her. Jane faked falling over at the edge of the bed, her bottom in the air and her legs open. Jasper smiled, he knew what she was doing, he got down onto his knees pulled her cheeks apart and buried his face into her bottom, he had wanted to lick her

was panting heavily as he pulled out of her, he crumbled down next to her laughing, both of them trying to catch their breath.

He pulled her into him and cuddled her.

"You are so perfect Belle, this is perfect".

They laid snuggled into each other for a while, enjoying the time together, Jasper had already decided he wasn't letting Jane up anytime soon, he wanted her here all day if he could. Jane sat up, their tea was going cold and she hated cold tea. They sat up drank their tea and laid back down, they turned to face each other. Jane's leg over his as Jasper caressed her back and she his.

He closed his eyes for a second, he stretched out his arm to find her, his eyes shot open, she wasn't there…… he sat up realising it was just a dream.

Chapter 7

Say goodbye

Jane woke up, her bladder was full, she was at bursting point. She didn't want to wet herself so she needed to ask him for help, after all he put a bucket close by. It would also give her a break from being strapped to the chair even just for a few seconds. She started to rock the chair and clap her hands hoping he would hear her. He did. He stormed in the door, rage on his face.

"What the fuck are you doing?"

"I need to pee, please." she spat trying to talk.

He laughed, "I should let you piss your knickers, but I don't think I want the smell."

He pulled the bucket over, pulled his knife out of his boot, his Glock still in his waistband at the back, He split the tape at her ankles and pulled her up.

The relief in her ankles was instant, she just wanted to rub them but knew he wouldn't allow it.

"Try anything stupid Jane and I will shoot you."

Not this time, she thought, *but I may next time.* She made mental notes of how he moved her, and how she had been taught to protect herself, if she could knock the gun out of his waistband she had a better chance of surviving this, or even being able to shoot him. Not that she had ever held a gun, let alone shoot one.

He pushed her down onto the bucket, it wasn't ideal but at least she was able to pee. When she finished he moved the bucket and pushed her back down onto the chair. He grabbed the tape and strapped her ankles back to the chair. Saying nothing he left.

"Thank you." she mumbled as he walked towards the door. He stopped and looked around. He didn't speak but she knew the fact he had stopped and acknowledged it gave her a smaller chance of more time.

He slammed the door behind him and went back to the internet. He had discovered it would take at least two days for her body to dissolve in the acid, that wasn't what he had planned, that annoyed him, but he didn't have an alternative. The other option was chopping her up in the bath but using an electric saw would certainly spike interest from someone. Feeding her to the pigs had interested him previously but he didn't know the area and didn't have the time to check the place out. He wasn't leaving Jane alone for long if at all, she would make too much noise. He just had to go with plan A and hope as she was so small and slim now it wouldn't take too long. At least if it were just bones he could get rid of those more easily. He just hoped this old place had a good drainage system and old pipes or he would be flooding the place with her fluids.

Jane sat quietly. Thinking about getting the knife out of his trousers, or the gun, she knew he had some force behind him, but she was nimble and could try and move around him. It had to be worth a try surely, she couldn't just let him take her life without putting up a fight. She was hurting all over, her face was swollen as was her lip and her jaw was out. She was bruised badly and sure she had a broken rib or two, she was used to that though he had done it enough times over the years, always leaving bruises where they couldn't be seen.

She played the scenario over and over in her mind, if he came in and helped her pee again, she was free to move, she could kick the knife out of his hand, she was a good kicker, she learnt well with G.
She knew then he would punch her, so she would have to go low straight away. The downside was the gun, he would go for it, she knew all guns had safety catches on them and he would

need to release it before he could shoot but she had no idea how you would go about it. She assumed it was as simple as pulling the trigger once, then he would have to pull it again to shoot. That would again give her seconds. She looked around the room for anything she could hit him with. There was nothing, only the bucket and that wouldn't do anything. She sat deflated.

The door flew open Mark just stood in the doorway. He had got bigger she was sure of it he almost filled the door, she wasn't sure if it was muscle or fat though. If it was fat that would slow him down.
Her head was going around in circles.
"So, it seems for me to get rid of your body I will be stuck with you for another few days, so I won't be able to play with you as much as I wanted too. But that's okay, it will still be slow. Any last wishes before I finish you, anyone you want to say goodbye too?"
Jane shook her head.
"Oh, come now, I am sure you would want to speak to Jasper or Moses? Wouldn't you like to say goodbye, let them hear you as you take your last breath. I know I would."

Jane felt the tears welling up in her eyes, she couldn't let him see her weakness. She had to do something.

He had brought a disposable phone and he was going to call Moses and leave him a little message. But not until she was almost gone. He would get so much pleasure out of destroying him at the same time. He knew he was in love with her and he couldn't wait to hear him down the phone. He had a grin on his face.

Mark walked towards her, his knife in his hand he was running his fingers up and down the blade.
"So where shall I start………?"

his phone out of his pocket. Deflated. Not wanting to make the call.

He decided to push this, he walked over to the TV and used the skype to call, He wanted everyone to see Jasper Moses and the guys, to see how bad it was out there.

The phone rang. Moses face appeared on the screen

"Hi Brother."

Everyone in the bar stopped and looked at the screen.

"I'm sorry Moses, we have all looked, it's not in the system either, he always rings in, nobody has it."

Helen stood still, not wanting to move in case she was seen.

Jasper appeared at the side of Moses.

"Guys this is Jasper, Jane's Fiancé, you know the woman who has been there for us all, the one everyone of you has turned to in your hour of need. The one who protected so many of you. Fuck sake guys, someone must have his number, if you don't want to admit it that's fine, send it anonymously. Just fucking help us get to Jane before she dies, if she hasn't already. If nothing else let us bring her home to be with Jasper."

The girls wiped their eyes. Lottie threw herself into Suzy, she couldn't cope.

She moved her tear stained face out of Suzy's shoulder, sobbing she echoed Moses words.

"Please everyone, check again, this is our Jane, the Doc, Half pint, please?" she sobbed

Helen didn't move. Gwen appeared in the screen, she was a bitch when she needed to be, she had tears running down her face.

"I know one of you in that room is protecting him, I swear if I find out who you are you will pay with your life too if Jane dies." She broke down. "Is this what you all want this man to win again?!"

Out of the corner of her eye Gwen noticed Helen move out of camera shot. She didn't think anything of it, just thought it odd at the time. Moses hung up, they all stood in silence in Jaspers kitchen.

James walked away, he needed to find another way, he had to find the right camera to show where he was headed.

In the UK the guys all went to the bar to get another drink. A few were pissed off because it was like they were being accused of helping Mark. Helen kept quiet. She nodded in all the right places when being spoken to. Everyone was talking about Jane and who could have the number, Helen was beginning to get a bit bothered by it so made her excuses and went home.

The drive home for her was stressful, she had been crying all the way, she didn't know what to do, she was fighting with herself again. As she arrived home she tried to put it out of her head and get on with some cleaning, she always cleaned when she was stressed or worried.

An hour later she hadn't got very far she put her cleaning things away, grabbed her bag and keys and got into her car, not sure where she was headed.

Chapter 9

I knew it

Gwen was sat quietly as was everyone else in their own thoughts. She suddenly jumped up and screamed.

"I knew it, I knew it. G, quick get back in here. James hurry."

Everyone rushed to her side, all talking at once.

"What the fuck is up your arse Gwen?" Moses barked at her.

"Get hold of Bill, send him to Helen's, G remember when she came in with bruises around her neck and she wouldn't tell us who it was? She was angry with us all, yet days before she was really happy?"

"What of it Gwen?" G frowned.

"It has to be him, today while we called them in the bar, she didn't check her phone. Why wouldn't she check her phone? Because she has the number...!"

"I hope you are fucking right Gwen, Moses grumbled, sighing heavily.

Jasper looked at Gwen, his world was falling apart his eyes showed the desperation, he was ashen.

"Are you sure Gwen, really sure?" He pleaded with her.

Gwen grabbed his hand and hugged it into her chest. The tears ready to spill onto her cheeks at a seconds notice.

"If I am wrong then I will beg for your forgiveness Jasper, but I know something isn't right, call it women's intuition. G please just ring Bill, send him round, get her alone she will fold I promise."

G rang Bill, he answered quickly. G told him what to do and they hung up within seconds.

Bill grabbed his crash helmet and ran out of the club. He was at Helen's within minutes. He almost let the bike drop, he ran up to the door and banged it with his fists.

"Helen open the door now!" he yelled.

Nothing, he pounded this time. Shouting at her

"Helen open this door, or I will put it in, your choice." Bill turned in frustration realising her car had gone. He kicked the door in anger.

"Fuck sake!!" he grabbed his phone out of his pocket and dialled her number. No answer, it went to voicemail.

"Helen it's Bill, wherever you are call me, we know you have been seeing Mark and you have his number. Don't mess me about love please. Nothing will happen to you, we just need his number." He hung up, frustrated, dialled again. Still no answer. Now he was getting angry, he dialled again and again. Still she didn't pick up.

His phone rang, he answered without looking. "Helen?"

"Bill, is she there?"

"Oh, no G, she's not in, I have been ringing over and over, I left her a message."

"Fuck sake, ok keeping trying Bill, keep in touch."

"Sure thing." Bill hung up and instantly rang Helen again.

Helen was in her car, she could hear her phone ringing but she didn't connect it to the car she didn't want to answer it. It continued to ring over and over, Helen was getting more and more upset, she began to cry again, she was begging and pleading her phone to stop, she began sobbing, all kinds of fear going through her head. She always liked Jane, but she knew they would kill for her and she couldn't let them know she had it. The club was all she had. Her phone stopped, she sighed wiping her eyes. She was on the motorway heading towards the New Forest she could hide out there in her car until the next day if needed. There was never a good signal out there so at least she wouldn't be bothered by anyone.

Her phone began ringing again, she looked over and saw it was Bill again.

"Shut up, shut up." She screamed. "Please leave me alone, I didn't do anything." her tears started again, her nose was running, she began choking on her tears, her mascara was now stinging her eyes she was struggling to see properly. She was in the middle lane, she was trying to wipe her eyes with her hand but it made them sting more, she knew she needed to get onto the emergency lane and sort her face out, she didn't look to her left just indicated and pulled across to the left lane, what she hadn't seen was the truck in that lane. He slammed his breaks on but it was too late, Helen collided with the front right of the truck, which spun her around, he caught her car again as he was trying to avoid her, the impact tipped her onto the roof, she rolled down the carriageway and slipped down the embankment into the bushes. The truck driver finally stopped the truck and jumped out with others, they ran down to where she had left the road. Men were trying to pull the doors open to get to Helen, they were all shouting at once. Helen was unconscious in the car. The truck driver shouted for someone to call the Emergency services. He was trying to wake Helen up but had been stopped by someone.

The Paramedics arrived first and assessed her, she was unconscious, she was also trapped inside the vehicle, it was an older car and the roof had collapsed trapping her. They needed to cut her out of the vehicle. The Fire brigade arrived shortly after and went to work cutting her out. They got her onto a stretcher and rushed her to the local hospital.

The car was left in the ditch, the local traffic Police were guarding it until the truck arrived to take it away, inside Helen's phone continued to ring.

Bill called G back to let him know he hadn't been able to reach her yet, he promised to stay at the house until she returned, they knew she didn't have any family, just those at the club.
He sat down on the pavement and took out his cigarettes. He sat with his head in his hands, dragging on his cigarette at a loss of what to do.

Chapter 10

Take me to my happy place

Jane laid on the floor in terrible pain. She was feeling sick and in desperate need of a drink.

The door crashed open and in walked Mark he had a bottle of Jack Daniels, Jane could tell he had been drinking heavy and if she hadn't noticed the smell followed him and he stank. He threw a bottle of water down to her and some biscuits.

"Get up slut." He slurred. "I decided as they think you are dead that gives me more time with you, so we can have a little chat and I can have more fun with you. After all, why would I come halfway across the world to kill you so quickly."

Jane got up onto one arm, holding her stomach, Mark was not a patient man, he stood tutting at her.

"For fucks sake you really are making a meal out of this." he moved into the kitchen and grabbed the first aid kit. He threw it down onto the floor and pulled a chair up to her.

"Sort yourself out Jane, they think you are dead so I have a few more days with you, so if you are going to be around then I need to keep you watered and sort your wounds out, but don't for one minute think I am going soft, I just want to make the most of my time saying goodbye to you. Then it will be a slow painful death and on top of that a nice little pay out."

Jane frowned, wondering what he meant by payout, he must have seen the look on her face.

He sat back on his chair rocking laughing his chair was on two legs leaning against the wall. He had his knife in his hand, he was sliding his fingers up and down the blade.

"Oh, of course, you don't know anything do you, how silly of me. Okay let me start from the beginning. You must be wondering how I finally found you, well let me tell you a little story."

He got off the chair and turned it around, sat back down and hung over the back of it looking at Jane, his knife still in his hand, he looked down at his nails while Jane tried to patch herself up. She sat back on the chair. Mark tapped her hands and legs back up.

"Well, when you left I took a life Insurance policy out on you, so when you died I would get a nice little payout, all I need is a death certificate or leave it a few years, report you as missing and then claim a nice little nest egg. I knew I needed to bide my time and one day someone would slip up. I was out shopping one day and bumped into that pathetic little club hoar Helen, I turned on my charm and within an hour she was putty in my hands."

Janes eyes flew open.

"Oh, you didn't think about that did you? Not everyone loves you Jane you know!"

Jane tried not to show any further emotion just listen.

Well before you knew it, I was at her place smoosing her, she was happy to please me, and she did on many occasions. We sat chatting one day and it all came out, where you were, what you were doing, I didn't even need to slap her about, well maybe a little I suppose, but then she liked it.

Jane felt repulsed listening to him.

"So once I get rid of you I will go back home get Helen to report you as missing and then I will be quids in, I just need to wait a few years for my payout." He sat laughing and gulping on his bottle.

Jane didn't comment, she just sat in the chair quiet.

"Do I detect a bit of jealousy? Does poor little Jane wish it was her underneath me?" He took another gulp of his drink and left the bottle on the floor, he walked over to Jane lifting her chin.

Talking in a childish voice and pushing his bottom lip out he spoke.

"Does poor baby want me still, do you want me to put another baby in your tummy?" He squeezed her face hard making Jane scream out in pain.

"No fucking luck you little slut." He spat at her. "Oh, but would you like to see me fucking poor little Helen?" He grabbed her face again and made her nod. He grabbed the chair and sat behind Jane, getting his phone out he found the first video.

"You will like this one Jane, she loves it up the arse." He held the phone in front of Janes face, she moved to look away knowing what was coming.

"Don't you fucking dare look away you little slut, watch it now." He grabbed Janes hair pulled it back and made her face the screen. Jane winced, he had hold of her hair at her nape twisting it.

Helen appeared on the screen sucking his cock, he was pushing her head onto him further as she gagged. Jane was feeling sick.

"Oh, you have to watch this bit. She really is a slut, she took everything I dished out."

Jane heard him unzip his jeans, her hair prickled on her arms, she was scared now, she didn't trust him at all.

Helen was on her knees facing away from him, she had a gag on and her arms were tied behind her back, her head was in the mattress, Jane could already hear her moaning, she knew she didn't enjoy this. Mark spat on his cock and rubbed it over the tip, he slapped Helen hard, she screamed out under her gag, Jane saw her body moving where she was crying. Mark hit her again and pulled her arms back so he could bring her head off the bed. Helen was sobbing, Mark let her go, she crashed down onto the bed. He rubbed his cock onto her ass and pushed in hard. The sounds that came from Helen Jane knew she had never experienced anal sex before. Mark didn't have the biggest of cocks but big enough to hurt someone. Helen wasn't a club hoar just one of the girls. Mark pounded into her harder and harder, she watched as Helen went limp. Mark grabbed her arms again and brought her head up high, he grabbed her around the throat and began strangling her. Jane heard Mark groaning behind her, she knew he was tossing himself off, she was repulsed by it. She could hear Helen gasping for air, she wanted to be sick, she had to stop this, before Mark made a move on her or she vomited watching anymore of this violence. She felt no anger towards Helen, she could see herself in her. She moved her chair shuffling like she needed to pee again.

"What the fuck are you doing you stupid little bitch?" Mark stood putting his cock away.
"I need to pee please, my legs have gone numb too." She mumbled, dribbling.
"Whine, fucking whine, that's all you ever fucking did, no wonder you got slapped as much as you did." He walked around the front of Jane, her head fell back as he slapped her, he grabbed her around the throat, she was choking on the air leaving her and the stench coming from his drink.
"Now listen to me my little pot of gold, try anything and I will shoot you and make this very fucking slow. If you are a good girl I will kill you before I put you into the acid." He pushed her head back letting go of her throat, Jane was gasping for air choking again.
Mark pulled the tape of her wrists and nodded to her to pull the tape off her ankles. She rubbed up and down her legs trying to get rid of the pins and needles, she stood up and stamped as gently as she could, in case he thought she was trying to get someone else's attention. But thinking about it she thought it wasn't a bad idea. But there was too much noise at the moment in the building. She moved over to the bucket and sat down. Luckily she was able to go or she would have taken another punch. Mark pulled her back up, Jane pulled her jeans up and went to sit down, she was holding her stomach, her ribs were aching.

"Don't sit I am not taking your piss to get rid of it." he pulled his gun out and put it into her back, Jane picked the bucket up and walked out of the room, she looked to the right and saw the bathroom, she emptied the bucket, flushed the toilet and washed her hands. Mark pushed her out of the room, as she walked past the kitchenette she noticed all the bottles of acid on the worktop, she began to panic, he really did mean to get rid of all the evidence. She was trying to breath and not show how panicked she was. Mark pushed her back into the bedroom dragging her back by her hair into the chair. Jane dropped the bucket onto the floor. Mark hit her around the head.

"Stupid bitch, watch what you are doing."

Jane kept quiet while Mark strapped her back into the chair. He walked off turning out the light and slammed the door behind him.

Mark slumped into the chair, he pulled his phone out calling Helen. When she didn't answer he became angry, he heard the voicemail beep.

"What the fuck have I told you about answering your fucking phone when I call. You better fucking call me back you little tramp or I will make you wish you had when I get back."

Jane heard every word, she cowered in her chair, bad memories of him came flooding back. She was waiting for the door to open and him to take it out on her, but nothing. She heard the main door shut, she was a little confused. Had he gone out?

Mark was hungry and angry, he walked out of the building grunting at anyone who looked at him the wrong way, he stopped at the local takeaway and grabbed a pizza and some fries. He walked back to the building all the time keeping his head down and his baseball cap covering his eyes. He wasn't sure where the cameras were and he wasn't taking any chances. He slammed back into the room, slumped into the chair, putting the TV on and gorged himself on the food. He fell asleep soon after Jane heard his snoring, she knew he was in a deep sleep.

She closed her eyes again thinking of Jasper. Taking herself to her happy place.

Jasper was sat on the chair, his eyes closed. Jane crawled up to him quietly, she sat watching him, smiling to herself, Jasper opened his eyes slightly so he could see her, but she couldn't see him, trying not to smile he waited. He closed his eyes again, knowing she would pounce soon, Jane got up onto her knees about to jump, Jasper jumped forward grabbing her, making her squeal. He picked her up sank his teeth into her neck making her giggle nibbling at her. He threw her onto the sofa sitting astride her. Jane was giggling beneath him. He moved down closer to her putting his hands either side of her face. Jane pulled him closer. She touched his face, his smile was so wide, she could see the twinkle in his eyes, she traced around them stopping at the crinkles, she traced them from the corner of his eyes down to the end. Jasper laughed, giving Jane butterflies seeing his smile. She pulled him forward. Her mouth slightly open, she slid her wet tongue slowly across her lips, he watched aching to touch her. To feel her soft lips and slide his finger into her mouth, while grazing his lips up her long neck, teasing her. Before claiming her as his own again, Devouring every part of her naked body. But he waited, watching her enjoying the teasing.

The door crashed open, Jane woke with a start. Mark was back. Her heart was pounding. She didn't move, just waited for it. She didn't wait long, her body moved as the impact of his fist hit her, knocking the wind out of her. She was desperately trying to breath, gasping for air.

"It wasn't that hard, so pathetic!" he turned and walked out slamming the door behind him.

Jane slumped into the chair, just wanting it over.

She closed her eyes again to try and get back to her happy place.

Chapter 11

I will find you, for her

It had been a couple of hours and no sign of Helen, Bill was beginning to think she wasn't coming back, it was past midnight. He paced up and down the street, he was running low on cigarettes but didn't want to leave in case he missed her. He decided to try few more times to call her.

He pulled his phone out of his pocket and dialled her again. Her phone just rang continuously, then went to voicemail.
"Helen it's Bill again, you can't hide forever love, just help us please, nothing is going to happen to you. I promise, do you really want Jane to die? Please I am begging you, just send me his number, I promise he will never hurt you again, we know this is not your fault." He hung up, sinking back down onto the pavement. He pressed redial and let the phone ring until it went to voicemail, hung up and redialled, still no answer so he redialled again.

"Hello, Bill is it?"
"Who is this, where is Helen, put her on please?" Bill was in shock and on his feet.
"Look mate I don't know who you are but I am sorry to say Helen is not here, she was in a crash and taken to Southampton General hospital, I'm at the compound where her car was brought, I heard the phone ringing constantly so decided to answer it. I can't help you any more than that."
"Can you get into the phone for numbers at all, I need Mark's number?"
"Oh she has a missed call from him too, quite a few missed calls and voicemails. Sorry mate it's locked, you would need to ask Helen for that."

"Tell me where you are I'm on my way to you now, I need the phone."

"Sorry mate I can't do that, I don't know who you are."

"Look mate I am begging you, this is a matter of life or death, I need Mark's number he is in the USA. I have pictures to prove who I am you can take my driving licence anything you like?"

"Okay come down we are in Marchwood, we will talk when you get here."

"I know it, will see you soon, thank you, thank you." Bill jumped on his bike, he was glad it was late there was very little traffic about so he was in Marchwood in no time.

He jumped off the bike, as the guard came to the gate unlocking it letting him in.

"Hi fella, thank you." Mark pulled his phone and wallet out of his pocket. "This is my driving licence, my credit card, look this is Helen stood next to her car after we sprayed it pink for her, that's the gang. I am begging you, please let me take the phone to her to unlock so we can call Mark."

"I'm really not sure about this, I could lose my job."

"Look, I understand you are nervous, I really do, but this is a matter of life and death, I am begging you. Take my licence, trust me this is real."

"Okay, but if anyone asks it wasn't me."

"Whatever you say." Bill was nodding like crazy. The guard handed the phone to him, he held it tight and grabbed the guards hand, he was shaking it hard.

"Thank you, Thank you, you really don't know how grateful I am, you are a life saver."

The guard smiled and stopped Bill shaking his hand, his arm was aching, Bill was a big man and didn't realise his own strength.

"Okay, look go, in case my boss comes round."

Bill pushed the phone into his pocket and jumped onto his bike, he went straight to the hospital.

It was now gone midnight and he knew they wouldn't let him in but he had to try. He walked into accident and Emergency and straight to the desk, there we others waiting, most had been drinking or got into fights, he pushed past them and up to the front, a few moaned but Bill just turned and snarled at them, once they saw his cut and the size of him they backed down. The receptionist looked up at him with disgust, Bill was used to it, most people thought bikers were trouble and sometimes it helped.

"Yes, how can I help?" she asked curtly.

"You have my sister in here, she was brought in a few hours ago after an accident, her name is Helen Tring, could you tell me where she is?"

"She is in resuscitation, but you cannot go in there, you will have to wait here until the Doctor has more information. Please take a seat. Next?" She looked past Bill and called the next person waiting.

"Hang on lady, don't dismiss me like a piece of shit on your shoe, I was still talking to you, who the hell do you think you are?" He slammed his hand on the desk making the receptionist jump.

"How dare you, I gave you all the information now move."

"But did you ask who I was? for when they have information, they wouldn't even know I was here, so I will be going through to find her." He walked away heading to the doors heading into the cubicles.

"Sir, Sir you cannot go through there." Bill turned and gave her the middle finger. She blushed sitting down calling the next person.

Bill walked past all of the cubicles finding his way to the nurses station. He stood waiting for someone.

"Hello there, can I help you?"

"Yes, I hope so, I am looking for my sister Helen Tring, she was brought in from a car accident earlier tonight. I'm told she is in resus?"

"Yes, that's correct, but I'm afraid she is still unconscious so you can't see her. If you would like to take a seat in the corridor there I will call you when she wakes up." She pointed down the quiet corridor where there were others waiting.

"How bad is she?"

"All we can tell you is just cuts and bruises, she is very lucky, her car barreled and ended up in a ditch. Hopefully she will wake soon, I will call you when she does."

"Thank you nurse, it is really important I speak to her, so the sooner the better." The nurse nodded and walked away.

Bill went to the nearest seat pulling his phone out. He knew it was early hours in Connecticut but he wanted to let the others know the situation. He texted Moses and G, knowing one would pick it up soon. He slouched back in the chair closing his eyes.

Chapter 12

I can't do this anymore

Mark woke up in the chair, his head was pounding, he had forgotten how much he drank or what he had done the night before. He stretched feeling a box slide off his legs, he looked down to see the pizza box from the night before sliding onto the floor, the pizza leftovers sliding out.

"For fuck sake." He yelled, kicking the box as it reached his foot sending the pizza across the room. He picked up the bottle of Jack and started to drink more of it.

Jane heard him, she put her head down, she knew this was bad news for her. Mark stumbled into the bedroom door pushing it open.

"Wake up bitch, I have decided today is the day." He walked over to Jane pulled her hair at the back lifting her head up, he slapped her face a few times making Jane wince. He let go of her head, walking around the back of her. He pulled out his Glock pushing it into the back of her head.

"So Jane, it's time to choose, you can either go in the bath with the acid and have a slow death until it eats away at you, that's my favourite, the thought of seeing your body eaten and see you take your last breath fills me with joy, but I would have to knock you out I don't want splashing when you writhe about. Secondly, I can put the gun in your mouth and pull the trigger, you even get to say when just by nodding. Or thirdly I will put it against your temple and pull the trigger. Either way you are going in the bath, I will have to break a few bones though to fit you in, so I either do that while you are awake before I put you in alive or do it once you are dead. What's it to be?"

Jane felt the colour drain from her face, her heart was pounding out of her chest, she was hot and cold, she was trying desperately to catch her breath but it wasn't working. She began to cry holding in her sobs, it was too late, they were never going to find her now.

She closed her eyes thinking of Jasper, Moses and the gang, she knew they would have done everything they could to find her, but time was up, this was it. All those years of looking over her shoulder were over. He finally got to take her life. Mark hit her on the back of the head with the gun.

He pulled her hair, dragging her head up from behind. Pushing the Glock into her temple.

"Come on Jane you know you want this over, just say the word and I will happily pull the trigger."

She let out a sob, she knew he would be mad.

"Oh, diddum's poor little Jane is scared." he walked around the front of hear punching her hard in the stomach, Jane folded, struggling to breath again.

"Get fucking used to it bitch, you pathetic creature, you know I hate wimps. What's the rule, no tears?"

Jane choked back more tears, Mark pushed her head back with the gun.

"Open your mouth." Jane looked up questioning him, dreading what was coming. She felt sick.

"Open your fucking mouth, have you forgotten I am the one in control here?" Jane shook her head and opened her mouth as wide as she could.

"Pathetic, you can do better than that, he grabbed her face.

"Open wider." Jane did as she was told, the pain ripping through her. Mark forced the gun into her mouth, Janes eyes opened as wide as they could, she was choking on the fear, her heart rate going through the roof, her chest was tight she could barely breath.

"Just nod Jane, then it's over, come on make my day, make Marky a happy man."

Jane kept as still as she could, scared to move in case he thought she was nodding.

"I have an idea."

He took his knife out of his pocket and released Jane's hands. Then pulled his phone out.

"Untie your legs, I don't want you to think I am evil, at least you can be free when I do it. It's no fun if you are tied up."

Jane undid the tape on her legs quickly, not sure what he had planned. She felt the tension leave her legs straight away, but she had been sat for a long time and knew she was going to struggle to stand.

"Get up." he waved the knife in front of her face. Jane struggled to get up, Mark put his hand underneath her armpit and dragged her up squeezing her arm.

Jane stood up not knowing why, Mark punched her again in the stomach, she collapsed back into the chair, falling onto the floor, she laid with her legs pulled up into her chest, Mark walked around her laughing.

"Oh, I am sorry did that hurt?" Jane didn't move.

Jane screamed out as his boot hit her in the back.

"Opps, sorrrrryyyyy." He laughed loving it.

Jane was laid with her arm out, the other holding her back, Mark stepped forward putting his foot on her hand, Jane looked up, she knew what was coming, he lifted his foot off and stamped down hard. Jane screamed out, the pain was unbearable. Mark looked down laughing.

He pulled his phone out of his pocket and dialled Moses. His knife still in his hand. He was stood next to Jane.

"Mark? What do you want?" Moses put him on speaker

"Well that's not a nice way to greet a friend is it?"

"Fuck off Mark, you were never that. Just tell me what you want?"

"Okay if that's how it is going to be, I was going to give you an option, but maybe I will just choose now."

"What options, what the fuck are you talking about?"

"Well your darling Jane is still alive and I was going to give you the option of how she goes today, but now I will just choose."

"Mark wait, listen."

"No Moses it's too late, you kept her from me for 10 years, she deserves this and more. If you were here I would do the same to you too."

"Mark take me, let her go, I kept her from you, kill me instead?"

"Ha ha ha, you think it's that easy, no thank you, but you are welcome to join her."

"Mark please, wait. What do you want, there must be something other than killing Jane, do you want to see your life out in prison? Surely not?"

"Moses, Moses, Moses, they will never know I did it, they have your word, but let's be honest what proof do you have. Once I am done with her there will be no evidence to show she was ever here.

It's your word against mine."

"Please Mark think about this?"

"Its too late, but as a kind hearted person that I am I will let you hear her go. All she has to do is nod and the gun will finish her off."

Mark put the phone down on the other chair and dragged Jane off the floor.

"Get up stupid. Someone wants to hear you die."

He pushed her down into the chair putting the knife under her chin.

"Be a good girl now and I might let you say goodbye." He grabbed the phone off the other chair and gave it to Jane.

"Moses." she mumbled dribbling on herself. She began to cry hearing the other voices in the room.

"Belle it's me darling can you hear me?" hang on love we will find you, I promise, we have some of Shadow's friends here. They will find you. I love you Belle." She could hear his tears.

"I love you." she mumbled. Moses had put her on speaker, the girls fell apart hearing her try to speak.

"Half-pint it's me G, go low darling, you know you can do this." Jane grunted in response.

Mark grabbed the phone from her. "That's enough, you are all so pathetic." He put the phone back to his ear. "See you back in the UK boys." He began to laugh, deep in his stomach, his mouth wide open.

Jane felt sick, she knew it was over for sure now. She sat in the chair waiting, thinking about how best to go, if she asked for a bullet to the head it would be fast. Yes, that's what she would do.

Mark put the phone down again. "Any last requests?" Jane shook her head and pointed to her forehead. "Oh, now you want me to shoot you in the head, good choice?"
Jane thought again about the safety on the gun and how easy it would go off but she had probably less than a second to knock him off his feet or the gun out of his hands. She sat in the chair waiting.
Mark turned away for a second, Jane threw herself onto the floor and kicked out her legs catching Mark off guard, he landed on the floor hard, the gun still in his hand, he pulled the trigger twice not sure where he was firing as the room was still quite dark with the heavy curtains closed. Jane screamed loudly and suddenly fell quiet.

Everyone heard the gun and Jane scream, they all began shouting at once. Mark struggled back onto his feet, he stumbled over to Jane kicking her, she didn't move.
"Stupid bitch, I will deal with your body later." He picked the phone up and disconnected the line.

Moses was screaming down the phone, G took it from him. She's gone this time Moses. It's over. Moses fell to his knees. "Noooooooooo!!" he screamed, holding his head, digging his fingers into his scalp. Jasper was sobbing, his whole body shaking, Gwen went across to him and held him tight, crying with him. James patted him on the back.

"Jasper I know that was hard to hear, but I need you to think straight now, we have to find her regardless there is a chance she is still alive."

Jasper nodded listening wiping his face, Gwen let go and stood with him, her arm around his waist.

G picked Moses up off the floor, they all turned wiping their faces and listened to James.

"There is every chance Jane is hanging on, we have to believe that, I know this is hurting you all, but come on guys we have to hope and pray. Has anyone heard anymore from Bill? We need that number to trace his phone, he wasn't on long enough to trace the last one and as we don't have a number, we can't trace it any other way?"

"I will call him now." G walked away from everyone and pulled his phone out. He dialled Bill and waited.

Bill woke with a start hearing his phone go off, he had fallen asleep while waiting for Helen to wake up.

"Yeah, who is it?" He was still trying to come too properly.

"It's me Bill. G. Any news Brother?"

"Hang on, I just woke up, I will go and ask and come back to you, give me 10 minutes."

"Thanks Brother, just so you know things have turned for the worst here, Mark shot Jane a short while ago, we don't know if she is dead or alive. We are banking on you now Brother."

"I will sort it, leave it with me." Bill stood up and dashed to the nurses station.

"Hi, can I help you?" the small nurse asked him.

"I came in early hours, my Sister is here, she was in an accident and was unconscious, the other nurse was going to let me know when she woke up."

"What's her name?"

"Helen Tring."

"Let's have a look, oh yes she was moved onto a ward for observation an hour or so ago, she must have come round. Let me see where she has gone for you."

Bill's heart was pounding out of his chest.

"Okay she is on D5, let me show you the way." Bill followed like a lost sheep, the nurse took him to the lift and left him to make his way up.

"Thank you nurse, I really appreciate your help."

You're very welcome, I hope she is okay." Bill nodded and walked onto the lift.

He felt like his legs were going to give way when he walked onto the ward, he stopped at the nurses station again and asked where she was, the healthcare assistant guided him to her.

He walked into the ward, she was sat looking out of the window, Bill walked up to her, she turned her head and saw Bill stood there, her smile changed to absolute fear. Bill put his hands up.

"Helen, I am not here to hurt you, come on you know me, I just need your help that's all, you heard what happened, I just need his number. Please?"

Helen began to cry, Bill pulled a chair up alongside her. Taking her hand.

"He will kill me if I tell you, he has already beaten me enough, I can't go through that again. Plus I don't have my phone it must be in the car still. You have no idea what that man is capable of, I didn't mean to tell him Bill, I promise." She began sobbing more.

Bill stood closing the curtains so others didn't see. "We do know Helen, he has shot her today, with his number we can trace his phone and hopefully get to her in time."

Helen began shaking. "Bill I can't help, I don't know the number, if I could help I would."

"Well it's a good job I have your phone then isn't it?"

Helen looked shocked, her heart was pounding. Bill held it in front of her.

"password please Helen?"

"2609." She put her head in her hands, she hoped he didn't look at her messages, Mark had sent her the emails when he beat and abused her, telling her he would release them if she told anyone.

Bill typed in the password and the phone opened, he went straight to her missed calls and found Marks number. He called G straight away

G answered without the phone ringing. "What you got Bill?"

"Got a pen Brother?" James came dashing up to him with his phone, 07779" he began reading the number, as James entered it.

"Thank you Bill, thank you, we will be in touch."

"Don't thank me, it was Gwen you said, please keep us posted. What do you want me to do with her?"

"Look after her Bill, she needs it, we will sort it when we get back."

"Anything you say Brother, take care, speak soon."

Bill turned to Helen, he moved close to her and kissed her head.

"Thank you Helen, we will look after you I promise. I will stay with you a while if that's okay?"

Helen nodded and began crying again. Bill took her hand and sat with her while she slept.

Chapter 13

Got you

G hung up and everyone looked to James. He was tapping away on his laptop as they heard a rumble outside.
Shadow and Animal stood up, they knew it was Axel and his friends. They opened the door as the guys approached, they hugged and shoulder bumped as they walked in.

"What have we got Shadow?" Axel asked
Shadow looked around at the room and stopped at Moses, "Brother?" he asked Moses
"Right now, we are tracing his mobile then we can pinpoint his position. James is working on it now. Then once we have a location we need to go in, we don't know if she is alive, so we have to hope and pray she is. He shot Jane earlier we heard Jane scream, but that's all we know."
"Okay, we need a plan, most of you know my team, Jock, Bullet, Ace."
Jasper stepped forward. "Hi, I'm Jasper Jane is my girl." He shook hands with Axel and the guys.

"Okay tell me, what is she like. Is she a fighter, will she try and protect herself?"
"She is a fighter now, she has many years of this before, she is stronger. She's sassy though and that could get her in trouble."
Axel and his guys nodded in unison listening.
"Okay", Axel pulled out his Glock, "Moses I assume you want this? Anyone else?"
G stepped forward, "I'm in, been a while since I held a gun, would be good to blow this arsehole to bits."
Bullet handed over his spare, G took it, turned it over in his hand, the metal was cold to touch, he rubbed his finger down the barrel.

"Feels good."

"Okay, Jasper I think once we get in there you just go for Jane when I give you the signal, and get the hell out of there, don't look around or look back. Just grab her and run."

Jasper nodded, "Whatever you say Axel, I have my own gun, I will grab it before we go."

"No you won't, I assume it is registered to you? Jasper nodded. "Leave it here, we can't have the risk of you firing it and the bullet casing being traced back to you."

"Okay I understand. But I don't like it."

"Jasper the important thing is you get your girl out, that's it, let us deal with him."

"Sure, whatever you say."

James came back out of the office, he was smiling which meant good news. Everyone stopped.

"Right guys I have traced the phone, all being well he will still be there.

He placed the laptop down on the table and everyone crowded around it.

Ok guys we have an address. Shadow did you get a van? "Yes it's outside. False plates too." We are going to need two trips. One to dispose of him. The other to transport Jane. We can't and won't have Jane in the same vehicle. However, she isn't far away. You get Jane to wherever you are taking her then come back for us. It's a bit tight for time depending on the noise we make but it's a chance we have to take." Everyone got close to the screen. James went through the route. Showed everyone where she was. Jasper stood. "Come on then, what are we waiting for?"

"Jasper I know you are desperate to get to her, but we need to make sure we go in properly. We know he has 1 gun. He could be ready for us. He could be using Jane as a shield too."

"I understand." he replied his head low.

"Okay everyone. The plan is, I will go first with Axel and the boys. We will check the room with my trusty friend here." James held up his tiny camera. Once we know the lay out and where he is, we will knock, as he approaches the door we will take him down. Then Jasper you go in on my say so with Moses and G. He could be alive and armed so we need to be aware still. Grab your girl and get the hell out. We will meet you back here after we have sorted the place out. Everyone nodded.

"Okay. Leave your cuts behind guys. We don't want anyone identifying you from your patch. Masks on all the time. Jasper you got one?"

"Yes, I have. Okay we go in 5." Everyone moved away. All those who had guns checked them and put them into their Jeans. There leathers were removed so everyone was dressed the same no markings on clothes. Face masks pulled up and they left the house and climbed into the van. The air was tense. Nobody talked. They were all sat quiet with their own thoughts. Within 10 minutes they arrived at the apartment block. It was 1.15am. Still noisy which was good cover for them. They all got out of the van.

There was nobody at the desk which helped too. Guns out, everyone crept through the building. No one to be seen. James got to the door and pushed his camera underneath. He moved it around. He could hear the TV. Mark was sat in the chair sleeping. "Excellent." he whispered.

That would help disorientate him when they knocked if he was half asleep. He moved the camera around further. He could see something in another room on the floor. It was blood. He turned and looked at the others. Signaling to them where Mark was, there was no gun to be seen on him but it could be close. He looked over to Jasper and Moses and indicated they go straight in and into the bedroom. Everyone nodded. James banged his fist on the door. Safety catches were off, everyone ready to fire at a seconds notice. Mark jumped up out of his chair completely confused. His head moving from side to side trying to work out where he was. James continued to bang. Mark grabbed his gun and headed to the door. As he got there Axel fired a shot through the door. It caught him in the arm, he stumbled back. The door was kicked open which helped to knock him off his feet completely. Axel went in first aiming his gun straight at his head. Mark was grappling for his but couldn't quite reach as he had dropped it when he was shot. "Fucking leave it arsehole!!" He growled. "Jasper, Moses get in here now. "Jasper ran in his heart pounding out of his chest. His mouth went dry as he rushed past Mark and Axel. The others were checking for anyone else. Axel walked over to Mark and placed his boot at his throat.

"I'm glad you're not dead. I think we are going to have some fun with you motherfucker. Let us see how you like being beaten. And my friend here is partial to shoving his gun up someone's arse." The boys laughed. Mark started to shake he was trying to hold it together. Jasper and Moses ran into the bedroom. Jane was laid on the floor. Blood surrounded her. Mark had caught her in the leg when he shot her. She wasn't moving. Jasper fell to his knees. Tears running down his face. Moses followed. His legs gave way when he saw her. "Belle baby hang on please," Jasper pleaded. "we're here baby, Moses too." He smoothed down her hair. He could barely see her jaw was out, but not the black eyes and bruises on her face. The anger was building inside him, he had to keep it together and concentrate on Jane.

Moses stripped his t-shirt off and ripped it. He wanted to stop the bleeding in her leg. This was a good sign. He tied it tight round her thigh and nodded to Jasper. He scooped her up as he always did and held her close. Kissing her forehead. "Stay with me Belle please. I promise you it's all over. We are going to get you well and get married. We will go wherever you want to go and just relax. Please darling don't leave me."

They rushed out of the door. G followed behind as they dashed down the stairs. They knew they needed to get her into hospital. They would sort their stories later, they knew the Police would be called but that didn't matter right now.

G opened the back doors threw his jacket in for her head. Moses helped Jasper to get her comfortable. He was stroking her hair as Jasper held her hand. "You ready back there?" G called out as he started the van.

"Go, go." Moses shouted back. The van took off down the street. The hospital was 10 minutes away. The longest 10 minutes of their lives. Moses bent down and kissed Jane's head. He whispered to her. "Half-pint we're here. Hang in there please love. You can do this. We are not leaving you. Please don't give up." He choked back the tears as they caught in his throat. He felt Jaspers hand squeeze his shoulder. He looked up at him and smiled.

Chapter 14

Revenge is sweet

Jock shut the door as bullet walked round the back of Mark's chair where Jane had been tied up.

They had gagged him and taped up his mouth. He was sweating badly and shaking his head. He knew this wasn't going to be good.

Axel grinned, his mask was off now, there was no way Mark was going to be alive to identify them so they weren't needed. He enjoyed inflicting pain on someone, especially when women or children were involved and being one of their own made it worse. They didn't know the condition of Jane and regardless this man would pay for all the pain he had caused Jane over the years.

Axel wasn't always kind to his women, he had watched his Dad treat women poorly so followed suit. He had fallen in love once before but she wasn't interested in him, just used him for fun when she wanted too. He earned his money doing jobs just like this one, his boys followed him and they worked well together, they didn't need to speak, they were used to each other.

Axel nodded at Jock, he grabbed Marks head and tilted it back, mark mumbled unable to talk.

"I can't hear you Mark!" Jock laughed looking down at him.

He pulled out his knife from his boot and licked the blade, he was a complete animal. He had lost count of the men he had killed for fun.

Bullet tutted and raised his eyebrows, he enjoyed riding with the boys but wasn't anything like these two. He preferred to clean up after them, he would kill if needed but he didn't do it for pleasure where Jock did. He was younger, Axel took him under his wing when they found him beaten in the street at 16, his father was a drunk and instead of allowing him to beat his mum he took it for her.

Jock slid the blade along Marks throat just enough to make him bleed, he started squirming in his seat, and screaming which came out as a mumble. Jock laughed. He had a roar for a laugh, it was evil.

"I know you want to do this slowly Jock but we need to get out of here soon, so we either take him to the old warehouse and walk him out of here or we deal with him now?"

"He has to suffer, I don't know this women but by all accounts she is pretty special to the club. So, I say we walk him out and you can leave him with me. I am happy to chop him up after and feed him to the pigs." He laughed again, he looked down at Mark, his eyes were wide, he looked terrified, he was shaking his head frantically.

Axel's phone rang it was G, "I'm heading back to you now, I will be with you in 5."

"Good man, change of plan we are taking him to the old warehouse, Jock wants to make it slow, we will drop you wherever and deal with him, then bring the van back when we are done and collect the bikes."

"Okay brother, whatever you like. I have dropped Jane, Moses Jasper off at the hospital, the boys are back at the house, they will pick up Jaspers car and head back with the girls. I would like to go back. See you in a few minutes downstairs, I will keep the van running."

They got Mark onto his feet, Jock kept his gun in his pocket pushed into Marks back, they put their masks on and covered his face. Bullet did a once over of the place ensuring nothing of Jane's or Mark's was there, they left the place as it was and walked out.

They got downstairs as G arrived and threw Mark into the back climbing in after him, he landed on his front, still moaning trying to release his hands, Jock turned him onto his back, he liked to look into the eyes of the man he was going to kill. "This kill is going to be an absolute pleasure."

Bullet pulled up outside the hospital. He turned to G.
"We will be back once we deal with him, I will call you when we are on our way, let us know where you are so we can head off once we know how Jane is."
"No problem, thanks Brother." They shoulder bumped and hugged as G climbed out and ran back into the hospital.

"Let's get this show on the road." Jock laughed rubbing his hands together.
 Axel sat next to him, "So what have you got planned for him then?" He asked looking out of the corner of his eye at Mark's face.
"A bit of this and that, a few fingers off, maybe a foot, his nose, might drill into his head that should finish him off, but before that I am going to beat the fuck out of him, so he knows how Jane felt. I promised Moses it wouldn't be pretty, she has suffered a lot at his hands so it's time he suffered at ours."

Mark's eyes grew wide again, he was moaning desperate to be heard. Axel hit him on the side of the head with his Glock. It started to bleed straight away. Mark crumpled in front of them.
"Shut the fuck up, nothing you have to say is of any importance, and I don't want to hear it anyway."
Jock laughed, "I do love the smell of blood and sweaty bodies, I am sure he will piss himself once I get him on the chains hanging from the ceiling."

Bullet pulled into the old warehouse and shut the lights off, it was out of the way, but he didn't want anyone driving past on the road to see them. Once inside they would have small lights on at the back which couldn't be seen.
They all climbed out and grabbed Mark, he was semi-conscious so between them they dragged him inside. Bullet worked out,

the guys knew it was to clear the tension from his body, he had a good body for it and was covered in tattoos.

They dragged Mark into the warehouse and between them they managed to winch him up on the chains. Jock pulled over the sheets of plastic they had stored there for times like this. He laid it down beneath Mark so he would wrap him in it when they were done and it would catch most of the blood making the cleanup easier.
They sat around waiting for him to wake up, then the fun would begin.

"So, what did he do to Jane then, did Moses let on and why?" Axel asked Bullet.
"By all accounts he's a psychopath, beat her quite regularly, Moses stood up to him once and put him on his arse, but he took it out on Jane, he has a sick pleasure in beating women, apparently he used one of the women at the club in Southampton to get the information out of her. She gave him up when Bill went to see her in the hospital. He killed their child too, Jane was pregnant, he went into the hospital and punched her over and over to kill the child."
Bullet felt the rage inside him build he hadn't felt like this in a very long time, his arms tingled and the adrenaline was rushing around his body, he pushed himself up off the floor and launched himself at Mark, pounding his stomach, roaring like a tiger in pain, he was like a punch bag hanging there and Bullet wasn't bothered that blood was starting to hit his face and body the more he punched him. He needed to get the anger out, it reminded him of his father.
Jock started to call him, he needed to stop him before he killed him, they all wanted their turn, it couldn't be too quick. Bullet slowed down, the sweat mingling with the blood on his own hands where he had split his knuckles and the blood from Mark. He was panting like he had done a marathon in quick time, he slumped onto the floor on his knees, his head laying on his arms cradling his head. He wept quietly. The guys left him, they knew

he would be okay, but he had to pass through the hurt and this had brought back some bad memories for him.

Axel went over to Bullet after a while and picked him up. "Come on Son, maybe we should have left you out of this one." he said as he lifted him off the floor.

"I'm okay, I'm not a pussy, just because I don't like killing the way you guys do."

"I didn't say you were a pussy Bullet, this is just a bad reminder for you of your past. You need to sort your head out Son." Bullet nodded, he knew Axel was right.

He let go of him and Bullet walked to the back door pushed it open and walked out into the night air. It was cool and the sky was clear, he looked up into the stars, the only light was from the moon, it was a beautiful night.

He could hear Jock, he didn't want to know what he was doing. He put his arms up against his head and gripped the back of his hair, he wanted to block out what was happening.

This is so fucked up he whispered to himself.

He walked over to a huge tree that was at the back of the warehouse, it stood proud, he turned and leant against it, slid down and sat underneath, listening to the night. He was far enough away from the warehouse now not to hear what was going on. He closed his eyes and as always saw his Mum's smiling face, she was beautiful, she was a tall dark haired women, she didn't have a perfect figure but to him she was the most beautiful person in the world, she had done everything to make him happy as a child and protect him from his father. He wanted to see her desperately. But didn't want to hurt her either. He knew she had a new man in her life and he didn't want to spoil that either. He just kept sending the money. He knew seeing her would bring back hurt and try and destroy him.

Axel came out of the back door, he took a deep breath and sighed. Bullet looked up at him as Axel walked towards him.

"It is done, He is just finishing, he will never hurt Jane again. She can now live in peace."

"Can she though Axel, he has almost destroyed her, we don't even know if she survived this?"

"Well hopefully G will call us soon, first things first we need to get rid of this body, I think the best option is to get him into the pig house and let them take care of him. They will devour him in a matter of minutes we just need to get rid of any belongings and clothes."

Bullet stood stretching his arms, took a deep breath and walked back towards the door.

"Okay let's do this."

Axel patted him on the back, "if we strip him you can go through his clothes then we can wrap him up and get him to the pig unit."

"Sure thing."

They got back into the warehouse Jock was just stripping Marks lifeless body, He threw his jeans and t-shirt which he had cut off him onto the floor, Bullet picked up his jeans and went through his pockets, he found his phone, he dropped it onto the floor, put his boot heel onto it grinding it into the ground, breaking it up into pieces, pulled out the sim card and broke it up. he found his wallet and credit cards, broke them up, he had a good place to get rid of things like this, they would be burnt beyond recognition. He bagged them up and put them into his pocket and zipped it up.

Axel and Jock finished wrapping his body, they grabbed his clothes they would go into the incinerator too with everything else. They loaded him into the van and headed off to the pig unit, it was still early so enough time to get rid of him.

Chapter 15

Belle

Jasper and Moses rushed through the doors with Jane in Jaspers arms, Moses was yelling at the top of his voice.

"Help please someone help us."

A porter came rushing forward with a trolley, they placed Jane on it gently, Jasper grabbed her hand as a nurse approached them.

"What happened, what did you do to her? straight into the ER." she shouted to the porter.

"We didn't do this to her, we found her, she was kidnapped, enough of the questions, we will answer anything later just please help her now." Jasper yelled at the nurse.

The porter was almost running with Jane as more nurses and Doctors approached.

"You need to stay out here, you can't come any further." she pulled at Jaspers hand to let go of Jane, he bent down to her ear.

"I'm here Belle. I'm not leaving you, please come back to me."

"What's her name?"

"Jane", both men answered in unison.

"Okay take a seat we will come back to you when we have more information, but I can't promise to be quick, we need to assess her first, just pray for her right now."

The nurse rushed away as both men stood in silence. They walked back towards the entrance and found a seat.

Jasper buried his head in his hands, Moses took his phone out, he had a few missed calls. He redialled the first which was Shadow.

"Hey Brother, where are you?"

"In front of you."

Shadow said as he walked up to them both, they both stood up as Shadow hugged them.

"Any news?"

"No, we just got here, they have taken her in, Moses put a tourniquet on her thigh as she had been shot and was still bleeding, it was on the edge so hopefully it hasn't hit anything vital."

Moses sat back down and returned the second call to Gwen.

"Hi babe."

"Moses how is she, where are you what happened?"

"One question at a time, she was in a bad way Gwen, he shot her, she has a broken jaw I think, she is covered in cuts and bruises. Her eyes are swollen where he punched her again.

"Nooooo, No, No, please tell me she isn't dead Moses?" Gwen screamed at him.

"I don't know babe, I'm sorry we are as much in the dark as you are, as soon as they come and see us I will call you."

I'm not sitting her waiting, we will come to you, where are you we will get a cab?"

"Gwen there is nothing you can do here."

"I don't care," she yelled, "she is my friend and I will be waiting with you all, so fucking tell me now where the hell are you or do I have to go to every damn hospital to find you?"

"Okay calm down." he gave her the details and hung up.

Gwen hung up and turned to the others. "I'm going are you coming?"

Matt and James had not long got back.

"We will wait here. Axel and the boys will want to collect their bikes and drop off the van."

Chicca, turned to James. "I'm going hun, I need to be there too."

"Listen girls, you need to do whatever makes you happy, if you feel you need to be there then that's fine, just keep in touch with us as things happen."

They both walked up to their partners and kissed them before grabbing their jackets.

"My car is here Gwen, come on."

They got into Chicca's car and headed to the hospital. Gwen sat wringing her hands, Chicca leant across and grabbed her.

"She is a tough cookie Gwen you should know that better than me, she is going to make it, she better anyway or I will kick her arse." they both laughed

It didn't take long to reach the hospital, Chicca parked and they both ran into the waiting area where the boys were sitting.

Jasper stood as they ran in. He grabbed Chicca as she ran at him, she started to cry as Jasper held her, he squeezed her tight, needing the hug as much as she did. He could feel the tears building inside too but knew if he let go now there would be no stopping him. They all sat holding onto each other, the hours ticked by. Axel and the boys returned, Jasper and Moses stood and went to greet them. Jaspers eyes asking the question without even saying it out loud.

"It's done Brother, he will never be found. She will never need to worry again, it's over for her finally."

Jasper felt the stress of him drain out of his body, his shoulders slumped. He grabbed Axel.

"Thank you Axel, we are indebted to you."

No Brother, it's a pleasure, he should have been dealt with years ago, but I hear you have a strong one there?"

"Something like that yes."

"Let's hope she has stayed strong and can pull through this. We will hang around for a while if that's okay, just to know what's going on then we will leave you."

"Yes of course, stay as long as you need to, the house is there if you boys need to get your heads down and get cleaned up. There is plenty of food, Linda and Jax are the with the boys too."

"Thanks Brother, we will do that before we head off, right now coffee is needed."

Chapter 16

Don't take my hand Darling.

Jane woke up in her bed, she looked down at the bedding, she was confused, she looked around the room.

"This can't be right, this can't have been a dream." She listened, she could hear her Dad singing badly in the kitchen, her Mum was laughing. She leapt out of bed and ran down the stairs. She was so excited, they were still alive, this had been a bad dream. She was crying as she reached the door, she rushed in and up to her Dad, she tried to cuddle him but went straight through him. She turned again.

"Dad, why did you move?" nothing, everything continued in front of her like a film.

She rushed out of the room crying. The door to the street was open, she ran out looking for answers. Everything went black again.

Jane woke to her name being called, she opened her eyes to see her Dad stood over her. She rubbed her eyes not believing he was still there.

"Dad?"

"Yes darling."

"It's really you and you can hear me?"

"Yes, we can. You have been hurt badly Jane, you are on the point of crossing over, but it's not your time darling."

"I don't understand Dad, I thought it was a dream, I woke up, you were in the kitchen?"

"No love that was a dream. You are crossing over love, but you have to fight now."

Jane stood up and walked towards her Dad.

"I don't want to go back Dad, I want to be with you and Mum."

Dance with my Father – Luther Vandross

"Do you remember when you were a little girl, and you told me you were going to marry me when you grew up?" Jane nodded the tears streaming down her face. "Because there would never be a man as special as me?"

Her Dad turned her around, Jane could see herself as a little girl, she had her Mum's spare net curtain on her head pretending to be a bride, she had taken the silk flowers out of the vase, she was dancing around the room singing to herself. Her Dad walked in the room, picked her up and swung her around. He stood her on his feet and they danced together. Jane sobbed remembering it all very well. Her Dad turned her back around again.

"Darling, Mum and I love you so very much, of course we want you with us, but it's not your time. You have to go back, you have a long life ahead of you. A very happy life now, you just need to go back love."

Jane fell to her knees sobbing. "Dad please, don't make me go back, he will find me again, I can't do it anymore, please?"

"Darling listen to me, you have a wonderful man waiting for you, do you want to break his heart?"

Jane looked up at her Dad and shook her head. He pointed behind her, Jane turned. She was with Jasper in the car going on their first date, they were laughing, she watched as they got to the restaurant and were seated. He remembered how nervous she was, she began to smile. Jasper came behind her, they were taking a selfie, she stole a kiss from him, she laughed at the memory. She turned to look at her Dad.

"He will find someone else Dad, it hurts too much, Mark will find me and kill me if I go back, I don't have the strength anymore, I can't go through my life like this."

Her Dad pointed again, Jane looked around. Her hand went to her mouth, she gasped and began to cry.

Moses was in the garden by the roses, she watched him crying, she couldn't hear him, she saw Jasper appear behind him. She turned to look at her Dad.

She turned back to see them at the hospital all sat waiting for her. They were all holding onto each other.

"Oh Mum?" Jane turned to see her Mum stood with her Dad.

"Hello love."

"Please Mum, let me stay?"

"Dad is right Darling, you have come so far, you can do this, its going to be okay love, I promise, Dad and I will be with you always."

Jane put her hand out to her parents, she sobbed desperate for them to take her hand. Her Dad shook his head, they stepped back away from her. Jane was on her knees begging them both. She couldn't see through the tears, she was frantically wiping her eyes so she could see them.

"Please just one cuddle Dad, I just need a cuddle."

"No Darling, if you take my hand there is no turning back and I can't do that to you." Both parents were crying, desperate to hold her.

Jane tried to stand, there was pain in her side, she couldn't breath properly. She saw blood on her clothes, she couldn't speak properly. She looked up her parents were moving away, fading in front of her. She put her hand out as they moved away, she saw a young girl and boy run up to them. Jane caught her breath, sobbing she closed her eyes, allowing the pain to take her back.

Chapter 17

It's up to her now

The doors opened and the nurse came out with the Doctor. They jumped up, hearts pounding. The Doctor took a deep breath, he pulled off his cap, they had come out of the operating theatre. He looked like he'd had a long night.

"Friends of Jane?"

Jasper moved forward. Everyone else stood behind him.

"I'm Jasper, Jasper Mitchell Jane's fiancée, this is Moses, her Brother."

Moses felt tears prick his eyes.

"Mr Mitchell." he put out his hand to shake Jaspers hand, "Moses." he took his hand and shook it. "Dr Roberts, I have been treating Jane, she is in a bad way, but she is alive, she is not out of the woods yet, she is asleep now, we have had to operate to remove the bullet, it hit her thigh, how it missed a main artery I will never know, she must have sensed it and moved, her jaw was dislocated we have had to put it back in, she can't speak for a few days at least, we want to make sure it stays in. She has 5 broken ribs, a bruised eye socket from what we assume is a punch, she has lost 2 teeth at the back which you cannot see. Her fingers on her left hand are broken and she is in plaster. We have removed her spleen, she looks like she was used as a punch bag it got damaged in the attack. She will need to be careful now she will be more susceptible to infections.

All in all she is lucky to be alive, how she is still alive I don't know, you have one strong lady there. Do you know what happened?"

Jasper cleared his throat, he was fighting the tears, Gwen grabbed his hand and Moses squeezed his shoulder.

"She was taken from me, I was knocked out, we don't know who took her, we had a call telling us where she was. We picked her up and brought her here. We thought she was dead."

The Doctor shook his head and squeezed his arm. "You may want to keep this safe then, he took his hand out of his pocket and handed Jasper Jane's engagement ring.

Jasper caught his breath. He didn't expect to see it again, he really thought Mark would have taken it.

"Thank you Doc" I didn't even notice it when we found her, I didn't think to look to be honest."

"That's understandable, we had to cut it off as her fingers we so swollen where he had either hit them or stood on them. Both I think."

"She is still asleep, we are moving her to a private room, if you would like to see her for a few minutes then you can but one at a time, and I mean just a few minutes in total. Jasper you and Moses can stay if you wish, we can put you up, but you must understand she will be asleep for some days yet."

Everyone nodded as they hugged and cheered. Moses looked around putting his finger against his lips to quieten them down. They all cheered in silence, Axel and the boys came forward.

"We will go back to the house now and get a few hours before we head off, give Jane our best when she wakes. Tell her never to be so stubborn again."

"Moses hugged them all, thank you all, I don't know how we can ever thank you properly."

"No need you just did, that's what Brothers and Sisters do for each other. We will see you around, keep in touch and let us know when Jane wakes up. We will be back some time to check in with you all. Shadow we will leave the van at Jaspers for you."

They all waved the boys off and followed the nurse to Jane's room. The nurse turned to them.

"I don't know what Jane looks like normally, but I need you to be prepared when you see her, she has a lot of tubes in her. She has drips too, her face isn't pretty at the moment and her eyes are very swollen, but a lot is superficial."

Gwen got her phone out and found a picture of Jane smiling, she turned it to show the nurse. She smiled sadly.

"She is beautiful, be prepared, like I said."

They got to Jane's room there was a small light on above her bed shining outwards. Jasper and Moses went in first, there were tubes and wires everywhere, the machine was beeping next to her bed and it was recording all sorts of things. Jasper stopped in the doorway, he couldn't breath for a second, he held onto the door frame, he thought his legs would give way.

Moses held his shoulder and beckoned him forward. There were leather chairs close to the bed, both men sat down, Jasper was closest, he leant forward and touched her forehead with his lips very gently, he felt a tear fall and land on her head.

"Oh Belle, I'm sorry baby, I'm so, so sorry, please forgive me." he whispered. He leant his head gently against hers, desperate to smell her, that familiar smell of her hair and her own natural smell. Sadly he could only smell the hospital.

He sat back in his chair as Moses moved closer, he kissed her head.

"Half pint we are here love. We are not leaving until you wake up. It's over love, he's gone for good this time."

He pressed his thumb and forefinger into his eyes to stop anymore tears and moved away.

They both stood and walked to the door, Gwen was waiting with Chicca they were holding onto each other. Jasper nodded as he left the room letting the girls know they could go in, he knew the Doctor said one at a time, but he didn't think anyone of them could cope alone, Jane was a mess and unrecognizable. The girls walked in hand in hand. Jasper heard as they both took a deep breath in shock and the beginnings of a sob escaped them both.

They came out a few minutes later crying and hugging each other, they both dashed to the boys. Shadow and G went next.

Shadow got down on his knees at her bedside and stroked her hair.

"Sweet lady, I am sorry we didn't see this coming. Hang in there, your High Tower here needs his sugar, come back to us soon please little lady."

He cleared his throat quietly faking badly, covering his sob, he moved away leaving a kiss on her forehead as G moved in. He took her little finger in his and kissed it.

"I promised you this would never happen again and I let you down, I don't deserve to be here with you Doc, but know, this is over, he can't come back again. It has finally finished. We love you so very much, heal beautiful lady and come back to us soon, we miss you."

He kissed her head before getting up and walked out of the door with Shadow, he openly cried and wiped the tears away as Gwen grabbed him. They came together in a group hug.

"Come on let's leave Jane to sleep" Chicca choked, "I will drop you off at the house you all need some rest. We can update the others." They all nodded and hugged Jasper and Moses.

"If you need anything guys shout, we will bring clean clothes and shower kits down later today, any changes let us know." Chicca asked.

Jasper and Moses went back into Jane's room and sat watching her, saying nothing.

The nurses came in every 30 minutes to check on Jane, the boys dozed in their chairs both trying to fight the exhaustion. Jasper held Jane's hand throughout just waiting for her to wake up and squeeze his hand.

He knew she had been sedated and it would take a long while for her to wake but he just wanted to see his girl open her eyes. He pulled his chair closer to the bed and laid his head on his arm holding her hand.

"Hey Belle, I know you probably can't hear me, and I will tell you this all over again, but I just wanted to tell you how much I love you. I just want you well so we can start again, I want you to heal this time and know that he can never get to you again. You never have to look over your shoulder. We can go away for as long as you want, I know a beautiful place which would be perfect. Do you remember me telling you about the farmhouse in the woods, where there was a stream, it would be perfect for us to go and relax, I had already planned to take you there, but now I will definitely take you there, we can stay as long as we want to. I just want my girl back. I know I let you down, I should have closed the door properly, I just hope you can forgive me. I don't think I will ever forgive myself. I could have lost you Belle. You are my everything, you have given me hope, life, you make me smile, make me laugh, make me want to be silly, most of all you make me fall in love with you more everyday, I can't get enough of you. Do you remember our first date? When you asked for a bib, I knew then I would love you for a very long time." He kissed her fingers and sighed, leaving his head on the bed and drifted off to sleep.

Jasper and Moses woke up a few hours later, they had slept through the 30 minute checks for most of the morning. As they woke the Doctor came in. They both stood up to greet him.
"Please sit, you must be both exhausted. Jane is a very lucky lady, we have been looking at her head scans from when you brought her in, there is nothing damaged, no fracture which is a blessing. You do understand though once the bones are healed and the bruises disappear Jane will need help with the mental scars?"
Yes, we know Doc, Jane is a Counsellor and she knows how it works, she has been through this before. We will get her the best help we can." Jasper replied
"We do have a great Counsellor here if it helps, she is used to dealing with this kind of issue, if you need her number then please let me know."
"Thanks Doc," Moses said, "we will let Jane make that decision, if she feels she wants to see her own Counsellor then we will fly her home to the UK, if not we will take you up on the offer."

"Okay, would you mind stepping away for a few minutes while I examine Jane, it would be a great opportunity for you both to grab a bite to eat and freshen up. I promise she won't be left alone for a moment until you get back."

Both men looked at each other and nodded. "Okay Doc, we will be back in 30 minutes."

"No hurry, I will be taking my time, the nurses will give Jane a freshen up too. You might want to think about getting her a night dress so we can make her more comfortable when she wakes up."

"Good shout Doc, I will call the girls and see what they can find for her." Jasper smiled.

They walked out of Jane's room, Chicca arrived with James they had brought clothes for them both and washing kit.

"Great timing you two. We were just going to grab a bite to eat. Will you join us?"

"Sounds good to me, you can update us on Jane."

They all walked down to the restaurant together, feeling a little happier than they had for a few days, they knew Jane was still not out of the woods yet but at least there was hope.

Moses filled his plate with cooked breakfast, Jasper looked around and raised his eyebrows and laughed.

"What?" Moses questioned.

"How many are you feeding Brother?" Jasper asked laughing. "Thought you were weight watching now?

"I am keeping my energy levels up, a man has got to eat you know."

They all laughed as he walked to the table with his food. They sat down and started eating, Jasper didn't realise how hungry he was until now, he devoured his plate of food in quick time.

"What's the update Jasper?" Chicca asked

"Well she's not out of the woods yet, the next 24 hours are crucial. She is pretty messed up but that will all heal, it's just her mental health which is the worry. But I don't care what it takes we will get her better and back to her old self again. I just hope she can forgive me, I have a lot of making up to do."

"She loves you Brother, she will come out of this. I know it will take a lot of time and patience and as long as you have thick skin you will be okay, I won't tell you it's going to be easy because it won't be and she will put you through hell, but you have to hang in there, let her work through this. Just stick by her and prove to her you can do it."

"Thanks Moses, I promise you there is nothing she could say that will make me walk away. I did this to her and I will make it up to her."

You didn't do this, yes, you forgot to close the door but he was going to get to her somewhere let's just be grateful it was then and not while we were all away, we have to be grateful for small mercies."

Chicca wiped a tear away from her cheek, James grabbed her hand and kissed her head.

"Sorry Jasper, I can't help it, I don't mean to cry."

"Hey, you don't need to be sorry, we have all shed tears and I am sure there will be more to come too."

"What are your plans Moses?" James asked

"At the moment I am not going anywhere I will wait until Jane wakes up and take it from there. I want to be here for both Jane and Jasper, I will get the others to go home, I might have trouble with Gwen but I am sure Matt can handle that." They all laughed.

Jasper choked back his tears and cleared his throat. He squeezed Moses's shoulder.

"Thanks Brother, I appreciate that, I know Belle will too. Right I need to go and shower and get back up there. Chicca I need another favour from you if you don't mind. The Doc has suggested a change of clothes some nightdresses for Belle, but she doesn't have anything suitable would you mind going out and finding something for me, I will give you my credit card, then give them a rinse out, you know how fussy Jane is about washing clothes before she wears them?"

"Yes of course Jay, I will do anything to help, any chance I can see her while you both get showered?"

"Of course, that would be great. I don't want her to get bored with the same voices and Moses and I can be pretty boring at the best of times." They all laughed again.

Jasper took the last mouthful of his tea and stood up, thy cleared away their dishes and headed back up to Jane's room.

Jasper and Moses went to shower and get changed while Chicca and James went in to see Jane.

As Jasper entered the shower room he pulled off his t-shirt which was covered in Jane's blood, he held it against his face, he didn't stop the tears this time, he dropped to his knees and let them come His body was aching from holding them in, he had held back for so long.

"Oh Belle, please baby hang on."

He continued to cry until he felt there were no more, he struggled onto his feet pushing his jeans and boots off and climbing into the shower. He leant against the wall as the water cascaded down his body. he felt the pressure of all that was ahead of them and of Jane being taken hit him at once. He wasn't a religious man, he believed in God but didn't go to church but the last few days he had never prayed so much. Whether it was God bringing Jane back to him or not he didn't know, but he knew there was someone somewhere looking out for her. He looked up to the ceiling.

"God if you are listening, please bring her back to me, don't let her suffer anymore, she has been through enough. Give all the bad stuff to me, not her. I am begging you."

The tears began again, he wanted to punch something or someone, he had so much pent up aggression inside. He needed to get to the gym soon and work it out of himself. He needed it desperately.

Moses walked under his shower next door, he stood looking at the floor, he was haunted by his past life, holding that gun, going into the unknown again brought back some bad memories of being in Afghan, he hadn't thought about it in a very long time, Jane had helped him with that over the years. But going in and not knowing if she was going to be alive or dead shook him more than he thought it would. He needed to shake it off. Maybe a few rounds with G in the ring would help him. He was worried he would start to have flash backs again, they took him to a very dark place and that scared him. He needed to be around those who cared and work this through. Or get laid. He needed something to distract him.

Chicca was emotional still, it hurt her to see the state of Jane's face, in the dark it didn't look so bad but in daylight it was quite shocking. She caught her breath when she walked in and felt her legs buckle under her. James caught her.
"Come on love, you can do this for Jane, a lot of the bruising is superficial, she will heal from that."
Chicca nodded. "I know I am too soft at times, but this is just so wrong, it's heart breaking."
Let's just be glad it's all over and now we have to be positive, no more negative thoughts, every time you come into this room I want you to be happy, smiling and positive for Jane."
Chicca nodded, wiping her tears away.
"That's my girl, Now sit yourself down there and talk to her like you normally would."
They sat down on the chairs next to the bed as the nurse finished up and left the room.

"Hey Jane, it's Chicca and James, isn't it about time you woke up and stopped lazing about in this bed, you have men to sort out and we need you lady."
James grabbed her hand, he could hear the emotion in her voice and knew she was going to break, but not in here. He had to keep strong for her.

Chicca leant forward kissing Jane's hand. "Come back to us Jane, we miss you. I need you, Jasper needs you. Hell, we all need you. We love you so much."

James stood and leant over Jane and whispered, "I'm glad you knew, I promise I will come and talk to you once you wake up. I'm so glad I was here to help you love. Get well soon beautiful." He kissed her forehead and sat back down.

Jasper and Moses walked back in looking clean and awake.

"It's amazing what a shower can do isn't it?" Chicca joked

"Cheeky mare, are you saying we looked rough?" Moses laughed

"Well if I saw you in the street I would have given you a few dollars." They all laughed, taking the pressure off the situation.

Chicca hugged both men, "you certainly smell nicer too."

Moses grabbed her the way he did Jane in a neck lock and rubbed the top of her head.

"okay, okay I will be nice." she begged laughing.

James hugged them both. "You guys need anything call you hear?"

"Yes of course, thank you Brother....for everything. We owe you."

"No you don't, we look after each other Jay, just look after her. I know she will wake up soon, she's a strong girl. Determined too."

"Thanks, she certainly is that, anyone who can go through the life she did with him and survive is a strong person, I just hope this doesn't leave any lasting scars, you know physical and mental that she will struggle with. I don't care what it takes though we will get her through this, I just want her to wake up."

"Same as Brother, we are all here for you. For both of you. He put his hand on Jaspers shoulder. Jasper put his hand on top and squeezed it.

"Truly, Thank you." James nodded.

"Chicca, Moses are you two finished fighting?" James asked laughing.

"Oops, you got me in trouble now Moses, Chicca said pushing Moses in the stomach, and laughing.

"You did that yourself, you started it." Moses said laughing

Chicca looked around and poked her tongue out at him as she walked over to James and into him cuddling in under his armpit.

"yes, I'm ready to go." she said looking up at James smiling.

"'Right, let's go, see you both tomorrow, like I said you need anything just shout and we will be over."

"Thanks Both, Moses and Jasper answered in unison and smiled. James and Chicca left and both men went back to the bed and sat down, both letting out a big sigh simultaneously. Jasper held Jane's hand again, leaning down and kissing her.

"Hey Belle, well we are both clean now and hopefully smell better for you, neither of us realised how bad we were." he said laughing. Moses sat nodding in agreement.

"It seems like you have been asleep forever, I know it's not that long. I think you will like this room though love, it's very bright at the moment the sun is streaming in the big windows just how you like it. The walls are a pale yellow. It's nice and big too, large enough for Moses and I to get our heads down at night so we don't leave you."

Jasper sat back and put his head in his left hand, sighing again. Moses moved across and got on his knees.

"Hey half pint. I'm getting to old for this kneeling nonsense, so please wake up soon, or I will be a cripple before my time."

He smiled as he said it feeling the pain in his throat again where he was trying not to cry. He leant over her and kissed her head. Jasper stood behind him and put his hand on his shoulder.

"Be back in a second, just popping outside to make a call."

Moses nodded and stayed where he was. He was happy to be alone with Jane for a few minutes, if he cried it didn't matter, she had seen him cry enough over the years.

He sat back on his heels and rubbed up and down Jane's arm with the tip of his finger.

"Hey beautiful. Come back to us please, come back to me. I need you. I can't function without you. I need to talk to you love. But I won't do it while you sleep, so knowing how intrigued you will be and how your mind will be working overtime you have no choice but to wake up." He smiled.

Jasper walked back in the room the Doctor behind him.

"Gents good afternoon, how is the patient doing? Behaving I hope? Good Afternoon Jane. I hope these boys are not boring you too much?" he smiled laughing as he spoke.

"Okay then let's have a look at you, how is that mouth feeling today? I think maybe tomorrow we can take the strap off, you will have mouth ache for quite some time but I think we can let you try without it so when you do wake up you can talk. He undid the strap at the top of Jane's head and carefully pulled it away to have a look at how the mouth was sat.

"Jasper it might be nice for you to rub some lotion into Jane's face when this comes off tomorrow. Just be careful around the joint but it may help her."

"Anything you say Doc."

"Let's have a look at this leg wound Jane, the Doctor unwrapped the top dressing, the nurse came in with fresh dressings. He slipped the gloves on to remove the dressing over the wound.

"Looks good Jane, shouldn't be any lasting scars, I think I did pretty well considering."

The nurse smiled, she loved the way he spoke so personably to those who were sleeping, he always made them and their families feel special and cared about. He changed the dressing after the nurse cleaned it up and redressed it.

"Jasper is anyone bringing in some night dresses for Jane to be changed into?"

Yes Doc, they will need washing though first, Jane is fussy about things being washed before she wears them so Chicca is getting them today, so all being well later she will drop them off."

"Okay great I would like to get her changed before we wake her up to make it less difficult for her and we can make sure she is nice and fresh. I would like to reduce the sedative in a couple of days so she can start to wake up naturally. It will give us a chance to assess her pain and movement too, if needed we can always put her back under, but I am hoping with what you have told me she will be okay, if she has been through this before then all being well she will cope well waking up, we just need to be aware when she does she won't know where she is and she may think she is still in the room with him after being shot."

"Understood Doc." Jasper looked around at Moses. "Can you remember the last time Moses?"

"Like it's embedded on my mind Brother, She had been beaten badly Doc, she called me and I went to her took her to hospital, we asked the staff not to let him in, but a change of staff at night and they didn't pass the message on, he beat her badly because she was pregnant, when he got into the hospital, she miscarried and they sedated her she was screaming badly, when she came round she was quiet, she knew that staying quiet and opening her eyes slowly to check if he was there was her best option to know how to handle the situation, I know when she wakes up she will do the same. Once she knows she is safe it may be different but as long as she can see Jasper and me she will be okay, well I say okay, but she won't lose it Doc."

"Okay, so you know who did this, I wont ask anymore questions just yet, I wont be reporting it either, I think Jane has been through enough, I just hope this is over for her now? Okay lets plan to reduce her sedation day after tomorrow in the morning." he said looking at the nurse, "then all being well early evening she should be awake.. The nurse nodded made notes on her iPad and walked away. The Doctor finished his checks on the rest of Jane's injuries and scars.

"We will have to continue with antibiotics while Jane is still with us, like I said she will be prone to infections and you will need to monitor it."

"That's fine Doc, we will be careful."

"I will leave you in peace. Try and get some rest, you will need all the energy you can muster once she is awake she is going to need a lot of help and patience too."

"Thanks Doc", Jasper said as he put his hand up and left the room.

They both sat back on their chairs letting out a long sigh.

"I ordered flowers for Jane, and some balloons. I want to cheer the room up for her when she wakes. It would be nice to get everyone to sign a card too, what do you think?"

I agree, let's ask Chicca when she comes back, she can get things sorted out for us."

"Do you think Axel and the guys will come back? I know Belle will want to thank them herself?"

"Yes, they will, Axel looks like a rouge, well, he is but his heart is in the right place. Bullet is the soft one, he could do with talking to Jane to be honest." Jasper nodded listening. "I feel for him this would have opened old wounds for him, Axel found him on the streets he was only 16, his father beat him and his mum for years, he took a lot so his mum didn't get hurt too badly, he killed his father and is still haunted by it. His mum is safe but he doesn't see her. He really is mixed up."

"That's awful, yes it is, he has come on a lot with Axel and the others, they all have their own stories, they do some dark stuff but it's for good if that makes sense. They are paid for it by others they are known as the Dark Angels for that reason."

"It would be nice to see them again, and thank them properly. I assume you have a number for them too, or do we go through Shadow?"

"I have it but not used it in years, it's a bit difficult for them to jump on a plane to many questions are asked."

"I understand, but thank god they were here for us."

"Absolutely, took the pressure from us for sure. I have done some bad stuff over the years but I don't think I could feed someone to the pigs, but then maybe I could." He laughed

They sat quietly for a while in their own thoughts. Moses was thinking of all that he had done over the years.

"How long are you staying Moses? I don't mean to say when are you going I just think we need to think about moving out of this room when Belle wakes up. We should maybe do shifts so she's not alone. You can take the spare room for as long as you like. I know she will want you around."

" I will stay as long as you both need me too, while she is recovering I won't even think about going home, financially I am okay, the job will always be there for me, I just need transport."

"Take your pick of the bikes or car Moses I really don't mind and I know Belle wont either, she would love you to be here. If you need any money please ask."

" It's fine Brother I have enough. But thank you. I will get the others to go at the end of the week as we were supposed to be anyway, that will give them chance to see Half-pint awake and hopefully on the road to recovery."

"Sounds like a plan, we could also take her home for a break when she is strong enough too, we could rent an apartment for us for a few weeks, but that's a long way off yet."

"I like that idea Jay, let's keep that in mind, a goal for her."

They sat watching Jane. Dinner time came and a soft knock came on the door, a huge bouquet of roses came in first it was a mixture of red and yellow roses. Behind it was a dozen balloons. Moses laughed.

"I know you said you had ordered flowers Brother but this is vast, you are crazy!"

"Nothing will ever be enough for her Moses, I just want to brighten the room up, normally it would be yellow roses but the room is yellow and they will get lost in the walls, so I added half red. I love giving her red roses but she prefers yellow."

"I can see that." he laughed "But how many are there Brother, I keep losing count?"

"Oh 50, 25 of each" he grinned

"Holy shit, you are fucking crazy."

"Crazy in love, yes I am." He grinned.

Jasper thanked the delivery man, gave him a 20 dollar tip and apologized for the weight they must be. He smiled and walked out. They cleared a space on the cupboard at the end of the bed and stood the flowers, they were in a huge glass vase. They tied all the balloons around the room and smiled at each other, it now looked happier and cheered the place up. Moses nodded.

"You're right Brother, it does look better, it's a good job she knows you are crazy already. I'm going to call G, and update them, I will grab coffee while I'm gone, do you want anything?"
"Tea would be good. Thanks."

Moses left and Chicca walked in with a bag of things for Jane. Jasper got up and hugged her.
"Hey Chicca, you okay love?"
"Yes thank you" she handed him his credit card. "Wow" she exclaimed looking around the room, "Someone has been busy, it puts these to shame." she said showing Jasper the bouquet she had for Jane, it was a beautiful summer array of colours and smells. It was hand tied in brown paper and clear wrapping.
"It's beautiful Chicca she will love it, mine is just over the top, you know what I'm like!, here let's put them on the cupboard next to her bed so she can see them clearly."
"Thanks Jay, anyway I hope you don't mind but I got a few more things on top of the night dresses, I got a dressing gown to match both of them and slippers, some fluffy socks as she gets cold feet. Some of her favourite perfume and body wash, and her shampoo. Oh and some wipes so she can freshen up when she needs too. Her hairbrush and comb from the house. I also took the liberty of getting some pictures printed from the BBQ, I hope you don't mind. She gave Jasper the tube she was carrying under her arm and he pulled out the rolled photo paper, it was A1 size, it was a collage of all the pictures that were taken at the BBQ, everyone was on there, all the guys from England, the club, Jane and Jasper in the middle, he was on his knee proposing. He felt the tears prick his eyes and that painful lump

in his throat as he forced back the tears, he grabbed Chicca hugging her tight.

"Chicca it's beautiful, she will love it." He held it up and walked to the bed.

"Belle look what Chicca did for you, isn't it something else, we will have it framed and put up in the house, but in the meantime it will go nicely on the wall here. What do you think?" He held it against the wall, knowing she wouldn't answer. Chicca came over with some sticky tape.

"I know we probably shouldn't use this on the walls but who cares."

Jasper smiled as he held the picture and Chicca stuck it to the wall. They both stood back admiring it as the nurse walked in.

"Wow did the flower fairy drop in here or something?" She smiled. "What's this?" she asked lifting her glasses out of her pocket and putting them on getting closer to the picture. "So, this is our Jane is it?" Chicca and Jasper nodded. "What a beautiful thought, this will certainly help her when she wakes up, it is really important to do things like this, to let her know she is loved, that people care, but once you start don't stop. So often people start with all good intentions and then drift off after a while, or when the patient is home and they think they are okay, that's when depression can set in. They both nodded.

"Jane is a counsellor, she has taught us all well, but thank you, it is important for us all to remember that." Jasper said

"Good so you know then. Right then let's fight through all of these balloons and flowers and see how she is doing."

"I'm sorry nurse we don't even know your name?" she turned and showed her badge.

"I'm Susan"

"Hi Susan, this is Chicca and I'm Jasper." Chicca smiled

"We all know who you and Moses are Jasper, two completely devoted men, we don't see that very often here." she smiled blushing.

"Thank you, Moses is Jane's best friend from the UK, she is my fiancé."

"So I see, it's unusual for a women to have a male best friend isn't it?"

"Yes, it's a long story, I will let Jane tell you all about it, I am sure she will want to."

"I look forward to hearing all about it, sounds like a plot for a book." they laughed. "Right then all good here, I will leave you in peace." As she walked out of the door she bumped into Moses.

"Oh, sorry nurse I wasn't looking, you nearly had this coffee all over you."

"That's Susan by the way Moses" Jasper said.

Oh, sorry Susan, pleased to meet you, I'm...

"Moses yes I know, we all know." he looked around confused. Jasper and Chicca laughed.

"Don't worry Susan we will explain."

She laughed and walked out. Moses came in and put the drinks down, he was carrying a bag.

He looked up at the picture.

"Wow where did that come from?" he asked studying the pictures.

"Chicca brought it for Jane, fantastic isn't it?"

"Perfect, she will love it. Thanks Chicca." he said kissing her on the cheek.

"Anytime, I just wanted to do something nice. Oh Jasper we were going to look at what I brought for Jane."

She went back to the chair and picked up the bag lifting the two night dresses out.

"I know they are nothing special or sexy which she will hate but she needed something with buttons so I thought this would be perfect, it's good that she is short it will be long enough to go down to her knees." They all laughed.

She held up the first, it was a cotton short sleeved night dress with buttons down the front, it had shirt tails and a collar.

"Well the colour is perfect, she will love the puppies on it too." Jasper smiled.

"I got a pink one with fairies on too." she laughed pulling the other one out.

"So. what matches these two then Chicca I am confused?" Jasper asked frowning.

She laughed and pulled out the dressing gown, it was covered in love hearts, in pink and red on a yellow background. They fell about laughing.

"Well it's yellow, so it matches, and the pink matches the fairy ones."

Jasper shook his head. You are as daft as she is Chicca, it's a good job I suppose, thank you she will like them all."

"I'm not done yet." She pulled out the socks, they were fluffy white with red love hearts. "These will keep her feet warm, there are 5 pairs all different colours, I can wash them for her weekly so she has enough."

"Thank you again Chicca, I do appreciate it and I know Jane will too."

She smiled and walked over to Jane, she bent over and kissed her head.

"Well I had to make you smile when you looked down at these didn't I? I will leave you in the capable hands of these two and see you tomorrow beautiful." She stood and walked to the men. "I will be back tomorrow, I hope you both get some sleep tonight." She kissed them both and left.

Moses handed Jasper his tea, I got some provisions for later, I wasn't sure if you were hungry so I got some things, he started to unload the bag, biscuits, chocolates, savoury snacks, and bottles of coke and water.

"Really healthy then Moses." Jasper laughed.

"Something like that." they both laughed as another knock came to the door. Moses opened it and in walked Gwen.

"Well first things first you can clear that junk food off the table Moses, and make room for this, someone has to look after you two." Moses stood looking dumfounded, pointing to his chest.

"Hang on how is it my fault all this junk food is here." Jasper laughed.

"Well did you see any in my house? and let's be honest Gwen knows you well." He laughed again.

"Come on Moses, don't just stand there, move it." Matt and G came in followed by Linda Jax and Steve laughing.

"Know your place Brother." Matt teased. They all walked up to Jasper and hugged him.

"How is she doing?" Matt asked as Linda walked round the bed to sit with Jane.

"As good as can be expected, they will reduce he sedative the day after tomorrow and hopefully by the end of the day she will be awake."

"Fantastic news, the gun shot?" Matt asked

"It's healing well as can be expected. She is very lucky by all accounts, but still very early days. Someone up there is looking after her." Jasper pointed up towards heaven.

"Probably her Dad, they were best friends, he was her world and she his. She still has a job to do down here then, they are not ready for her yet."

"Thank god, I'm not ready to lose her yet."

"None of us are Brother." G chipped in, they all nodded.

Linda sat quietly holding Jane's hand, the tears slipping down her face, it was the first time she had seen Jane, she had heard about her injuries but never imagined how bad she would look. She was rubbing her fingers softly.

"Oh Jane, I'm sorry we never saw this coming. That bastard deserves to die a very painful death, I hope it comes to him one day soon so you can enjoy life without looking over your shoulder.

G squeezed her shoulder, bending down whispering.

"Linda, he has been dealt with. Jane is free now." She looked around in shock, she hadn't been party to the conversation the outlaws had with him and the others.

"I don't understand?"

"The outlaws sorted it Linda, you don't need to know any more than that."

She held her chest in shock, her mouth open. "Really? Oh my God, nobody said anything." she felt the tears fall again, she leant into Jane and kissed her fingers. "Did you hear that love, He's gone?"

G sat on the edge of the chair with Linda, he put his arm around her. "I'm sorry love, we didn't mean to leave you out." She smiled

"It's okay, I'm glad, Jane can heal properly now. I am just an old lady I don't get to know the important stuff."

"You are important Linda all of you, you are not "just" and old lady" please remember that. With all that's going on I just forgot to tell you as did Steve I'm sure." Linda nodded her eyes filling with fresh tears.

"Come on we have to be happy when we come and visit, Jane will be awake in two days, we have to be grateful for small mercies and keep smiling." Linda nodded again and wiped her eyes. She stood up.

"Okay then what have we got I can do to help?"

"You can pop down to the restaurant and grab some plates for the boys so we can feed them?"

"Okay, I'm on it."

"I will come too." G said, "I will show you where it is, drinks anyone?" Everyone replied with their orders.

"I hope you will remember that Linda because I won't, Jax you better come too?" he laughed as the three of them walked out. They were back in a few minutes with a bag full of cold drinks and enough crockery to feed an army.

"Great, who's eating?" Gwen asked. She had made a chicken casserole and brought a huge pot along with some French stick. She dished up all the bowls the girls and G had brought up and everyone tucked in. Susan the nurse poked her head in the door and shook it.

"You lot keep the noise down or I will have to throw you out."

The men saluted her which made her smile, she put her index finger up to her mouth to shush them, they all nodded and started to whisper, which was nosier than when they were speaking.

They finished eating and sat chatting quietly to Jane, sharing memories with Jasper about the silly things Jane did. They were laughing, Jasper thought he would share their first date with them all, but just the silly things Jane did.

"I know she will kill me when she knows I did this, but it was the moment I fell in love with her." They all cooed together making Jasper laugh.

Moses looked at his watch, it was just after 9pm.

"Guys I don't mean to break up the party but Jane has a big day tomorrow and I think we could all do with a good night's sleep." They all agreed and got ready to move.

"Leave the dishes Gwen I will get them down to the restaurant when you go."

"Thank you for the food, it was delicious, and very welcome, it would have been junk food with Moses otherwise." Jasper smiled.

"Anytime Jasper, it feels good to be of use, and I have to say I love the kitchen, so it was an absolute pleasure to use it." she smiled, looking over at Matt.

"What did I do?" Matt exclaimed, they all laughed

"It's probably what you didn't do." Steve said and patted him on the back, "If I remember rightly Gwen has been on to you for years now about a new kitchen."

"Thanks Brother." he said grumpily looking at Jasper.

Jasper looked shocked and pointed at himself. "What did I do?" everyone laughed.

"You have the perfect kitchen, and I bet Jane loves it too?" Moses said laughing

"Yes she does."

"See that's all Gwen needed to know to dig at Matt."

Gwen walked up behind Matt and hit him across the back of his head.

"You might want to pick up some tips while you are here Mr."

Matt sat rubbing the back of his head as they all laughed and got up to leave. They hugged each other and blew kisses to Jane and left. Moses went down to the restaurant to return the dishes, when he got back Japer had the cots out ready for them to bed down for the night. They both got ready for bed, exhausted.

"Jasper was closest to Jane, he bent over and kissed her. Goodnight my darling Belle. Sleep well my angel, can't wait to see you wake up." He kissed her forehead and moved away.

Moses got close to Jane. "Yes I know it's not a pretty sight me being in shorts but while you are sleeping you just have to deal with it Half-pint, good night love. See you tomorrow." Moses kissed Jane's head too smiling and went back to his cot.

Chapter 18

The long wait

Jasper woke early, it was 6am, he heard the nurses outside the room doing their rounds. He pulled on his jeans and t-shirt and bent over Jane.

"Good Morning my beautiful Belle, how are you doing today? I am just going to shower, I will be back soon."

He grabbed his bag and went out to shower, the nurses all turned to watch him walk away, he felt their eyes in the back of him so turned as they quickly looked the other way giggling. He smiled to himself, "Don't let Belle catch you she will eat you for breakfast."

He showered and returned to Jane's room with two drinks, as he walked in Moses was just stretching and yawning.

"Morning Brother, coffee?"

"Great thanks Jay, how did you sleep?" he asked yawning.

"Not bad actually, you?"

"Great, me too, I will take this to shower with me will be back soon."

"Sure, I better open the windows and let some air in here, Belle will be kicking arses before we know it, and your arse isn't pretty smelling even with all these flowers."

Moses laughed as he walked out the door. Jasper sat next to Jane as Susan walked in to do her morning checks.

"Good Morning Jasper, how are you?"

"I'm ok thank you, slept okay so feel better than I did yesterday."

"That's good, you both need to stay well, or you won't be any use to Jane you know."

"I know once she is awake, we will take it in turns, it will be easier then, but neither of us want to leave her at the moment. Daft I know."

"You are far from daft Jasper, it shows how loved she is, especially as her best friend is a man and he is here too. A lot of men wouldn't accept it. They would assume there is something going on."

"When she first told me before I knew the story, I found it a little odd, but to be honest I think it's great. Wait until you see them together, they are like Brother and Sister, it's beautiful. It's all about trust too. I trust Belle 100% if she didn't want me, she wouldn't be with me and certainly would have said yes when I proposed."

"That's so lovely Jasper. I'm sorry to be so personal. I like to understand and get to know my patients so when they wake up I know them a little and as Jane will be with us a little while I want to make sure she is happy, tell me about her nickname, where did it come from?"

"Which one, she has many?" he laughed

"Oh of course yes, I meant Belle?"

"Oh, when I first met her I couldn't believe how beautiful and funny she was, I asked her if I could give her a nickname of my own, she agreed and I wanted to call her Belle, it means beautiful and it fits her perfectly."

"That's so beautiful, thank you Jasper. I can't wait to meet her and get to know her, she is certainly well loved."

"Yes, she is, you will see why when she wakes up."

"Right I better get on, I will pop back in a while so you can go to breakfast."

"Thanks Susan we really do appreciate it." Susan smiled and walked out.

Jasper sat holding Jane's hand lost in thought when Moses came back in.

"You okay Brother?" Moses frowned looking at Jasper.

Jasper turned to Moses. "I'm good, just lost in thought that's all. It's going to be a long day today."

"Yes, it is, if you want to get out for a while I am happy to stay?"

"No, I'm cool, but the same if you want to get out, please do?"

"I might later, we will see."

"I expect the gang will be up later anyway?"

"Wild horses Brother, especially the girls, I will have a tough time getting Gwen to go home though, she's a tough one and bloody stubborn too. Probably where Half-pint got it from, she was a pain in the arse for a few years."

"I can only imagine, she's bad enough now." They both smiled thinking about Jane.

"It took her a while to relax, especially when she first moved out of mine, she needed her independence. I found her a place that had an entry phone, she was in the middle of the building with no balcony, there was no way in without buzzing the right apartment, it was a small block and I knew most of the people, so they were warned not to ever buzz anyone in. I had keys for it too so could let myself in as and when needed. I did one last tour to Afghan and G looked after her, that's when he began training her, he followed her everywhere, she never knew. She wrote to me everyday I was away, I wouldn't have got through it without her. When I got back I turned to her, with all the other places I had been it all came to a head, and Half-pint fixed me. I will forever be in debt to her."

Japer put his hand on Moses arm. He turned and smiled at him.

"Thanks Brother, you know, for understanding….."

"Listen to me Moses, I get it, honestly I do, I can't believe how lucky I am. She is very special to you, I am glad she has you too. She wouldn't be Belle without you."

Moses pushed his thumb and index finger into the corner of his eyes to stop the tears. Jasper patted him on the back and squeezed his shoulder.

The Doctor came in with Susan to check Jane, he was happy with her progress and to wake her the following day.

Both men sat with Jane for the day until the gang arrived later in the afternoon. They sat chatting to Jane, laughing and joking until Susan came and asked them to leave, she wanted a peaceful evening for Jane and the men, she knew the next few days would be hard on her.

Jasper got the cots out early, both men decided on an early night.
"Our girl has a big day tomorrow and it's a big one for us too, I don't know about you Brother but I am nervous as hell?"
"Me too Moses, I don't know what to expect."
"Well lets hope for a peaceful night so we are ready for whatever comes tomorrow. Goodnight Brother."
"Goodnight Moses."
Both bedded down and were asleep in no time.

Chapter 19

Come back to me

Jasper woke first excited about the day, he got up and went straight into the shower. He walked back to Jane's room, Moses yawned, and stretched as Susan came in behind Jasper. She looked straight at Moses, he was bare chested, she gasped when she saw him blushing a little.

"Morning Susan, a big day today for our girl, so a little excited to see her open her eyes."
"Good Morning Jasper, Moses, don't expect too much from her though, she has a long road ahead of her, one day at a time."
"I know, just having her eyes open so I know she is alive is good enough for me." Jasper smiled, Moses nodded in agreement pushing the bedclothes off pulling his jeans on

"Good Morning Jane, let's check you out before the girls come in and freshen you up and put one of your fetching new night dresses on, I think we need to change these drips too, what is it to be today, pink Gin or Champagne?!
Jasper laughed, he loved the way people here treated her, she would love it too.
"Wow, Pink Gin it is then, the hard stuff today, good girl I am proud of you." Susan grinned at Jasper. He smiled back nodding in thanks.
"Right then, the Doctor will be round at 10am, to reduce the sedative. Then it's the waiting game."
"Great. Can't wait."

"If you two want to grab a bite to eat I will happily sit with Jane while you are gone, I need a break anyway and I can read to her if you like?"
"That would be lovely, are you sure you don't mind?"

"Of course not."

"Thank you, Belle will love that. She's been reading one of those naughty books, something about a billionaire."

Susan laughed "Oh I know the series, yes very good, I won't read that to her thank you very much a bit raunchy for her healing, I think we will stick to a Mills and Boon or Jane Ayre."

They both laughed. "Glad to hear it, we don't want gossip up and down the nurses stations do we?, you will have a queue of men wanting you to read to them otherwise." They laughed again as Moses returned without his t-shirt on just his jeans, which were undone at the waist.

Susan stared at him a little too long, she could see his tattoos and his ripped chest and stomach. He didn't have a defined six pack but more a soft version but still a thing of beauty, his skin was soft and smooth and lightly tanned, his tattoos went around his body. He smiled his cheesy grin which lit his face up. Susan couldn't help herself she sat grinning back at him.

Jasper noticed she was growing red from her neck and up to her cheeks, he laughed to himself and turned away.

He slapped Moses in the chest, "You need to put that away Brother or you will have nurses dropping at your feet."

Moses buckled the slap was a shock. He laughed, he had forgotten how much work he had done on his body, he hadn't been this toned since he was in Afghan.

"Not a chance Jasper, this body is too old now. My bones creak I think they will be looking at you first." Jasper smiled, raised his eyes at Moses trying to signal Susan but he didn't catch on to what he was doing, he shook his head and turned away.

He looked up at Susan she was looking slightly flustered trying to find her book in her bag.

"Susan has offered to sit with Belle while we go down to eat, she is going to read to her."

"Oh wow, that's cool, thank you Susan" She turned and looked at him as he pulled his t-shirt over his head. She blushed again staring at his body. Moses didn't have a clue.

"You're welcome. Take your time."

They headed out of the room and Jasper put his arm around Moses neck.

"Brother we need to talk, that lady in there has the hots for you, didn't you see it?"

"Don't talk about Jane like that, no she doesn't"

Jasper laughed," Oh boy, this is going to be harder than I thought. Susan, I'm talking about Susan!"

"Susan?"

"Yes, the nurse who is looking after Belle, the one with the big brown eyes that blushes when you look at her."

"Oh shit! You're fucking with me Brother?" He looked at Jasper wide eyed.

"No, I'm not. Check for yourself when we go back to the room." He laughed again shaking his head moving his arm away, he patted him on the back as they entered the restaurant, Moses was looking confused and shaking his head. They were both hungry and again Moses stacked up his plate.

They sat and chatted for 10 minutes while eating and headed back to Jane. As they walked in Susan was just finishing the chapter she was reading to Jane. She turned and looked as they entered the room, she looked at Moses and her cheeks turned pink. Jasper smiled, Moses didn't see it again.

"Is that the time already? I better get going, Dr Robinson will be here soon." Jasper nudged Moses.

"Thanks Susan, that's really kind of you."

"Oh yeah, thanks Susan." Moses nodded.

"Anytime, it makes me take a break so I will continue if she wants me too when she wakes?"

"Right I will be back in a while with the Dr, see you later."

They both put their hands up and acknowledged Susan as she left the room.

"You are useless Moses."

"What are you talking about?" he looked at him confused.

"Didn't you see her cheeks go pink when she looked at you, Christ man you make her all of a dither?"

"No, I didn't."

"Jeez, okay, I will have to do your dirty work for you then by the looks of things." he laughed shaking his head and walked away.

They sat down Jasper leant across to Jane and kissed her head.

"We're back love, it looks like Susan your nurse has the hots for Moses, she blushes whenever she looks at him it's quite funny. Think we will have to do some matchmaking. What do you think?"

He kissed her again and sat back in the chair. He had a few jobs he needed Ernie to do so he set about finding the things he needed. Jane had sent him the poem that they had put down for the babies that was his first job, he needed to find a glass company who engraved on glass then he needed Ernie to make a place for it to be cemented in. Then the base for the chair that she loved so much.

He stood and called Ernie, walking out of the door, he knew Jane was asleep but he didn't want to give away the surprise.

"Ernie it's Jasper, how are you?"

"Hi Jasper, we're okay, any news on Jane? I went to the house and found you had a few people staying, they told me what had happened, I am so sorry, is there anything I can do to help?"

"Thank you Ernie, that's kind of you. Yes there is actually I want a few things doing in the garden for Jane when she gets home, there is no rush, firstly I want a base putting in across from the rose bushes, it's for a double seat, it's made of wicker and has a hood that you pull over. Once you have the base in I can order it, Jane would like lights in it too, I would rather do mains lights so can you get connected to the shed from there?"

"Sure thing, that's no problem at all, I can run it along the fence line and dig it into the ground it won't take long for the grass to grow back over."

"Great okay and secondly I have found someone who can engrave the poem Jane wrote on glass, I just need you to make a plinth for it as close to the three new bushes as possible, in the middle would be ideal. But I will leave that to you."

"No problem at all, I will get onto it straight away, I will drop you a line once it's done, if you let me know where the engravers is I will go and collect the glass too.

"Thanks Ernie I really appreciate that. Catch up with you soon, let me know how much I owe you and I will put it into your bank."

"Will do Jasper, give our best to Jane, if you need anything at all please just call."

"Thank you will do Ernie."

Jasper was happy he could get something moving, until he knew the extent of Jane's rehab he didn't want to jump the gun and get Ernie doing anything else. He walked back in the room as the Doctor came up the corridor.

"Good Morning Jasper, Moses how are you both. Did you sleep well?"

"Morning Doc, not too bad thank you all things considered."

Moses looked up, Morning Doc, all good thank you."

The Doctor walked over to Jane , looking down at her smiling.

"Good Morning young lady, how are you feeling today, are you ready to join us?"

"Right then Susan, can I have a look at Jane's obs?"

Susan appeared holding her Ipad, she handed it to him. Dr Robinson looked down the checks nodding his head.

"All looks good to me." he handed it back to Susan.

"Okay no time like the present, let's do this. Remember that she may wake temporarily after an hour or so a bit like when you have a general anesthetic, but it will take a good few hours for it all to sink in and for her to feel anything like normal, she will probably drift in and out of sleep for some hours, once she does speak she will get very tired, her jaw won't help either, so we need to be patient, okay are you ready?"

"Readier than I have ever been Doc", Jasper grinned.

"I second that." Moses agreed

Okay. Let's remove the sedation nurse please.

Susan moved into the IV and stopped the pump.

"Okay I will leave you in peace. Susan will be on hand if and when she wakes up."

"Press the nurse call button and I will be straight in, I am just doing paperwork for Jane anyway so I am only feet away."

"Thanks Doc", Jasper put out his hand to shake the Doctors.

"My pleasure Jasper, she has a long way to go, don't exhaust her when she wakes let her make the decision to speak but any problems Susan has my number give me a call."

"Will do, thank you."

Moses put his hand out and the Doctor shook it too. "Thank you Doc" he smiled and walked away.

Both men sat down looking at Jane willing her to open her eyes. Jasper took Jane's hand in his pulling his chair closer. He bent down to her gently kissing her forhead.

"I love you Belle, I can't wait to see you open your eyes. The excitement is bubbling up inside me."

He turned to Moses. "You okay Brother?"

"Yeah good thank you, just worried about what she will say."

"I'm trying not to think about it. I am hoping she has forgotten the worst of this, apparently people who have been sedated after something traumatic can forget what happened, that would be so good if it were the case."

"Yes it would, we can live in hope, I'm going to call the guys let them know Jane is off the sedation."

Moses walked away and called G, he updated him on Jane and said he would call back later to let him know what the situation was. He didn't want her overwhelmed with lots of people but a quick hello would be ok if she was awake.

As he walked back in he was met by a delivery man with more flowers. He signed for them and took them into the room.

Jasper took the first card. "Hey Belle, the grumpy boss has sent you flowers. Wow, he must be feeling kind." he laughed. Moses pulled out the second.

"This one is from the gang, we need to find room for all these.

"The window sill look favorite I think Moses?"

"Agreed." he put both vases down on the first window and stood the little cards in front of them so Jane knew who they were from. The room was beginning to smell lovely.

"This room is starting to smell like a woman's bedroom." Moses complained pulling a face. Jasper laughed at him.

"You are funny Moses, unless it stinks of oil or leather you really don't care do you?"

"Nope" he replied grumpily.

He sat back down and slouched in the chair sighing heavily.

"How long did the Doc say?"

"He didn't Moses, it's all up to Belle, she will decide when she wants to open her eyes, we just have to be patient."

"You want a drink?"

"Tea would be good if you are going?"

"I'm going I can't stand waiting for anything, this is driving me nuts, I need to be doing something, I feel useless." He pushed himself up out of the chair and strode towards the door.

"Be right back."

"Okay fella, see you soon."

Jasper leant forward and kissed Jane again on her forehead, this time she frowned, Jasper jumped back, he hadn't expected that.

"Belle?" he said excitedly and waited......................nothing.

He kissed her again, and again she frowned. He was grinning like a Cheshire cat when Moses walked back in.

"Moses quick" Moses put the drinks down and rushed over.

"What?"

"Watch." he leant over and kissed her, she frowned again.

Moses stumbled back, and grabbed his head, he brushed his hands over his face.

"Fuck, did that really just happen?"

"Yes it did, you try."

Moses got closer, "it's me half pint." He pressed his lips against her forehead and as he did he felt her brow frown. He jumped back, clapping his hands and punching the air.

"Yes!!, Thank fuck for that, go girl, you can frown as long as you want, just open those beautiful eyes please?" He kept laughing and watching her like a hawk, Susan walked in seconds later. He rushed over to her picked her up, span her around and kissed her cheek. Susan laughed and blushed.

"Did she wake up?"

"No, she frowned Susan." Jasper laughed.

"Oh okay, well god knows what he will do when she opens her eyes."

"You may want to stay by the door." they both laughed as Moses continued grinning walking around the room."

Jasper watched Jane's face with determination to see the slightest movement. He didn't want to miss a thing. Moses kept leaning in just to see if anything new had happened. He couldn't settle he was feeling really restless.

Jasper pulled his chair closer to Jane and bent over her so he could whisper in her ear, still holding her hand.

"Hey Belle, if I could get into this bed with you I would, I can't wait to hold you in my arms and feel your warm body against mine, to feel your bare skin touching mine. To kiss you softly and tell you how much I love you. Please open your eyes and tell me you're ok Belle. My heart is pounding out of my chest right now just needing to know you're okay, to know we are okay, I promise I will look after you everyday, I will carry you anywhere you wish to go, you are my world, my everything."

He sighed close to her ear and kissed her nose softly as he moved away. She wiggled her nose just a little, he almost missed it.

"Belle? Baby if you can hear me do that again." she wiggled her nose without him doing anything.

He leapt out of his seat, "Moses!" he screamed, he came rushing to the bed. "Belle do it again baby please." She did it again. Moses leapt up and ran towards Susan, this time she was ready. He squeezed her tight, "she wiggled her nose Susan, she wiggled her nose."

"Let me see then." Moses carried her to the bed, Susan was laughing at him, he put her down so she could get closer to Jane.

"Hi Jane it's Susan your nurse, this crazy man her tells me you can wiggle your nose, will you show me please?" They all watched intently............. and there it was, Jane wiggled her nose. Moses was out of his seat again, punching the air.

"Yes, yes, yes, she did it again." He looked over at Jasper and saw the tears streaming down his face.

He rushed over to him grabbing him, hugging him from behind.

"Jasper she's going to be okay, our girl is waking up." Moses openly cried as he hugged Jasper tighter.

He let go after a few minutes and sat down, he put his hand on Jaspers shoulder. They looked at each other without speaking, the nightmare was almost over, they just needed to hear her speak the rest they could deal with, whatever was to come.

Jasper sat back in his chair still holding Jane's hand and closed his eyes for a minute, he was trying to get his head right, the last week had been traumatic for everyone especially Jane, he knew this was far from over but just having his girl back he could get her through anything.

He drifted off into a heavy sleep.

Jane pulled back the covers and got out of bed naked, she walked round the room to see him. He was sat in his chair watching her. As she approached, he opened his legs and brought her in closer, she was just the right height that he could suck her nipples. She cuddled him into her as he sucked cupping her breast in his hand. She ran her fingers through his hair pulling him closer to her, he grabbed her bottom and pulling her closer. Her head fell back as he sucked harder, she moaned softly. She felt his hand grip the other breast as he swapped over, he sucked and squeezed, they were so sensitive, he stroked the sides making her tingle.

He span her around licking down her back, bending her over he continued down to her bottom into her crease and opened her cheeks, Jane groaned pushing her bottom at him, he kept licking pushing his fingers into her cheeks to open her up so he could see her fully, she loved the feel of his fingers digging into her skin. She bent over onto the bed and spread her legs further, his face squeezed between her cheeks his tongue touching her rose, the electricity shot through her body, she was on fire, his beard tickled her as his nose rubbed the outside, she screwed up the bedclothes moaning loudly.

"Jasper, yessss don't stop." She hissed.

He continued licking and slid a finger deep into her pussy, she was so wet, she pushed her bottom up into his face as his finger went further inside her.

"Jasper" she moaned again.

Jasper woke with a start, realising it was a dream and someone was calling him, he was brought fast forward back to the present as he looked down at Jane, he could see her eyes barely open through the swelling as she called his name again, it was croaky but it was there. It took him a few seconds to come to properly. He had been deep in sleep for minutes, but it still took time to wake up. He felt her squeeze his fingers. Moses hadn't heard her, he looked down at her, she tried to smile but it was too painful. He squeezed her hand.

"I'm here baby, can you see me, squeeze if you can." she squeezed his hand, the tears came hard and fast.

"Moses quick!" he span around rushing over, he could see her eyes barely open.

"Oh fuck she's awake, Oh fuck, thank God, he prayed looking up to the ceiling, thank you God, thank you, I owe you one."

Jasper laughed through his tears. Moses got down onto his knees, getting as close to her as he could.

"Hey Half-pint, can you hear me okay?" Jasper let go of her hand and nudged Moses, he took it, Jane squeezed, and opened her mouth to speak.

"Yes" she croaked, trying not to cough.

They both cried openly again. Moses jumped up, Susan was already walking in the door, she had gone to call the Doctor. Moses grabbed her face kissing her hard on the lips. Susan's legs almost gave way as he continued to kiss her. Jasper laughed loudly he couldn't help it.

"Put that poor girl down will you?" Moses stopped and walked back over to the bed.

Jane was looking around her, Jasper could see the questions in her eyes. He knew he needed to tell her lots of things, but she wasn't ready for all of them yet, so the important things had to be said first. He took her hand and bent forward kissing her head and nose, Jane blinked.

"Belle darling, I know you have lots of questions." she squeezed his hand.

"I will give you a few things, I don't want to tire you then you can sleep. As you may have guessed you are in the hospital." She squeezed "Mark will never bother you again, he has been taken care of, I promise you there is no way he could ever hurt you again."

He watched as tears slid down the side of her face. Jasper wiped them away gently brushing her skin with the back of his hand.

"He shot you in the leg, but it's okay, you have had surgery, on your leg. Your spleen has been removed, your jaw reset, so you need to be careful for a while. You have broken ribs, lots of superficial bruising and cuts. Your eyes are very swollen but no breaks, your nose is fine too. You have a broken hand and fingers." She tried to speak.

"Okay, thank you" she whispered. "You heard me, didn't you?" Jasper moved closer, he could barely hear her. I prayed for you to come, I called you, I begged you." she coughed.

"Oh Belle, yes Baby I heard you. I'm sorry, I love you so much."

"I love you too." she whispered.

Moses came back over and sat down taking her hand.

"Hey Half-pint, we missed you. I'm sorry love, we let you down, that should never have happened." He was choking back the tears. Jane put her hand on his to stop him and gently shook her head.

"It's ok." she whispered

The Doctor walked in. "Well, well, welcome back Jane, how are you feeling?" she nodded.

"Okay." She replied smiling.

"Try not to talk, your jaw is still delicate and I don't want you overdoing the talking if you can help it, I assume the boys have told you all that has been done, in a day or two we will have a proper chat about your injuries and how you need to heal. We nearly lost you and I need you to be aware of what you have been through inside."

Jane nodded. Saying nothing.

"For now, I will leave you alone, please rest as much as you can, don't let these boys keep you awake, and no wild parties tonight please?"

The men just looked at each other confused and being silly. Pointing fingers at each other making Susan and the Doctor laugh.

"I can see you have trouble with these two Jane?" The Doctor smiled.

She nodded smiling back.

"Right I will leave you in peace."

Susan walked in and smiled at Moses, her cheeks turning pink.

Jasper walked back to Jane, he leant over and kissed her head.

"Hello gorgeous women of mine". She smiled as best she could.

She whispered back. "Hello gorgeous man of mine."

Jasper felt like his heart would burst. He never imagined today would be this good, he knew she had a long road ahead but this was perfect.

Moses rang G and told them the good news, he said they could pop down but it had to be a quick visit as Jane had to rest and not try and overdo it, he knew once they arrived it would all go the wrong way, and Nurse Susan would kick them out, well he was hoping she would then he would have to make it up to her.

They sat next to Jane while she slept, both with huge smiles on their faces. This sleep was good they wouldn't disturb her now, they wanted her to rest. Susan popped her head in.

"If you two want to grab a bite to eat I will sit with Jane?"

"Are you sure?"

"Of course, I wouldn't have offered otherwise."

"That would be great Susan thank you."

"Let's go now before she wakes Moses."

"Sure thing, thanks Susan." he smiled at her

She blushed again and looked away, Jasper grinned he saw it too.

They went down to eat, Jasper piled his plate high this time he was suddenly ravenous. Moses did the same and they sat at the usual table eating in silence.

They walked back up to the room after finishing their food and clearing the table to find the gang had arrived. They were all sat quietly talking to Susan while Jane slept. The room was filling quickly with flowers and balloons, there was a huge card sitting at the end of the bed, it looked like everyone on site has signed it. Jasper smiled feeling happier than he had in days.

Jasper's phone rang, it was on vibrate in his pocket, it was Graham

"Hi Jasper, how is she? Can we see her?"

"Hi Graham, yes of course but to be honest I don't think the girls should see her, she is in a pretty bad way right now."

"Christ okay, can I pop up later?"

"Sure, it's a house full here but I am sure they will kick us out later, come up when you are ready."

"Thanks, see you later Jay."

"See ya, Oh Graham, please be prepared, she doesn't look anything like Jane at the moment just the hair."

"Oh, okay, thanks for the warning."

Graham hung up and threw his phone onto the settee next to him. He put his head in his hands and dug his heels into his eyes, he cried for the third time in a few days. He let the tears fall, his chest ached from holding them back whilst on the phone.

He went and got changed. He wanted to get this over with now. He headed out of the house, the hospital was 20 minutes away from home and with the traffic it would be more like 40 minutes, he joined the traffic and got lost in thoughts of Jane. He reached the hospital within 30 minutes, his legs were feeling heavy as he got out of the car, he took a deep breath and pushed himself out. He was desperate to see Jane but scared about what he was about to see.

10 minutes later he was stood outside her door, he had sent flowers earlier that day. He knocked lightly and Moses opened the door, he looked in to see a sea of faces, he sighed heavily relieved others were there too. They all spoke softly to him as he walked in, the women hugging him, the men shoulder bumping. Jasper stood up and came round the bed. The men were good friends now. They hugged hard.

"Thanks for coming Graham, Jane will be pleased to see you."
"Thanks Jay, can't say it was an easy walk coming up here." everyone nodded in agreement
"I hear you Brother." Moses replied patting him on the back.
Everyone moved out of his way as he walked towards the bed with Jasper, he took a seat next to the bed. He looked over at Jane and his choke of fighting tears again caught in his throat. He bit into his fist looking at her, she didn't need to see more tears, he was trying to pull himself together as her eyes opened slighty, he could see the beginnings of a smile.
"Hey cupcake." he whispered
Jane screwed her nose up. and shook her head, she hadn't lost her sense of humour. He took her hand and squeezed it gently. For the first time he was lost for words, he knew what this man had done to her in the past, now this was more of that and worse. He lifted her hand to his lips and kissed her.
"How's my girl?" he asked looking at her deeply
"Okay" she croaked. "You didn't need to rush down here, how are my girls?"

He choked back the tears again. "They are okay, they send their love, we didn't tell them everything, just that you had surgery and you are a bit bruised."

Jane nodded in agreement. "It's okay, it's over." Everyone dropped their heads, choking back tears, not knowing half of what she had been through but imaging the worst, but looking at her was bad enough.

"So do we get to push you around in a wheelchair for a while, we can have races with you, what do you say?" Graham asked looking around at the others as they smiled and joined in. Jane smiled again.

"Trust you." she whispered

"Well someone had to ask, I'm game if you are, these hallways are lovely and slippery we could have so much fun." Everyone began to laugh as Susan walked in.

"Oops we're in trouble now." Moses smiled.

She put her hands on her hips. "Okay I know you are all worried about Jane but this is way more than two at a time round her bed. How are you Jane, if they are bothering you I will kick them out?"

Moses turned and poked his bottom out at her, everyone laughed at him.

"Oh and don't think I won't Mr" she said blushing. Everyone cheered.

Jane wasn't daft, she may have been half asleep and in pain but she knew flirting when she heard it.

She made a note to ask Jasper what was going on, she felt a pang of jealousy, Moses hadn't had a girl all the time she knew him, he had slept with plenty but nothing else. She didn't know how to feel about it either.

Susan came to her side to do her checks. "How are you love?"

Jane nodded. "okay thank you." she whispered. "A little tired."

"Would you like me to get them to leave?"

Jane shook her head. "it's okay, a few more minutes."

"Whatever you say love."

"Thank you Susan." Jane swallowed hard, she was very dry, Graham leant across to her with a straw in her glass of water.

"You certainly have them trained well love." Susan said smiling over at Graham

Jane smiled and nodded as she drank some water and laid her head back on the pillow mouthing thank you to Graham.

Jasper put his hand on his shoulder. "Not so bad when you hear her voice is it Graham?"

He looked up at him, "no, it's not, scary to start with, but happier now, thanks Jay."

"No need to thank me, she would have killed me if I had said no to you coming down, you know how special you are to her."

"Thanks Jay, is it okay to hang around with you guys for a while?"

"Yes of course."

He stood, bending over Jane as she was laid with her eyes closed and kissed her head.

"Love you little lady, get well soon, the girls are desperate to see you."

He moved away and went over to the others to chat. Jasper sat back down with Jane and took her hand. "Hello Belle."

He leant forward as she turned her head his way and he kissed her nose. He remembered her telling him how special it was to be kissed on the forehead and nose. She had told him how her father and grandfather did it to her all the time, she had missed it until he did it the first time, He wasn't about to stop it now.

Moses spoke up an hour later. Right, you ugly lot it's time to go, we need to let Jane rest properly, I will come back to Jaspers tonight too, leave these love birds alone. Anyone got a spare lid?"

"I will drop you off Moses." Graham offered.

"Thanks Brother that's kind of you if you don't mind?"

"Of course not."

"Let me grab my things and we will all head out."

Jasper let go of Jane's hand to say goodbye to everyone and get out of the way so they could all say goodbye to her. They all kissed her head and said a few words of encouragement before they filed out of the door. Moses was left with Graham.

"I will leave you both now and come back in the morning so you can go and get a few hours sleep and a proper shower and change."

Jasper nodded, "Thanks Brother, much appreciated."

The three men hugged and the two left leaving Jane and Jasper alone. Suddenly he felt quite nervous. He pulled his bed cot out of the cupboard and bedded down for the night.

Chapter 20

Healing time

Jasper woke to screams from Jane, he jumped up out of his cot, his heart racing, feeling like it was going to pound out of his chest. He flicked the low light on and pressed the nurse call button, Jane was fighting with someone, she was sobbing, begging to be left alone.

"Please Jasper don't leave me, I want to die in your arms, not here. Please god let him hear me, Jasper please" she pleaded, he could just make out her words.
Susan rushed in and turned the button off.
"Jasper you need to talk to her softly, let her hear your voice but don't rush to wake her, just reassure her, without touching her."
"Can I kiss her head while I talk to her? she loves that it reminds her of her Dad?" Susan nodded.
"Belle baby it's me Jasper, I'm here sweetheart, it's all okay, he has gone now, he can't hurt you anymore. He kissed her head gently as she began thrashing about again.

"Don't touch me, I hate you, I hated you for years, I won't be happy until you are dead, you bastard, you will pay, you don't scare me anymore, do what you like I won't cower away."
Susan nodded beckoning Jasper to continue, he was really worried.
"Belle baby it's okay." he repeated. He kissed her head again as she fell silent. He got closer to her ear.
"Baby I love you, come back to me, I promised you I would come for you and I am not leaving you now, it's a bad dream Belle love."
She quietened and began to frown.

"That's my girl, do you remember when you caught your foot in the car rubber and I had to carry you everywhere,? well I will do it every day if it makes you happy. You make my heart sing beautiful girl. Please come back to me."

Jane opened her eyes slowly, her breathing still deep, but slowing down.
She looked around slowly at Jasper and smiled, looking confused.
"Hi, it's okay it was a bad dream, you are still in hospital, Susan is here." Jane looked around and smiled at her.
"Drink please." she whispered
Jasper was quick to respond holding the straw at her lips, she took a huge drink gulping it. Jasper looked up at Susan.
"That's great, well done Jane, that's the most you have drunk since you woke up." She looked over at Jasper and nodded. "All good."
Jane pushed the straw out of her mouth, Jasper put the glass down, moving closer to her, he sat stroking her hair, it still had traces of blood in it still, he made a mental note to comb it out for her in a day or two when she was more awake.

"I will leave you both now, if you need anything just shout."
"Thank you Susan." she smiled and walked away, Jasper laid his head down next to Jane's, he heard her moan softly in appreciation. That was his mind made up he was staying right here with her for the rest of the night, he heard her smell him which made him smile. He looked up and gently kissed her lips.
"I love you Belle."
"I love you too." she croaked.
Jasper smiled, kissed her once more and laid his head back down. They both closed their eyes and went back to sleep.

Jasper woke as Susan came in with the day nurse to do handover checks, he had a stiff neck as he sat up, he was bending his head from side to side stretching it out. He still had hold of Jane's hand.

"Morning Jasper, looks like Jane slept through after her nightmare, that's a good sign."

He nodded. "Yes, it was scary to watch though. I hope she doesn't have too many of those."

"It's all part of it I'm afraid. Jane will tell you the same, in her field she will see that a lot."

He nodded. "I guess so, are you going to be here a while if so I will grab my shower and a cup of tea."

"Of course, go ahead, we need to redress her leg anyway so we can do that now, and freshen her up."

"Thank you Susan." he smiled at the other nurse, who he hadn't met yet.

Jane woke up as Jasper was picking up his things.

"Good Morning Belle." he kissed her head, she smiled up at him.

"Hi, I'm Alison, I will be your day nurse for the next 4 days."

"Nice to meet you Alison." Jasper replied, Jane nodded smiling.

"I will be going home and getting some rest for a couple of days, you will have a new night nurse too." She smiled.

"Well I know someone who won't be happy about that." Jasper smiled.

"I think you are teasing me Jasper." She blushed.

"No not at all, if you like you can leave your number for him, I am sure he will like to call you, after all he isn't the patient?"

"I will have a think about it" she smiled.

"Well I am sure he would love to take you out and you will be doing us a big favour anyway. It will get him to relax and stop worrying about Jane." Jane nodded in agreement.

"Oh okay you have twisted my arm." she ripped a piece of paper out of her notebook and scribbled her number down and passed it to Jasper.

"Thank you Susan, he may look a bit rough on the exterior but he is a good man."

She laughed "You have sold him already no need to keep on."

Jasper laughed, "Sorry." He kissed Jane again, grabbed his bag and headed out of the door.

"Won't be long Belle." He smiled at Susan and left.

Alison was just coming back in with a fresh dressing. She stood and watched him walk down the corridor. "Wow, he's a bit hot Susan." She laughed

"You don't stand a chance with that one, he adores our Jane here."

"Oh, believe me I am just looking Jane, I have my own at home, but wow he isn't as sexy as yours and it's quite clear he doesn't have eyes for anyone else." The girls laughed and got focused to clean Jane's leg.

"So Jane I hope you are going to share the gory details with us when you are feeling a little better, we need to know how you bagged Mr Adonis there. Jane nodded laughing.

"Leathers and a trike." she whispered, smiling.

"Oh, wow you are a biker chick then?" Alison asked her eyes out on stalks.

"Wait until later when Moses and the gang turn up then you will see more of them." Susan laughed.

"Oh, I can't wait. Are they rough and ready, I have this image of being carried off by a biker and taken into one of the bathrooms and given a good seeing too."

Jane was bashing her hand on the bed desperate to laugh, Susan was almost wetting herself.

"What!, it's true. Have you seen that guy in Sons of Anarchy, with all the tattoos?, my god he makes me wet just watching him, I keep rewinding his sex scenes." Both girls were beside themselves laughing at Alison.

"Well you are a darkhorse Alison, I never imagined you coming out with something like that. His name is Charlie Hunam."

"That's him, come to mumma, my god I wouldn't say no to him, you got any friends here that look like him Jane that fancy making an old lady happy?"

Susan stood with her mouth open, in total shock.

"Well I would go for Chibs if it was me, that Irish accent does things for me, but then so does an English."

"Now you're talking Susan, let's be honest they are so polite and they drink tea." both women burst into giggles, Jane was holding her ribs. They were trying to calm down as Jasper walked back in to leave his bag.

"I'm just popping down to eat and grab a cup of tea, can I get you ladies anything?"

Both of them roared with laughter holding their stomachs, Jasper looked at Jane, she just raised her shoulders pretending not to know. As soon as he walked out Jane lost it too.

They were all feeling very hot and flustered as a knock came to the door. Susan looked around as G stood poking his head in the door.

"Sorry to bother you ladies, Hey Jane, how are you? I just popped in to catch up with Jasper, I need to see him quickly, I will be back to see you when these lovely ladies are done with you. Moses will be back soon too."

"He went down to the restaurant for some breakfast." Susan smiled.

Okay great, I will be back shortly. Jane waved as he walked away. He blew her a kiss and left.

Alison looked back at both girls, pointing at the door with her mouth wide open.

"Who….was….that….hottie…?, Oh my god, get him back here right now."

Susan and Jane laughed at her. "That is G."

Susan replied, looking at Jane for confirmation. Jane nodded.

"He is one of Jane's friends from the UK MC."

"MC?"

"Motorcycle club, Oh, my God you mean we have a real life Hell's Angel in this bed." Jane and Susan laughed again.

"No silly, they are members of the Skulls MC of Southampton England, it doesn't mean they are Hell's Angels. They have another club here in Connecticut too which is connected. They had some other guys here that are outlaws when Jane was brought in." She looked at Jane confirming what she was saying was right. Jane nodded.

"Wow" real life "Sons" then how exciting, he can carry me off anytime he likes."

"Alison! and you a married women."

"Well I never got married, isn't a ring on my finger." She sang bending over dancing and slapping her hip as she held her finger in the air as G walked back in with Jasper. Alison didn't see them but Susan and Jane did, they fell quiet as Alison continued singing, Jasper cleared his throat, G stood watching with a big smile on his face.

"They're behind me aren't they?" Alison asked stopping in her tracks blushing from head to toe.

Both girls nodded at her, she buried her face in her hands as everyone laughed.

"You both could have warned me."

Jane shrugged and made movements across her throat to show she had no voice smiling. Susan just smiled, desperately holding in her giggle.

They busied themselves finishing Janes leg and left. Alison hanging her head in embarrassment as both men smiled. Susan said cheerio to Jane as she was off for a few days and as she reached the door she bumped into Moses coming in. She looked up at him blushing as their bodies collided.

"Oh, so sorry, I wasn't looking." Susan apologised embarrassed.

"No sorry it was my fault" Moses replied smiling down at her.

Susan brushed her uniform down composing herself clearing her throat and walked away. G looked round and started laughing.

"Looks to me like you have a fan there Moses?"

"Something like that yeah, she's a nice lady so watch your mouth"

"Ooooohh listen to you, been a long time since you said anything nice like that. Something tells me you are interested in this one"

"Like I said, watch your mouth"

Jasper walked over to Moses and handed him the piece of paper. Not saying anything. Moses looked down at the crumpled paper in his hand and noticed at the edge part of Susan's name. He looked up at Jasper wide eyed. Jasper nodded and walked over to Jane and sat down.

"Did you girls have fun, there was a lot of giggling going on, I could hear it down the corridor".

Jane nodded smiling.

"Good I'm glad, it was good fun, it was so nice to see you laughing again, I am going to head off for a while, check in on site and the office, I will be back in later on to have dinner with you. Moses will be here and G is hanging around for a while."

"Okay," she croaked "you need to get away from me and this room for a while."

"No, I don't, I just don't want you getting bored with the both of us day and night."

Jane shook her head. "Never."

He leant over and kissed her, "I will be back in a few hours, anything you fancy or need picking up?"

She shook her head. If you think of anything get G or Moses to call me."

"Yes boss." she smiled

"Cheeky girl, I love you Belle."

"I love you too." she whispered

"Right then you two, look after my girl, I will be back later."

"Our girl you mean?" Moses corrected him laughing folding his arms across his chest.

Jasper nodded. "Yes, our girl" Moses smirked and nodding.

Chapter 21

Homecoming preparations

Jasper got home, G had told him the glass memorial plaque had arrived and the seat for the garden. The guys wanted to make themselves useful and were helping Ernie get everything sorted. Jane was going to be off her feet again for a while so Jasper wanted to make sure the house was accessible for her. With all the guys there this would be easier to get things done, Jasper walked into a full house, it made him smile he wasn't used to seeing it this busy, it was a good feeling.

"Hey Jasper, how is Jane?" Gwen shouted from the kitchen.
"Hi, she's doing okay, better this morning, she was giggling with the nurses this morning."
"Oh fantastic" has to be sex talk then?"
Jasper raised his eyes. "Yes, I imagine so, they were laughing when G and Moses walked in, a new nurse is with her today, she seems to be a little naughty, so god help those two."
"Oh, can't wait to meet her then."
"I need another favour Gwen please?"
"Sure love, what can I help with?"
Jane could do with some more clothes, get her out of her nighties, I wondered if you would come and take a look at what she has and if we don't think it's suitable would you come shopping with me to find something, you know her taste better than I do?"
"I would love too."
"Great let's go and have a look."

They wandered into the bedroom and started to go through Jane's things.

"I think she needs shorts for sure so they can get to her leg easier, and something with a zip up the front or short sleeves, what do you think Gwen?"

"I agree love."

"I think we better bite the bullet and just go shopping and get some of each don't you?"

I think so, any excuse to get around the shops anyway." Gwen laughed.

"Let me go and see the boys and Ernie then we can get going, I want to pop into the jewelers too."

"Oh? You have her ring don't you?"

"Yes I do but I want something making for her, let me show you."

Jasper pulled out his wallet and slipped a piece of paper out, drawn on it were two capital J's, of different colour, one appears to be behind the other, slighty to the right, the bottom one is higher by dimension they are equal in shape and size, each have a slim line with a diamond half way down from the frontal roof of the letter.

 "Oh Jasper that is beautiful!, did you draw that?"

"Yes I did, I was going to wait a while but as she can't wear her ring I thought It might be nice to wear this on a necklace."

Gwen felt the tears prickle her eyes.

"Oh Jasper, are you truly real? Promise me you will never hurt Jane?"

"I promise Gwen, I can't explain how much I love her, I know some may think I am a soft touch or weak and stupid, but I really don't care. She is everything to me and I will do everything in my power to show her that, the bad stuff is over for good, we just need to get her well both mind and body now, I know she is going to have bad nights like she is having for a while and that's ok, I will take the rough with the smooth."

Gwen cried openly and threw herself into Jaspers arms, "you are far from weak or stupid love, soft touch maybe." she said through the tears laughing.

"Cheeky mare." He hugged her tight and wiped the tear from her face with his thumb. "Come on, let's go and see what the boys have been doing, but you might want to wipe your face, first, what is it you say to Belle, you look like a panda?" he laughed as Gwen wiped her eyes frantically. And she punched him in the arm.

"Oww, what was that for?"

"You made me cry so it's your fault."

"Women's common sense always throw's me." he laughed and walked to the patio doors.

As they walked outside Ernie and the men were at the table drinking tea. They all stood and walked to Jasper hugging him. All wanting to know how Jane was doing. He gave them an update, they all nodded and smiled happy to hear there was a small improvement.

"So what have you guys been up to?"

"Come on let's show you."

They walked down the garden together, Ernie leading the way. They stopped at the rose bed and Jasper could see the sun shining onto the glass, causing a rainbow to bounce off the corners, his sob caught in his throat, he really wished Jane was here to see this with him. He walked around the front of it and stood in silence for a few seconds, he knew the words off by heart but still wanted to read them allowed.

Our beautiful Angels,
You were too beautiful for earth,
You are a thousand winds that blow.
The diamond glints on snow,
The love that surrounds us,
In every breath we take.
You will be remembered and loved,
As our hearts break.
We will visit you in our dreams,
Forever in our hearts.
Love Mummy and Daddy.

Everyone stood in silence with him as he read the poem. Gwen caught hold of his hand and squeezed it, he looked down at her and kissed the top of her head.

Matt put his hand on his shoulder and squeezed it. After a few seconds Jasper spoke.

"Wow, it looks perfect. Belle is going to love it, it's better than I imagined and I love the way the sun catches it too."

"You want to thank Ernie for that, he moved it so many times, he wanted the morning sun to catch it." Matt smiled patting Ernie on the back.

Jasper turned and hugged him. "Thank you Ernie, Belle is going to be overwhelmed when she sees it, I have to take some pictures not that it will do it justice though."

"You're very welcome Jasper, the wife has asked if she can come and take a look later?"

"You don't need to ask Ernie, you are both part of the family to me."

Ernie smiled feeling the tears pricking his eyes, he blinked furiously trying to stop them, cleared his throat and turned away.

"Right the chair is here, the lads and I have laid the slabs and got it ready. Matt has done the feed for the electric already, come and see."

Jasper felt a leap of excitement as they headed around the corner, Matt had gone ahead with Gwen and turned the lights on and pulled the canopy over it. It was like a little cave inside, the lights were low to give it that romantic feel.

"Oh wow!" Jasper exclaimed. "That is perfect, Belle is going to go nuts, I won't be telling her this is here until she's home and I can bring her around here. Thank you all so, so much."

"There is more." Matt smiled looking smug, he walked over to the swing and bent down under the tree flicking a switch, the swing lit up with 1000s of tiny lights.

"Well we couldn't miss this out could we, Jane is a child at heart and I know she loves this swing."

Jasper felt a huge lump in his throat, he grabbed Matt and hugged him.

"Thanks Brother." he walked to Ernie and the others and did the same.

He stepped back, "I really can't thank you all enough, I don't know how I will ever repay your kindness."

"No need Brother, that's what families do for each other." Everyone nodding in agreement.

"Thank you Matt, right Gwen and I have some shopping to do for Belle, anyone need anything?"

"We will join you, we could do with stretching our legs and finally looking around this town of yours."

"Great, sounds like a plan, Gwen grabbed Matt's hand and kissed him.

They went back into the house grabbing their keys and jackets before getting the bikes out.

Jasper led on his Harley and the others followed.

"Can someone really miss this feeling", he asked as he rode out onto the main road. "I can't wait to get you out with me Belle."

He looked into his mirror and smiled as he saw the lads behind him, Ernie had gone home to collect his wife so she could look at the garden too.

They pulled into the shopping centre and parked up. They locked up the bikes and left their gloves and helmets locked up.

"Right then let's go and spend some of Jasper's hard earned then." Matt laughed, rushing along in front of them. Jasper laughed.

"Whatever you want Matt it's yours." Jasper shouted ahead to him.

Matt stopped as Jasper and the others caught up, Matt put his arm round Jaspers neck and bent him over rubbing the top of his head.

"We need to toughen you up Brother, repeat after me when a woman or anyone wants anything, "Fuck Off."

Jasper laughed, sorry Brother, no can do, if my girl wants anything and I haven't already thought about it she can have it."
Matt tutted and shook his head laughing. "Jasper Brother, you are letting the side down."
Gwen linked arms with Jasper. "Ignore him love, he is talking out of his backside, I can bring him to his knees if I want too."
"Oh, this I have to see." Jasper replied smiling and stopped walking turning to look at Matt.
Matt laughed nervously. "Come on sugar, you know I am only teasing." He said looking down at Gwen with his hands outstretched. She was stood with her arms across her chest tapping her foot, with one eyebrow raised. Everyone laughed at him as he walked across and cuddled Gwen.
"Wow that's control you got there Gwen, I think he forgot you were here." Jasper laughed.
"Oh probably yes."
"I don't know what you mean Gwen?" he said putting his arm around her as they walked through the shopping centre.
Jasper stopped at the jewellers. "I need to pop in here and have a chat with them, do you want to have a wonder and I will catch you up?"
"Sure, come on you lot let's go and have a look around. We will just stick to the left-hand side Jasper, you will probably hear this lot before you see them." Gwen smiled.
"Great, see you shortly."

Jasper went in the door, the old bell chimed over his head. It was an old shop that had been built many years ago. He had only been in once or twice for Christening gifts and special Birthdays for friends. The old man came out with his glasses on the end of his nose, Jasper thought he must be 80 at least. He was bent over slightly with wispy grey hair, it was combed across the top of his head where he was trying to cover his balding head. The rest was scraped back into a ponytail that looked like a cat's scraggy tail. He had long dirty finger nails and you could tell he had been working on a piece his hands were dirty.

"Good Afternoon Sir, how can I help?" the old man asked

"I was hoping you could help with two things?" he pulled out Janes ring. "My fiancé had her ring cut off and I need it repairing and secondly, a pendant for her. I have drawn it out if you wouldn't mind taking a look for me?"

"Of course, let me take a look, yes I can do the ring no problem at all. Now let's have a look at this drawing."

Jasper handed the drawing over to the old man, he took it from him like it was a rare jewel into his crooked old fingers he looked at it carefully and nodded his head.

"Is this to scale?"

"Not perfectly no, but I wouldn't want it to be any bigger if you can help it."

"Okay, he pulled the half worn pencil from behind his ear and licked the end.

He looked at Jasper. "Do you mind if I draw on this?"

"No please go ahead"

He added to the picture like he could read Jaspers mind. Jasper stood with his mouth open watching the old man.

"Oh my god, that's it, that's perfect." He gasped

"I suggest two different colours of gold for each J, do you agree?"

"Whatever you say, you're the expert."

"No Sir, you put this together not me, it's your dream I just helped bring it to life. It will take a week, it won't be cheap either, is that okay?"

"Yes, yes whatever you say and please call me Jasper."

"Thank you Jasper, I will need some details from you, and I will also need a deposit."

"Oh of course, it goes without saying. Here is my business card, you can get me on that number anytime or leave a voicemail if I am at the hospital. Here take my card, I am happy to pay the full amount now."

Jasper hurriedly took his wallet out and pulled out his card handing it to the old man.

"Half is good enough now then we can settle up. I will need you to pop back in a few days to look at the pendant before it is polished to make sure you are happy with it, can you do that?"

"Yes of course, that's wonderful."

"Okay let's say Friday afternoon."

"Perfect."

The old man took his card, that will be $80, I hope that's okay?"

"Of course, yes, whatever you need, would you mind if I took a photograph of what you have added?"

"Okay if you want to, you youngsters and your technology." he shook his head. "I will never understand it."

Jasper smiled at him. "It's beyond me sometimes too, I can just about work this phone and that's enough for me." the old man smiled and nodded, "Anyway I will see you Friday, thank you for helping me to make a dream come true."

"You're welcome Jasper, see you in a few days."

Jasper walked out feeling very emotional. He had this pendant in his head since he met Jane, he thought about doing a J and B but knew it wouldn't look as good, he was so excited to give it to Jane, hopefully she would be home by then too.

He walked back up to meet the others and find Jane some clothes. Gwen spotted him first, Steve wandered up to him and grabbed him around the neck and rubbed the top of his head, Jasper started laughing.

"Hey Jay, what kept you Brother?"

Sorry guys it went better than I thought." He got his phone out and showed them the picture of the pendant. They all nodded in agreement at how beautiful it was.

"You're spoiling her Brother, you want to rein that in." Steve joked. Linda hit him in the stomach, as he wasn't expecting it he buckled over. The others laughed at him.

"That will teach you Steve, you know the women wear the trousers and we are there just to please them."

"Are they fuck, my woman knows her place." he moaned looking around at Linda, she scowled at him.

"That's you out of favours now, Matt laughed, "those legs of Linda's are going to be shut tight now."

"She wouldn't dare, she knows who's boss."

"I am fucking here you know, you don't need to talk to me like I am back at the house, and "she" is the cats fucking Mother! Arsesole."

She stormed off in front, Jax ran after her. Jasper shook his head, Steve raised his shoulders like he didn't know what he had done.

"Those size 12's of yours are going to get you in serious trouble Brother, you might want to go and make peace with her."

"Nah she will come around, anyway I will have her if I want to, she has a big enough mouth she can still talk when she is full of my cock."

"You mean your cock is that small?" laughed Matt and Jasper joined in.

"Don't add to it Matt or you will be going without too." Gwen said as she rushed up to Linda to check on her.

"Hey love, you okay?"

"I'm fine, he just pisses me off at times, and I think all the worry about Jane and lack of sleep is getting to me."

"I understand that love, I have been feeling a bit like that too. Why don't we go and find some nice things for Jane and have some fun with her when she is a bit better, get the guys to go out and have a few beers so we can spend time alone with her?"

"Sounds like a plan, Jasper could do with a break too, I know he doesn't really drink but he could do with letting his hair down. He could get his friends over with Graham and James too."

"Right come on then, what shop shall we try first?"

Gwen linked arms with Linda and Jax and they marched off leaving the boys moaning behind them, Jasper was trying to persuade Steve to talk to Linda but he wasn't interested.

The girls stopped outside a sports shop, and signaled the boys to let them know they were going in.

They picked out shorts and t-shirts and little zip up jackets and left. Jasper followed on to pay the bills.

They found a small lingerie shop that had some pretty lace nighties and underwear in the window. Linda nudged Gwen.

"Come on let's do it". They giggled and walked inside, the boys followed.

For Linda this was payback, she would have Steve eating out of her hand later and she wanted to find something pretty for Jane for when she got home with Jasper.

Matt and Steve were very vocal, they had their leathers on which made everyone look at them as they walked in. the staff looked concerned as they were looking through the bras and knickers.

Jasper wanted to let the staff know it was okay that the guys were harmless so he walked to the front of the shop to talk to them.

"Hello ladies, please don't be alarmed about my friends, we are all harmless I promise, they are visiting with my fiancée and I from the UK, she is currently in hospital, so we are looking for nice things to cheer her up."

The girls nodded and relaxed in front of him.

"Well if you need anything please just shout."

"Thanks we will."

Jasper went back to the others, Gwen and Linda were holding all kinds of nighties up and shaking or nodding, they had put a huge amount to one side, which they would show Jasper when they were ready. They remembered his favourite colours were black and red.

Jasper was looking around himself and found a pair of shorts and a button up top which was nice enough for the hospital it wasn't sexy but functional, he knew she would like it even if it was just for home. He decided to ask the girls.

"Girls, help please"

"What's up love?" Gwen said as they both walked over to him.

"Would you wear this in hospital?" he asked holding up the red satin shorts and top.

"I would yes but not for moving around in, I would need a dressing gown."

"Do you think it's okay for people visiting to see it?"

"Of course, she's covered it's pretty and will make her feel good, it's also functional."

"Okay it's in the bag, what you girls got there, you trying to break the bank with the boys?"

They laughed. "Umm, no yours actually." Linda replied smiling.

Jaspers eyes almost came out of their sockets. "you mean that's for Belle?"

"Of course, once you are happy then we will shop for ourselves."

"We better have a look then, he said reaching for the basket, they headed over to the changing area and the sofas and sat down. They lifted most things out.

"Wow, you don't mean for Belle to wear this in hospital do you?" he laughed

Both girls tutted, "No we just want to take it in to show her, we've decided next week you boys are going out, give your friends a call and meet up with this lot and go and chill out, we want some time with Jane alone too and we will take all today's purchases once we wash the stuff for her to wear."

"Oh are we, you made that decision, do the guys know?"

"They will in a few minutes when you go and tell them, first you need to decide what you want to keep out of this lot?" Linda grinned at him.

Jasper started to go through everything, he felt his cheeks go pink, there were crutchless knickers, peep hole bra's, some with half cups where the breast was free just a piece of fabric underneath pushing them up. He then choked as he picked up a leather cupless basque, it had chains and buckles on it, it didn't take much for his mind to wonder and his cock to wake up thinking of Jane dressed in it with stockings and heels on.

He put it into the basket and covered it up, "I will take it all, let Belle decide."

He loved all of it and he knew they could have some fun, his thoughts were straying again.

The girls giggled he hadn't spotted the toys at the bottom, they decided not to tell him and have some fun. "Here let me take it to the till and get it packed up for you then they can call you once they are done."

"Okay, thanks Gwen." she nodded and both girls got up and walked away.

They were laughing when they reached the till. Can you please put this through Jasper will come over and pay once you are done and he hasn't seen the toys, they both burst into laughter again knowing he would be blushing when he realised, but first they wanted to show Jane and have some fun with her.

The girls walked off to buy their own things and torment their husbands. Jasper walked over to the till to pay the bill, both shop assistants smiled as he got his card out.

"All done for you Jasper." one of the girls said, as she handed him the bags. "That is three hundred and fifty-seven dollars and forty four cents."

Jasper choked as he slid his card into the machine. "Thank you, I think." he laughed nervously realizing he hadn't looked at what he had brought properly. He wasn't bothered about the cost at all, just the amount they had found and he had agreed to it easily, before his cock really woke up and he embarrassed himself, he was horny all the time now he knew Jane was on the mend and not being able to have her was killing him. He had to have a play later in the shower after looking at all this sexy clothing and seeing images of Jane in it. He shook his head smiling, took the bags and his card and walked over to the men. The girls went to the till with their purchases and paid returning to the gang.

"Time to eat I think" Steve suggested.

"Whatever you say, we could go to the diner we use if you like."

"Sounds good."
They all nodded and walked out of the shop waving at the assistants as they left.

Jasper managed to squeeze Jane's new things into the leather bags on the side of the bike and he led them to the diner. They parked up and headed inside, the boys were nodding in approval. Jenny walked across to greet them.
"Hi Jasper, wow nice bikes, and who have we here?"
Hi Jenny, thanks, these are some of our friends from the UK, we are all in need of food and I wanted to give the guys something traditional."
"Okay, how about the booth then you should all fit in there?", Jasper nodded.
she grabbed some menu's and led the way, everyone was looking around impressed.
"They all started to move round the booth seat squeezing in, I will give you a few minutes then be back for your orders, can I get you all a drink while you check out the menu?"
"Thanks Jenny, can I have a coke?"
The rest of them added a coke too and Jenny walked off to get them. They had all decided once she returned. "Right what can I get you?"
Jasper laughed, "You might regret asking that Jen."
They gave their orders. Jenny shook her head shocked by the amount of food they were ordering.
"Are we done then? She smiled.
"That will do for now thanks." Steve replied rubbing his stomach.

Did you hear we are all going out next week, the girls tell me they want Belle to themselves?"
"Oh really? Where are we going?" Matt asked
"Depends what you guys want to do, we can go to the club or find a bar somewhere?"
"The club sounds good." Steve said
"Are your friends coming down Jasper?" Linda asked

"I haven't called them yet. But I'm sure they will."

"Well no time like the present." she laughed.

Jasper raised his eyes and got his phone out of his pocket. He dialled Tony, he would get the boys organized.

"Hey Tony, the guys and me are going to the club next Wednesday, Belle should be doing much better and the girls want some time with her so we have been ordered out, we wondered if you guys would like to join us for a few beers?"

"Hey buddy, sure I will call the other two, what time you heading down there we will grab a cab?"

"About 8pm suit you?" he asked looking around the table, everyone nodded.

"8pm seems to be a good time if you are ready then or meet us there?"

"That's perfect, we will see you then. Unless you are going to the gym before then."

"Great I will let the boys there know you are coming so they will let you in, I will call Graham and James let them know too. I'm sure Chicca will go down to the hospital with the girls. I might pop in I could do with a good workout, feeling a bit tight, I will call and let you know if I go."

He hung up and rang the others. Both were in agreement and James said he was sure Chicca would join the girls.

"It looks like Chicca will meet you at the hospital, that okay with you ladies?"

"Yes perfect, she is great." Linda smiled.

"Okay great, that's sorted then, I may go down to the gym if any of you guys are interested later?"

The boys nodded, all in agreement. "We can go and see Jane then, give Moses and G a break too."

Jenny arrived back at the table with huge plates of food, she managed to get it on leaving no space at all. Matt and Steve were grinning like kids in a sweet shop, there were extras of everything, the guys picked up every extra piling up their plates. The table went quiet as they all began tucking in.

They finished up with their lunch Steve and Matt sat rubbing their stomachs.

"Wow that was good Jay, how are you not as big as a house man?"

"Probably because I limit my intake and workout most days, but if I'm not careful and hang out with you guys anymore I will end up like that." The guys laughed holding their stomachs and wobbling them.

"Jenny can we have the bill please love?" Matt asked

"Sure thing, I will be right back."

All the men got their wallets out as Jenny came back with the bill and took her card reader out of her pinny.

"Matt put his hand up, here Jenny I will settle it."

"No, come on Matt at least let me split it with you."

"No Jay its cool, I got this."

Jasper put his card away as did Steve. "Don't argue with him Brother, no point."

Jasper raised his shoulders, "whatever you say, but I am happy to pay."

"Right then, where to now?" Steve asked as they all got up.

"Can you drop us girls at the hospital in a while and you boys can go off to the gym, but you better let your food go down first?"

"Good shout Jax, let's go back to yours Jasper and chill for a while then head over to the gym."

"Sounds good to me." Jasper texted Moses to let them know what they were doing and what time they were dropping the girls off.

They got back to the house going into the garden to chill out, the girls made drinks and sat around talking.

"Jasper tell us more about when you first met Jane, what was the first date like?"

"Well I'm sure she told you I was expecting a guy, I was told he was a biker and Counsellor, I wasn't sure what to expect but always got fed up being the babysitter. Well the first time we set eyes on each other was a few days after she arrived, she had picked up Red and was heading out for a ride, I haven't been in a relationship for quite a few years and to be honest I really wasn't interested. I had been burnt and happy on my own. Anyway, I was sat at the roadworks and heard the bike next to me, I turned to look and the beautiful leather clad woman in control of that machine was smiling back at me, I'm not ashamed to say it had a good reaction." He blushed making everyone laugh.

"Carry on Jasper please?" Gwen begged

"Well when she pulled off I was gutted, I then saw her trike in the market and went looking for her, I felt like a damn teenager! I thought she had gone when I didn't see her again until the day I pulled up onto site and there she was again. Let's just say I remember I was a hot blooded man when she climbed off and bent over. I'm sure you guys know exactly what I am talking about with the girls?"

Steve was on his feet, he rushed over to Jasper patting him hard on the back teasing him. He gripped his shoulder.

"I think what Jasper is trying to say is when he saw our Jane bend over his old man woke up from his sleep and did a happy dance."

Everyone roared with laughter, Jasper was blushing covering his face nodding. Steve slapped him again on his back before returning to his seat.

"Okay, okay yes something like that. I can't believe I am talking like this, especially in front of you ladies."

"Hey Brother, you are part of the family, you don't need to hold back on us now. Continue" Matt laughed.

"I fell hook line and sinker within days…..well maybe the first night actually." he laughed

We went out to dinner, she was hot in her leather, real hot, but wow! When she opened the door and stood there in that dress I was done for, that girl really doesn't know how beautiful she is and I love that about her." Everyone nodded.

"She is a rare one Brother, you got lucky, none of us thought she would ever have another relationship again, she has been asked out enough but she always laughed it off. The party we had for her when she left, seeing her dressed up like you say she looked a million dollars in a dress, all she ever does is where jeans and leathers, but when the girls had finished with her it was like a different girl stepped out of the room." Jasper smiled, remembering the black-tie event, he wasn't going that far though.

"I agree with you Steve, she is pretty damn special. I know it has all happened very quickly and you probably all thought she was crazy and so was I to propose so quickly, but I didn't want to wait, I think when you know you know. This has all proved it all the more."

"The moment I saw Linda walk into the bar with Gwen all those years ago I knew she was the one for me, our wedding was quick too, wasn't it love? I know I can be a bastard at times, but I would walk over hot coals for her." Linda moved across kissing his head and sitting on his lap.

"I remember it well, he had a good few drinks before I arrived, it was another party, all the girls were dancing when he came up behind me, he grabbed my hips trying to grind into me, this lot were laughing at him," she gestured around the gang. "the next thing I knew he picked me up in his arms and carried me outside, he kissed me the first time while I was in his arms and I was smitten, we spent the night together and every night since."

"Wow you mean there is a soft side to you Steve?" Jasper laughed

"Yeah just don't let anyone else know, I don't want them thinking I am a wimp." Everyone laughed at him.

"What about you two Matt?"

Matt laughed looking at Gwen. "We knew each other for years before, she brushed me off all the time, I liked her no nonsense attitude, she takes shit from no one, you know where you stand with her, but she made me wait, I chased her every party we had, she was seeing one of the others on and off, he was a bastard but she gave as good as she got didn't you love?" Gwen smiled nodding, she was enjoying this.

"I think I caught her off guard one day, it was coming up to Christmas and she was organising the decorations, she was up a ladder hanging lights, I climbed the ladder behind her freaking her out, so I grabbed her jumping off and we both fell in a heap on the floor, she sat on top of me slapping me about, her eyes were on fire. I grabbed her hands and brought her down closer to me and stole a kiss, that was it, the rest is history. It's not easy for the girls being old ladies, we keep a lot from them, but they are highly respected."

'What about you Jax, anyone special in your life?" Jasper asked really interested, Jax was a lovely woman and he hoped she didn't have a bad story.

"I was married to one of the club, we drifted apart, we got married very early and I had my Son. He is the best thing that ever happened to me, he is at University now. He doesn't want to be part of this life and to be honest I am pleased. It's not an easy life and not for everyone. He loves these guys we are all family after all, but he wants to do something special, to make a difference. My ex and I are still friends, great friends to be honest. Yes I miss having someone around at times, but I have my toys they take care of my needs." Jasper choked on his tea.

"Jax, a little too much information there."

"Why, we all do it, why hide from it?" Jasper sat with his mouth open, Gwen walked over and hugged him closing his mouth.

"The thing is Jasper we love to talk about it, we don't hold back, we girls are hot blooded women too and before we dry up, we are determined to take as much as we can." The guys were nodding behind Gwen, smiling.

"Okkkaaayyyy" he blushed. They all laughed together the girls all hugged him kissing his blushes.

"However, you did get the shy one Jasper, we need to work on her a bit more."

"I think I am happy with who she is, we can work on that together thanks all the same, he smiled feeling like his face was on fire."

Jasper cleared his throat. "Right then guys I am going to hit the gym, anyone want to join me?"
They all stood, the girls cleared the cups away heading back inside.
"Let's do this." Steve slapped him on the back.
"Moses and G are going to join us, apparently they have stuff in their bags, they are going to pick it up and meet us there."
"Jax you coming with me again?" Jasper asked her, "I would take the car, but it still means one of us has to ride."
"Sure, G will pick me up later from the hospital then when you get back." She waited for him and the others to grab their kit and they headed out to the bikes.

They dropped the girls off and headed over to the gym, Jasper got them in as guests. They worked out for an hour and went off to the showers. Jasper closed the door behind him, sighing, it all felt normal again and then it hit him, Jane was still very poorly and they had a long way to go.

He stood under the shower closing his eyes, the water cascading down his body, it was just on the warm side, his mind wandered to Jane, talking about her earlier had him wanting her so badly, he loved seeing her when he closed his eyes, he thought of the times they had been together.
His mind wondering. They were on the beach sunbathing laid close together. It was beautiful and sunny not too hot with a slight breeze. They had a holiday hut on the beach. It was secluded from others. They had been teasing each other for a while, laying naked, enjoying the freedom of it, and the air across their bare skin, Jane opened her legs, the air teasing her

more. She was laid on her front Jasper on his back, his arms behind his head. Jane began walking her fingers up and down his chest. Occasionally teasing his nipple pinching it. She walked her fingers down to the start of his cock, then moved away making Jasper inhale sharply. She did it again, his cock getting harder each time. Her mouth watered wanting to suck him as she watched his cock get harder, making her pussy wetter. She pushed her hips into the ground needing pressure, grinding slowly. Jane looked up at Jasper their eyes locking, the sexual tension building. Jasper moved his arms down stroking her back. Barely touching her, teasing her, Jane's eyes close as she drifts off, his touch sending signals to her pussy making her wetter. She moans softly, Jasper moves onto his side. Jane opens her legs further desperate to be touched. Jasper moves his fingers further down her back caressing her spine then down the side catching her breast. He pushes himself further down alongside her body getting closer to her breast. He gently places his lips onto the side and kisses her softly, biting gently making her jump, she turns onto her side as he takes her nipple between his wet lips. His hand cupping it, like he is feeding from her. He lets go with a pop moving down to her stomach, stopping at her hip. Pushing her onto her front he spanks and bites her, she feels him smiling as he does so. Jasper gets onto his knees spreading her legs. He starts kissing her bottom, lifting her by the hips onto her knees. He kisses down her bottom pulling her cheeks apart. Jane buries her head into the towel groaning loudly as he slides his finger into her waiting pussy. She is so wet, he moves his head to get closer to her lapping at her. Janes body is on fire, He whispers to her to lay down on his face as he lays on his back, his head between her legs, pulling her down onto him. His tongue pushing into her wet pussy eager to catch every drop of her, his darting in and out. Jane screws the towel her face buried into it, her moans getting louder. The cool breeze is teasing her more as he licks her making me more sensitive. She pushes her pussy onto him rubbing against his beard, his nose hitting her clit giving her the friction she needs. He moves slightly his tongue is catching her clit each time she moves back. She grinds into him her orgasm building ever closer. She feels his arms wrap around her pulling her further onto his face and tongue. He slides his finger inside while his tongue flicks over her clit. Circling biting and sucking. His finger plunging deeper as she feels her orgasm hit. Her body tenses for a few seconds as she begins to tremble as it moves through her body. Jasper laps harder sucking as she cum's with force. His face his wet as he continues to drink her. Janes pussy becomes very sensitive as she comes out of her orgasm. Jane moves away from Jasper sinking onto the towel panting to catch her breath. Jasper gets back onto his knees, turning Jane over onto her back, pulling her towards him. His cock rock hard. He opens her legs sliding inside her holding her legs against his body as he pounds into her fucking her hard chasing his own orgasm.

Jane clenches around his cock as you groans. "Fuckkkkk." Hissing through his teeth as he comes hard. Jane feels it fill her as he pounds harder into her. His balls hitting her bottom. He has tight hold of her legs as he rides this orgasm, groaning, his body pounding her again and again. He finally begins to slow as it subsides, he bends down moving Janes legs, kissing her stomach before crashing down with a thud on the sand. They both lay panting, hot and sticky together. Jasper opens his eyes, his cock in his hand, he rubs harder, his balls aching.

"Oh Belle, I love you baby, I want you so badly, I wish you were here up against the wall, arghhhhhh." he groans as he comes hard, he squeezes his balls, not letting up on the speed still rubbing his cock, he begins to pant as it subsides laughing, his legs feeling like jelly.

He isn't sure how long he had been in the shower, he quickly gets washed and dressed embarrassed now expecting the others to be waiting outside for him. He opens the door, Moses and Matt are waiting G and Steve were still showering.

"Feel better for that Brother?" Matt asks.
Jasper wants to bury his head with embarrassment, he didn't realise he had been so loud.

"Well you said you needed a workout to clear the tightness in your body?"

"Oh yeah right, yes thanks." he stutters.

"You ok?" Matt frowns.

"I'm good, sorry, lost in thought."

Matt slaps him on the back, I understand Brother, no fun having blue balls is it, you need to pull a few off, clear the backlog so to speak."

Moses shakes his head. "Only you Matt...."

Steve and G come out of their showers and join the rest of them.

"Right then, are you going to collect the girls and see Jane for a while before you head off?"

"Yes of course, but we won't stay long the girls will have exhausted her by now." G pipes up. "She was tired when we left her. I will wait down here for Jax if you two want to go up with Moses and Jay?"

"Sure thing, we won't stay long then, just a quick hello." Matt adds.

They all get onto their bikes and head for the hospital. Jane is sleeping when they walk in, the girls put their fingers against their lips letting them know. They all gently kiss her head before they tiptoe out leaving Jasper with her.

Jasper sits down with her holding her fingers as she sleeps, he closes his eyes for a few minutes enjoying the calm. He feels Jane squeeze his fingers and opens his eyes.

"Hi baby, you ok?" she nods

"Can I get you anything?"

She shakes her head trying to push herself up the bed. Jasper stands gently sitting her up and fluffing her pillows , Jane sighs feeling more comfortable.

"Did you enjoy having the girls with you?"

"Yes, it was lovely." she croaked "Thankfully they did all the talking, they told me about the shopping trip and how much they boys ate at the diner." She smiled remembering how much they could eat.

"It was nice to get out with them for a while, do Matt and Linda always fight?"

"Yes, they adore each other but Matt isn't sensitive to Linda's emotions, he forgets sometimes thinking she can read his mind. He's a grumpy sod, a bit like you." She laughs holding her side.

"Cheeky madam, if you were not so bad I would be blowing raspberries on your tummy right now.

We had a nice chat in the garden, they asked about when we met and how I felt, it was really nice to relive it. Matt and Steve were honest about the girls too. I didn't know about Jax, that's quite sad really."

"Yes it is, he is a nice guy, but they just couldn't make it work. Cooper is a great kid, he has worked hard to get into University, they should be proud, they never argued in front of him, always took it out of the house or waited until he was at school. Their house has always been a calm environment for him. Neil comes to the club still, he's single as well, I think secretly they get it on sometimes, you can see it in their eyes when they catch a look at each other. I hope one day they both find happiness.

Jasper laughed. "Oh really well she was telling us her toys do the trick!" Jane started to laugh again holding her ribs.

"That girl honestly she doesn't care."

"I did blush a bit, I'm no prude as you know but I am not used to someone coming out with it like that."

"You have much to learn love." Jane grinned, pulling his hand to her lips kissing him."

"Did the girls tell you they were coming up next week to spend the night with you? Apparently us boys are going out."

"Yes they did, it will do you good, get out and let your hair down."

She closed her eyes again falling to sleep almost instantly as Alison came in.

"Hi Jasper, have you had a good day?"

"Hi Alison, yes it's been good, I went shopping with the gang, that was interesting and cost me a pretty penny." He laughed.

"So I heard!" She smirked. "The girls fills us in."

"Why am I not surprised? Is Belle okay."

"She is doing great, tired but okay, this time next week you will see a great change in her. Just keep doing what you are all doing."

"Thanks Alison, we will, we won't leave her alone at all."

"That's lovely, I will just check the machine and get out of your way, would you like a cuppa while Jane is sleeping, I can bring you one in shortly?"

"That's really kind Alison thank you."

"You're welcome, no point in going to the canteen just for a drink, I will be back soon."

Jasper sat quietly with Jane while she slept, he checked his work emails and cleared a good amount. He messaged Henry and Lilian at the cottage, updating them on Jane. He drank his tea and closed his eyes. He felt drained. He knew Jane was okay, but also knew she had a long way to go, he wasn't bothered by it, he loved her unconditionally and would never let her down he just worried about her.

Jane woke briefly while Jasper was sleeping, she didn't want to wake him so laid watching him, it wasn't long before she went back off too.

Chapter 22

Coming together at last

The next week went as the past couple of days had, Moses spent the days with her and Jasper the evenings and nights. The gang came up everyday to give her someone else to talk to, they had all been out for a ride with Shadow, he showed the girls more of the area to get them out and about.

Jasper was on his way back to the hospital, he had been back to the jewellers again to collect Janes ring and check on the necklace, it was stunning, it just needed the stones putting in and polishing so he could collect it at the end of the week.

Jasper walked into Jane's room, G and Moses were sat chatting and laughing with Jane, it made him smile to see it. Jane looked over as he moved further in.
"Hi baby, how are you doing?" he walked to her bed and kissed her on the lips.
"I'm okay, how are you?"
"Good Belle, the girls are coming up shortly, I wanted to spend some time with you before they arrived and we went out for the night."

"Sounds good to me Brother, let the girls do their thing." Moses smiled, "We may have trouble getting this one out though he is smitten with a certain nurse who likes shaking her arse in his direction." They all laughed except for G. he sat pouting.
Jane nodded as Jasper looked round at her. "He is too, never seen him like this before."
Jasper was so pleased to see Jane laughing and smiling again.
"You got it bad G?"
"No, I'm fine, she's a nice lady, a bit of fun that's all."
"Oh I see, okay then." Jasper smiled over at Jane.

"Right then little lady we will get out of here and give you some time with Jay. We will see you tomorrow." Moses leant over Jane and kissed her head, G followed. She hugged them both.

"Thanks for spending time with me, I know it must be getting boring now."

"Hey never think that Half-pint, I would be here all night if Jay wasn't here you know that."

"Me too." G agreed.

They hugged Jasper, kissed Jane and left.

Jasper pulled the chair close to Jane's bed and sat down, he put his head on her pillow and rubbed noses with her.

"I've missed you Belle." he said kissing her lips

"Mmmmmm missed you too baby, did you have fun today, it looks like you have been shopping?"

"Not guilty. I paid the bill the girls did the rest, so if there is anything you don't like then you can tell me and I will take it back, this is what they brought last week."

"Do I get to take a look?"

"Sure, I don't know exactly what's there, the girls kept somethings hidden from me."

Jane started laughing knowing what the girls were like, so she was careful to pull things out. She found the leather cupless bask and held it up.

"Okay, did you see this?" she laughed holding it against herself in bed.

"Jasper looked down, be careful Belle or I will be jumping in there with you."

She started to giggle, he loved making her laugh. She pulled out another negligee it was black, sheer and very short. It had lace around the breast area.

"Oh, I love this Jasper, can I wear it now?" she made a serious face.

"Do you think that is wise Belle?" Jasper looked at her for a second believing she was being serious. It then dawned on him she was teasing him. Jane started to laugh and covered her face with it.

"If you weren't laid in this bed lady I would be tickling you right now until you begged me to stop."

Jane was holding onto her ribs trying not to laugh too much.

"No sympathy Belle." Jasper laughed looking down at her.

She pouted at him which always made him melt. He leant into her and kissed her, catching her lip in his teeth.

"I love you Belle, I've missed us."

I love you too, I just want to be better, seeing you not being able to touch you and lay with you it's so hard."

"I know what you mean, I am so damn horny for you. I am going to have to do something about it later before I go out."

"Oh really, why is that, are you worried you might grab one of the club girls?" She folded her arms across her chest raising one eyebrow questioningly at him. She was teasing him again.

"God no Belle, you know I only want you, how could you even think that?"

She couldn't help herself she started giggling again. Jaspers face lit up, he should have known better, she wouldn't believe he would do that, she knew he only had eyes for her.

He growled at her "grrrrrrr!! Just wait until you are better Miss Belle, you are in trouble lady."

"Oh, I can't wait, bring it on." she grinned at him

"Such a bad girl. Come on, what else have we got in this bag of yours? You know whatever you wear it won't last long anyway I love you naked."

Jane loved that, she always loved being naked around him. She dug deep and pulled out some eggs, they both laughed remembering the black-tie evening and how they teased each other all night.

"Mmmmm, maybe you should put them in now Belle?"

"Oh you would love that wouldn't you?"

"Hell, yes I would, but I can wait. That was an amazing night love wasn't it?"

"Yes, it was, I loved teasing you, that was so hot. First time I have ever gone out without underwear too."

"Well we have plenty of time to do more of that when you are better, something to plan for don't you think?"

Jane nodded. He could see she was getting tired, he took the bag from her. "Let me take this you and the girls can have fun later with the rest of it. Do you fancy a cuddle?"

"Jane frowned up at him, "Can you shuffle over a little, I will climb on the bed with you and we can cuddle for a while."

Jane didn't need to be asked again, she moved across a little, her drips were out now so she was freer than before. Jasper closed her door, and climbed into her bed, he put his arm out as Jane curled into his side and snuggled in. Both of them sighed as they joined together finally.

Jasper kissed her head again. "God I have missed this Belle. I really thought I had lost you, I thought you would want me to go."

"Never, it wasn't your fault, it was going to happen and at least now it's over. G and Moses told me everything. Well I think they may have left a few things out, but I don't mind, I know enough."

Jasper squeezed Jane as hard as he could dare too. "I can't wait to get you home."

"I don't want to go back there Jasper, I want to be with you all the time."

"Okay I will sell the house, we can find somewhere else, I just want you to be happy and we can take the roses with us, I understand Belle."

"No, I meant my apartment." She could feel the tears pricking her eyes. "I love your house baby, I will be nervous for a while, but I want to be there always, I don't want to leave it, or you ever again."

"Oh, Belle you just made me so happy, are you sure?" he said moving away from her to look into her eyes properly.

"Yes of course I am, as long as he can't come back again."

"I can guarantee that, one hundred percent Belle, I will even step up the security. I have already put a closer on that door so if we don't close it then it will close itself."

He cuddled back into her. "I will get your place packed up and moved over then and hand it back, I'm sure the guys will help me." He kissed her head.

"There is one thing Belle" She looked up at him frowning, worrying about what was coming next. "It's our place, our home, promise me you will call it that from now on, I want you to make any changes you like, I want you to be completely happy there."

"I promise." she said choking back tears.

Jasper put his finger under her chin and lifted her head.

"I love you Belle, I never want to be without you."

He dug into his pocket and pulled out her ring, he slid it over the end of her finger, Jane gasped when she saw it again, looked up at him and moved to his lips kissing him hard.

"I thought it had gone, I really thought he had taken it."

She was crying softly looking at her ring, she couldn't wear it yet but just having it on her finger for a while knowing she still had was perfect.

"So did I Belle, the surgeon gave it to me and I had it repaired, they had to cut it off for you."

He wiped her tears away with his thumb and kissed her face catching those that had already reached her cheeks. She squeezed him as tight as she could.

"I love you so much I just want to be at home with you, please ask them when you can take me home, I know I will heal better there, I promise to talk to someone about the attack, I just want to be with you, I will do whatever it takes."

"Okay baby, when the Doctor comes in later we will have a chat with him, if we have to pay for someone to come in and redress your wound we will, if it gets you home. Now rest please you have the girls coming later you need to rest so you are up to it."

"Yes Boss," she grinned. "I do love it when you are so masterful."

"Cheeky girl." he laughed, kissing her hard.

She laid her head onto his chest and drifted off to sleep, Jasper laid his head on hers and fell asleep with her.

Alison came in to check on Jane and saw them both sleeping, she stood for a few seconds watching them, Susan was right she thought they are so in love. Jasper stirred he sensed someone was watching him. Alison tried to get out of the room quickly but Jasper saw her.

"It's okay Alison come in if you need too, I was just enjoying a cuddle with Belle and wanted her to sleep for a while, her girls are coming later to spend the night with her." He whispered.

"I hope I didn't wake you up?"

"No, you didn't, I was dozing more than anything." he lied, he hadn't settled since he had been knocked out, he was hoping now Jane was better that things would change once they were home.

"I will come back, no need to disturb her now, it can wait."

"Thanks Alison, I appreciate that." He smiled at her and laid his head back down onto Jane's.

Being this close to Jane Jaspers body started to respond, he could feel his cock getting hard. He looked down at himself and whispered.

"You always let me down, this is not the time nor the place for this."

Jane stirred, and opened her eyes, she looked up at Jasper and kissed him.

"Someone else is awake I see, glad to know I still have that effect on him, even in my hospital bed."

Jasper laughed, "Belle, it doesn't matter where you are you will always have that effect on me."

She kissed him again more passionately.

"If you don't want me pulling your nightdress up and making love to you then stop that because my cock is aching to be inside you."

Jane continued, her jaw was aching but she didn't care, she was aching for him too.

"Belle we can't do this," she slid her hand down between them feeling his hard cock.

"Why not?" she pouted.

"You are in hospital for one, secondly we will make a mess on your bed."

"I have an idea. Please could you ask Alison to come in?" Jasper frowned at her. She just smiled at him.

"I need my cock to go down first Belle, I am not going out there like this." he bent backwards and showed Jane how much he was tenting in his jeans.

She started to giggle and held her face.

"Oh, funny is it? This is your fault Belle."

"I didn't do anything, you got into bed with me."

"You touched it."

"No, I woke up with him sticking into me."

"Well you shouldn't be so damn sexy and he wouldn't respond."

"How am I being sexy, I am laid in a hospital bed looking like I have done a few rounds with Muhammad Ali?" she moved her hand up and down her body showing him.

"He laughed, "it's not all about the outside Belle you should know that."

She raised her eyes at him teasing him and pressed the nurse call button at the back of her.

"Belle!" he exclaimed.

"Just lay into me, it will be fine, if you get any harder then I know you are perving over Alison." she laughed.

Alison came in looking worried. Jane everything okay?"

Jasper shrugged his shoulders.

"Yes all good, I just wanted to ask if it's possible for me to have a shower?, I feel so dirty and I know if will make me feel so much better, Jasper will come in with me and wash me down, won't you love? She said looking around at him.

"Sounds like I don't have a choice," he laughed. "Of course Belle yes." They both looked at Alison

"Well, we will need to cover your arm and leg, we have a dressing for your leg and a plastic bag that slips over the arm. But you need to promise me you will look after her Jasper, no standing on that leg, until the Doctor says so?"

"I promise, we have done this before when Belle sprained her ankle. I will carry her."

"Okay I will go and get the waterproof dressings and extra towels for you Jasper, I will be back shortly."

"Thank you Alison, I really appreciate it." Jane was smiling looking really excited.

"Are you sure about this Belle?"

"Damn right I am, we can kill two birds with one stone."

Jasper looked at her confused. "Two birds?"

"Did that bang on the head make you forgetful or something? Think about it love. You won't make love to me in bed so we can shower and make love."

Jaspers eyes opened wide. "You are such a bad girl, you must be feeling better?" he said kissing her and smiling.

"Well we can't waste your hard on, can we?"

"Obviously not." he smiled. His cock reacting to the thought of being inside her again. He got off the bed and went into the en-suite to look at the shower, it was big, it had room for a wheelchair and had it's own chair.

"Perfect." He looked down at himself again. "Please just for a few more minutes will you just go back to sleep while the nurse comes in?"

"Jasper who are you talking to?" Jane called to him

"Nobody Belle just myself, he looked down again. "You really do get me into some bad situations." He undid his jeans and flicked the head of his cock a couple of times, it went down quite quickly as Alison returned.

"Right then, let's take the dressing off your leg and put this one over it, that will keep the leg clean and dry then we can do your operation scar, I know that is looking really good but we need to keep it dry too."

Jasper stood and watched, he hadn't seen her wound, the nurse pulled the dressing off and the gauze covering the wound. He felt a gasp escape him. He was trying not to cry for her. He was shocked at how much damage a bullet could do.

Alison covered the wound with a fresh gauze and the waterproof dressing.

"Make sure you don't rub it, or it will leak, try and keep your leg out of the shower as much as possible, and your tummy, I know it doesn't leave much of you under the water but you know what I mean don't you?". Jane nodded. "Right then, this will keep your arm dry, it has a rubber seal so slip your arm inside here. Jane put her arm through a rubber circular diaphragm seal, into a plastic bag. She turned her arm round looking at it and laughing.

"Very sexy I must say." she laughed. Holding it up to show Jasper.

He smiled at her shaking his head. "Trust you Belle."

"Right not too long Jasper, if you are going to wash her hair make sure you move her out of the heat of the shower, I don't want her passing out in there."

Jasper saluted Alison. "Yes ma'am."

Alison smiled. "Okay I will leave you to it, if you need anything at all press the button in the bathroom and I will come straight in."

"Thank you Alison, we will."

Alison left and Jasper started to undress, leaving his boxer shorts on just in case someone came in.

Jane sat on the bed eagerly waiting for him. He came over to her and undid her top, he hadn't seen the bruises on her ribs either, this was going to be hard for him, but he needed to see it. Then he was going to make love to her as gently as possible. Jane laid on her back and lifted her bottom as he slid her shorts off. He loved seeing her naked, apart from the bruises that made him want to cry and hurt someone he was enjoying looking at her again.

"Are you ready your ladyship?"

Jane nodded, "Yes, yes I am." she said smiling.

Jasper put his arms out for her to scoop her up. He lifted her up with no effort and she wrapped her arms around his neck, kissing him as he turned into the bathroom, his cock getting hard again in anticipation. Jane leant forward and turned the water on. He put her down onto the chair and pulled his boxers off putting them on the shelf.

"If I push you into the shower Belle on this chair and I can wash your hair, then I will lift you out and wash you?"

"Okay, that's fine with me."

"Great, he pulled her across the tiled floor and sat her head under the shower. She leant back enjoying the water as it cascaded down her face. She smiled.

"That feels so good." Jasper walked behind her and put the shampoo into her hair and massaged her scalp. Jane laid back further enjoying it and feeling relaxed with his fingers in her hair and on the nape of her neck.

"Is that good Belle?" he asked

"Mmmmm perfect thank you, just perfect."

"That's good to hear."

He rinsed her hair off and tied it up out of the way for her.

He picked her up out of the chair, she wrapped her arms around him.

"Can you put your legs around me Belle?" she nodded and did so.

He leant into her and kissed her, his tongue opening her mouth as he ran it along her lips, Jane moaned softly as her tongue joined his, kissing deeply, Jane put her fingers into his hair pulling him closer to her, his hand on the back of her head supporting her. His cock now ready to slip inside her. He moved his hand away from her bottom and slid his fingers deep inside her, Jane pushed herself up moaning loudly, she was soaking wet, he really wanted to taste her but that wouldn't be easy, he slid his fingers in and out of her.

"Jesus Belle you feel so good, you are so wet, I want to taste you, can you grip your leg around me?" He asked tapping her good leg, she did so as he pulled his fingers out of her and into his mouth.

"Mmmmm, you taste so good."

He mumbled licking his fingers clean, Jane was smiling at him as he made a meal of out sucking his fingers. He kissed her again and pushed his tongue into her mouth.

"Can you taste yourself on me love?"

She sucked his tongue and could just taste herself. She grinned as she sucked his tongue into her mouth hard.

He gripped her bottom and moved his fingers further round to her pussy and opened her up, he lifted her a little higher and slid her down onto his waiting hard cock.

"Oh god Jasper!" she moaned as he filled her. She sank her teeth into his shoulder.

He lifted her up and slid her down again getting deeper inside her.

"Fuck Belle you feel so good."

"Oh, I have missed you." she moaned.

He moved them to the wall under the shower, he didn't want her getting too cold. He put her back against the wall and slid in and out of her slowly. They were both moaning, enjoying the time alone.

"You okay Belle?" Jasper asked breathlessly.

"Yes baby." she said nodding. Her head falling back as he slid into her again pushing her up the wall.

She sank her fingers into his back, Jasper arched pushing himself further into her. She clenched her pussy around his cock making him moan loudly.

"If you keep doing that you will make me cum." Jane smiled and continued.

"Oh Belle, please stop I don't want to cum yet, I don't want to stop unless you need me too." Jane stopped and shook her head, she loved hearing his honesty.

She bit his lip and sucked it into her mouth. As Jasper forced himself deeper inside her, faster and faster he was becoming more aggressive, she knew he was close, he couldn't hold out much longer she knew it. He grabbed the back of her head and moved away from the wall, he pushed her head back and sank his mouth onto her long neck, he growled into her.

"God, I love you so much Belle." he kept sucking her neck not wanting to leave any marks on her. He moved down to her breasts, taking a nipple into his mouth and sucking it, Jane moaned, she loved her nipples being sucked, she knew it would make her wetter as did Jasper, she looked down at him as he glanced up at her, she felt her juices seep into her pussy.

"I love you too Jasper." she moaned quietly as she felt his cock rubbing her pussy wall. She knew she was going to cum, she needed the release as much as he did.

"Faster Jasper please, make me cum baby?" She moaned.

Jasper moved faster, pulling her hips up and pushing her down hard onto his cock.

"Yes, baby don't stop." she moaned.

"Fuck Belle I am going to cum," he moaned loudly as he felt his balls stiffen. "squeeze me Belle please?" he begged

Jane tightened her grip around him and released him, he ground into her harder.

"Yes, Jasper don't stop, Oh, god oh god." she moaned as her orgasm hit her. She was squeezing harder around him as she came all over his cock. Jasper felt her juices hit his cock and he pushed hard into her as he came, he pushed faster and harder, as Jane rode him. Both moaning loudly as their orgasms slowed down. They were both exhausted. Jane wrapped her arms around his neck. Breathing deeply, he felt her smile.

"Are you okay baby?"

"Yes, I am, couldn't be better." she laughed.

We better get you washed and back into bed before Alison comes in to check on us, I don't really want her seeing my bare arse."

Jane laughed. "That would make her day believe me."

"Oh, something you want to share?"

He asked slipping out of her, Jane moaned at the loss of him. He put her down onto the chair and kissed her lips.

"Alison was admiring you the other day as you went down to the restaurant, then she saw G and she has the hots for him, she apparently likes a bad boy, she has someone at home but said he's really boring. She wants to be carried off into the bathroom by G and taken advantage of." she laughed.

Jasper looked at her. "You women are worse than men, I dread to think what else is in that bag of yours, I know Gwen was covering something up, God only knows what it is."

Jane laughed, I wouldn't put anything past Gwen, didn't you watch at the till?"

"No I didn't they kept me talking, that's probably why."

Jane couldn't help laughing, "Oh this is going to be funny, I won't open it until I am with them later, I won't be able to look surprised otherwise, but I have a good idea."

"Do I want to know?"

"Umm it depends how opened minded you are to be honest."

"Oh, shit really, maybe I don't want to know?"

Jane was holding her sides as she was laughing, she couldn't wait to check the bag and see if what she thought was in there, actually was, if not she was going to get one herself for him. It could be fun.

"Ready to be washed off Belle?"

Jane nodded, "Yes please, I'm feeling tired now, you have worn me out."

Jasper laughed and grabbed the scrunchie and shower gel. Jane spun on her chair so Jasper could reach her back. He went down her arm and leg then onto her back, when he moved her around to the front he bent down and licked her nipple as the water was cascading down her body. He put his tongue out just under her breast, below the nipple and caught the water as it dripped off.

Jane smiled "You are so daft."

"Probably yes," he laughed. "but I can't get enough of you." He licked up her breast and onto her nipple sucking and biting softly as Jane smiled looking down at him again.

He finished washing her body and quickly washed himself off turning off the shower. He grabbed two towels, wrapped Jane's hair in one and her body in the other. He pulled another off the rail and wrapped it around his body and carried Jane to the bed. He laid her down, quickly dried himself off and got dressed. He dried Jane off removing her cast cover, he couldn't do anything about the one covering her wound on her leg, but once she was dry and dressed he would let the nurse know, he was also going to dry her hair, he has missed that.

Jasper helped Jane get dressed into clean clothes, she sat on top of the bed waiting for the nurse to come in and redress her leg. Jasper climbed onto the bed behind her and started brushing her hair drying it for her as Alison came in.

"Oh, I wish my other half would do that for me." she smiled looking at Jasper, he had a big smile on his face while he did it.

"I know I am very lucky, he does it most of the time for me." Jane replied smiling.

"Well I must say you look bright eyed and bushy tailed Jane, that shower did you the world of good."

Thank you Alison, Jane smiled desperate to laugh. "I feel much better, what do you think the chances are of me going home in the next day or so?"

"I wouldn't like to say to be honest, you would still need around the clock care just in case and someone to dress your wound every day. We can ask the Doctor when he comes round, it's his decision, you have made great progress though, so let's keep our fingers crossed."

"I will be at home with her anyway and Moses is staying until Jane is back on her feet properly, I am happy to pay someone to come in and do the dressing on her leg and stomach"

"Well like I said it's up to the Doctor, Jane you still have a lot of healing to do, I know you feel good at the moment, but you are not healed completely yet."

Jane smiled. "I understand that Alison, I'm not taking this lightly honestly, I have been in this position before, granted I wasn't shot the last time but I did get beaten badly and I lost my daughter after my ex-husband beat me in hospital. I understand I have to heal, but I know I will do better at home in my own surroundings."

"We will chat to Dr Robinson when he comes later and I will support you with him too, how does that sound?"

Jane felt tearful. "Thank you Alison, thank you so much, I promise I won't let you down, I just want to be at home with Jasper."

"Yes, thank you Alison, that really does mean a lot, whatever it takes I promise we will do it."

Alison smiled. "Okay, Okay, we will ask. Let's wait and see, now get some rest please Jane."

Jane saluted Alison which made her laugh.

Jasper had just finished her hair and climbed off the bed he pulled her hair up as Jane laid down so it fanned out across the pillow.

"What's that for." she laughed.

"I just want to make sure it's dry properly, I don't want you laying on damp hair."

"Oh, Jasper you are so perfect, what did I do to deserve you?"

Alison smiled, she would love some of that kind of attention, Jane was fortunate to have found him she thought, but look what the poor woman had been through, she certainly deserved some happiness.

Alison redressed Jane's leg for her and covered her with the bedding, she could see how tired she was looking, Jasper sat in the chair holding her hand as Jane drifted off. He placed her hand under the bedding and crept out, he needed to make a couple of calls to the office and site which he hadn't done earlier, he walked down the corridor into the relative's area and pulled out his phone. He made his calls and once done walked back up to Jane. She was still sleeping when he got back, he had spotted the Doctor making his way down the corridor, he wanted to catch him first and ask him what her chances were, she was so excited at the thought of going home he wanted to be prepared if the Doctor said no before he said it to Jane.

He walked back out into the nurses area as he heard the Doctors voice talking to them.
"Hi Jasper." he said putting his hand out to shake his.
"Hi Doc."
"I was just checking on Jane's progress with Alison, how do you think she is doing?" he beckoned him to take a seat outside her room.
"She's doing great Doc, her attitude is much better, she is talking much easier too. I showered her today which she said has made her feel so much better, she is sleeping at the moment."
"That sounds great, Alison said her wound is looking good, the stitches can come out in a week, she is off the intravenous antibiotics now too. She has certainly recovered very quickly which is great, she certainly has a positive mind."
"She is determined Doc, I wanted to talk to you before you see her, she wants to ask when she can come home, she is really excited about it. I don't want her being deflated by you saying no, which I know will knock her for six, so I would rather know your thoughts before she asks you."
The Doctor looked deep in thought. He rubbed the bottom of his chin and looked at Jasper with a serious look on his face.
"Okay Jasper, Jane has been hurt badly, you know her injuries, let alone her mind and how this is going to affect her. She needs her leg dressing daily, she needs medication every four hours, yes she is off the intravenous so that's not an issue, she still needs to be on bed rest and then needs physiotherapy to help with her legs and arm once the plaster comes off, that will be another month yet though, her leg won't be until the stitches come out.

She would need around the clock care, a nurse daily to check on her, and dress her leg. She would need personal care too, are you really up to that?"

Jasper smiled. "Doc without being rude, Jane and I are very tactile, we shower together daily, when she sprained her ankle, I carried her everywhere and I would do it again until she is well enough to walk. I can give her the medication, I will happily pay for a nurse to come in and redress her leg, and then a physiotherapist. She can be in bed as long as she needs too, she can also be moved into the lounge for a different set of four walls or go out into the garden on her lounger. I am sure she would love the fresh air, I will hire a wheelchair too so she can move herself around if she wants too. I won't lie to you Doc, I am desperate to have her home. Moses is staying on until she is on her feet so there will be the two of us to look after her. I won't be going back to work until she is ready, I can do most of it from home and if needed Moses will be there if I have to pop out. We have plenty of friends who will also be over to take the monotony out of her day. She has already agreed to talk to someone of her choosing about the attack. Please just think about it before you go in to see her."

"I appreciate your honesty Jasper, I know you would take great care of her that is obvious, I have never seen such devotion for so long to be honest."

Jasper was getting excited it looked like it was going the way they wanted.

The Doctor looked down at Jane's reports on his tablet. He scrolled through the nurses notes as Alison came over to them.

"Dr Robinson, I heard Jasper asking you about Jane going home, I just wanted to say I have been with Jane a couple of days now and I have to be honest, she is doing really well, seeing her spirits lift today at the thought of going home has done her the world of good. Of course, it's your decision but Susan and I have been with her day and night and we think she is ready, I called Susan earlier and spoke to her about it too."

"Thank you Alison, I appreciate your input." He turned to face Jasper. You can guarantee 100% she will be cared for around the clock, you will do everything we say, if you are unsure of anything you will call us and we will be out to you, we will also send either Susan or Alison to dress her leg, so we know she is doing okay, it will go on your bill of course."

"Doc whatever you say, I will get everything you tell me she needs before she comes home."

"Okay, Alison please would you draw a list up for Jasper of things he will need including the overbed lifting pole so she can straighten herself up if needed."

"Yes Doctor." Susan replied grinning from ear to ear.

"Okay Jasper, you have persuaded me, if you can get everything ready in a couple of days then Jane can go home for the weekend."

Jasper felt tears welling up in his eyes, "Doc I could kiss you, but I won't." he said laughing.

The Doctor put his hand up, "No there is no need for that, okay let's go in and see Jane now, I want her to ask me though Jasper, unprompted."

"Understood Doc."

They walked into the room together as Jane was waking up, she smiled at the Doctor as he walked in.

"Hi Dr Robinson."

"Hello Jane, how are you feeling?"

"I'm doing great thank you, I had a shower today which has made me feel so much better."

"So I heard, how is the pain?"

"It's okay thank you, the medication is keeping it at bay and I feel I don't need as much, I am not counting the hours now until the next dose."

"That's good to hear, Alison said you wanted to talk to me?"

She looked around at Jasper and he nodded. "Yes I wanted to ask when I could go home, I really do think I will get on much better at home Doctor, I know it's still early days but it will help me, I feel so good just having a shower, Jasper will be home to look after me and Moses is staying for as long as he is needed."

The Doctor looked thoughtfully at her. "Would you do as we told you, if Jasper or Moses said no would you listen?"

"Yes Doctor, I promise I would. I just want to go home now, I promise I will speak to someone about the attack, I know I need to talk about it to a professional, I am a professional in that field myself and know plenty of people I can talk to. Albeit in the UK, but I can Skype with them."

The Doctor was nodding listening to her, Jasper was stood at the back of her grinning at him.

He looked at Jasper. "And you are happy to have Jane at home now Jasper?"

Jane spun her head around to look at him. "Yes Doc, more than anything."

"You will do everything we ask of you?"

"Yes Doc."

"Jane, will you?"

"Yes, I promise."

Alison walked in with a list in her hand and passed it to the Doctor. "Okay then, Jasper please ensure these items are at the house waiting for Jane when she arrives, if you can get them sorted then Jane you can be home for the weekend, we will let you leave Saturday morning."

Jane's hands shot up to her face as she started to cry, she didn't expect to get a yes from the Doctor, Jasper bent down and hugged her tight.

"Thank you Doctor, thank you so much." she said through her tears.

"You're welcome Jane, I will be honest if it wasn't for this man here you wouldn't be going home, he has managed to persuade me already, but I needed to hear it from you to know it was you who wanted to go home. I will leave you to talk, Jasper has his list and orders. Susan and Alison will be across every day to check on your dressings and change them, you will need physiotherapy too, but we can sort that out nearer the time. So now rest."

"Yes Doctor I will. Thank you again."

Jasper stepped forward and took the Doctors hand again and shook it. Thank you Doc, I won't let you down."

"I know you won't."

"I will see you tomorrow Jane."

Jasper came around the front of Jane's bed she was still crying, he hugged her tight.

"Can you wait a couple of days Belle?"

"Yes I can, it's something to work towards too."

"Good I will start on this list now, firstly would you like to tell everyone?"

She nodded frantically "yes please."

Jasper got his phone out of his pocket and pressed facetime on Moses number. Within seconds it connected. Jasper sat next to Jane as Moses spoke.

"Jane, everything okay love?"

"She nodded, is everyone there?"

He looked around, "yes hang on."

He covered the microphone and called out to everyone, they all came into the kitchen and joined Moses.

"Okay love we are all here, you have me worried what's wrong?"

"I have some bad news for you all, I am coming home at the weekend."

Everyone erupted cheering at the other end, Jane started crying, Jasper hugged her as tight as he dare.

"Just for the weekend Jane?" Moses asked

"No for good, Jasper has lots to get sorted over the next couple of days and we will be relying on you too Moses if you are serious about staying on?"

Everyone cheered again. Moses had a huge smile on his face, his girl still needed him.

"It goes without saying Half-pint, try and get rid of me."

Jane was laughing and crying again.

"Well you have made our day love, now go and get better, we will see you tomorrow, the girls will be up later, we better get this man of yours drunk then if he has to behave and look after you for a while." Moses laughed.

Jane blew kisses to everyone and Jasper hung up.

Jasper sat down on the chair and looked at the list the nurse had prepared. He knew there was a few shops in Hartford that had this kind of thing, he would give them a call in the morning and get things organized.

"Is everything okay love?" Jane asked feeling concerned.

"Yes love, why?, I was just looking through the list the Doctor said we need for you to come home, there is a place local I can get it all from, so I will get it sorted tomorrow."

"Are you sure you are prepared for me to come home, I am being serious now?"

"Yes Belle of course, I am more than prepared, I want you home, I can look after you better there and you can relax better too. We can snuggle up at night so I don't fall asleep in the chair we can both rest properly."

Jane put her hand out to him, he took it and kissed her knuckles.

"Thank you Jasper, for everything you do for me."

"You don't need to thank me Belle."

"Well, it seems since you have known me you have now had to look after me twice, this wasn't what I had planned you know."

"I don't think any of us had this planned Belle, but it's okay, you will heal soon and we can get on with our wedding and the rest of our lives in peace."

Jane felt the tears well up in her eyes again, she was an emotional wreck at the moment, she knew it was due to everything that had gone on, but she hated feeling like this.

Jasper got up climbed onto her bed and cuddled her into him, he wiped the tears away with kisses.

"Hey beautiful girl, you don't need to worry about a thing.

Jane smiled and looked up at Jasper, "I am so lucky to have you. Thank you baby."

Jasper kissed her head and slid down the bed, so they were nose to nose. She grinned at him when he was level with her.

"I like this, I can't wait to be home and be able to do this every day and all night."

"Me too Belle," he smiled rubbing noses with her. "so, what are you girls going to do tonight?"

"I don't know what they have planned, chatting I expect, I hope they bring some nice gooey cake with them, I could murder some chocolate or cream."

"You are funny Belle." Jasper laughed.

"Well you better message them for me or I will be like a thing possessed."

"I will before I leave, I am sure Chicca knows where to go, when you are well enough we will go to Junior's in New York City. They do the best cheesecake in the world and they ship it anywhere in the US."

"So what are you waiting for then?" she said pretending to push him off the bed.

Jasper started laughing loudly, "Oh my girl is feeling better."

"I am a poorly girl, you know poorly girls need looking after, so go, go, go, get me some of this amazing cheesecake." she said grinning at him.

But he knew there was a serious tone in her voice, she was feeling a little better and he would do anything to please her.

"Whatever my girl wants my girl gets." he thought to himself.

He smiled at her, kissed her softly and rubbed her chin. "My beautiful Belle."

They snuggled back in and Jane fell asleep, Jasper just loved being this close to her, he couldn't wait until they were back in their own bed where she would be comfortable and they could cuddle without being disturbed.

Jasper left Jane for a short while once she woke up and Alison came in, he knew it wouldn't be long before the girls arrived and he needed to make some calls and get things ready at home. He was excited knowing in two days Jane would be home with him.

Chapter 23

Time to let your hair down

Jasper got home as the girls were leaving to go and see Jane, they were loaded up with goodies.

"Jane is in need of cake girls, chocolate or cream, so if you don't have any you may want to stop on route, she is feeling better and you know what she's like for cake."

The girls laughed. Gwen opened the bags.

"She can take her pick from this little lot, I don't think she will be disappointed."

"Hell, how many are you feeding?"

Well just us, but anyone can join in, I hear Alison is a bit of fun so she can join on her break. We have DVD's too, both Jane's favorite and a naughty one."

"Oh, don't tell me it has to be something smutty, you know she has been reading some Billionaire series!"

"Oh yeah, that was me who recommended that one."

Matt stood up and came over, "Hi Jay, believe me you won't be disappointed, that stuff is good and these ladies get off on that."

Japer laughed, oh really, well once Jane is back on her feet I will have to get her to read it to me then."

"Great idea, that's what Gwen does."

"Right girls, have fun, don't lead my girl astray please?"

"Too late for that sweetheart." Linda replied laughing.

"I will just go and shower guys and get changed, give me 15 minutes."

"Sure, no rush, the night is young, I hear we have a treat in store too." Matt laughed as he replied

"Oh really, what's that then?"

"Ahh wait and see, let's just say this lady is full of surprises!"

"I'm not sure I like the sound of that, but I will go with it, be right back." He laughed nervously.

Jasper was washing his chest thinking back to his shower with Jane earlier that day. He felt his cock stiffen remembering how good it felt to touch her again, and how much he missed the feel of her skin and her smell. He didn't have time to play he would have to wait until later. It was a shame the girls were there all night, or he would have gone back or called her for video sex.

He finished up, got dressed and went back to the guys, everyone was ready. Moses had called a cab for them and he was waiting outside.

They arrived at the club to loud music and bikes two deep outside, it was a warm night, lots of the guys were moving outside. They walked in and were met by Shadow, the place was packed, Jasper hadn't seen it like this before, his friends were at the bar with Graham and James.

"Hey guys, how is our little lady doing?"

"Good Shadow thank you, coming on well, she is hopefully coming home on Saturday, so we have a lot to get done so the house is ready for her."

"You need anything you shout Brother, we are here for you both."

"Thank you Shadow, that means a lot."

"Right now it's time for you to let your hair down and relax, she is in good hands tonight, so get a beer in you and enjoy the show."

"What show?"

"Oh wait and see." Shadow laughed walking away.

They moved towards the bar and met with the others, Jasper picked up his first beer and it went down smoothly, to easily. He wasn't a drinker so it surprised him.

They found a table and all sat down, everyone asked about Jane and then relaxed back to watch the show. Shadow had fitted two poles on the stage and two cages were hanging either side, there were two couples inside dancing, the girls were topless with just leather lace thongs on, the men were in leather pants that were barely covering their modesty. They were up close and personal with each other, the women at the front pushing their bottoms into the men's cocks, you could see they were enjoying it.

A slim tall girl dressed in a leather short skirt, waistcoat and bra, with thigh high boots and long dark curly hair, approached the pole slowly, she bent down holding her ankles and slowly ran her hands up her long legs and began swinging her hips, walking seductively along the stage, she was smiling at the crowd who were cheering and going wild for her, she swung her leg around the pole pulling herself to the top, she bent backwards from the top looking into the crowd. She moved up and down with ease continuing to make love to the pole and the guys were on their feet, she finished on the pole sliding down with her legs wrapped round it, until she reached the bottom dismounting and crawling like an animal about to pounce to the front of the stage. She beckoned one of the guys to join her, he was huge with a long beard, he was one of the club members. She whispered in his ear and he walked to the pole. She turned around lifted her skirt to show the crowd as she pulled her knickers off. They went crazy as she climbed the pole again, she spun upside down did a 360 opening her legs and slid down to the bottom. The guy on stage with her was nodding his head with a huge smile on his face rubbing his hands together, as she dismounted he moved towards the pole, she nodded at him, he went around the back of it so everyone could watch and ran his tongue down the pole slowly. The noise got louder everyone was shouting and cheering. He finished up, walked towards her, kissed her cheek, took a bow and left the stage, his friends waiting for him slapping him on the back.
The dancer continued as another rock song S.E.X by Nickleback played. She moved slowly around the stage rocking her hips and wiggling her bottom, she stopped and started to strip, her waistcoat came off first, she was smiling at the crowd as she

slowly let it drop down her arms to her wrists, she took it off, and slid it along the stage, turned around and undid her bra, she span it above her head and let it slide along the stage too. The crowd were yelling for her to turn around. She undid her skirt and shook her hips as it slid down to the floor. She kicked it off and bent over looking through her legs at the baying crowd, she stood up and caught a whip that was thrown from behind the curtain still with her back to the crowd, she slid the whip through her hand and whipped the floor. She turned and looked at the crowd, they went wild, she was stood naked, no embarrassment at all, she put her finger to her lips like she was thinking, then pointed her whip at Tony, the guys went wild.

He pushed his way through the crowd and was lifted onto the stage. She beckoned him towards her and pushed him onto his knees. She told him to take his shirt off and pass it to her. She went behind him moving his arms behind him like a sub. She held one end of the shirt and put it through her legs grabbing the other end, pulling it up to her pussy. She rubbed herself across it over and over as Tony grinned, his cock tenting in his trousers, he could smell her juices which made him worse, the crowd roared in appreciation. She gave him the shirt back and told him to smell her, Tony didn't disappoint he made a show for the crowd of offering it others, then held it against his nose and inhaled her and licked a particularly wet patch. He was nodding happily, she told him to stand and hold the shirt up and put his arms out as far as he could reach, he did as one of the bouncers came behind him and covered his face to protect it. Blaze flicked her whip and it ripped through his shirt, the crowd erupted, she held her hand against her ear asking for more, the crowd got louder so she did it again, the shirt was now in shreds in his hands, the bouncer uncovered his face and Tony stood with his mouth open looking at his shirt. The crowd were laughing, many were shouting at him asking him to throw it into the crowd wanting bits of it. Blaze walked across to him as the bouncer handed her a bag. She whispered in Tony's ear.
"Thank you for being a good sport, here take this t-shirt."

"No, thank you it was great fun." he smiled kissing her on the cheek.

Tony put his arm around her as he faced the front, all of the guys had been filming him. He took a bow, Blaze kissed him on the cheek leaving a huge red pair of lips as he jumped off the stage. He got back to the guys who were geeing and cheering slapping him on the back, pointing at his now hard cock which he was trying to cover. He ripped open the bag and pulled out the t-shirt pulling it on. He put his torn shirt in the bag and put it out of the way.

Blaze gave a bow and left the stage leaving the men wanting more. Blowing kisses as she walked off. The compare a biker himself jumped onto the stage and quieted the crowd. "Okay well you loved Blaze so hopefully you will love our next lady too. She really does have a treat for you, please make some noise for Amber." The crowd roared as the music started. The dancer came out dressed in a white basque, stockings and frilly knickers. With white lace up boots that came up to her knees. She was beautiful with red curly hair down to her shoulders. She mounted the pole like she was no weight at all. She began by wrapping her leg around it, spinning slowly, she leant outwards and hung at an angle then moved back into the pole, spinning again, she slipped down onto her feet and gyrated sexily at the pole, crawling on her hands towards the crowd. You could see she was enjoying it she was certainly a pro. She went back to the pole stood up, wrapped her leg around the bottom spread her hands up the pole and span round lifting herself up to the top, she laid down the pole looking into the crowd. She was blowing kisses at the men as she span again and dismounted.

Gyrating her hips to the beat of the music she turned away, slipped off her frilly knickers showing her bare bottom. Opened her legs and bent down looking through her legs. There was something hanging from her pussy, everyone could see it, many were pointing, she pulled on it slightly to show fake pearls on a string, it got longer, the room fell quieter as everyone was in awe of what she was doing, as she pulled again it got longer, the crowd got louder. The men were wooing and geering, she continued to pull them out slowly, she stopped and stood straight, looking around she pointed at one of the bikers, he was wearing his cut and chaps over his jeans, he pointed to himself and she nodded, he pushed others out of the way and jumped onto the stage as Tony had done. She walked him over to the pole and stretched her leg up the pole, the crowd went crazy. The biker got closer and fell to his knees with his tongue almost hanging out of his mouth. She beckoned him over, he crawled on his knees closer to her, she held up the string of pearls and placed it in his mouth, he lifted his arms cheering, the crowd joined in. She told him to move back slowly, he inched back as the string got longer, it was soaked in her juices, the biker could see it, he could feel his cock getting harder and his mouth was watering to taste it. He reached the edge of the stage, others were leaning up to pat him on the back. Amber beckoned him back to her, she asked him to stand up, she took her leg down from the pole and placed it in his arms, she continued to pull the string out and told him to run it through his lips he didn't waste a second, his friends could see he was rock hard but he didn't care, just like Tony he was lost in the moment. He sucked hard on the pearls as Amber laughed getting off on it too, the last pearl came out and the crowd were shouting, she moved her leg back to the floor and he finished sucking the pearls and handed them back to her, she ran her hand down his body but not touching his cock, that was against the rules. She wasn't a prostitute either. She tiptoed and kissed him on the cheek, whispering in his ear.

"Thank you for allowing me to tease you, sorry for the hard on, I do hope you think of me when you finish it, please don't waste it."

He looked down at her and grabbed his hard cock, bent towards her ear and whispered back to her.

"Listen little lady, you will be every one of my wet dreams from now on, you ever need a bodyguard or need help you let me know." He pulled a card out of his cut pocket and placed it in her hand.

She kissed him again as he jumped off the stage and went straight to the toilet cheering as he did as everyone watched where he was going. Amber finished up her set and left the stage to huge applause and cheers from the crowd, the band came back on and the crowd headed back to the bar.

The guys headed to the bar too, all laughing at Tony, his t-shirt had the Skulls MC club logo on and the Connecticut chapter, he was quite proud of it, he had earned it after all.

"Hey Shadow, I had an idea, I wondered if these guys would be interested in bidding for my shirt? We could raise some money for the ward Jane is in. As it's in pieces we could sell parts off to make more money?"
It's worth a try Tony, great idea, these guys will buy anything related to these women, I will give it to the guy who is hosting this tonight."
"Thanks Shadow."

Shadow walked over to the biker who had organized the stripper event, with Tony's shirt in his hand.
"Hey Brother, Tony the guy who had his shirt shredded asked if we could auction it off? One of the girls from the UK chapter who is working out here for a few years is in hospital, she was beaten and shot by her ex a week or so ago and Tony suggested raising money for the hospital for the care they have shown her."
"Hell yeah, we can do that, these guys are drunk enough to buy it and will do anything for one of their own. I remember Jane, she's a friend of Moses. Give it to me, let's have a look how many pieces there are."
Together they pulled it out of the bag to have a look at it. It was shredded but there were five decent size pieces so they both got onto the stage and took the microphone. The biker started.

"Guys and girls can I have your attention please, Tony who was lucky enough to have his shirt shredded tonight has offered to auction it off, now the reason for this is one of our club members who many of you already know Jane, was shot and beaten a week or so ago by her ex and is still in hospital, Tony would like to raise some money for the ward she has been staying in for all of the help and support they have given her and her partner Jasper and friends from the UK. So dig deep guys and girls, it's not about the shirt really it's about one of our own. I know Jasper is here tonight and her friends from the UK, so guys come up here and join us. Some of you may remember the night Jasper proposed to Jane so you will know who we are talking about."

Jasper and the guys put their drinks down and headed to the stage with cheers from the crowd, they joined the biker and Shadow.

"So, Jasper tell us how Jane is doing, give us an update and do we know where this scum bag is, as I know a few of us would like to dispose of him." the crowd roared in anger.

"She is doing great thank you, she has a lot of recovering to do but in the main she is okay, it was touch and go, he beat her pretty bad this time, thankfully he is no longer around he has been taken care of." Jasper looked into the crowd he could feel the anger coming from the men.

"Are you telling me he is a goner?" Jasper nodded, The crowd roared and cheered. "Let's get this shirt sold then and give some money back to the hospital. You will bring her down when she is up to it won't you, and we will let this lot know so they can come and see her."

"Yes of course, it's her second home." Jasper laughed

"Okay boys and girls we have 5 pieces of this scented shirt from the lovely Blaze, so where are we going to start the bidding for the first piece."

The bids rolled in and within 15 minutes all five were sold, with a few scuffles in the crowd about who won the bid they had raised three thousand dollars, a pot was put on the bar for loose change, they were going to collect it over the next couple of weeks and present it to Jane to give to the hospital. Jasper was determined to make it more and he knew the same thought was going through the minds of his friends.

The party continued the band got back on stage and played for another couple of hours, the boys went back to their drinks after being stopped by most of the crowd as they made their way back to the table. Jasper was feeling quite emotional, he never expected anything like this at all.

Moses was quiet which was unusual, Jasper walked over to him.

"Hey Moses, you okay?" he put his arm around his shoulder

"Sure Brother, why?" he said turning around to look at Jasper

"You just seem a bit quiet?"

"Just thinking about Jane and what could have been I suppose, annoyed with myself for letting it go on for so long, but she is a hard women to say no too. I should have known better though."

"Listen, I think we all feel somehow we are too blame, Christ, I relive it every day but if we have learnt something from Belle it's how to let it go, we need to do that to help her heal. If we keep hold of this anger and continue to question everything we won't get anywhere, and wasn't tonight about letting our hair down and relaxing?"

"You're right." he laughed, "So get me another beer." Jasper slapped him on the back and walked toward the bar, he didn't ask who wanted a drink just got another round in and had them brought over. As the drinks were put down onto the table Jasper picked up his beer, he knew he had drunk too much, but he wasn't bothered he could sleep it off.

"Let's make a toast to friendship and Belle of course." The guys cheered

"To friendship and Jane." they all replied and clinked drinks.

Jasper took his phone out of his pocket and started a text to Jane.

Hey Belle, just checking in baby to see how you are doing and if you are enjoying your time with the girls. I miss you like crazy,

but I will be back early tomorrow. I think I have had a few too many to drink too. It's been a crazy night, I will tell you all about it tomorrow. I love you darling. Call if you need anything at all.
xxx

He sent the text and stared at his phone until it was delivered, happy that he knew she had it now. He was enjoying himself but felt a bit disjointed being away from Jane. His phone vibrated almost straight away.

Hi Baby, I'm good, the girls have arrived and we are having an amazing time, but I miss you being here, miss looking at your face and being so grateful to still be here knowing I have you to look after me. Can't wait to see you tomorrow, go and get drunk and have fun with the boys, just don't get chatted up or I will have to send the girls in :-). I love you more than you can imagine. xxx

Jaspers face lit up, he was grinning from ear to ear reading Jane's message, a few of the lads looked around and smiled. He locked his phone, as he was putting it back in his pocket Tony snatched it from his hand.

"Enough of being a pussy, tonight is your night and we still have plenty of time to party, Jane is in good hands so get this down you and stop dwelling."

Tony passed Jasper a shot, all eyes were on him as he knocked it back. Tony knew he didn't drink but also knew how far he could push him. The shots kept coming, they were all getting slowly drunk and laughing at the slightest thing. Jasper felt himself really relax and enjoy the night.

Chapter 24

Girls night

Jane smiled at the text from Jasper and put her phone down after replying. She was pleased he was out enjoying himself, she missed him, but she had missed time with the girls too.

"Right no more phone lady, leave Jasper alone with the guys, it's our time tonight."

Jane laughed. "I know I was just replying."

"Yeah, yeah heard it all before." Chicca added "We all know what you two are like, smitten, makes you want to be sick." she said laughing with the others.

"Cheeky bitch, I can go a night without talking to him."

"Okay give me your phone then, let's see how you get on."

Jane picked her phone up and checked it before handing it to Chicca, she was laughing but nervous at the thought of missing a text from Jasper.

"Here you go then, you think I can't do this." she said slapping the phone into Chicca's hand.

"I tell you what ladies, I think it's only fair if we all do it, phones in the middle of the table upside down so we can't see them." Linda suggested.

They all did the same. It was their time now. Gwen started unpacking the bags she had brought in, Victoria sponge, chocolate and carrot cake, chocolate, popcorn and chewy sweets. 2 bottles of wine for the girls and a non-alcoholic for Jane. Jax had also packed plastic cups and started to pass them around.

"Forget the drink open the damn cake." Jane laughed

"Patience women we don't want you gorging yourself on it."

"You might not want me to, but I do." Jane giggled. "Any way if I spread it all over myself and send a picture to Jasper he will come and lick it off."

"A bit difficult without your phone and I don't really want to see your boobs out smothered in chocolate cake either and I don't think the girls will?" Gwen giggled

"Right then a game." Chicca said, she passed around the paper and pens. "Place this paper on your head and draw a cock, when you finish place it upside down on the table."
The girls laughed. They put the paper on their heads and began drawing, giggling trying to concentrate.
They all finished and put their drawings upside down.
"Okay, let's see shall we. When I say turn, everyone together turn yours over." They all nodded
"Okay turn."
They all turned at the same time and burst into laughter, they all barely looked like cocks to start with.

Gwen picked up Jane's "so this is what keeps you so excited is it Jane?" she said looking down at Jane's drawing.
It wasn't straight, he only had one ball and it looked like he was a gorilla with hair right up to the top.
"I wasn't drawing his." she giggled. "He doesn't look anything like this."
"I hope not, who would want to give that a blow job with all that hair?" Chicca was laughing she could barely breath as she said it.
Jane picked Chicca's up. "Well it has to be better than this, how would that work you can't even see it, I hope it grows, he has just one ball too." Jane was holding her chest, she was desperate not to laugh too much but she couldn't help it.
They grabbed at Linda's you couldn't even see what it was, there were no balls and it was really skinny.
"Oh boy, I will never be able to look at your old man in the same way again, that's teeny tiny." She burst into a fit of giggles.
Linda picked up Gwen's "And this is what? Poor Matt, does he know what a real cock looks like?"
Chicca grabbed Jax's, it was the longest of them all with a bend at the top.

"Hey I think we ought to get the men to drop their pants and see who this belongs too, don't you girls?"

Jax blushed she was laughing hard trying to tell them it wasn't anyone's

All the girls were giggling and holding their stomachs they couldn't breath with laughing so much.

Chicca opened Jane's cupboard and pulled out the bag they had brought at the shops. She dug deep and brought out the box of chocolates all cock shaped and handed one to each of them. That started giggling again.

"Okay ladies, it's picture time, you have to give it your best effort to look like you are sucking your man's cock and I will send them all the picture."

"Oh Jesus," Jane said looking at the chocolate cock, "that's unfair I can't open my mouth properly."

They all started giggling again.

"Okay Linda you are first up."

Gwen got her phone and Linda got into position, she gave it her best, with her lips just touching the tip her tongue on the underside. The girls were trying not to laugh at Linda as she posed.

"Chicca, your turn." Chicca swallowed the whole thing, so asked for two pictures one showing how big it was and another when she swallowed it.

"Damn James must love you girl!" Linda exclaimed

"Come on Jane your turn."

Jane opened her eyes wide as she always loved looking into Jaspers eyes. She ran her tongue around the chocolate and finished with her tongue at the tip, she knew Jasper would know what she was doing.

Linda took the phone from Gwen "your turn!" Gwen placed the chocolate into her cleavage and pushed her breasts together, they all fell about laughing.

"What?" she asked, looking round at the girls. "It's what he loves."

Come on Jax your turn, we will send this to one of the boys of your choice."

She blushed again. She pouted and held the tip on the edge of her lips and cradled the base in her hand, all the girls laughing. Linda took the pictures and they all had a look through giggling at each other. Gwen sent them to the guys with a note stating they had to reply to their respective other half with the naughtiest comment for their girl to win. Jax had hers sent to G, he would give a great answer.

"What else is in that bag Linda? Jane asked. The girls laughed.

"They started to unpack it. Linda pulled out crutchless knickers, holding them out and shaking them. The girls laughed, next the peep hole bra, then what looked like a dress made out of lace, with cut out cups so the whole breast showed. It had a halter neck fastening and a low scooped back. Jane grabbed it, she loved it. The lace was soft she couldn't wait to wear it for Jasper.

"I guess you like that then?" Chicca laughed.

Jane blushed and covered her face with the dress. They all laughed at her.

"What did Jasper say?"

"Ahh he didn't see it, we kind of got it all behind his back, he saw a few bits but not the best stuff and we just let him pay for it."

"Oh goodie he is in for a treat then." she smiled laughing.

Chicca grabbed the bag and pulled out a new vibrator.

"We thought you might like a new one, you know back and front."

Jane's mouth dropped open. "Chicca!" she exclaimed.

"Don't tell me you haven't had anyone touch your backside Jane?"

Jane could feel her cheeks heating up again. "No I haven't!" she squeaked

The girls were all laughing now.

"Oh girl you are missing out."

Jane covered her face, she was so embarrassed, she loved sex with Jasper but she hadn't ever been adventurous.

She looked through her fingers feeling like a wimp, the girls were nodding at her, Jane covered her eyes again, really blushing.

"We do too Jane, don't be embarrassed." Linda said.

She took her hands away from her face. "okay, okay. I'm a wimp I know, God I feel like a virgin with you lot."

"Well, let us be your guide Jane." Gwen grinned.

"Oh god! get it over with, tell me how it feels?" she blushed again.

Chicca laughed, Jane you really don't know what you are missing, there are so many nerve endings, it will give you an orgasm so damn fast. Hell, when James slides in its heaven, I push back onto him and my head goes, I feel like I am swallowing him. At first it can be painful, you need lots of lubrication though. How about a butt plug to stretch you a bit first?"

Jane's hands shot up to her face again, the girls were laughing. Chicca put her hand into the bag, putting her finger over her lips to the others. While Jane had her face covered she pulled out a butt plug and left it hanging off her fingers by the label.

"Jane come on, we have been friends for years, you know me and Steve have a very open sex life and I enjoy talking about it."

Jane moved her hands, "I have only been kind of touched." She looked round at Chicca, "oh my god what is that a dummy?"

All four girls fell about laughing, not at her but at the naivety of it all. Jane looked around.

"What's so funny?" she said looking confused.

"Jane darling it's a butt plug, you use it widen your bum so it doesn't hurt, it's a nice feeling too, some women and men wear them all the time it's quite erotic."

"Oh, good god, I feel so stupid." Jane said laughing, she took it from Chicca.

"So how do you sit down?"

"Easily, you will know it is in there, but as long as you have a flat end like this you will get used to it." Jane felt her face redden again.

"My god where have I been all these years? I thought I was doing well when I put in my vibrating eggs in on a night out." The girls smiled.

"Not everyone likes it Jane, but it's worth a try, why don't you try it when you get home and surprise Jasper when you get used to it."

"I don't know, don't think that's me."

The girls laughed, "Well you can always try it, if you don't like it then get rid of it." Chicca smiled.

"Okay what's next in this bag of wonders?" Linda asked.

Chicca dug deep, "Well now you have two sets of eggs Jane."

"Jane clapped her hands, feeling a bit more normal. "that I can do."

Next came the cat o' nine tails. It was soft leather strips and a nice wooden handle.

"How about it Jane, it doesn't have to hurt, and if you tease the right way with it you will get a great response?"

"I sense you have done this before Chicca?" Gwen asked laughing

"Hell yeah, I like to get the most out of my foreplay, it's not all just about a quick fuck or licking my pussy, I like to prolong it and get the best for both of us, if that means using lots of toys then I won't complain."

"I like foreplay too and Jasper doesn't complain, we have a great sex life."

"This is about spicing it up Jane, believe me you will love it. Come her give me your arm and close your eyes."

Jane gave her good arm to Chicca and closed her eyes, Chicca gently ran the "cat" up and down her arm slowly just touching her skin, Jane shuddered.

"Ohhhh I like that" she giggled.

"So imagine you are naked laid on the bed blindfolded and you are having that ran up and down your body with the odd soft whipping across your arse."

Jane blushed, "I think that would be nice, am I really discussing my intimate sex life with you girls?"

"Did someone mention sex? I'm in." Alison laughed from the doorway.

"Hey Alison come and join us, we were just talking to Jane about anal and whipping." Chicca smiled

"Oh, now you are talking my language."

Jane's mouth dropped open. "Alison you surprise me!" she squealed

"Well I better keep my stories clean then Jane." she said laughing

"Oh no you don't Alison, we need the dirt." Jax begged, she was a bad girl herself but enjoyed more smut.

"Welllllll, okay, me and my old man were in a very stale relationship and we decided to do something about it so went to a voyeurs club." Jane screwed her face up looking confused.

Alison laughed. "Jane the club is a really safe place, people go there to watch and to take part, we had to go through lots of questions, and an interview, it's taken very seriously. The first time we went was just to watch, it was amazing, I was turned on so fast."

"Isn't it seedy though seeing all those men with hard cocks?" Jane asked screwing her nose up.

"No, not at all, we have masked Balls quite regularly, why don't you come along with Jasper, you girls are welcome too, it's an open event as long as you complete the security forms, and go with us."

Jane looked around at the others. They all nodded grinning like teenagers.

"If we are here then yes for sure." Gwen said, Linda agreed nodding furiously.

Jane shrugged her shoulders, it can't hurt can it. I can just watch, can't I?"

"Yes of course, there are men and women who love to put on a show, you would love it I promise."

"Okay I will mention it to Jasper, there is nothing wrong with our sex life, but I suppose variety is the spice of life and I get to buy a new dress from that lovely lady Chicca." They all laughed. "Great can't wait to introduce you."

"Now give me some of that cake please." Jane pointed at the table.

Linda got up and cut the cakes, handing it to the girls.

"So, come on Jane what is the most amazing thing Jasper does for you?"

Jane sat with her finger against her lips she was thinking hard, she wanted to impress them but she knew what she was about to say wasn't going to.

"Don't tell me I am playing safe, but it has to be the way he kisses me."

The girls smiled and leant in listening.

"It's hard to describe, but when he kisses my head or my nose it's so romantic, it means so much to me. I am not used to being kissed and it does make me melt. But when he comes up behind me and pulls my hair away from my neck his right hand on my boob, not squeezing, he seems to find my nipple without any problems and just rubs it, his lips touch my neck and I feel his hot breath over my skin, his left hand is under my chin holding my neck, pushing my head up, it's such a light touch. He licks up my neck and runs his wet lips up to my ear, it gets me every time, it's so hot."

The girls were listening intently. Gwen rubbed her neck.

"Stop that now I am having all kinds of images going through my mind and I want my husband here so I can try it with him, or Jasper……, I'm not fussy." She teased, Jane threw her napkin at her across the bed.

The girls all laughed. "Come on then Gwen what does yours do for you?"

"It has to be when he comes up behind me when I'm in knickers and t-shirt, he pushes his hand under my t-shirt and cups my boob, then his other hand slides down my tummy his fingers spread out and into my knickers, by that stage I am already hot and wet, his knee pushes my legs apart, not that he needs to but I love him doing it so pretend he has too, then his finger slides straight into me, he never talks just does it."

"What about you Linda?" they asked in unison

"Definitely has to be when he takes me wherever we are in the house, we had a fight one day because he has this thing about squeezing my boobs, I hate it." Everyone nodded in agreement.

"Anyway, he came in one night, I was in the kitchen bending over in the dishwasher, I just had my normal clothes on, he bent over me and kissed me on the neck. Then rubbed my bum really gently, I stood up, he grabbed me from behind turned my face and kissed me hard, next thing I know he has my clothes off on the floor and he is bending me back over the work top, dropping his trousers and sliding inside me. It was amazing. It was not the norm, it was unexpected and perfect."

"Christ girls it's getting warm in here, good job the boys are out." laughed Chicca.

"Come on Chicca, what does James do for you?"

"Oh God!!, well when I see him pull up on the bike its instant wet," she laughed covering her blushes with her hands. "he comes in the door, puts his crash helmet down, smiles, he has this smile, that's what did it for me, then he takes me in his arms and kisses me, whatever I am wearing and it's normally not that much, he pulls it off there and then, his leg pushes between mine as his hand goes straight to my pussy, I am normally soaking wet, Christ am I really saying this?! He pushes his fingers inside so deep while kissing me, it makes my legs go weak, then he slides them out, sucks off my juices making lovely moaning noises and kisses me."

"Jax, your turn, come on, what does it for you."

It's definitely when I am bent over and my legs are pushed open and my arse and pussy are licked from behind, I was seeing this guy, I won't name him to save him but he used to come in the house as I went to make a drink he would pull up my dress or pull down my shorts and spread my legs. He would be licking and sucking within seconds. It was incredible."

"Jesus women, you are not doing us any favours with that, I think we need to change the subject." Linda laughed.

"What about G and Moses, I see the way Moses looks at you Jane, have you been there, or would you?" Alison asked, the girls laughed.

"I love Moses very much and G, but they are like brothers, I wouldn't even consider it with either of them."

"But you must see the way Moses looks at you, that man is in love with you Jane." the girls didn't say a word.

"Don't be silly, he feels the way I do, doesn't he?" she asked looking at Gwen and the others for confirmation.

Gwen spoke first. "Sorry love I have to agree, that man adores you, why else would he keep your secret for 10 years and do what he does for you. There is more than friendship for him, the way he holds you, the forehead kisses, he never takes his eyes off you and questions any man that goes near you, I am sure Jasper has been through it a few times." The others nodded.

Jane put her hands over her face. "Oh my god, no! I would never consider that, I adore that man, he is my best friend, but I don't fancy him, are you sure?" She looked around at the girls, shock written all over her face, they nodded again.

"Oh my god, what do I say to him?"

"Nothing Jane, he has to deal with it himself, he knows you are going to marry Jasper, hell, he has had 10 years to do something about it." Gwen banged the bed in frustration. "Don't say a word, you have to be normal with him Jane."

Jane covered her face again bending over, shaking her head.

"Did I lead him on?"

"No you didn't, it's a fact of life Jane, it happens. G adores you too, yes he probably fancies the arse off you too, but he isn't in love with you."

"Shucks." Jane said disappointed, slapping the bed, "I thought I had a pair then."

"Greedy bitch." Alison said laughing. "I would if he was on offer."

"You're married Alison, I thought you were happy?" Linda exclaimed. Looking shocked

"Me and my old man have this deal, if someone turns me on and I want him and he's game, then I can go and play, the first sign of feelings we have to be honest with each other, so far I have only done it once but to be honest G does it for me." The girls whooped and giggled. Alison looked at each of them laughing.

"Hey, this little lady has needs." she said pointing to her pussy.

The girls fell about laughing. Gwen was banging the bed holding her tummy.

"I have to pinch that Alison, next time he has a headache I will tell him, this girl has needs."

"Well now I have given away all my secrets I will leave you to it, I must get back to work, on a serious note Jane, don't overdo it, you are far from hundred percent, we don't want you going backwards especially if you plan on going home in a couple of days."

"She's right Jane, let's relax and watch a film. Which do you want?" Linda asked holding up the DVD's.

"The Notebook, I love the scene in the rain when he kisses her." the girls laughed.

"The Notebook it is then, her ladyship has spoken." Linda walked over to the TV and put the DVD on, Linda and Chicca grabbed the popcorn and chocolate and took the chairs, they all settled back in, Gwen got onto the bed with Jane. Alison blew a kiss and went off back to work.

Within minutes of the lights being turned down Gwen heard Janes breathing change and knew she had gone to sleep, she smiled knowing she needed the rest and she was so happy to be there with her, she picked her phone up off the cabinet, held it above their heads and took a picture of her and Jane and sent a text to Jasper.

Hi Jasper, I just wanted to let you know Jane is sleeping like a baby, we have had a lovely evening, and now she is resting. I hope you boys are having fun. Give my husband a kick up the arse from me. See you all tomorrow. x

Hi Gwen, thank you, she looks peaceful, hope you've all had a great time too. I've missed her so much tonight. Yes, we have had a great time. Arse kicked and almost got punched until he realised it was from you after reading the text. Lol. See you in the morning, sleep well, mind she doesn't kick you out of bed :-) x

Gwen settled back down put her phone away and laid watching the film, she was happy she was here and able to help, she felt a tear slide down her cheek, she wiped it away and sniffed pretending it was a yawn. She wasn't about to cry now her friend was okay.

Chapter 25

Getting ready

Jasper woke with a thick head, he lifted his head off the pillow.
"Shit did I get hit across the head again?"
He heard groans coming from the other side of the bed, he jolted up and looked around quickly.
"Shit Tony, what the hell are you doing in my bed, and you better have pants on, or I will kick your arse?"
Tony groaned holding his head. "You don't have a pussy, don't fucking flatter yourself, if it was Jane laid next to me then that would be another story."
Jasper picked up his pillow and hit Tony across the head.
"That's my fiancé you are talking about." he scowled at him.
"Fuck Jay, that hurt man, my fucking head is pounding, go easy."
"Shit, I haven't felt like this in years, now I know why I don't drink." Jasper sat at the edge of the bed feeling queasy, his head in his hands, his normal perfect hair was a mess, he rubbed his chin and wiped down his face.
"Shower, I need a shower, my mouth feels like the bottom of a bird cage." he pushed off the bed and stood, his headache now pounding.
"Shit, I need to get rid of this hangover."

He walked into the bathroom shutting the door behind him, pulling his t-shirt off over his head and dropping his shorts to the floor, he turned the shower on and stood leaning over the sink looking in the mirror.
"Shit Jasper, you look like hell, how much did I drink last night? I better do something with this face before I go and see Belle." he rubbed his beard again and turned getting into the shower.
The hot water hitting him in the face, he moaned at the feeling as it cascaded down his body. He was feeling a little better already. He washed his hair and soaped up his body, moving

under the shower as it pounded his body into waking up. He could feel his cock getting hard, he looked down at it shaking his head.

"No point you waking up now, I am not touching you with my best friend the other side of the door!"

He rinsed his body, turning off the shower, he used his hands to wipe off the excess water, he opened the door and stepped out grabbing a towel wrapping it around his waist. He opened the cupboard and took his trimmer out.

"Right then Jasper, we need to get you looking half decent to see your girl this morning, you look like hell, what must she have been thinking, this beard is wild!"

He went to work on his face, trimming his beard, shaved his neck and trimmed his moustache. He felt better already. He cleaned his teeth, put his hair product in and left the bathroom feeling more awake but still with a cracking hangover. Tony was laid flat out on the bed still snoring. Jasper shook his head and smiled, he remembered this from when Tony lived with him after getting kicked out by his wife.

He opened the drawer and took out his clothes stepping back into the bathroom he dried himself off and got dressed. He walked back out putting the towel in the basket.

"Tony, Tony, wake up fella, do you want coffee?"

"Ugh, what, yeah, yeah, please. Thanks." he replied rolling over, groaning as he pushed himself up, holding his head again.

"You got any headache pills, my head is pounding?"

"Sure thing."

Jasper went to the kitchen, a few more bodies were laid in the lounge on the sofas, he didn't remember everyone coming back but it looked like they did. He put the kettle on for his tea, grabbed the mugs out of the cupboard for when the others woke and made coffee for Tony. He left his on the side and walked back to the bedroom leaving Tony's on the side with 2 tablets and went back to the kitchen. He took a couple of tablets himself and opened the curtains. A few moans and groans came from the guys on the sofas, it was a bright sunny morning, Jasper squinted too as the sun hit him.

"Shit brother, you trying to blind us or what?" complained James as he rolled over burying his face in the cushions.

"Sorry James, didn't realise it was so sunny out, well you're awake now so do you want a drink, kettles on?."

James picked up the pillow on the floor and threw it at Jasper, he laughed and ducked out of the way, walking back to the kitchen.

"That's a yes then with headache pills." he said laughing as he went to make more coffee.

James staggered into the kitchen with just his jeans on rubbing his face.

"Give me water please, by the bucket load, I feel like I have a mouthful of sand."

Jasper put a glass in front of him and turned the tap on, James filled the glass and emptied it within seconds and went back for more.

"You trying to drown yourself James?"

"If I could, I would, shit what did I drink, this must be what a Nuns pussy is like, dry as the damn dessert?"

Jasper spat his coffee out and coughed trying to swallow what was left in his mouth.

"Not the image I really wanted today James, thanks buddy." he laughed wiping his face.

"Sorry Brother, I don't remember much about last night and I really would like to know what has left me so dry."

"Can't help you there, think we are all in the same boat."

I doubt that you look pretty good for someone who is hungover."

"Ahh, but I showered already and need to look good for my girl so made the effort."

Moses stumbled into the kitchen in just his boxer shorts scratching his chest and yawning.

"Did someone say coffee?"

"Morning Moses." Jasper smiled. "You look like hell too."

"Who's stupid idea was it to do shots?"

"That would be G, he had all the bright ideas last night."

"Someone call my name?" G walked into the kitchen looking like he hadn't drank at all

"You fucker, how come you get to look so good the morning after, when we all feel like shit?"

G laughed, "you can either handle it or you can't, and some of us can." he laughed raising his arms smiling.

"So Jay, what's the plan for today? What do you need us to do?" asked James

"Well I'm going in to see Belle shortly, let the girls come back and get some rest and showered. The equipment I ordered should arrive I could do with someone staying here until it does."

"Sure thing, we can do that? Is Ernie coming in today, we need to get the garden finished to lay the ramps down by the doors?"

"I assume so yes, I will give him a call shortly, we need to get the house cleaned too, Belle will be home tomorrow mid-morning."

"Don't worry about the house we can sort that, we will pack our shit away and move it back to the apartments later today, then you are free to do what you need once we are gone, but we will leave it spotless later, what equipment are we expecting J?" G asked

There is a wheelchair, the rest of the ramps and an overbed table, I have a TV being delivered for the end of the bed, can one of you boys set it up? I know Belle won't want to stay in bed for long but just in case she is having a rough day. There is also a leg raiser, she still needs to keep her leg elevated."

"Okay well we will all be here. I will set the TV up. If you want shopping doing Chicca and I will go when she is back with her car?"

"Thanks guys, I really do appreciate all you are doing for us, Belle is going to go nuts when she sees the garden, it's the first place she is going to want to go." Jasper was feeling choked, he had a huge lump in his throat, G spotted it at the same time as Moses, they both dived on him rubbing his head.

"You big softie." That's what friends do Jay, you need to get used to it Brother, we will be around a lot."

"What he said." G laughed wiping his eyes.

"Don't you start as well, Jesus you lot are turning into a bunch of pussies." Moses laughed slapping G across the back.

"Fuck you arsehole." G grumbled. "You might want to remember when Half-pint left."

"Yeah well we don't need to go into any of that, unless you want knocking out." everyone laughed and finished their drinks leaving the dirty cups on the sink.

"Right, I am off, I need to pop to the shop before I see Belle, catch you later."

"See you later, call if you need anything." Moses called after him, the others raised their hands as he left.

Jasper grabbed the keys to his bike and threw his car keys to Moses.

"Use the car later if you need to. I'm taking the bike."

Cheers Brother that will help, it will save us filling Chicca's car up."

Jasper slipped his boots on and grabbed his jacket from the boot room, he opened the garage door and fired the bike up. Smiling like the cat who got the cream he swung his leg over and slipped his helmet and gloves on. He pulled out of the driveway and settled in, the jeweler was only 15 minutes away, he was so excited about picking up the necklace, it was perfect timing, he was going to try and hold out giving it to Jane until the morning. But he knew he was rubbish at keeping his excitement locked away.

He pulled into the parking area at the back of the Mall and walked around to the jeweler. He walked in, the bell above him sounding, it had the familiar musty, dusty smell, it felt good coming in, he knew the guy was a perfectionist and he didn't like using big named stores, after all they couldn't do anything like this. They were simply pretty faces to sell the goods.

The old man came out of the back of the shop wiping his hands. He smiled at Jasper and went to a drawer behind him to get the necklace out.

"Good morning Jasper, how are you?"

"Very well thank you, are you?" Jasper smiled

"I am yes, I have your ladies' necklace ready for you, I hope you like it, if you do you can take it away?" he pulled open the velvet pouch and slid the necklace into his hand.

Jasper was itching to take it from him. He handed it to him placing into his hand gently. Jasper was in awe.

"Oh wow, this is beautiful, it's so delicate" he rubbed his fingers over the top of the bottom J, tears welling in his eyes, just seeing his drawing come to life had him feeling emotional, thoughts running through is head that it almost never happened. looking up at the old man he wiped his eye.

"I'm sorry, I don't mean to cry but this has just reminded me how delicate life is and it was almost taken from me a couple of weeks ago. You have really worked your magic here, I can't wait for Belle to see it."

The old man beamed with pride. "You are very welcome Son, I hope she loves it as much as you do."

"Oh, she will I can promise you that." Jasper pulled his wallet out of his pocket cradling the necklace in his palm, he let the wallet drop open and put it down on the counter pulling his card out handing it over.

"Give me the necklace let me clean it up and put it into its box then you can take it away, it will take a few minutes if that's okay?"

Jasper handed it over reluctantly watching every move the man made, now he had it he was very protective over it, even to the man who made it. Jasper looked around the old shop while he waited, there was a layer of dust on all the shelves but the old man had a great customer base and he wasn't worried about cleaning anything, he did it for the love of creating things. 10

minutes later the old man came out with it polished and sitting in its box, Jasper took the box and his mouth fell open.

"My god I didn't think it could get any more beautiful!"

The old man smiled with pride, "any problems at all come and see me."

He put it into its box and handed it to Jasper, took his credit card for the remaining amount and handed him the receipt. Jasper put his hand out to the old man.

"I can't thank you enough, it's incredible, Belle is going to love it."

"You're very welcome."

They shook hands and Jasper put the box in his jacket pocket zipped it up and walked out. Biding the old man goodbye.

He went back to the bike and sent a text to Jane

Good Morning Belle, I will be with you in about 15 minutes, anything you want love? Xxx

He got back on the bike while he waited for Jane to reply

Good Morning baby, no thank you, just you :-) xxx

Jasper smiled, put his phone in his pocket and got ready to leave. Within 10 minutes he was back at the hospital. He parked the bike up and walked in, he was excited to be seeing Jane, he felt like he had been away from her for a long time. As he got to the door he could hear the girls laughing, he knocked and opened the door. All the girls turned and looked at him smiling.

"Well you didn't drink last night obviously because you look like a proper ray of sunshine this morning Jasper" Gwen said holding her hands on her hips.

"Oh, believe me I did, but I got up early and made myself look better for my girl." He walked over to Jane, took her face in his hands and gave her a long lingering kiss.

All the girls swooned, making kissing noises at him.

"I bet my old man wouldn't do that for me, he probably got up scratching his balls, farted and went for coffee." Linda moaned
Jasper laughed. "Well the first two I can't confirm, yes he had coffee."

"Come on girls let's leave these lovebirds to it, I need a shower." Gwen said sniffing her underarms.
They all got up and grabbed their phones and bags, hugged Jane and kissed Jasper on the cheek before leaving.

Jasper walked around the bed to sit the other side of Jane away from her bad leg, she leant forward so he could put his arm around behind her, she laid back and snuggled up to his chest.
"Oh, you do smell nice." she said smelling him again.
"Are you trying to say I have been smelly lately Madam?" he asked turning her head up to him to look at her.
"Well….. let's just say you haven't really bothered of late." she said screwing her face up waiting for the tickle or the bite from him. She wasn't disappointed.
Jasper sunk his teeth into her shoulder biting gently over and over making her giggle, he knew he couldn't tickle her she had too many stitches to worry about. Jane was out of breath laughing.
"Stop please Jasper, stop…." She begged over and over loving every minute, even though her face was aching and her stomach hurt.
Jasper continued, he wasn't letting this go to easily. He loved her silly laugh and it felt good to make her laugh and see her so relaxed.
"Please baby no more I need to pee." Jane begged him
Jasper stopped, "You better not be playing me lady or you will get it twice as bad." He teased
"I promise I'm not." she begged and pleaded still laughing.

Jasper stopped and got off the bed, "Hang on Belle, let me take you."

He walked around the other side of the bed. Jane put her arm up ready to be lifted so she didn't hit him on the head with her plaster, he slid his hands underneath her and carried her to the bathroom. He stood her up taking her weight so he could get her shorts down and sat her onto the toilet.

"The lengths you go to just to be carried like a princess." he laughed.

Jane swatted him with her good hand laughing, "You cheeky sod, you will pay for that when I am better."

"Ooooooo, promises, promises." He grinned at her knowing she would laugh at him. He bent down and kissed her, he didn't care if she was peeing. They were passed that the first day they met.

"I was going to ask if you wanted a shower but I think you may have already had one?" he questioned.

"Yes, I too wanted to smell and look as good as I could for you today."

"Belle you could never look anything but beautiful to me, well maybe when you cry and have mascara running down your face or you leave your runny nose all over me."

"This time Jane caught him perfectly on the backside as he didn't expect it, she started laughing at him as he yelped and rubbed the spot where she caught him. He pouted at her while she laughed.

"Turn around I will kiss it better for you?" she grinned with a glint in her eye

"I hope you are not trying to get my boxers off young lady?" he smiled.

"Hell yes!" Jasper turned around and dropped his jeans, Jane giggled and leant into him leaving a huge kiss on his bottom, making lots of kissing noises. He pulled up his jeans turned around and kissed the top of her head.

"I love you so much Belle, I really do."

"I love you too Jasper, and I would love you even more if you helped me off this toilet my leg is going to sleep." she grimaced.

Jasper laughed and lifted her up so she could clean herself, he pulled her shorts up and lifted her to the sink to wash her hands.

"All done baby thank you." Jane said kissing his cheek.

Jasper smiled and walked her back to the bed, he put her down gently and joined her on the other side. Jane snuggled back into him. He held her tight wrapping his arms around her, smelling her hair, he could smell her normal scent which he loved, he just realised how much he had missed her smell. He kissed the top of her head over and over making her look up and smile at him.

"Belle." Jasper whispered into her hair.

"Yes baby?" she replied looking up.

"I have never been so scared in all my life when you were taken, I really thought you were dead." he could feel tears building, but he needed to tell her how he felt. "My heart felt like it had been ripped out, I could barely breath as I ran around the house calling for you."

He wiped his face, pushing his fingers into the corners of his eyes, squeezing hard. Jane pulled his head down and kissed both his eyes catching his tears, she was fighting her own, she wanted this conversation, they both needed it.

"Talk to me love, please" Jane pleaded

Jasper smiled sadly. "If you're sure?"

"Yes, I think we both should, I am well enough and I want to hear it."

He took a deep breath and sighed. "When I woke up and I realised I had been hit on the head, but you know that don't you?" Jane nodded, "I remember seeing the fear on your face as I went to kiss you, the hair on the back of my neck stood on end. Then it all went black. When I realised you were gone I ran around the house calling you, I didn't know what to think. I never imagined it would be him, when I went to the door I realised I had left it open, Belle it was my fault, I had left the door open when I picked you up to carry you across the threshold. I thought I had kicked it closed but I didn't kick it hard enough." He started to cry openly, not realising how much he had buried. Jane pulled his face down and kissed him. She whispered.

"It's okay love, I knew it was going to happen, I was ready, I had a feeling the week before something was going to happen, when the guys arrived I had a feeling he was around, I didn't want to say anything I kept it buried, I didn't want you thinking I was being paranoid." Jane started to cry too, their heads touching, looking deep into each other's eyes, they kissed softly as tears began again.

"Please tell me you forgive me Belle, if you don't I will try and prove my love to you for the rest of my life, if you want to leave that's ok too, but promise you will stay until you are on your feet, I will move into the spare room or I will pay for someone to look after you in your apartment?"

Jane pulled away from him looking scared. "Do you want me to go?" fresh tears falling.

"My god no!!" he grabbed her face, Belle you are my world, my life. I don't ever want to spend a moment without you by my side."

Jane started to sob openly, "neither do I. This isn't anyone's fault, you carried me out of love, we should be safe. I want to start again and know it's over."

"I promise you Belle it is over, there is no way he can ever come back."

Jane nodded, "I believe you. I don't need any details."

"Belle. You know how much I love you?" She nodded. "When you were taken. I was terrified. My heart felt like it had been ripped out. The pain was awful. My head was scrambled. I don't function without you. I was completely lost. I kept shouting to you to hang on I was going to find you. I promised you I would never let you down".

"I heard you baby. I did the same. I kept whispering to you, asking you to wait for me, to find me, even if it was just to die in your arms, or to be back with you, I didn't want to be washed down the drain. I was terrified, he was so angry, he knew everything, he told me about Helen, he made me watch videos of them, I need to know she is okay, nobody has mentioned her yet?" Her sobs caught in her throat the thought of what could have been.

"When we got the call from that psycho and I heard your voice I knew we would find you. The guys were amazing and worked hard. James is the guy I will be indebted too for the rest of my life. The other four guys they are known as the Dark Angels , were amazing too, they took him off after. I am so glad you hung on Belle, G kept telling me you were stronger now. I don't think anyone realises you know about Helen, she had a crash after rushing out of the club, she was trying to get away and hide. Bill is looking after her until the others get back. She had concussion."

Jane nodded. "Yes, he did, he put me through self defence, but not for women, it was more intense than that, they knew him and knew what he was capable of. They helped me to change my thoughts too. It's what got me through, I couldn't have done it otherwise, and knowing I had you, knowing how loved I was this time, I just needed to get back to you, I didn't want to die. Before I would happily died, just to get away from him. He told me he had a life Insurance policy in my name too, he was going to registered me missing when he flushed me down the drain." She sobbed harder.

"Belle, what do you mean? Flushed you."

"In the room was the acid to get rid of me, he was going to break my bones to fit me in the bath, and leave me in the acid until I disintegrated, then flush me away, he said any other bones left he would put in the rubbish shoot." Jane began to shake.

"Oh, my darling, I don't think anyone knew about that. Oh sweetheart, thank you for telling me, come here." He held her tighter as she sobbed, I'm sorry Belle, truly."

Jane nodded again looking into his eyes. "Thank you for coming to look for me."

"There was never any doubt Belle." He kissed her head, the thought of what she had gone through made him feel sick, he was so relieved the guys had killed Mark.

Jasper took Jane's face in his hands, he looked deep into her eyes, rubbed her nose which always made her smile and kissed her softly. He suddenly had an idea. Jane wanted to start again, he wanted to give her a good memory, just their memory and he was going to give it to her. He needed to organize a few things, he felt butterflies in his tummy thinking about it, he loved to surprise her. It meant he had to keep the necklace for another few weeks or so but it would be worth it. Jane snuggled back into his chest sighing, he wrapped his arms tightly around her his mind working overtime.

Jane fell into a peaceful sleep, Jasper smiled as he felt her body relax into him, he loved the noises she made when she slept. He didn't dare move or she would wake up, he managed to get his phone out of his pocket, putting it on silent and one handed sent a couple of brief messages. The first to the couple at the cottage, he wanted to rent it for a long weekend. He messaged Moses and told him what he wanted to do, he was hoping he could get the cottage in a few weeks. It would give her enough time to be used to being out of the hospital and used to her restrictions while she healed. Moses thought it was a great idea. He felt his phone vibrate on the bed, he picked it up, it was a reply from the couple, it was available, they were happy to help out. He replied quickly and said he would call to arrange everything later. He turned his phone off and laid his head on Janes and went to sleep, happy she was in his arms and looking forward to the following day when he could take her home.

Back at the house the guys and girls had packed up their things and taken them back to the apartments. The girls had cleaned the house from top to bottom. They had been out and brought some banners, Shadow came over with a hand made one on a sheet of white plastic that said welcome home Doc in bright colours, they hung it from the bedroom windows so she would see it when she came into the street. Flowers had been sent by many of the guys at the MC, the house was awash with them, the smell overwhelming as you walked in the door.

Once the house was back to normal and all the banners were up they all stood back arms folded smiling.

"Right let's get out of here, I think we should all leave them alone at the hospital tonight and come over for when she arrives tomorrow."

"Great idea," Gwen agreed, "we can bring some food over too, so Jasper hasn't got to think about it. I will text him and let him know. Come on you lot let's get out of here" She walked over to Moses and kissed his cheek.

"See you tomorrow love; get some rest you look like shit, she's going to be fine now you know that don't you?"

"Cheeky bitch, yes I do but I can still worry."

"Tell me something Moses why have you never told Jane how you feel, you are watching the one woman you ever loved be taken away from you, why?"

"She was never going to be mine, yes I am in love with her and I always will be, but she sees me as a Brother, nothing else."

"But you never told her, how do you know that?"

Gwen was frustrated, she could see how much he adored her, she had watched it for years, this last month had proved it even more. He hated being in the UK without her, he was so different being around her.

"She is with Jasper now, I am happy for her, as long as he treats her well then I am happy with that, she is still in my life I can see her whenever I like and I will always look out for her, I would never tell her, I wouldn't want her to know either." Gwen put her head down. "What have you done Gwen?" he looked at her quizzically.

"We were talking about men last night and Alison mentioned how you look at her, she said she could see how much you are in love with her, she thought Jane knew. We just confirmed it for her, I'm sorry Moses, she had a right to know."

"No Gwen, no, no, no, this can't happen. He grabbed the sides of his head screwing up his face, pressing his temples, he began pacing round the kitchen. He wasn't angry, just scared, he didn't want to lose her.

"How the hell do I face her tomorrow? What do I say to her, Jasper caught me talking to her the day after she was taken in the garden, I was telling her how much I loved her and he was stood behind me. Fuck, Fuck, Fuck!!!"

Gwen walked up behind him and put her hand on his shoulder. "What did Jasper say?"

"Nothing, he did what you did and put his hand on my shoulder and squeezed it, he's not stupid. I can't lose her Gwen, Fuck, what am I going to do?"

He walked off again pacing, everyone else had left the room.

"You have to talk to her Moses, not right away but when she is on her feet. You both need to clear the air."

"What if she doesn't want me staying here when she comes home?"

"She knows it's fine, stop worrying."

"Stop worrying, are you fucking kidding me?, I could lose the one person that is everything to me Gwen, do you understand that? Of course you don't, nobody does because you are not me. That girl is my world, she is everything to me, I chose to keep it under wraps, that's my decision and you have all blown it out of the fucking water now! Why couldn't that fucking woman keep her fucking nose out, arghhhhh." He screamed, looking up to the ceiling, he pushed the heels of his hands into his eyes and walked around the kitchen again muttering to himself.

Gwen stood with her arms across her chest. "Listen to me Moses, Jane knows, so what, you two are closer than any couple I know. Nothing can spoil that unless you allow it. Stop being a drama queen and sort it out. Talk to her, get it out of the way, she loves you too remember, you are her best friend, nothing will ever change that."

"Just leave it Gwen, please."

"Fine," she walked over kissed his cheek again and walked away, "see you tomorrow. Let Jasper know the bed has been changed."

Gwen left with the others, Moses locked the doors and walked back into the house. He didn't know what to do with himself, he was feeling sick, the thought of losing Jane. He went into his room undressed and walked into the en-suite. He needed a shower and was going to try and relax in front of the TV, if he could work out how to even switch it on, let alone find something. He turned the shower on and stood waiting for it to get warm enough. He looked down at his body, his flat stomach he did that for Jane, he could see his feet now, not looking over his beer belly. He rubbed his flat stomach and his chest. His thoughts going to Jane.
"Could it have worked Jane?" he said aloud, "If I told you? Maybe if I hadn't been such a slob back then things may have been different?"
Without thinking he ran his hand over his cock, he sucked in air through his teeth, "mmmmm, I need this". He licked his thumb, wrapped his hand around his cock and rubbed his thumb over the tip, his head rolled back.
"Fuck that's good". He closed his eyes, rubbing the tip sucking in air again. His other hand rubbing his chest, he pulled on his nipple, he liked it rough, he loved being bitten, a few women had done it for him in the past, he loved it when he had two of them, he was younger then, in the army, they would fall at his feet back then. He let his hands wander across his body imagining a woman at his feet, he pulled his cock up, gripping his balls and pulling on them imagining a brunette sucking on them as she pushed a finger into his bottom. He opened his legs sucked his middle finger and pushed it into himself, "oh yesssss" he hissed, his eyes still closed.
"Suck me you bitch." he whispered, he squeezed his balls to hurt himself, he loved the pain, then moved his hand back up his shaft, he rubbed it slowly up to the top and over the head, back down again, his hand getting tighter around his cock. His

finger going deeper inside himself, he knew just how far to go. He got a little faster pumping his cock, his balls getting harder, his cock was straining, "Yes, yes, oh fuck yes." he repeated, getting faster, his finger now getting faster pushing in and out of him, he could feel the warmth creep up his body as he was ready to cum.

"Oh fuck, yesssss." he didn't want to cum so quick, but he needed it. He pushed deeper into his bottom, pumping his cock harder, his hand running up and down the full length. He imagined he was on his knees on the bed with the brunette behind him licking his hole and pushing her vibrator deep inside him while her other hand wanked him. The other girl was laid in front of him with her legs open, her bare pussy glistening with her juices as he licked at her, pushing his finger inside her. She moaned loudly as he ran his tongue around her clit. Flicking it fast.

"Yes babe, I want you to cum for me, squirt into my mouth, let me drink you."

The girl raised her bottom off the bed, digging her fingers into the sheets as she came hard, he sucked on her, lapping up her juices his tongue going deep inside her licking at her, he wanted her to cum again, she was begging him to stop, he hadn't finished with her yet so kept going, he felt her go rigid again as another orgasm hit her, this time she came harder, his own body responded, the girl behind him pushing harder into him as she felt him cum, "Oooh shittttt" he yelled as his cock went rigid, his finger pumping into himself as he came hard. He came covering his own chest in his cum. It was dripping off him onto the floor, his breathing was hard and erratic his body tingling as it contracted over and over, he took his finger out of his bottom laughing feeling better and more relaxed, he stepped into the shower to clean himself up.

Chapter 26

Going home

Jasper was sat awake watching Jane sleeping when Alison arrived, she came in smiling looking at them both. Jasper put his finger to his lips to let her know Jane was still sleeping. She smiled and backed out not wanting to wake her. Minutes later she came back with a cup of tea tiptoeing in and leaving it on the bedside cabinet. Jasper mouthed Thank you, she smiled and walked out closing the door. Jasper knew once Jane was home he would have trouble keeping her in bed so the more rest she had there the better, but he also knew she would heal better at home.

He picked up his phone and checked his emails, he wanted to know everything was in hand for the long weekend away to the cottage, they had both slept well even though they were in a small bed. He had several emails confirming everything was sorted. He had a text from Moses letting him know the house was ready and everything was in place. He just needed 30 minutes to get the gang there ready. Jasper replied letting him know he would text giving them an hours' notice to give them time to get to the house. He drank his tea and felt Jane stirring, she made little noises when she woke which he loved, he turned to look at her and kissed her on the head, she smiled at him and curled into his chest.

"Good Morning Belle, how did you sleep?"

"Mmmmmm," she moaned into his chest smiling. "like a baby thank you because you were with me."

Jasper smiled, he felt the same too. "Are you sure you want to go home today, we can delay it if you like for another week?"

Jane grabbed his nipple through his t-shirt and twisted it.

"That's a no then?" he asked laughing.

Jane looked up to him and he bent down to kiss her, he loved his morning kisses and more so than ever now, he knew they had a long way to go on her recovery and mentally she would need a lot of time, but he felt good, he had his girl back and today they were going home.

Alison came back in to do Jane's observations with a cup of tea for her.

"I could get used to this service, I hope you are taking note Jasper?" she teased

"Cheeky mare you get that anyway." he replied.

We shall miss you both, I know I get to come and see you at home but it won't be the same without you here. All being well the Doctor will be round for 10am to give you the all clear to go home. Then we need to get your medication dispensed and you are on your way, we won't keep you any longer than necessary I promise, I know you are itching to get home."

"Thank you Alison, you have been so kind, I can't thank you enough, you have let us get away with a lot."

"Well it's not every day you get a room filled with bikers and gorgeous looking men at that, how could I refuse?"

Jasper and Jane laughed, "I just hope they won't disappoint me when I get to come and see you at home?"

Jane looked at Jasper, "Are the guys staying longer?"

"I know Moses is staying until you are back on your feet, I think the others will be heading home later this week, we will find out later I'm sure."

Jane nodded. And fell silent.

Alison finished her obs, "I will leave you alone to sort yourself out unless you want one of the girls to help you shower?"

"No, it's fine I can help, happy to, we both need a shower anyway."

"As you wish. I will grab your waterproof dressing and come back and sort you out." she said giving a naughty smile, she knew exactly what was going to happen. She closed the door behind her and left them alone.

Jasper passed Jane her tea, she was deep in thought.

"Penny for them Belle?" She sat silent. "Belle?" silence. He bent and kissed her head which made her look up, she was holding her tea in her hands.

"Are you okay darling?"

She looked up, "Yes I think so, I was just thinking about going home, just a bit nervous I suppose, am I doing the right thing?"

"Yes Belle you are, the Doctors are happy for you to go, they wouldn't let you if they weren't."

Jane nodded. "Okay." she half smiled. Hiding from the real reason she was nervous about going home. She passed her empty cup to Jasper and he put it on the side. She snuggled back into his chest, smelling him.

"Are you enjoying yourself Belle?" he laughed

"Yes thank you, just getting my fix of you before we shower, I think we should bottle your smell, and call it Eau De Jasper, it would fly off the shelves."

He started giggling, "Belle, I don't smell very nice, I think you have lost your sense of smell, I think we need to get your nose checked out."

Jane pulled his t-shirt up, licking up his chest around his nipples making him moan.

"I will be the judge of that, and I say you smell delicious." she continued to lick his body

Jasper laid back enjoying it, he couldn't wait to get her home.

"Oh Jesus Belle, if you don't want to be put on your knees then you better stop that." he groaned begrudgingly, he wanted her so badly, and not just a quick one in the shower, he wanted to enjoy her.

Jane looked up smirking as she ran her tongue around his nipple and bit it. Her hand travelling down his chest over his stomach and down to his cock, he was rock hard already, he was still wearing his jeans, he now felt dirty having slept in them. Jane started to undo them and he grabbed her hand.

"No Belle, let's go and shower, I have been in these clothes overnight."

Jane pouted, "Why baby, you never stop me, don't you fancy me anymore?"

"What did I just say to you, does my hard cock not tell you how much I want you? But I am not having you going down on me when I have been in these clothes for 24 hours."

"It wouldn't stop you licking me though would it?"

"No because you haven't been doing anything and you only have shorts on, so you have air getting to your pussy."

"You are getting boring in your old age." she pouted again

Jasper sprung off the bed walked around to her side, picked her up and walked her into the bathroom, Jane was smiling, she knew it would do the trick.

He opened the shower door and Jane leant across to turn the shower on, he put her down, as she balanced on one leg, he pulled down her shorts. He sat her down on the stool and pulled her t-shirt off, her put her into her shower protection then stripped himself off, Jane reached over and stroked his body, trailing her fingers down his abs reaching the start of his cock.

"Jesus Belle."

"I'm not sucking it, just touching it."

"Baby you just have to look at and that's enough for him, he gets a sniff of you and that pussy and it's game over."

Jane looked up smiling pulling him to her, she kissed his stomach and flicked her tongue across his belly button, which made him laugh. She continued downwards and stopped at the start of his cock.

"You are such a tease Belle." he moaned.

She nodded grinning at him. "You told me I couldn't, so I won't."

"Get up her now and in that shower." he growled, gritting his teeth playing with her as he put his arms out to her to climb into.

"Can you manage to put your hair up Belle?"

"Sure I can." She said leaning over and grabbing the hair slide off the side.

He walked her into the shower and sat her down on the seat. He directed the jet lower to not soak her hair and picked up the shower gel.

"Ready when you are." he said rubbing the shower gel into his hands making bubbles.

Jane looked up at him grinning, "bring it on big boy" she said leaning into him, pulling him closer, she still couldn't open her mouth too wide, but she wasn't going to let that stop her especially as when she pulled him closer his cock was level with her face, she looked up at him and smiled, then took a long slow lick of the length of his cock. Jasper sucked air through his teeth as her tongue slid up and down.

"Fuck Belle, that feels so good." He moaned his head dropping back.

Jane was desperately wanting to lower her mouth onto him but knew it would hurt so instead she ran her tongue over her lips to make them wet gently running them across the tip, she knew Jasper would react...and he did.

"Jesus woman are you trying to kill me, fuck don't stop please."

Jane smiled. "I thought you didn't want me to touch him, you said you felt dirty?"

Jasper quickly washed his cock off and stood proud smiling down at Jane, with his hands on his hips, Jane began laughing at him, licked her lips again and went back to the tip of his cock. She opened her mouth as wide as was comfortable just to take a little of him and slowly lowered herself. She knew she was overdoing it but so desperately wanted to please him. Jasper knew he was going to cum soon, he didn't want to exhaust her by making love to her in the shower, they had plenty of time and she needed to heal.

"Belle if you don't want me to fill your mouth you better stop." she smiled up at him and continued. Jasper felt her hand go to his balls and squeeze gently, she was only sucking the head of his cock but it was driving him nuts.

"Oh, fucking hell Belle." he moaned as he felt his cock stiffen. He was moments away from filling her mouth, "Oh god yes don't stop baby please." Jane moved her hand further round past his balls to the soft stop he loved her touching, the water was running down his body so gave her good lubrication, the sensation was pushing him over the edge as he felt his balls tighten again and the tingle in his cock rise, he felt like he was losing all his senses, his body was on fire, Jane continued sucking just the head and rubbing just below his balls, before he could warn Jane he exploded into her mouth, Jane felt him cum before he did, she was swallowing as fast as she could still smiling as Jasper yelled out.

"Oh, my fucking god Belle, Jesus Christ!" he groaned his body on fire.

Jane giggled as she licked the tip to make sure she had captured it all. She looked up at him, his head was still back, he was trembling all over as he rode through his orgasm. He came back down to earth and looked down at Jane and laughed.

"The fact you can't open your mouth very much and you still manage to do that Belle. Jesus woman. I love you."

Jane looked up smiling, "I love you too, now get me washed and take me home before they change their minds."

Jasper saluted smiling. "I would kidnap you Belle. No way are you staying any longer." He turned and grabbed the shower gel and body scrub, "Arms up love."

Jane did as she was asked and put her arms up out of the way while Jasper washed her down. Once done he washed himself turned the shower off, grabbed the towels wrapping them both up and carried Jane back to her bed. He dried them both off and Jane got into her new leggings and zip up top before resting back on the bed while Jasper went to get dried off and dressed.

Alison came in shortly after with breakfast for them both, Jasper looked at her.

"What's this Alison?"

"Well I didn't see any point in you leaving Jane to go and eat as she is going today so I brought it up for you while I grabbed Jane's, so eat please."

"Wow, that is really very kind of you, you didn't need to do that." Jasper was shocked, after all this was a hospital.

"I know I didn't need to do it Jasper, Jane has been an absolute pleasure to look after and you guys have been fun, there is no harm in it, I shall miss you both."

Jane beckoned Alison she was feeling really emotional and a little scared about going home. She hugged Alison tight and whispered to her.

"Thank you so much for everything, I wouldn't have got this far without you." She sniffed trying not to cry.

"Oh don't start me off, I will be a blubbering mess otherwise." they both laughed at each other wiping their eyes.

"Come on girls, you will see each other again, Alison is coming home to see you remember."

"I know she is, it's just emotional leaving here that's all."

Alison hugged her again and Jasper leant over and squeezed her tight.

"Come on Belle, let's get you packed up so we can leave as soon as the Doctor says yes. I will take the flowers down to the car too, then I just have to take her majesty." he turned and gave her his best smile. Jane laughed at him.

"Cheeky! If I could find something to throw at you I would." She said laughing.

Jasper walked back to her pushed his hands into her hair holding her head and pulled her towards his waiting lips, they were barely touching, just the breath between them, they were looking into each others eyes, their breathing matching each others, as Jasper brushed his lips against Jane's, he moved his lips back and forth over hers teasing her. Jane moaned into him, he kissed her once more then pushing her face up taking her bottom lip in his and biting gently, Jane's breath caught again as he moved down onto her chin leaving another bite, he released her head with one hand and moved her head to the side pushing her hair away with the back of his hand, he smiled as he kissed her neck just below her ear, Jane could feel his breath and his lips touching her so softly, her breath catching every time he touched her. She felt his teeth graze her neck, she moaned loudly, she could feel herself getting wet. They were both lost in each other for a few minutes when the door knocked which brought them back to the present moment.

"We will continue that later" he said as he kissed her lips and turned as the door opened.

"Good Morning Jane, Jasper, how are you feeling, ready to go home?"

"Good Morning Doctor." she replied with a huge smile, "Yes I certainly am, a little nervous if I am honest and hope I am doing the right thing?"

Well if you weren't feeling a little nervous I would also question allowing you to go home, but I am more than happy for you to go, you have an excellent support network, we will see you every day to change your dressings and as Jasper said you will heal better being at home, we all do. So let's not delay this anymore, I have already finished your paperwork, your obs are perfect I have no question about sending you home, so continue packing, I want you out of here before 11am." he smiled at them both left her paperwork in an envelope on her bed and walked toward the door. "Let Alison know when you are ready so we can arrange to take you down to the car."

Jasper walked back to the Doctor and shook his hand, "Thank you for everything Doctor Robinson, I can't thank you enough for saving Belle, we will forever be in your debt."

"Jane did the hard work Jasper, she fought to stay alive, we just repaired her, you have one strong girl there."

Jasper nodded. "Don't I know it." he laughed

"I'm sure she will have you all running around for her as soon as you get home."

"Oh, I have no doubt about it, why do you think Moses is staying?" Jasper laughed. The Doctor patted him on the back

"I will see you before you leave, Alison will have the appointment ready for you to come back and see me next week."

 "Thank you Doctor." Jane replied. Grinning widely

As the Doctor walked out and closed the door Jane squealed and patted the bed in excitement.

"Right then love we have a couple of hours until you turn into a pumpkin, you heard the Doctor, let's get you home." Jasper had butterflies, he was dithering around not sure what to do first. He was grinning as he wandered around Jane's room. He hit the side of his head as if to get it into gear and spoke to himself.

"Come on stupid sort your head out."

"Did I do something?" Jane frowned looking down the room at Jasper.

Jasper turned around, "No Belle I was talking to myself, sorry, I am so excited, I have butterflies and I don't know where to start to pack you up." he began laughing and walked back to the bed. He leant onto the bed and kissed her head.

"You are my world, my joy, my life. Taking you home today is the happiest day of my life."

Jane looked up with tears in her eyes. "Promise me no matter how bad this recovery is and whatever I might say you will never stop loving me?"

"Belle baby, there is nothing on this earth you could do or say that would ever stop me loving you, we are in this together and we will take everything in our stride that is thrown at us."

He looked at her, the tears ready to spill at any moment. She was looking down and fiddling with the bedding. He put his finger under her chin and lifted her head.

"Listen to me Belle, no more tears, you could have pimples all over your face and be toothless and look like a balloon I will always love you regardless. Now wipe those tears away and sort my head out, what do you want me to do first, maybe I should do a few trips down to the car with your flowers and balloons?"

Jane laughed wiping her eyes, and sniffing, she grabbed Jaspers hand and pulled him close.

"If you lose all your teeth and grow nose hair and have long hair in your ears I promise I WILL stop loving you" she laughed. "And don't get me started on your losing your mind and dribbling, you will be in a home before you can say Jack Rabbit."

"Oh I see, you just want me for my good looks and charm, and when I get old and grey you will trade me in for a new model. I got you all worked out Belle, it's okay. Don't you worry about me." he grinned, he loved teasing her as she did him.

Jane grabbed his face, they were both smiling, she went to kiss him and took his lip in her teeth and bit it softly, he tried to pull way.

"Ow, ow." he moaned with his lip trapped, Jane let go giggling. He rubbed his lip with his finger pouting.

"That will teach you for being cheeky."

"That's fighting talk Belle, wait until I get you home."

"Bring it on big boy." she teased, grinning at him naughtily.

"Right I need to get you packed up." He kissed her nose and walked to the door in search of Alison. He was in need of help or a trolley to move the flowers and balloons.

He went to the nurses station, Alison wasn't around but there were other nurses, he knew if he turned on the charm he would get some help.

"Good morning ladies, how are we all today?" He gave his best smile.

They all stopped talking and looked at him, "I wondered if I could borrow a trolley or something to put all the flowers on to take down to the car?"

They all jumped to their feet. He smiled laughing to himself. He was going to tease Belle with this one. One of the nurses he had seen a few times rushed off and grabbed a trolley for him.

"Would you like some help, I don't mind?", she purred.

"Thank you that's very kind but I think I can manage, if I need anything though I will be sure to let you know." she grinned at him fluttering her eyelids. *Jesus are all these nurses the same?* He laughed to himself. He hadn't noticed in the past the way women drooled over him, but now he saw it. He wasn't sure he liked it but at times like this it didn't harm anyway to use it. He grabbed the trolley and went back into Jane's room, she was sat sorting out her little cupboard. He loaded the trolley and filled the sack with balloons to take them down to the car so they wouldn't fly away.

When he got back Alison was with Jane packing her bag. She had brought her medication up for her. So all that was left was to pack the bathroom and get Jane in the wheelchair. He walked out of the room and pulled his phone out of his pocket and dialled Moses.

"Hey Brother, everything okay?" Moses said as he answered
Yes, just letting you know we are almost ready to leave so see you in around 45 minutes."
"Great we will be ready."
He walked back into the room. "Right then, just the bathroom to do and we are ready to go Belle."
She looked up and grinned, "I'm ready."
He walked into the bathroom grabbed everything and packed it away before walking out and putting it into Jane's bag.
"I will call Dr Richardson so he can see you before you go, and I will grab your wheelchair at the same time to take you down to the car."
"Thanks Alison." they said in unison.

Jane was sat on the top of the bed with her boots on and small jacket waiting to go when Dr Richardson walked in with Alison pushing the wheelchair.
"Right then Jane, remember what I said, look after yourself, Alison will be in to see you tomorrow any issues you call me, you have your medication make sure you take it."
"Yes Doctor." she grinned
"Right, now get out of here, I look forward to seeing you looking even better at your appointment."
Alison pushed the wheelchair to the bed and Jasper lifted her into his arms and sat her in the chair.
Jasper turned to Dr Robinson chocking back tears and shook his hand.
"Thank you again Doctor for everything."
"Just look after her Jasper, that's thanks enough for me."
Jane looked up at the Doctor with tears in her eyes and took a deep breath. He took her hand and patted it.
"Take care Jane."
"Thank you Doctor, I will, I won't let you down."

They walked down the corridor Jasper was carrying the last of Janes things and Alison was pushing the wheelchair, Jane was feeling a little nervous, they got to the car, Jasper put everything in the boot and opened Jane's door. He lifted her up and sat her in the seat, Alison moved the wheelchair out of the way while Jasper strapped her in.

He turned to Alison "Thank you Alison for taking care of Belle, we will see you tomorrow?"

"Yes, you will, it's been a pleasure Jasper."

She walked to Jane and hugged her, as she turned away, she opened her arms and looked at Jasper, he smiled walking into a hug with her too.

"Oh, I will make the girls jealous now when I go back up to the ward." she teased. Jasper laughed

"Behave yourself woman."

Jasper walked around to his door and climbed in. He looked over at Jane and squeezed her hand, lifting it, kissing her.

"You ready to go Belle?"

"Yes, please take me home."

"Your wish is my command." he grinned

They drove in silence, holding each other's hand, Jasper was rubbing Jane's fingers with his thumb. He was nervous and excited. The traffic was light so it didn't take long to get to the house. As they pulled into the drive Jane saw the banner above the door, she squealed when she saw it. Feeling tearful again, Jasper squeezed her hand. He stopped the car and walked around to her side.

He opened the door, Jane was frowning.

"You okay Belle?"

"Yes, I just thought...oh it doesn't matter." she looked down at her hands fiddling with her nails, she thought her friends would be here to welcome her home, but she told herself off for being selfish and needy.

Jasper grinned to himself. "let me take you in first then I will unload the car."

"Okay." she said climbing into his waiting arms.

"Welcome home sweetheart he said kissing her softly."

"Thank you."

He gave her the keys to open the door and carried her in closing the car door behind him with his back.

Jane opened the door, she took a deep breath as they walked in. She looked around, nothing, nobody was there. She felt a little low again, really hoping to see her friends.

Jasper sat her down on the sofa, "I will just go and unload the car, can you just wait here for a few minutes then we can go and get some fresh air outside?"

"Yes please I would love that."

He dashed outside grabbing as much as he could and walked back into the house leaving the flowers in the kitchen, went back and grabbed her bags before locking the door and coming back in.

"Right then." he said wheeling around her wheelchair. "Your carriage awaits your ladyship."

He picked her up and settled her in, adjusting the footplates before wheeling her towards the door. He opened the doors and wheeled her out, the ramps were in place. Jane took a deep breath and inhaled the fresh air.

"Oh, that's better." she said.

"Can we go and see the roses please baby?" she asked looking up at him.

"Yes of course we can." he smiled, mouthing thank you God looking up to the sky.

"As Jane walked past the flower beds she brushed the plants as they walked past with her hand.

As they turned the corner where the roses were, her hands shot up to her mouth and she squealed. Sat on the swing and in the lovers seat were all her friends.

They all cheered "Surprise, Welcome home."

Jane started crying happy tears, Jasper stopped and bent down kissing her on the head.

They all came dashing towards her, hugging her in turn and then Jasper.

She slapped G and Moses. "I thought you had gone home."

"No fear of that little lady." G replied. Hugging her again.

"Come on we have things to show you." Jasper said, he wheeled her to the roses the sun was shining catching the glass. They all stopped and fell silent for a few minutes as Jane wiped a tear from her eye, she put her hand up grabbing Jaspers. He held her shoulder with the other hand and kissed her head again. "The boys all helped Ernie with everything you see."

Jane looked around and wiped her eyes again, clearing her throat.

"Thank you all, it's so beautiful."

They all smiled at her, "come on there is more, if you haven't already spotted it." Jasper grinned

He pushed her around to the lover's seat he had brought, Linda leaned across and turned the lights on.

"Oh my god! You remembered?", she squealed her hands at her mouth. Everyone laughed.

"You can sit up here now as often as you like love."

She looked up at Jasper, took his hand and kissed it. "I love you so much Jasper."

"I love you too Belle, would you like to sit on the seat?"

She nodded furiously, everyone laughed, Jasper walked around the front of her and picked her up, they moved away so he could get to the seat and sit her down, she moved herself back and patted the seat, everyone dived on making her giggle. Jane looked around at the seat, then at her friends, she touched each one of them taking a deep breath trying not to cry.

"I love you all so much, thank you for being here."

"We wouldn't miss it Half-pint." Moses replied. They all agreed, patting her feet and arm.

"Right who wants a drink?" Gwen asked. The girls jumped up ready to help her. They all replied and the girls went off to get the drinks.

"Do you want to stay here Belle or go up to the house?"

"We better go to the house, we can all sit comfortably there at the table."

They all climbed off and Moses looked at Jasper asking permission to lift her up. Jasper nodded, he needed to get used to it if he was staying to help.

Jane moved herself to the edge and Moses put his arms out for her.

"Come on love, I will move you across."

Jane grabbed him around the neck as he lifted her into her chair. She kissed him on the cheek making him smile, he knew he needed to talk to her but that could wait. He wheeled her up to the house and onto the patio, the girls came out with the drinks.

"Well, as you are all up here is anyone hungry?" Linda asked.

Everyone put their hands up, shouting me, me, me she smiled.

"We better bring out lunch then." she smiled.

"Just salad for half-pint girls, she's heavy enough or she will be breaking our backs." Moses laughed

"Cheeky pig, if I could throw something at you I would."

"Why do you think he is brave enough to say it." Steve laughed grabbing him in a headlock. Everyone started laughing, Jasper looked across at Jane, he smiled, this is just what she needed he thought to himself.

The girls brought a huge spread out and they all dived in. They talked and joked enjoying the time together and cleared most of the food.

Jasper could see Jane was getting tired, he wasn't going to let her push herself. He walked behind her and kissed her head.

"Would you like to get some rest Belle?"

"Yes please if you don't mind?" Jasper pulled the chair out and lifted her up. She blew kisses to everyone and snuggled back into his chest as he walked her into the house.

"Where would you like to go, the sofa, the bed?"

"Our bed please if you will stay with me until I go to sleep, but leave the curtains open?"

"Of course love."

He headed to the bedroom, he felt her tense up in his arms. He walked into the bedroom, it was full of more flowers and new white bedding with tiny flowers on it. He knew she loved Laura Ashley so went a bit crazy buying cushions and bedding for her, he wanted it to feel very different.

"Oh Jasper," she smiled, "you really do spoil me," she hugged him tight and kissed his cheeks. "Thank you baby."

"There is nothing in this world I wouldn't do for you Belle." he put her down on her side of the bed. She ran her hands over the bedding.

"This is beautiful, you didn't have to do this."

"Yes I did, the girls washed and ironed it for you too. Gwen almost ripped it out of my arms when I brought it in, to make sure it was washed first."

Jane laughed. "Am I that bad?"

"I'm not saying a word he laughed. Right do you want to get changed? Or are you happy to stay as you are. You have plenty of shorts and zip up tops?"

"I will get undressed and get into bed." she said undoing her top.

Jasper stood watching her wanting to help, his hands going towards her then stopping, she needed to do somethings for herself. He grabbed his t-shirt for her, and she took it to her face and inhaled.

"It doesn't smell of you! She pouted.

Jasper laughed, "Sorry Belle."

"You don't need to be, take off this one please." She said pulling on the bottom of his t-shirt.

"You're kidding right?" he asked, she shook her head. He laughed and pulled the neck of the t-shirt over his head sighing, pretending to be frustrated by it, but really he loved it.

Jane smiled and took it, putting it on and inhaling deeply at his smell. "Thank you baby."

"You're welcome love." he said turning to grab the other one he had passed to her.

Jasper pulled back the covers and helped Jane get underneath, he pulled the blinds and opened the window to give her some air. He climbed onto the bed and she cuddled up into the crook of his arm.

"This is better don't you think?" Jane nodded, he kissed the top of her head and held her tight, within minutes he felt her breathing change as she fell asleep. He stayed a little while longer until he knew she was in a deep sleep and moved away slowly, he left the door open a little. He wasn't sure how she would cope being back in the room.

He went back down to the gang, as he walked back out everyone looked up.

"She okay?" Gwen asked.

"She's good thank you, she went out like a light."

"Did you have an accident or something Linda asked pointing at his t-shirt?"

He laughed. "No Belle wanted it to sleep in."

"Oh, your smell, I get that." The men looked at each other frowning. "You wouldn't understand Moses, it's a girl thing."

"Say no more Linda, you girls are odd."

"Wait until you find the one, you will be the same, that familiar smell when they are not around, the memories it gives you of when they were there last." Jasper chipped in.

"Oh you do it to then?" he asked

"Yes, especially after the attack." Moses nodded.

"Right then, more drinks?" Gwen stood.

They all gave their orders and the girls cleared the table before going in to make more drinks.

The guys sat down chatting when they came back out.

"We found these two on the doorstep." Gwen said as James and Chicca followed. Everyone stood and greeted them.

"Jane is sleeping, she hasn't long gone." Jasper added.

"That's okay, we just wanted to make sure she was okay." James said sitting down, they all moved around the table to fit everyone in, they kept their voices low as to not wake her.

"What's the plan then Brother?" Matt asked

"Well I spoke to the owners of the cottage up in the woods and I have booked a week up there for us, I thought she could do with a change of scenery and I know we will be spoilt up there."

Shall we all head off soon and leave Jane to get settled in, we can come back tomorrow" Steve said. They all nodded, Jasper was a little relieved, he wanted time alone with Jane and a bit of quiet. Moses was staying but he was happy to come and go when he was needed.

They sat chatting a little while longer and the girls cleared everything away washing dishes before they said their goodbyes and headed off.

Jasper and Moses sat in the garden and both let out a huge sigh.

"You okay Brother?" Moses asked

"Just relieved I think to finally have her home, I just hope she settles here. I hope being here doesn't give her nightmares and change her mind, we both love this house I would hate to leave it."

"I'm sure it won't come to that, Jane is a strong girl, hang in there Brother."

Jasper nodded. They both fell silent enjoying the quiet.

Jasper heard a faint cry, he looked at Moses. "Did you hear that?"

"Yes, I think I did." They were both on their feet in seconds, running to the bedroom, as they walked in not knowing what state Jane would be in they found her sat up crying wiping her eyes.

Jasper got onto the bed and cuddled her. Cooing to calm her, stroking her hair. Moses stood at the foot of the bed.

"Hey Belle, what's wrong?" he said wiping her eyes with his fingers rubbing her nose on his.

"I...I had a bad dream you were taken from me." She sniffed taking big gulps of air.

"I'm here love, I'm not going anywhere." he held her tight, her head buried in his shirt sniffing hard. She nodded and wiped the side of her face roughly with her hand.

"Would you like to get up, it's just us three now, everyone has gone home." she nodded.

Jasper grabbed her shorts, Moses turned, "I will see you in the lounge, can I get you a drink Half -pint?"

"Tea please Moses." she sniffed again.

"Consider it done." he walked away and headed to the kitchen.

"Come on then, let's get you into these and I will take you down." Jane nodded.

Jasper leant forward and kissed her head. "Just a bad dream Belle, they will soon stop love."

Jane nodded, "I'm sorry." her head hanging down while she put the heels of her hands into her eyes wiping the tears.

"Belle, you don't need to be sorry. We are here for you." He slid her shorts up her legs and Jane lifted her bottom so Jasper could pull her shorts up properly.

"Ready?" he smiled brushing her hair away from her face tucking it behind her ears. Jane nodded. "Come on then." He put his arms under her legs and Jane held him around the neck as he carried her to the lounge. He sat her on the sofa and Moses came in with tea for them all.

"How you doing love?" Moses asked as he sat down in the arm chair leaning over to take her hand.

"I'm ok now thank you." she said squeezing his hand. "Just a bad dream again."

"I remember those well love, and thanks to you they went away, so please make sure you get the help you need. We want you back 100%, no less."

Jane nodded again feeling the tears prick her eyes. Jasper pulled her into his side so she was laying against him outstretched on the sofa.

"Would her ladyship like a blanket?" Moses grinned.

"No thank you love, I'm good."

"So little lady what plans do you have?" Moses asked.

"Nothing really, just to get back on my feet and back to work, I want to get some help too before you say anything."

"Well you know who you are happy talking too, and we will do whatever it takes to get you what you need." he replied looking over at Jasper for confirmation. Jasper nodded in agreement.

"If you want to go home to England Belle we will make it happen, but we need to get your body healed first."

Jane looked around at them both, "Would you really do that for me?"

"Of course, we would." They answered in unison. She hung her head again fresh tears escaping.

"Come on sweetheart, you know we love you very much and nothing is out of the question if it means getting you better."

Jasper wrapped his arms around her hugging her tight, Jane bent down kissing his arm, the hairs tickling her nose.

"I don't know what I would do without you two." My knights in shining armour.

"Ahem, don't you mean, your knights aka bikers in dirty leathers?" Moses replied laughing.

"Of course, how silly of me." She laughed.

"Well I'm not sure about this one here." he replied pointing at Jasper, "I think we need to drag his leathers up the road to make them a little dirty, they are too clean."

"Cheeky sod at least they don't smell, those gloves of yours are stinking out the boot room."

"Hey that's plenty of sweaty road miles in those."

"Yeah don't we know it." Jane chipped in. "You gave me new leathers so maybe we should get you new gloves."

Moses held his hands up. "Okay, okay no need to gang up on me he laughed."

"You heard that Belle, we will have to take him to see Shadow then and get those dirty smelly things burnt." They all sat laughing.

"Right then I am on kitchen duty tonight Half-pint, what do you fancy to eat, nothing too complicated, anything that can go in the microwave is good for me?"

Jane sat with her finger against her lip deep in thought. "hmmm, well I think chicken and something would be nice, what do you think babe?", she smiled looking up to Jasper.

"I think that sounds perfect Belle, how about Chicken Stroganoff, not to heavy and quite easy to make?"

"Perfect, yes I think so. Stroganoff please Moses."

"Piss off the pair of you." Moses grumbled. "I will go to the supermarket and buy it from the freezer."

Jasper and Jane started laughing.

"I can help you Moses, it's easy."

"Yeah for you I'm sure it is."

"Well if you want to impress the ladies you need to learn to cook."

"You can fucking stop that right there, I have had no issues so far, once they get a taste of me there are no problems."

Jane knew he was touchy when it came to talking to women, she was laughing hard and holding her side, she could barely breath, she loved seeing someone else wind him up.

"Stop please it hurts" she begged, giggling and moaning.

Jasper was getting used to Moses and his grumpy outer shell, he had seen him at his weakest when Jane was taken he knew when to stop and when to carry on.

They all laughed. "Come on seriously, what do you want. I can do Chinese Indian, Pizza, anything you like."

Jasper laid his chin on top of Jane's head. "Belle, you chose, we will go with whatever you want?"

"Hmmm, well as you say anything, then I think you should get me some cheesecake from that fancy place in New York." she smiled at them both.

"Now you're getting cheeky, if you didn't have these injuries, I would get you in a headlock right now little lady."

Jane smiled at him, trying to give him her best cheesy grin. "A girl is allowed to try, I am poorly after all." she said pouting.

"Oh lord how many times are we going to hear this Brother, I think we are going to be fed up hearing it before the week is out?" He said looking at Jasper tutting and grinning.

"Oi" Jane scowled at him. Jasper and Moses started laughing knowing they would get a response.

"Now you can go to New York and get me cheesecake." she pouted

"I promise before I leave here to go home you will have your cheesecake Half-pint but for now what can I get you?" he asked smiling hugely at her walking across and kissing her on the head.

"Chinese please, we can all share then." Moses scowled at her. Pretending to be upset about sharing his food.

"Menu is in the middle drawer under the hob Brother."

Moses went to grab the menu and a piece of paper from the wall before Jane changed her mind.

He came back to the lounge and sat down "Right then Ms Jane, what will it be, the usual?"

"Yes please, deep fried salt and pepper chicken with fried rice."

"Jasper? What can I get for you?"

"Beef in Black bean sauce, with fine noodles, and some prawn toast."

"Got it, can I use the phone in the kitchen?"

"Sure of course, help yourself." Moses walked away to order the food and Jasper pulled Jane closer to him, he inhaled her smell deeply, "Mmmmmm you smell good enough to eat Belle, I think I might just eat you instead."

She snuggled back into him loving the closeness and being home. Laying her head against his chest.

Jasper leant down and kissed her bare shoulder, digging his teeth in gently. "Did I tell you how much I love you today Belle?"

"She grinned, he never failed to make her smile. "Actually, no you didn't." she lied but loved playing his games.

"Well my love, when I get you back into the bedroom I will show you exactly, but for now I will tell you. I love you with every fibre of my being and I want to squeeze you so damn tight, but I know I can't. He finished gritting his teeth and growling at her.

Jane laughed she loved how she could say what she wanted and so could he to her, she loved the honesty and openness of their relationship.

Moses came back into the room, sitting back on the chair. "Food will be here in about 40 minutes."
"I'm hungry now." Jane replied rubbing her tummy.
"Good then maybe you will eat plenty and sleep well with a full belly." She nodded in agreement at Moses.
They sat back listening to the music lost in their own thoughts. It wasn't a painful silence, they were all happy together and comfortable with it.

Jasper broke the silence. "Where would you like to eat Belle?"
"At the table I think, we can spread the food out then."
"Okay let's go and get the table ready he said sitting up."
"Stay, it's my turn." Moses said standing
"You will domesticate him before he leaves you know." Jane said smiling.
"Let's hope so, he looks well for losing the weight he really needs to get to grips with cooking properly to keep it going."
"I expect G has been doing all the cooking or the girls do it at the club for him."
Jasper laughed, "I can see that too."
Moses come back into the room shortly after, "Dinner is served Madam." Jasper laughed.
Jane looked at him. "I am not or never have been a hoar house owner." Both men laughed, Jasper hadn't heard that one before.
"Sorry your ladyship." he laughed. "Can I escort you in?" he asked putting his arms out to her, she held him round the neck as he lifted her up. Jasper got up off the sofa and watched as the two walked into the dining room. He felt a pang of jealousy watching them laugh together.
Moses had spread the food out on the table leaving Jane's closest to her. They all tucked in not saying much as they ate.

Once they finished they sat back chatting about their plans for the next couple of weeks, how they would work together to look after Jane and her needs. Jasper knew he needed to trust Moses to be able to care for Jane, after all he had done it for years before he came along.

They sat for hours chatting and laughing until Jane started to yawn.

"Tired Belle?"

She nodded, "Yes sorry, do you mind if we call it a night?"

"Of course we don't, this is all about you love, you call the shots, you both go and get to bed I will clear this lot away, I can do the dishwasher now, Gwen taught me well."

Moses stood and started collecting the empty trays and walked around to Jane as Jasper picked her up, he kissed her on the head and ruffled her hair.

"Goodnight love, Jay, shout if you need anything you two."

"Thanks Moses we will." Jasper replied. Jane smiled and blew him a kiss.

Jasper put Jane onto the bed her pillows stacked behind her, he passed her Kindle to her so she could read if she wanted to, it helped her sleep.

"Will go and get you some water love, anything else you want?"

"No thank you love, just you." she grinned

Jasper left the room and went down to the kitchen to get Jane her water, he loved hearing her say she wanted him, he was going to devour her tonight if she wasn't too tired. He ached to be in her, to taste her. He walked in the bedroom, she was naked laid on the bed he hair fanned out across her pillows, kindle in hand looking like she had been there for ages waiting, what he didn't see was the frantic movements Jane had made to get her shorts off, and pulling her t-shirt off, she was out of breath but trying to look cool and sexy, she didn't feel it with her plaster on her arm and her dressings on her stomach and leg, but she knew Jasper didn't care about those he loved her hair and she had spread it out so he would see it, she knew he couldn't resist touching it, which was her plan.

Jasper stood looking at her, he loved her perfect soft skin, she was pale which he loved, he followed the curve of her body, the way her breasts were shaped so perfectly, her hard nipples waiting to be touched, he loved her legs, so smooth, her good leg was bent up, the other slightly outstretched towards the middle of the bed. He wanted to explore her again, it had been so long, he thought.

Jane was pretending she didn't realise he was back in the room, she made a deep sigh and opened her other leg letting it fall down onto the bed exposing her, she was horny, desperate to feel him between her legs, to feel his tongue tease her, his beard tickle up her thigh.

Jasper smiled, he could see she was wet he moved around the bed ignoring her open legs, he wanted her to make the move. He loved teasing her. He put the water down on the bedside table and bent over kissing her on the head. He stripped off his clothes putting them into the washing basket and walked around to his side of the bed. He climbed in beside her.
"What you reading Belle, more smut?" he smiled.
She looked at him, "It's romance, not smut"
"So, tell me is this your Billionaire romance?"
"No this is Russian mafia actually, the girl is sold into slavery as a virgin and the guy has to buy her, which he does and makes her his. It's a nice romance."
"With smut added in I'm sure?" he laughed teasing her.
"No just a few nice sex scenes." she smiled, "they don't turn me on if that's what you are asking as they are not that detailed like some I have read."
"Oh really, tell me more, maybe you should read it to me then, see if it gets me hard.?"
"Baby you don't need that, I only have to touch you and you get hard." she giggled
"Oh you think do you?"
"I don't think love, I know!"

Jasper laughed, laid down his cock laying down his leg, he was horny just being near her, but he was trying hard not to get hard.

"Prove it then." he said giving her his naughty smile.

Jane reached out her hand and touched his stomach, caressing him with her nails. He put his right arm behind his head and stretched out. She continued to glide her nails up and down his body, his stomach moving as it tickled and excited him, he laid watching her every move.

He looked down at his cock, "No reaction Belle, think you need to read to me, you've lost your touch."

Jane didn't speak, her fingers moved down his stomach to his V and to the beginning of his cock, almost like a feather she glided her fingers past his cock and down to his now open legs to his thigh, he sucked in hard trying not to let it show he was getting turned on. Jane smiled, she knew it wouldn't be long before he was hard, she moved her fingers into the crease of his legs, so close to his balls, but didn't touch them, she saw his cock twitch, grinning she carried on teasing. He fingers moving slowly in and out of the crease. She moved her fingers in and gently allowing the tip to brush his balls, he barely felt it, but his cock responded as she knew it would. Grinning she did it again. This time he sucked in through his teeth, his head laying back on the pillow. He was hers, who needS naughty books she thought. But it wasn't a bad idea if she found the right thing. Smiling she carried on, two fingers now grazing his balls for a second, Jasper groaned.

"Fuuuck, yessss" he whispered. His cock growing harder.

Jane continued, her fingers moving up his balls and onto his waiting growing cock. As she touched him, moving her fingers up his length his cock got harder and stood to attention, throbbing and ready. Jane sucked her finger and ran it across the head.

"Jesus! okay Belle you win." he whispered, grabbing her hand bringing it to his lips and kissing them.

"You know I could never not get turned on by you."

Jane looked smug, "I know, but I do love to tease you."

"Oh really, well let's see how you like being teased shall we?" Jane frowned.

He moved down the bed moving her bad leg out of the way so he didn't knock it, pulling her down the bed gently he grabbed a pillow and lifted her bottom up, he pushed the pillow underneath her and looked up at her grinning. He moved her good leg out further. Smiling to himself he was going to enjoy this. She was going to be begging him to let her cum.

He ran his hands up her legs, Jane was laughing nervously, she knew he loved being at her pussy, he blew air onto her, she flinched, not expecting it. He looked up at her grinning and went back down to look at her pink wet pussy. He kissed along her thigh like a butterfly so gently making Jane tingle, she was already wet, he could see it. He wanted to dive in but wanted to take his time. Jane could feel his beard teasing up her leg. She loved the feeling. She felt his tongue moving up her thigh.

"Oh god." she mewled.

Jasper smiled, *perfect* he thought just the response he wanted. His tongue moved up closer to the crease in her leg. Jane could feel her body heating up already, she was desperate to touch herself, her juices already soaking her outer lips, glistening for Jasper to see. She moved her hand down, she needed to feel the pressure on her clit. She reached the top of her pussy and Jasper moved her hand away slowly.

"I don't think so Belle." he said smiling, Jane pouted pretending to be upset.

Jasper ran his finger down her opening touching her gently, pushing in deeper as he went down, his finger being coated in her juices, his mouth began to water, he was desperate to taste her. Jane arched her back off the bed.

"Oh Jesus! don't stop please." she begged.

Jasper grinned, bringing his finger to his lips, he licked his finger tasting her. "Mmmmm Jesus Belle you taste so good."

Jane smiled down at him. He moved his fingers to her lips leaving her juices on them, Jane ran her tongue along them as Jasper put his finger on the edge.

"Suck it Belle." he whispered. She sucked her juices from his finger like she would his cock.

"Naughty girl Belle." he growled pulling his finger out, his cock reacting to her, he wanted to be inside her, but he wanted to taste her too.

Jasper pushed his finger back inside her. Jane gripped the bedclothes moaning. Again he moved his finger down teasing her but pushing it in deeper. He crooked his finger to collect more of her juices. Pulling his finger out he watched her juices run down his finger, he licked them hungrily.

"Oh my beautiful Belle, I could never tire of the taste of you. So, so good."

"Jasper please." Jane barely whispered, growing desperate to feel his mouth on her lips.

Jasper smiled and opened her lips with both hands, he sucked in his breath as he looked at her.

"So pink, so tight, so smooth and perfect." He growled again.

His index finger slid inside as his other fingers held her open. Again, Jane arched off the bed as his finger slid deep inside her.

"Oh god, oh god, please don't stop." she begged, gripping the bedclothes her fingers turning white.

Jasper pushed his finger in deeper and slid it out and back in, Jane was losing her mind, she was so sensitive. He moved closer to her open pussy and slid his tongue from the bottom to the top lapping at her juices, he could feel his beard getting wet. He couldn't wait any longer, he sucked at her lips, his tongue moving to her clit, teasing her, flicking across the top.

"Jesus Jasper." she panted.

Jasper didn't speak he was too lost in her now, his lips moving up and down so his beard teased her.

He loved the taste, he tried to describe it in his mind, but he couldn't, it was sweet, like a piece of fruit, juicy like a pear. The more he licked and sucked the more juices he got from her, Jane was writhing on the bed. Desperate to cum, but didn't want to yet, she was loving every moment of it but was losing her mind at the same time. Jasper pushed his tongue deeper, his lips covering her pussy he sucked hard, fucking her with his tongue, his beard was soaked with her juices, he could smell her, the smell that drove him nuts like now. Jane was clamping around his tongue, they were both moaning, Janes hands went to his head, pushing him closer to her, desperate to get the pressure she needed. Jasper smiled again, *not yet Belle* he thought. He stopped and moved away looking up at her. Jane looked shocked.

"You stopped?" he nodded "No baby please, she is desperate for you, please darling?"

Jasper winked at her and went back down, Jane sighed with relief. He wasn't going to give her what she wanted though. He pushed his fingers back inside her and turned his hand, he was stroking her pussy wall, Jane was moaning again, lost in the ecstasy of it. He continued to rub her, he pushed harder. Jane was bucking on his finger, her hips joining in with the movement of his fingers. She needed the pressure on her clit, she was moving trying to get to his hand, but it didn't work.

"Baby please, touch my clit, I need to cum, pleaseeee." she begged.

Jasper continued, he wanted her on the edge, he knew she was almost there.

"Oh God, Oh God, yes, yes. Oh………Jesus Christ!" She moaned as Jasper suddenly stopped and pulled his finger out.

"Are you trying to kill me?" she begged laughing. She was exhausted, so wet and so horny, desperate to cum.

"What's wrong Belle?" he asked innocently.

Laughing she replied. "Grrrr, you know what you are doing to me, you are such a tease."

He smiled at her and went back down to her pussy, he opened her lips again and sighed.

"I will never ever tire of you." He said to her pussy.

"Oh so that's all you want me for is it?" she laughed

He didn't reply just licked her waiting pussy again, then he thought about where he was and wanted to push things a little. Her bottom was in the right place, she was on a pillow, her bottom in the air. He could see her rose, he wanted to touch her, spread her cheeks and lick her. He pulled her gently a little further on the pillow so her bottom was higher. He pushed his hands under her bottom and lifted her, his tongue on her pussy he began licking again, his face wet from her juices, he sucked hard on her, making her moan louder, her hands knotting up the bedclothes again. He licked up and down, teasing her clit, flicking and sucking it, Jane's eyes clouding over, her body heating up and tingling she knew she was close, she loved this feeling so much, just as she thought she would cum he moved his tongue down her pussy to the edge. Her breathing was erratic, he moved down to her perineum, he loved the softness of the skin there, he had never gone any further, he teased it with his tongue, Jane opened her legs wider for him, pushing herself at him. It was so sensitive there, then his tongue moved further down, his mouth was wet at the thought, he pulled her cheeks apart further, her rose ripe for the taking, gently he slid his tongue just on the outside and circled her opening.

"Oh my fucking god!" Jane whispered as she lifted off the bed, she never swore. Unless she was mad. But this was so very different, had he done it by mistake she thought? then she felt it again, the tingling went straight to her pussy, the nerve endings on her opening on red alert. He didn't stop, he continued to circle it. Jane wasn't sure what she wanted him to do, did she want that? Then she felt it, his tongue slide across her rose.

"Oh, Oh, Ohhhhhhh……….." she felt her pussy contracting, she was soaked again. She wanted to touch herself but knew not too. Then she felt his fingers slide inside her pussy, Jane almost blacked out, her rose being teased, her pussy teased by his fingers. She felt his hand on her cheeks opening her rose, her head all over the place. Then the warmth as his tongue broke her open and slid in.

Jaspers cock was rock hard like a steel rod, he was aching to be in her, this was so different, he was loving her reaction. She was bucking on his fingers, his tongue invading her, he pushed it in a little further, he was barely breaking past the opening, but it was enough for now, he stopped and sucked his finger. Circling her rose and went back to her pussy. He pushed his tongue inside her as deep as he could. Jane was lost completely, his finger circling her rose, pushing in slowly, she liked it, he smiled. Now he wanted her to cum. To see her reaction while he teased her bottom too. He slid his finger into her bottom a little further, Jane lifted higher off the bed, his tongue going deeper inside her, he pulled out and went back to her clit, he got himself onto his elbows, his finger still in her bottom, his other inside her pussy rubbing her wall, his tongue and lips sucking and teasing her clit, Jane felt like she was losing consciousness, her whole body on fire. Jasper wanted to taste her cum, he flicked faster on her clit, Jane moaned louder.

"Yes, yes, baby please don't stop. Oh God yes." He smiled he loved this. She was wetter than ever before, he was gulping her juices down as he sucked harder, she was tasting sweeter than before. He flicked and sucked her clit, rubbing his beard up and down her pussy.

Jane felt her orgasm close, the heat in her body intensified by him touching her bottom, his finger slowly in and out of her, her clit being sucked and licked like his life depended on it. Jane went rigid seconds before her orgasm hit, then her body convulsed, she came harder than ever before, feeling like it was never going to end. The bedding was being pulled and pushed as she came over and over, Jasper wasn't stopping, his fingers inside her, his tongue not stopping, just as she thought it was finished trying to catch her breath she felt another one hit her.

"Jasperrrrr………. She screamed, trying to bite her lip to be quiet so Moses didn't come running in.

Her orgasm hit just as hard, she was exhausted, her pussy pulsating making her giggle as it slowed down. She was so sensitive she was trying to move away from Jaspers mouth but he was still licking her juices up which made her giggle more, her nerves were on fire. He sucked the last of her juices, his cock throbbing. He got onto his knees, Jane could see his beard was covered in her juices, he was licking around his lips still tasting her. He moved closer to her, she looked down at his cock, her pussy waiting to be filled by him. He had to be gentle but he didn't want to be. He rubbed his cock on the outside of her pussy, looking into her eyes, she blinked, he knew she wanted it, slowly he pushed himself inside her, her pussy pulling him in.

"Oh Belle….., fuck you feel so good." He pushed further, his head rocking back, "So, so good……."

He held her good leg up against him so he could get deeper inside her. They were both moaning, Jane put her hand on his chest as he slowly pushed the remainder of his cock inside her. His balls against her bottom, he pulled out slightly and pushed back into her.

"Fuck….I love you Belle….." slowly and gently he made love to her, not wanting to hurt her. She was exhausted. He didn't want this moment to end but he didn't want to hurt her.

Jane looked up at him. "Cum for me baby please?"

"Oh yes, don't stop Belle tell me."

"Cum for me Jasper, fill me up, I want to feel you fill me with your cum.

"Oh fuck yes Belle, I'm cuming…….." he hissed.

He felt his balls go hard as his orgasm hit, his cum filling Jane's pussy, his head fell back as his body was alive, Jane was clenching her pussy around his cock, draining him. He laughed, he was sensitive now and Jane wasn't letting him go, his cock still rock hard.

"Jesus woman, please stop." he laughed.

Jane stopped as he slid out of her. He bent down and kissed her, she could taste herself on his lips and his beard.

"I love you Belle." he said rubbing her nose with his.

"I love you too Jasper." she smiled, yawning.

"Let's get you cleaned up and snuggled up so you can sleep.".

She nodded.

Jasper got off the bed and went to the bathroom returning with a warm cloth and towel and a fresh pair of shorts and t-shirt. He cleaned them both up helping Jane into her shorts before he pulled on his own, he climbed into bed behind her pulling her into him. He bent and kissed her shoulder, lingering taking in her smell.

"Goodnight Belle."

"Goodnight baby, sweet dreams" she whispered, exhaustion taking her as she drifted off to asleep.

Jasper went off quickly, he was exhausted, relieved to have Jane at home.

Chapter 27

Settling back in

Moses was laid awake, he couldn't sleep, his mind drifting back to when Jane came out of hospital after she was beaten before, she had terrible dreams, he was concerned this time would be the same. Especially being in the same house. He could see she was trying to be brave, but he knew she was struggling with it. He could read her like a book as she could read him. Hell, he had been in the depths of despair when he met Jane for the first time. He took to her straight away, he vowed then he would always be there for her, he never realised how important she would become over the years. He sat up in bed, swung his legs out and got up, he went to the kitchen to get a hot drink, hoping it would help him sleep. He hadn't struggled like this in a while.

He got a cup out and put it on the side, then he heard the screams. He ran as fast as he could to their bedroom, not caring if either was naked. He pushed the door open, Jane was laid screaming throwing her arms around, sobbing to be left alone.
"Please, please, I can't take anymore, just let me go, just finish me I can't do this anymore, you fucking coward, why won't you kill me?"
Jasper was on his knees on her side of the bed stroking her hair and talking softly to her, he
remembered Moses telling him never to restrain her, she couldn't cope with that. He ran around the bed and got on his knees next to Jasper.
"Keep talking Brother don't stop." he panted, his adrenaline pumping around his body.
"Belle baby it's a bad dream darling, it's okay love, wake up, he can't hurt
you anymore."

Jane was throwing her arms around kicking her legs, both were concerned she would hurt herself, she was really deep in her nightmare. Jasper grabbed his pillows and put them under her arm to stop any damage if she hit the bed with force.

Moses got closer to her. "Jane love it's me, you are safe. It's a bad dream." He was stroking her head. "Half-pint come on, you can shake this off, wake up love. Please. It's just Jasper and me." She slowed down, growing silent, Moses nudged Jasper to talk again.

"Belle love, wake up, we need you love, come on baby."

She began moaning quietly, laying still, she was screwing her face up. They both sighed she was okay. Jasper stroked her head again. Humming a tune to her.

She started to sob again. "My baby, you took my baby, one day I will kill you, one day you will get

what's coming to you and I hope it's me who gets to do it."

She wrapped her arms around her stomach and sobbed quietly. "I'm sorry baby girl, I am so sorry, I

love you, wherever you are. Mummy loves you with all her heart."

She turned and coiled into a ball and went off to sleep peacefully. Moses beckoned to Jasper to follow him outside the room, they closed the door behind them.

"Don't wake her Brother, she is peaceful now, the nightmare has passed, let her sleep." "How long did this go on for last time Moses?"

Months, but then she didn't get the help she needed. Now it's different. She knows in her own mind he is gone. She will settle I'm sure, probably being here for the first night has started the nightmare off."

Jasper nodded. "Tell me what you think I should do, you have been here before with her."

"Just do as you are doing, nothing more you can do, but we need to push her to see her counsellor."

"Agreed, sooner rather than later." Jasper nodded.

"Get back in there, I was just making a drink when I heard her."
He patted Jasper on the back. "Goodnight Moses, thanks for
being here."
"Anytime, Brother." He smiled walking away.

Jasper climbed back into bed, Jane was still in a ball curled up
tight, He laid next to her facing her, he kissed her nose and
closed his eyes, hoping she would settle now. He was
heartbroken seeing he like this, the guilt crept back in, he
couldn't shake it off, he knew it didn't matter where she was,
that animal was going to get to her, but it didn't help knowing
he made it easier. Maybe he needed counselling too.

Jasper woke at 7am, Jane was still sleeping, he didn't want to
get up and leave her, so he stayed in bed, she had uncoiled
herself during the night and gone back to sleeping on her side.
Jasper curled back into her and laid there cat napping.
Jane woke up a short time later, she turned onto her back and
smiled at him.
"Good Morning my beautiful man, did you cuddle me all night?"
"Good Morning Belle" he smiled at her, "Yes I did, how do you
feel?"
"I'm okay I think, I ache a little, but I just need my pain relief and
I will be fine." "That's good to hear, fancy a cup of tea before
your shower?"
"Oh yes please." Jasper went to get out of bed as a knock came
to the door.
Moses stood with a tea towel over his arm with 2 cups of tea.
"Morning both, I heard you moving around so thought you
might like tea in bed. How did you sleep
Half-pint?"
Jane stretched. "Morning Moses, I think I slept okay, I told
Jasper I ache a little but I'm okay thank
you."
"That's good news love." he walked around the bed and left
Jane's tea on the side and handed Jaspers
too him, "See you in a while."

Jane sat up properly and cuddled into Jasper.

"It feels good to be home in our bed, would like to get out today if that's okay?" "Of course Belle, where would you like to go?"

"To get some fresh air would be nice, can we go to the park, get the others to meet us?"

"Sure, we have a wheelchair and many willing bodies to carry you, we could have a picnic or go to the diner for something to eat?"

"Yay, would love to do." she smiled, "Come on then let's drink up and call everyone." "Remember you need to rest too Belle, no pushing your luck."

"I know I promise. I just want to get out."

"Okay as you wish, let's get showered and dressed and talk to Moses then, he can call the guys and get them to meet us for a few hours."

Jane sat up straight and grabbed her tea, she drank it down quickly, turning to Jasper and smiling, waiting impatiently for him to finish.

"Can you ask Moses to take Red out for a spin too please, she can't sit there all this time." "I'm sure he will, he has been using her back and forth a few times anyway."

"Okay good, come on then, shower time."

"okay, okay Miss impatient." He laughed, getting out of bed and strutting around to Jane's side.

He stripped out of his shorts and put them in the washing basket and Jane moved to the edge of the bed, she pulled her t-shirt off.

"Lift Belle." Jasper said as he grabbed the edge of her shorts, Jane grabbed him around the neck as he lifted her and pulled her shorts down, he carried her into the bathroom , sat her down on the seat and put her arm into the shower cover and her leg, he dressed her stomach wound in the waterproof dressing and Jane grabbed her hair tie as they passed the sink and tied her hair up, Jasper turned the water on and they waited for it to warm up before he walked them both in sitting Jane on the ledge.

They showered quickly and Jasper wrapped them both up in towels and carried Jane back to the bed. He grabbed some clothes for her, helped her dry off and get dressed.

"Remember we can't go anywhere until Alison has been to redress your wounds."

"I know but she said she will be here around 10am so that's plenty of time before we meet everyone. I can sit in the garden until then too and have my breakfast."

"You can do anything you please Belle, it's your home too, remember."

She smiled up at him. "Kiss me please, I love you so much, I am the luckiest girl on the planet."

He bent to kiss her as she wrapped her arms around his neck. "I am the luckiest guy on this planet too." They rubbed noses and Jane giggled.

"Right let's get you to the lounge or garden wherever your ladyship pleases." Jane smiled. "Garden please."

They got to the kitchen and Moses was busy making another drink, Jasper bent over so Jane could put the cups down.

"Her ladyship would like breakfast in the garden this morning Moses." "Oh really, well we better make sure it's warm enough for her then." Moses opened the patio doors, the sun was shining it was already warm. "Can we go and look at the roses please?" Jasper smiled

"I knew that was coming Belle, of course" He walked outside and the three of them walked down to the roses. As they got to the rose bed the sun was shining on the glass plinth, rainbows were being made on the roses, Jane went quiet, her hand at her mouth. Both men looked at each other and smiled. It was perfect. All of the roses were ready to bloom, each bush had a few roses waiting to open, Jane was overcome with excitement waiting to see them.

Jasper put her down on the love seat so he knew she was comfortable. They all sat together enjoying the early sun.

"What time is Alison due Half-pint?" "This morning so anytime I guess."

Okay I will go back up to the house just in case she knocks, leave you two love birds to it, I will bring

her down once she arrives."

"Thank you Moses." she said as he bent and kissed her cheek. "Anything for you love."

Jasper smiled as Moses walked away, "Thanks Moses." he turned and nodded as he walked up the

garden.

They sat and snuggled for a while, the canopy was down on the chair so Jane could look around at the garden.

"I love it here so much, this garden makes me feel so glad to be alive." Jasper smiled. "If you want to add or change anything you know you can Belle?"

She smiled. "I know baby, but I am happy the way it is, it's like you read my mind before you even knew me."

Jasper pulled her close and kissed her head as Alison and Moses appeared in front of them.

"Well look at you all relaxed and looking like the Queen of England on your seat." Alison smiled. Jane's face lit up seeing her. "Oh Alison, welcome, come and sit down." as Jane patted the seat next to her.

"Drink Alison?" Moses asked putting his hand on her shoulder.

"Tea please Moses."

"Coming up love."

Well I can't really do your leg and tummy out here Jane I wish I could, so we better go back inside, as much as I could sit here all day we better get on. Moses tells me you have plans today. I hope you are going to take it easy?"

Jane nodded as Jasper climbed off the seat and waited for Jane to wrap her arms around his neck.

"Yes, we are going to the park for a picnic and to just chill out, this lot will probably play football or

something and me and the girls will probably just chat."

"How lovely. Erm Jasper, I don't mean to be a spoil sport but please be careful carrying Jane, if you fell over anything could happen, she should really be in her wheelchair."

"I know Alison, and you are right, that's why we put the slope in, but I prefer to carry her, saves me

going to the gym anyway." he smiled as Jane elbowed him.

"Ow what was that for?"

"I'm not that heavy" Jasper laughed, he loved teasing her.

"I didn't say you were, it's a good work out that's all"

Alison laughed as they reached the house, "You are a tease Jasper, be careful or someone will be

beating you when she is well enough."

"Can't wait." he winked, as Jane blushed. "I will leave you ladies to do what you need to do, shout if you need anything Alison."

"Thanks Jasper, think I have it covered." Jasper nodded and left as Moses came in with her tea. "Wonderful, thank you Moses" she smiled as he put her tea down on the side and Jane's next to her. "You have them trained very well I can see that."

"I'm just a lucky girl I think." Jane smiled.

"Right then let's have a look at this." she said tending to her wounds, she cleaned her up replaced the

bandages on all of the wounds and checked her bruising.

"You're healing well Jane, in the next day or so we can take your stitches out of your stomach, and next week your leg. Then it's just the healing process of getting your muscles to work, so a lot of physio and then get you out of plaster. However, your arm will be another month I guess, but I think Dr Robinson will x-ray it again in a couple of weeks to see how it looks."

Jane was happy to hear about her stitches coming out, it was restricting her a lot, she wanted desperately to be back on her feet.

Thank you Alison, you have made my day. Will Susan be coming again at any time or can you drag her around, it would be lovely to see you both."

"I'm sure we can sort something out" she sat back drinking her tea.

Jasper and Moses came back in. "What's the diagnosis then Alison?"

She smiled up at him. "All good Moses, I was just saying in the next day or so I will take out the stomach stitches and next week the leg, hopefully in a couple of weeks we can x-ray the arm and get the cast off in a month. That will make it easier for showering then too."

"Fantastic news", Jasper smiled bending over the back of the sofa to kiss Jane on the head.

"Right then I better make a move and get in, I will be back tomorrow to see you about the same
time. Fingers crossed I can take out those stitches too." She stood, Moses took her cup from her.

"I will see you out Alison."

"Thank you Alison, for everything, see you tomorrow." Jane said holding her hand.

"Look forward to it, you can tell me all about your picnic." She let go of Jane's hand after squeezing it. Moses walked her out, "Thanks again Alison, see you tomorrow."

"Don't let her overdo it today, keep her sat please."

"Of course, we will all be keeping an eye on her no fear of that."

"Good, see you tomorrow then."

Moses went back into the lounge, Jane and Jasper were chatting about her stitches coming out.

"Remember Half-pint, regardless you still have to take it easy, that muscle still has a lot of healing to do."

"I know and I promise I will. I'm not going to hurt myself I promise."

"Right then I will call the gang, get them to pick up some things for the picnic and we can head off. Jasper said he has everything we need so it's just the food we need the others to get."

"I will go and get another couple of blankets for the ground and some of the cushions from the garden and put them in the car with the basket, anything you need Belle?"

"Maybe a jumper or my shawl please, just in case I get chilly, thank you."

"I will get that sorted and the wheelchair Brother." Moses went off to get Jane's shawl and jumper.

Jane sat looking around the lounge while the boys went off getting everything ready for the picnic,
she felt quite tearful, but in a good way, she sighed heavily.
"God I am so lucky to have so many wonderful people in my life, I love you guys so much." she whispered.
Moses came back into the room, "you ready Half-pint, hey what's wrong?" He could see the tears in
her eyes, her face was a giveaway, she was red around the eyes and her nose was like Rudolphs.
"I'm okay."
"How long have I known you Jane? I think I know better?"
"Wow that's serious you used my name."
"Well you know you need to talk love, tell me what's wrong?" he brushed a stray tear away from her
cheek as he sat down on the sofa edge with her.
"I was just looking around watching you two getting us ready to go, thinking how lucky I am to have so many incredible people around me, you will never know how grateful I am. I love you all so
much." She choked back on her tears, not wanting to cry, sniffing trying to stop them.
Moses held her face. "Listen to me Half-pint, you are a very special lady to us all, you don't need to be grateful at all, we love you too, that's why we do it. So wipe those tears and get up here so we can get out of here." He stood bending, holding his arms out ready for Jane to hold on so he could lift her up.
She laughed wiping her face and running her hand through her hair.

"okay I'm ready." She put her arms around his neck and he picked her up. Heading towards the front door. Both men had discussed taking her into the garage and decided against it until she could walk out there herself. Jasper had pulled the car out and locked up the garage. Jane hadn't thought anything of it as

Moses put her into the front seat of the car and he climbed into the back.

"Right have we got everything?"

"Wheelchair, jumper, shawl, full picnic basket, blankets cushions, yep think we have it all Brother."

"Great. Let's go." he smiled at Jane grabbing her hand kissing her fingers.

"Remind me Belle I want to take you to Elizabeth Park Rose Garden, you will love it." "Oh okay, is it full of roses then?"

"Yes love it is, there are these archways which have had roses grow over them which lead down to a beautiful pergola, definitely your kind of thing."

"Oh wow it sounds beautiful." She smiled.

Within 15 minutes they arrived at the park. They pulled in, there were already lots of people there, the car park was quite full, they spotted Shadow and the others, Gwen climbed out of the van with Shadow, the others were on their bikes parking up, Shadow opened the back doors and they all grabbed bags of food and drink heading towards them.

Jane was excited waving like crazy at everyone. "Come on, get me out please?" she squealed
excitedly.

Jasper and Moses laughed and did as they were asked. Moses grabbed the wheelchair and Jasper went around to lift Jane out, they put her in the wheelchair and grabbed all the bits out of the boot, Jasper put Jane's camera on her lap.

"Think you can manage to carry this Belle?" he grinned

"Oh my god, thank you baby, I can take lots of pictures of you all now, thank you, thank you." She
was so excited.

"Ready when you are Brother." Moses was loaded down with things. Gwen came across and hugged Jane, she was laughing at Moses who was trying to carry everything telling Jasper he could manage.

"Come here Moses, give me something for Gods sake before you do yourself an injury."

"I'm fine I can manage." he scowled at her.

"They don't give out Yorkie chocolate bars in the US for trying to be strong, so you will just have to stop pretending and give me some things." He huffed at her and handed some of the cushions and a bag over. She smiled and walked on to catch Jane.

"Ohhhh you remembered your camera, you haven't used that in a long time Jane, be good to see

some nice pictures from today."

"It wasn't me Gwen, Jasper brought it."

"Well hopefully it will keep you out of trouble then."

"Fat chance of that Gwen, you know her better than that." Jasper scoffed behind her whilst pushing Jane. "Right Belle, decide where you want to go and we will follow."

Jane had her finger against her lips looking around trying to decide, then she pointed.

"Over there please under the tree."

"You heard the lady." Moses shouted as they all walked across the field towards the big tree.

They unpacked, laid the blankets and cushions down and all collapsed on the ground. Jasper picked Jane up out of her wheelchair and placed her on the ground, he sat behind her with his back against the tree and pulled her between his legs. Jane was already unpacking her camera swapping lenses. They all started to tuck into the picnic, laughing and joking. Jane started taking pictures as Jasper fed her from behind. She put her camera down and laid back into Jaspers chest. He kissed the top of her head wrapping his arms around her.

"You okay Belle?" "mmhm" she murmured.

He smiled squeezing her gently, the guys laid down as the girls sat talking, there was a gentle breeze blowing which cooled the air down.

"I could quite easily fall asleep out here." Jasper moaned.

"No time for that Brother, come on, it's time to play football, not quite 5 a side." Steve said slapping Jasper on the leg.

Everyone pushed themselves up as Jane leant forward so Jasper could get up, he placed a big cushion behind her so she could lean back comfortably for a while. He kissed her on the head and ran off with the others. Jane was smiling watching all her friends having a kick around
laughing, she knew it wouldn't be long before they all went back home to the UK. She missed them
all but wouldn't change being with Jasper and being in the US.

She sat watching and taking pictures of everyone laughing and being silly.
Her mind wandered back to the party and Jasper proposing to her, to how happy she was and the fact all her friends had helped pull it off for him. She was so proud of him learning to ride, shocked he did it all for her.
She shivered suddenly as the memory of being taken came flooding back, her breathing became erratic, she could feel her heart pounding, she suddenly felt sick and dizzy, she was having a panic attack and knew it. She needed to calm herself down before someone spotted her. She started talking to herself trying to talk herself down, she put her head between her legs. She wished Jasper was with her he would stroke her hair or talk to her to make it go away. She looked up watching everyone trying to concentrate on them and regulating her breathing. She felt herself relax, she knew her trigger now, she needed to work on that and made a mental note to talk to someone about it. She grew frustrated that he took her on the day Jasper proposed to her, he took that away from her, she would never forget the heartache that followed now, she began feeling faint again and her breathing was getting out of control. She put her head between her legs and started to cry between gasps. She felt like she was going to faint, her arms were tingling, she was struggling to
breath, she was feeling scared, her brow was sweating, she began talking to herself, trying to bring herself out of it again and trying not to think about it.

A few minutes later Gwen came over gasping for air, she was bent over her hands on her knees trying to catch her breath.

"Jesus love, they are trying to kill me I swear." Jane looked up, feeling sick still smiling at Gwen.

"You will join in, so you only have yourself to blame." she laughed trying to hold it together.

Gwen got onto her knees holding her sides trying to catch her breath laughing. Then she looked into Janes face. She didn't say a word just moved closer to her and took her hands. Lent her head against Janes and whispered

"Breath with me, love, it's going to be okay, I promise. It is all over, he can't hurt you anymore, it's just the memory of it." Jane nodded. "Don't think about anything else, just on this moment with me, think about my voice and our breathing.

Jane continued to nod and her breathing became slower, she squeezed Gwen's hands letting her know she was okay. Gwen continued talking, Jane had shown her a few tricks years ago after a friend of hers had told her she struggled with her mental health. Jane looked up and let go of Gwen's hands, Gwen leant forward and hugged her.

"Thank you Gwen." Jane choked back her tears.

"Don't thank me, you showed me what to do. I was watching you I knew something was wrong

that's why I came across. I didn't want to worry the boys I told them I was knackered. Well I was but

it was a good excuse." both girls laughed.

"We are heading back to the UK in a few days, if needed I will stay if you want me too? They can

cope without me." Jane smiled tears welling up in her eyes.

"No, I will be okay, I promise, thank you though. I need to get myself sorted I will call a few friends that are counsellors in the UK and see if I can get some help, we can Skype to do it."

"If you are sure, I know you have Jasper and Moses, and I am sure they will take perfect care of you, but I am allowed to worry and I will."

"You can come back whenever you want, anyway you promised Alison you would come to her club
remember."

"Oh my god yes!, I could go without Mr of course and maybe have some fun." Jane slapped her leg "You wouldn't?"

"In my dreams yes, but no he maybe a pain in the arse but I adore him. Well it's a date, once you are back on your feet properly out of plaster and that chair we will definitely do it, would be lots of fun." "Thank you Gwen, for being you, for not hating me for not sharing things with you and still loving me." Jane smiled fighting fresh tears hugging her again.

"What's all this then?" Jasper asked from behind them. Jane looked up and smiled wiping a stray tear.

"I was just telling Jane we were going home in a few days that's all, you know us girls get emotional." She winked at Jane and turned to face Jasper, he put his hands on Gwen's shoulders looking at Jane. "I promise we will look after her Gwen, you will have to come back soon for a visit anyway and you can stay at the house with us, we can do that ride out too."

"Sounds good to me, you may want to get a separate diary though, I think you may have all of us coming backwards and forwards, and of course you need to bring him to us Jane?"

"Of course I will, wild horses wouldn't stop me."

Jasper kissed Gwen's head. "Excuse me, that's my girl, you have your own.", Steve joked behind
Jasper patting him on the shoulder.

"Yes doesn't he know it." Jane said laughing. They all sat back down on the blankets, the boys grabbed the drinks and passed them around.

"Did you get any pictures then Jane? While you sat here pretending to be injured." G teased her. Jane hit him on the back and pushed him over. He feigned injury as he laid on the ground. Making everyone laugh.

Yes, you can look when we get back home if you like, that's if you are all coming with us? Jane
looked at Jasper for conformation realising what she had done, he smiled nodding.
"Sounds good to me."
Everyone looked around at each other and all agreed it was a good plan.
"The biggest decision is what you want to eat of course, we could be really unhealthy and have Chinese or Pizza?" Or we could stop off and grab some bits for the BBQ?"
Gwen laughed, "We know what your "bits" are Jasper, maybe we will stop and do that, you can get Jane home and sort the BBQ out, we will stop off and get the food."
"Agreed" they all said in unison packing the picnic bags away. G picked Jane up and put her into the wheelchair.

"My turn for a bit of fun with you Half-pint, I wonder how fast we can get this chair going, maybe we need to convert it and add a small engine, give you a set of handlebars?" he was teasing her as he span her round. He began trotting with her across the field back to the car as everyone else picked up the bags and cushions. He stopped at the car and span her round to face him.
"Right little lady, talk to me, none of this I'm fine, shit." He crouched down in front of her holding her hands.
"You saw me didn't you?" she asked looking into his eyes, not wanting to cry again.
"Jane I know you better than you know yourself, we are expecting it, all of us, we are not going to wrap you in cotton wool you know better than anyone how you need to deal with this, but we are here, don't hide it from us." Jane nodded as he kissed her forehead. "I might be across the pond love but I will always be here if you need me, at the end of the phone or on the next flight out, I know you have Jay, but you have us too, we love you more than you can imagine, and we want to see you well again and able to cope with it all."

"Thank you, I love you all too, you are my family, I suppose I didn't want to worry you. The panic attacks have only just started, honestly. I told Gwen I would make some calls to friends in the UK who can help."

"Good, okay, that's a start, shit sorry love, I need to get up my knees are bloody killing me sitting like this." He got up rubbing his knees, Jane laughed at him, it took the pressure of the conversation.

The other arrived back, Jasper opened the doors on the car and G picked Jane up out of the chair and sat her in, she hugged him tight and kissed his face.

"You know when you call me Jane I know I'm in trouble, thanks for not being hard on me. I can never thank you for all you have done for me. I love you so much Grayson." She cowered laughing waiting for a slap. Like Jane nobody ever called him his full name. not many people knew it, he hated and hadn't allowed anyone to use it in years, only his Mum of course. He put his hands around her neck and pretended to strangle her, they were both laughing like children when Jasper walked to the front of the car with Moses.

"What did she do this time?" Moses asked, "It has to be serious you putting your hands round her
throat."

"Nothing much." she squealed as G growled at her.

"Come on get in you two." Jasper smiled across at them. He knew why G had taken her away in the
chair. They all did, they just played ignorant, if it helped her then that made them all happy. G climbed in the back with Moses.

"Oh, you're coming with us are you? Don't you want to go and get the food then?" Moses looked at
him.

"Nah, they can manage, they don't need me. I will help get things sorted at the house with you guys, Jay can sort Half-pint then."

"Oi. I am here you know!" and its only my legs that are not working at the moment."

G started laughing, "Get off your high horse Half-pint I was being nice." He pulled her hair through
the seat teasing her, she grabbed his hand and squeezed it.
"Children, children please." Moses laughed "Enough already or we will have to separate you." "She started it." he replied laughing, Jane started to giggle.
"Tell him why." she laughed.
"Shut up Half-pint!" he laughed back, swatting her again.
"This sounds really interesting, I think someone needs to tell us what is going on between the two of
You?" Jasper smirked.
"No need Jay brother, it's done."

Jane laughed patting Jaspers hand, "I will tell you later."
"okay, okay, J, my name is Grayson, yes you can laugh, get it over with and make sure you don't use it, not many know but her ladyship here decided to say it earlier."
Jasper looked at him through the rear view mirror, "Listen G when you have grown up with a name like Jasper you kind of get it, I won't say a word. Your secret is safe with me Grayson."
The car erupted into fits of laughter. Moses grabbed G around the neck and rubbed his head with his fist.
"Sorry G", he sniggered "I couldn't resist, I won't do it again." Jasper apologized laughing.
"It's okay, get it out of your system before the others get back."
He grumbled pushing Moses away. Jasper pulled up outside the house and they all got out, Moses and G unloaded the car as Jasper carried Jane out and into the lounge. He kissed her as he put her on the sofa.
"I missed you today Belle, how are you feeling?"
"Missed you too. I'm ok, had a blip but you all seem to know about that." she smiled
"Yeah, we do, but it's okay and we don't need to talk about it unless you want to?" Jane shook her
head.
"We will talk when you are ready then, just promise you won't lie to me about being okay at the moment?"

"I promise" she smiled being honest with him "Good, what can I get you love?"
"Nothing, I'm ok here thank you, just need some time out."

Jasper kissed her on the head and headed out to the patio doors opening them as G and Moses followed, they went outside and unwrapped the barbecue . G got his zippo out of his pocket, he hadn't smoked in years but still kept it, Jane had brought it for him years before for his Birthday. He turned the gas on and lit up all the burners.
"Well it's about time this got used properly."
"It sure will get that today J." G laughed

"I have some chips somewhere let me go and grab them then we can leave it to warm for when the
others get back."
Jasper went out into the garage, he always felt odd going out there, he opened the cupboard and pulled the bag out, just as he turned he felt something behind him. It moved slow. The hairs on the back of his neck stood up. He turned quickly, nothing, he heard a rustle. He picked up the stick from the corner ready to beat whatever it was.
"I will have you, whatever you are, show yourself." he snarled.
Waiting for a huge rat or mouse to
crawl out. His skin was crawling he wasn't bothered by them if he could see them but he didn't know
what he was up against.

Moses and G came walking into the garage seeing Jasper stood there with a stick over his back waiting to hit something. They both started laughing.
"What is it Brother?" Moses laughed.
"If I knew that I wouldn't be stood like this would I?" he grumbled back. "Something is in here, could
be a mouse or rat, but it sounds that kind of size."
"Okay you little skunk get out here and show yourself." G sniggered getting down on the ground.

Moses stood in the doorway watching, his hands in his pockets.
"Pull out the box G, I bet its behind there." he offered watching.
G pulled out the box, nothing. He moved the pots of paint, nothing. Then they heard a scurry and a tiny noise, like a yelp, they all looked up at each other, eyes wide. Moses jumped down off the step into the garage, they all moved around looking.
"If I'm not mistaken that sounds like a dog?" he said shocked, "But how the fuck would it get in
here?"
"Well we had the garage open to wash the cars and bike a couple of days ago, could have been
then" G replied pulling more things out. They stopped and went quiet as another yelp was heard. "shhhh" G motioned putting his finger to his lips, they heard it again coming from behind them. They all turned, nothing there.
"Hang on a minute, Moses lift the tarp off my bike will you please, but slowly, I think its trapped
underneath."
They held their breaths as Moses lifted the tarp slowly, then stopped as a pair of big eyes looked up at him, he put his hand out showing the palm of his hand to the tiny ball of puppy on the ground. "Hey little fella what you doing in hear, someone must be missing you?" The puppy sniffed at his hand and licked his finger, he lifted him gently off the floor, they all started laughing.

"Well what do we have here then?" Jasper smiled stroking his head.
Let's get him in the house, I will check just to make sure there are no more under here to be safe." Moses walked into the house heading to Jane, as G and Jasper removed the tarp checking for any more. All was clear so they headed into the lounge.

"Oh my god, where did you find it?" Jane squealed kissing it on the head, "Let me look at you" she said holding him in the air, "it's a little boy." she smiled. "Someone must have lost him, we need to ask around."

"He doesn't look like a pure breed, I would say he's a mongrel, might be worth looking in the front garden Brother just to make sure a stray bitch hasn't brought her pups here for safety."

"Good idea, there are plenty of bushes out there she could have hidden under." They headed out as

the others arrived.

"Good timing you can help with the bags." Gwen smiles.

"Sorry love, more important work to do than that, we found a pup in the garage, it's with Jane looks like a mongrel so we are checking in case Mum is out here with any others." Moses says with his hands on his hips.

"Girls grab the bags let's unload while they look around." They grabbed the bags and walked into the house putting them onto the worktop heading back out for more. They finish up and head into the lounge to see Jane cuddling the puppy.

"Well let's have a look at this little beauty that's got the guys hunting for more." Linda asks, Jane

holds him up grinning.

"Say hello to Harley."

They all begin to coo over him.

"Named him already Jane, that's not a good sign love?" Gwen says smiling at her.

"I think it was meant to be actually, after all he was under Jaspers bike."

The boys come back in. "We found Mum and one other pup, she is very dirty, looks like she hasn't been fed properly in a long time, she's in the kitchen with G having a drink, I am going to give her some of that chicken breast from the fridge Belle?"

"Oh my god, take me to them please I want to see them." She begs, feeling tearful.

"We're not keeping them Belle" Jasper tries to be firm.

"Please?" she asks again moving to the edge of the sofa desperate to see the other two.

Jasper scoops her up and carries her into the kitchen, he sits her in the wheelchair as G hands her the other puppy.

"It's a little girl Doc."

"Oh my god one of each!"

"No Belle." Jasper says again behind her.

G looks down at her and smiles, she looks up and winks at him.

"Let me see mum please?" she says straining to look past the island.

G pulls her closer and she sees mum stop drinking and look at her. Jane doesn't speak just puts her hand out and the dog moves towards her, the others get down onto the ground so not to scare her. The dog moves closer to Jane and G and sniffs at her hand.

Gwen passed the puppy to her so she can show mum she has her. She comes over to her sniffing at her and licks her son. Jane holds her hand against her heart, too scared to speak. G smiles as she gets closer and sniffs at Jane's plastered hand and licks it. They all begin cooing. Jane smooths her head and she let's her.

"Move me out please, give her space, let's have a proper look at her." They all back up and put the pups down for mum. They all stay sat down on the ground and watch. Mum lays down as the pups go to her to feed. She is skin and bone, dirty and in need of love.

"Looks like she may have been kicked out after getting pregnant. She has a collar but not name or contact details. We will keep her here tonight and get her to the vet tomorrow, they will try and trace the owner."

"You think anyone cares about her? She's a mess. Her fur is matted where she has been living on the streets for a while, she needs a good bath and some good food inside her so she can feed the pups properly, they can't be more than 5 weeks old, we saw plenty like this out in Bosnia didn't we G?" "Sure did. He's right nobody has cared for her in a long while, she's skinny enough you could probably feel it if she has a microchip, come here beautiful." he says putting his hand out to her as she sits up, she walks over to him.

"You can feel the chip between the should blades if you feel deep enough." he starts to push around her back searching for it but finds nothing.

"Well let's give her some chicken and plenty of water, what about the pups, isn't porridge good for them?" Jasper asks standing slowly, putting his hand out to the dog, she sniffs his hand and licks it. "Yes, porridge will be good in addition for tonight Jay." Steve says. "My friend who has Dobermans feeds his pups with it."

"That's settled then, let's get them outside and feed mum, don't fancy clearing up the mess these little two will make with porridge." G picks them up and Moses temps mum outside.

"Jasper stays in the kitchen with Jane and pulls out the porridge, he is searching around for a dish they can eat out of in the cupboard.

"What will happen to them if they don't have a chip love?"

Jasper smiles from inside the cupboard, knowing what's coming next, he knows Jane adores any animal dogs more than anything, but he has to pretend to be firm for a little longer, to be sure. "They will go to the pound and put up for adoption love, I would say mum is a good few years old so should find a home, the pups will have no problem at all. However, they have quite big paws so they won't be little. I think mum has some Labrador in her and maybe some German Shephard amongst other things, so they will be big too."

"She is beautiful and so are they, why would anyone want to kick her out?"

"Who knows Belle, there are some cruel people in this world as you well know. But we can't keep them all, we work long hours and it wouldn't be fair."

Jane pouts at him, looking sad.

"Don't give me that look lady, you know as well as I do it wouldn't be fair. Not 3 of them." Jasper replies trying to be hard, he would love another dog but 3 wouldn't be practical.

He finishes up with the porridge grabs the chicken and places them on the worktop as he lifts Jane out of her wheelchair and heads outside, he gets Jane seated with the others and goes back in for the food.

"Right then, let's see how hungry these little pups are shall we?" he smiles putting the porridge on the ground. Mum is sat between Jane's legs being petted while she watches the pups get taken to the food. G puts them on the ground and they both start eating, the little girl gets her front paws
into the dish as the little boy stands in the middle, they all start laughing. The little girl gets tired and her full belly is showing, she sits down as she is falling asleep. G grabs her laughing and rubs her face and paws off with a towel. He passes her to Jane who cuddles her while he picks up the little boy and does the same. Chicca comes over and grabs the little one from G, she nuzzles into him and sits down next to James.
"Don't you get any ideas lady." He says stroking the dogs head.
"His name is Harley if you don't mind." Chicca replies stroppily.
Everyone begins to laugh, "And who may I ask is the little one then she can't be Davidson now can
she?" Moses asks.
"Well we could call her Harley and him Davidson?" she begins to giggle, Moses shakes his head, as
everyone begins to laugh.
"And this beauty, is Lady" she says patting mum on the head. Lady looks around at her and sniffs
Harley, then licks her. "I think she likes it." she giggles.

"Right now they are fed and watered what about us?" Steve stands up rubbing his stomach. Gwen
stands up, pats his tummy and laughs.
"I don't think you will ever starve dearest."
The girls get up and go and grab the food out of the kitchen as the men take the dogs onto the grass. Lady lays down in the sunshine and stretches out, they lay the pups down next to her who quickly fall asleep.
"Seriously Brother what are you going to do? I think Half-pint has her heart set on one of these if not

all of them." Moses asks

"Damned if I know. We can't have three dogs, but I know it will be a fight to take any away from her,

but how do you choose one?" He rubs his head looking at the dogs.

"Hey things happen for a reason Brother, maybe this was meant to be, I would take one if I knew Chicca and I were going to be long term then she could look after it in the evenings and when I go away at short notice."

"What do you do, I don't remember you ever telling us?" Steve asks

Moses jumps in, he has an idea. "He told you, IT in the forces, that's all we need to know."

James nods at him in thanks, he knows he can't tell them, none have been cleared anyway even if he wanted too, he can't.

"Spot on Moses, I work in IT, which is how I managed to trace the twat who took Jane so quickly." "Okay Brother, just wondered, seems you do all the dark shit that most of us know nothing about, or don't understand, just glad you were here to help out. We owe you big."

"Not at all, I was just one of all of us who found her and got her to safety, we all had a big part to

Play."

"Enough of that guys, let's see what these girls are doing I am sure we can cook better than they can,

looks like the pups are resting anyway." G got up off the grass and brushed his knees off.

"Right then ladies, the G master is here, move over let me show you how you cook on a barbecue."

Everyone laughed and the girls handed him the utensils and walked away, he looked around realising he was alone.

"I didn't mean leave me, I do need some help you know." The girls went back patting him on the back.

"You big girl G, what's your name Gail lol?" everyone laughed, G turned around and stuck two fingers

up.

"Fuck you arseholes." All the men laughed at him.

The girls were back and helping him cook, he looked back at the others and grinned, he had a hundred percent attention from the all the girls, he was loving it.

Jane was sat with Chicca preparing the salad and rolls as the others came across with the meat which was ready. Everyone came back to the table and tucked in. They were enjoying the evening sun and being together, it was one of the last nights they would all have together.

Lady came over and sat next to Jane, putting her head on her lap. Jane automatically began to pat her, Jasper nodded over to the others who looked over smiling.

"She needs a good bath and a big comfy bed to sleep in don't you think?" She said nudging Jasper "I'm sure she will get that at the pound love too. Or when she gets home to her owner."

Jasper looked away, he was trying to be sensible and protect them both, he had lost his best friend his

German Shephard years back and he never wanted to give his heart to another dog again, it hurt too much.

Jane pouted at him. Continuing to pet Lady and eat her food.

The puppies woke up and started playing on the grass, they were play fighting making everyone laugh. Chicca went and sat with them, she was hooked on Harley already.

"Don't you get attached either woman." James shouted over, "They are going to the vet tomorrow and then to the pound if not back to their owner, there could be a small child who is desperate to find their dog."

Chicca ignored him. Moses patted him on the back, "£50 says you will be taking a dog home in a few

Days."

"Don't you start Moses, I thought I could count on you."

"Well we all know what girls are like around puppies."

"Well there are other puppies I prefer to be around and right now that dog is cuddled into them!"

They men roared with laughter.

"Oh, jealously will get you in trouble James.", Moses laughed hitting him on the back. You better go
and rescue your woman before Harley there steals her heart."
"Too late for that, I can hear you, she already has."
"Ha, ha, ha, ha, looks like you will be sharing your bed in future then Brother" Moses laughed ruffling
his hair.
"Fuck you, no animal sleeps with me and my woman, it will be leashed up outside and like it." "Oooohhhh he's so tough and butch." Moses teased changing his voice making everyone laugh. James shrugged his hand off his shoulder, grumbling to himself as G passed him another bottle.

"If all else fails hit the bottle, that will sort things out, she will soon change her mind."
"I can still hear you G, and SHE won't change her mind, SHE has her own place and doesn't need any man telling her what she can and can't have."
"Oooooooooooooo, that told us." G laughed. "You know I am only teasing don't you Chicca?" "And I am just telling you G." she smiled letting him know she knew and so was she.

"Right I think it's time we called it a night, it's getting late, let's get these things cleared away and the barbie closed down so Jane and Jasper can get the pups to sleep, I'm sure you must be exhausted Jane you have had a long day love?"
Jane nodded, "Yes I have, it's been perfect though, thank you all for spending the day with us, but now I think I need to go to bed."
Jasper moved Jane out from the table and everyone else started to clear up and take things in the house, outside was clear in no time, Moses and G went into the garage looking for something to pen the dogs in with and keep them warm overnight. They came out with some boards and a few old blankets Jasper used around the cars when he was working on them. They were clean and good enough for one night. They made a pen in the garage, it was warm enough for them, and collected the dogs

from the garden. Everyone patted them before they were put to bed, with water and the door was locked.

The girls loaded the dishwasher and wiped everything down, Steve took the bin bag out, they were ready to leave. They all hugged each other and left. Jane slumped in the chair. She was exhausted and just wanted to lay in bed. Jasper came up behind her. Kissing her on the head.

"Is my girl ready for bed?" Jane nodded yawning. "Come on then let's go then, he bent down in front

of her scooping her into his arms, she curled into his body and laid her head against his shoulder. Moses followed with her water and left it on the side, he kissed her head as Jasper laid her on the bed.

"Night Half-pint."

"Night Moses" Jane yawned again he eyes already closed.

He left the room as Jasper climbed on the bed, "Come on Belle we need to get you undressed."

Jane grumbled as Jasper sat her up so he could pull her t-shirt off. It always made him laugh when she was so tired. She became like a grumpy little girl, he pulled her t-shirt off and wrapped his arms behind her undoing her bra.

"Mmmmm, you feeling frisky baaaabbbbbyyyy." She teased.

"I'm always turned on by you Belle you know that, but when you are this tired no, I can wait." She rolled over onto her side, raising her leg to look sexy, rubbing her thigh, "Are you sure honey, don't you want this sexy body anymore?"

Jasper laughed. "Belle you are so cute, I love you, but you are tired and need to rest, and if you are a

good girl and get your stitches out tomorrow then I have a surprise for you, so get under these

covers now and sleep." He pulled the sheet up for her to roll under, she looked up and pouted at him.

"Yes, I know that beautiful pout normally gets you everything you want but not tonight. Sleep!" "Yes bossy, but you are getting in too aren't you?"

"Of course."

"Oh good." she pushed her bottom out towards Jaspers side of the bed so he would have to wrap himself around her. Jasper smiled and walked around the bed, knowing exactly what she was doing. He undressed went to the bathroom and climbed into bed. Wrapping himself around Jane. She pushed her bum further into him knowing she would be pressing up against his cock. Jasper laughed. He could feel his cock getting hard but wanted to let Jane sleep. He sighed and kissed her shoulder before laying down.

"I love you Belle, Good night love."

"I love you too, night night."

Jasper pulled her closer and they both smiled as they closed their eyes.

Chapter 28

A New beginning

Jane woke first, she was still in the same position as when she went to bed, Jasper was wrapped around her, she loved the feeling of being so close to him. She smiled pushing her bottom into him, she ground it into him softly, she wanted him as she always did, and she was going to get what she wanted this morning, she pushed again into him feeling his cock getting hard, she smiled knowing it wouldn't be long before he woke up.

"Mmmmm. Good Morning Belle." Jasper moaned softly, pulling her by the hips closer into him.

"Morning my love, I'm sorry did I wake you?" she giggled knowing full well she did. "No Belle your bottom did pressing into me." he grinned pushing into her.

Jane giggled again, putting her hand behind her grabbing his head and pulling him down, she turned her head and kissed him. She let go and he kissed her shoulder, moving her hair from her neck, pushing it up the pillow, he kissed up her neck and bit her gently, Jane mewled loving the feeling of his lips on her neck, she moved her hand down into his hip rubbing her nails up and down his thigh. He pushed his thumb into her mouth pushing her tongue down, she closed her mouth sucking his thumb. Jasper pushed her bottom away from him, his cock was so hard he needed to move slightly before he crushed it. She lifted her leg over his hip so her legs were open.

Jasper moved his mouth close to her ear, biting on the lobe. "My bad girl, tell me what you want Belle?"

"I want you, touch me baby please?" she whispered begging him, opening her legs, she could feel her pussy getting wetter for him.

"Tell me Belle, I want you to tell me exactly what you want." He had hold of her neck pushing her head up, his lips rubbing across her ear has he whispered to her.

"I want your fingers in my pussy, she is so wet for you."

"And?" He whispered.

"Slide your fingers deep inside me, rub your thumb over my clit, please baby?"

"Come here Belle." Jasper moved away from Jane sitting up against the headboard. He helped her move into sit between his legs. He pushed her legs apart one hand around her body holding her breast, his other hand moving down her body, he rubbed over her tummy as Jane moaned, desperate to feel his hand between her legs. He bit her ear again, her head fell back against his shoulder. She moaned desperate for his hand to move further down. He slid his hand down across her tummy to just above her pussy. he teased her running his fingers across her body. Jane mewled again.

"Please baby please, I can't take anymore."

Jasper smiled, and walked his fingers down to her opening, she was wide open for him, at the top of her pussy he could feel her wetness, he wanted to taste her. He slid his finger in, touching her clit, Jane moaned loudly.

"Yes baby, please don't stop."

Jasper ran his finger down inside her pussy across her clit and down to her hole.

"Belle you are so wet." he groaned, he slid his finger slowly inside, Jane clenched her pussy around his finger holding onto him. He pushed his thumb against her clit, circling it. He felt her body relax under his touch. She released his finger and he pulled it out slowly. Jane took his hand sucking his finger wanting to taste herself.

She smirked, wanting more, sliding her fingers into her pussy coating them in her juices, she took her fingers out and sucked one, Jasper grabbed her hand taking both her fingers in his mouth sucking the remaining juices off.

"Grrrrrr, such a bad girl." He growled, pushing his fingers deep inside her making her groan. He slid two fingers in and out, slowly, building up his speed, Jane could feel his fingers against her G spot, her orgasm building. Jasper stopped, he leant her forward so he could move from behind her and slid down the bed, his cock standing proud and rock hard for her. He grabbed the pillows and pilled them up on top of each other, he grabbed Janes legs and spun her round and laid her across the pillows so her bum was in the air and her thigh was off the bed, Jane giggled, she knew what he wanted, he loved taking her from behind. He got onto his knees behind her and spread her legs, he slid his finger inside her coating his fingers in her juices again and moved them up to her bottom, Jane bucked off the pillow, he had only touched her there once and she still wasn't sure. He circled her hole and slipped across the opening teasing her.

"Oh Jesus." *What are you doing to me* she whispered talking to herself more than him. Jasper continued, dipping down into her pussy for more of her juices then back up to her bottom, teasing her again. He bent down to her bottom and slid his tongue from her pussy to her hole. Licking her gently, he circled her hole with his tongue the way he did with his finger, he opened her cheeks up and went deeper, his face buried in her bottom. Jane had her face buried in the pillow, half was embarrassment the rest was pure delight.

"Oh my god Jasper, oh please don't stop." she begged squeezing the life out of her pillow burying her face. Jasper grinned as his tongue teased her more, he brought his finger up to his mouth sucked it making it very wet then slid it inside her. Her back almost bent in half in pleasure.

"Oooohhhh my God Jasper!!!" his finger went deeper, he was so desperate to push his cock in but

didn't want to rip her apart, they need more lubrication before he could do that.

He got onto his knees and crouched behind her his cock aching to be inside her wet pussy, he straightened his legs out and placed his hands either side of her lowering himself down to her pussy, Jane pushed herself up to meet him as he slid inside her slowly, her juices coating his cock the deeper he went.

He threw his head back as Jane clenched around his cock.

"Oh, Belle fuck you are so fucking wet, I could explode right now deep inside you."

Jane clenched and unclenched her muscles around his cock making him crazy, he started laughing he

couldn't cope, he bent his head and sunk his teeth into her shoulder growling at her.

"Grrrrrrrrr, fuck, fuck, fuck woman you drive me crazy." He growled again. Jane stopped and released him, he rammed into her not wanting to hurt her but to claim her again and again.

"Yes, baby please fuck me hard, harder baby please, don't be gently I need this." Jane begged. Jasper got harder and faster pushing as hard as he could into her.

"Yes Belle, I fucking love you and this hot sweet pink pussy of yours. I just can't get enough of you,

cum for me Belle please?" Jasper got onto his knees, he wanted as much force as he dare to fuck Jane the way she wanted and he was going to tease her hole too. He held her hips and pushed into her deeper, Jane was moaning loudly, he didn't care if Moses heard her either. He felt his balls tighten the deeper he got, he knew he couldn't hold on too much longer, he slid his hand across her bottom and down onto her hole, circling it again, Jane bent upwards again and began pushing into him.

"Yes baby fuck me hard, don't stop please, push your finger in." Jasper didn't wait to be told a second

time. He gently pushed his finger inside her as Jane yelled out.

"Oh fuck yes, yes, don't stop please, slide it in further, please I want to cum." "Yes Belle, cum now for me please baby. Let go baby and come with me."

"Ooooohhh yes, oh yes don't stop Jaaasssppperrrr, she screamed slowly as her orgasm hit.

Jasper kept his finger deep inside her as her pussy clenched around her while he continued to pump into her as his cock head swelled as his own orgasm hit him.

"Arghhhhhh" he yelled, pushing into Jane, his body jerking into her, while Jane pushed back onto him. He felt her juices wash

over his cock as hers mingled with his. He started to slow down as he
caught his breath and Jane collapsed onto the pillows, exhausted. Jasper pulled out of her, kissing her shoulder and back.

"Jesus Belle, where did that come from?" he asked trying to catch his breath.

"I don't know, but wow it was wonderful." she blushed into the pillow. Jasper moved off her and turned Jane over laying next to her and putting his arms over her. He lent down and kissed her.

"I love you so much Belle, you are my world."

"I love you too baby, so, so much." Jasper kissed her shoulder and laid his head down on the pillow. "Christ I need another sleep." Jane laughed.

"Me too." they both laughed and laid cuddling for a few minutes to catch their breath.

"Think it's time we got up before Moses comes in with Tea."

Jane stretched out pouting, "I just want to spend all day in bed with you."

Jasper kissed her nose. "I know Belle, we will soon, I promise. But first we need to get the pups to

the vet and get them sorted out."

Jane looked up at Jasper still pouting. "But you want to get rid of them by sending them to the pound." Jasper smiled.

"Let's just get all three of them seen to first then we can talk about it." Jane grinned like a Cheshire

cat. She sat bolt up in bed.

"Come on then, shower time quick." Jasper laughed at her, climbed off the bed and scooped her into his arms.

"Hair up Belle." He reminded her as they past the sink, Jane grabbed her hair grip and twisted her hair up putting the grip on. He put her cover on her arm and body turned the shower on and walked them both in, he showered them both quickly and carried Jane back out to the bed wrapping her in a towel and drying her off before he helped her dress. They went into the kitchen, Moses wasn't about he saw the door open so knew he would be outside with the dogs. Jasper made the tea and sat with Jane when Moses walked in from the garden with Lady and the pups.

"Morning you two, I thought I would put these little ones out for some fresh air, I put some paper
down so they could do their business and it didn't ruin the grass and lady went out the side, I cleaned it all up for you."
"Oh Moses, you didn't have to do that." Jane cooed putting her arms out for the pups.
"Come here Lady." she called to Mum, Lady dashed over wagging her tail she jumped up putting her feet on Janes legs so she could be fussed.
Moses put the pups in her arms and Jane snuggled them into her. Jasper walked away shaking his head at Moses who just laughed.
"I'm off to shower, will be back soon, I will come to the vet with you too so you can have your hands free for Half-pint."
"Thanks Moses, that would be great. I will give them a call now and get an appointment."

Moses came back Jasper was getting ready to leave for the vet, he had a box in the boot of the car for the pups and Mum. He put Jane's wheelchair in the boot and they were just waiting on Moses. "We ready to go then Brother?"
Yes, we are, they can see us straight away."
"Great just grab my boots and I'm ready, where are the pups?"
"Do you really need to ask? Jasper said raising his eyebrows. They both walked into the lounge, the pups were on Jane's lap and Lady was laid at her feet at the end of the sofa. They both snapped a picture before Jane saw them.
Jasper cleared his throat. "Don't mean to disturb you, your ladyship but we are ready to go."
"Oh, ha, ha, I was keeping them quiet nothing else."
"Of course you were Half-pint." he laughed "Lady come on." he called and she jumped off the sofa and followed him. He put the pups in the box and lifted Lady in.

Jasper carried Jane to the car and they set off.

"Right I had a call from James, he has gone soft on Chicca and if these pups don't belong to anyone then they want to take Harley. I also rang Ernie to ask him to come and check out the fencing and he would also be interested in Davidson, they lost their dog a couple of years ago and he has been lost without one." He looked out the window smiling, he knew what was going through Jane's head.

"Oh my god, what about Lady?"

Moses put his hand on her shoulder from the back seat, he had read Jaspers mind he knew what he

was doing. "I am sure someone will take her from the pound, they will feed her up and get her healthy."

Jane put her head down, saying nothing.

"Yes, she is a beautiful dog, someone will take her." Jasper echoed Moses. As they pulled into the vet

and parked.

They got out of the car, Moses took the pups and Lady walking in ahead holding the door open with his foot. Lady went in and sat down waiting for Jane and Jasper. They followed in and Jasper went to the desk, they waited a few minutes until the vet called them in.

"So, tell me where did you find these pups and mum?", he asked ,while checking Harley over.

"We were in the garage and we found one of the pups under the bike cover mum was outside under a bush with the little girl, we don't know where they came from, we were hoping she was chipped, or not as the case maybe, she may well have been kicked out for getting pregnant." Jasper replied.

The vet nodded. "I agree, well these pups are around 5 weeks old, very under nourished and need to be with mum another couple of weeks really before they can be put up for adoption. Right let's have a look at mum then. Well she looks quite poorly to be honest, I would say she is dehydrated and

could do with a drip for a couple of days, what has her waste been like?" "She hasn't been, has she Moses?"

"She had a piss earlier but that's about it, the pups have been more than she has. But that could be
the porridge last night and the milk from mum."
"Okay let's scan her then, see if she has an owner." He said leaving the room to get the scanner to
check her out. Jane sat with her fingers crossed saying nothing. Moses looked at Jasper and raised his eyebrows, Jasper didn't say anything. The vet came back and checked lady over.

"No chip, I'm afraid, we will have to treat them all and then send them over to the pound. Thank you for bringing them in, we will take it from here." Jane looked up fear across her face.
"Hang on a minute, Jasper please tell him about Chicca and Ernie."
"Yes Doc, our friends are interested in the pups how do we go about them adopting them?"
"You will have to do that through the pound as mum will be there and they will want to keep them there a couple of weeks. So they need to go down and make their claim. We will have to get mum well and then make sure she won't be having any more pups before she is put up for adoption, they will all need a good bath, flea treatment, worming and their injections. Thank you again, leave it with me, if you leave your number at the desk I will let you know once they are going down so your
friends can go and do the relevant paperwork."
"Okay, thanks Doc, really appreciate your help. Do you mind if we say our goodbyes?" "Not at all I will leave you to it."
Jane sat with her head down, the tears brimming ready to spill any moment Jasper excused himself and went out of the room leaving Moses and Jane with the pups.
"Hey come on, they will all find a great home, you will see the pups again anyway." Moses soothed Jane as she cuddled Lady kissing her on the head. She sniffed and let her go. Moses patted mum on the head and the pups and wheeled Jane out. Jasper was waiting for them when they came out of the room.
"You ready Belle?" Jane nodded sniffing. Jasper bent down and kissed her on the head and they headed towards the door.

"Mr Mitchell Sir." the vet called. They all turned round. "Yes Doc?"

I forgot to say, if you call tomorrow afternoon we can let you know when you can come back and pick the dogs up, hopefully by then they will all start to look better and you can take them home." "Great thanks Doc, let me know what I owe you." He grinned nodding at the vet who stood with a huge grin on his face.

Jasper knelt down in front of Jane as she threw her arms around his neck crying openly. She was

squeezing the air out of him.

"Did you really think I would leave her to go to the pound? I saw the way you bonded with her, I know it will be difficult to manage but I don't want to let her go either, if the others hadn't taken the pups then we would have a big family."

"Oh my god, I can't believe you did that, I really thought you were going to leave her behind and when you left the room I really couldn't believe how hard you could be." She was still crying and

squeezing him. Everyone else in the vet was smiling and laughing. The receptionist came over with a tissue for Jane, she took it laughing, as the lady helped her wipe the mascara under her eyes. "Panda is not a good look babe." She smiled walking back to the desk.

"Oh my god you sound just like my friend." she laughed through more tears.

Jasper walked over to the vet, shook his hand thanking him for his help in surprising Jane and they left agreeing to call the following afternoon.

"Thank god that's over I couldn't hold back much longer, seeing you cry is a bloody killer." Moses

moaned.

Jasper laughed patting him on the back, "Sorry Moses, I appreciate your help though. Looks like we need to go shopping then?"

Jane clapped her hands cheering in her chair. "Now please, can we go now?"

"Yes of course." Jasper laughed. "You can have the pleasure in calling Chicca and James if you like too?"

"Oh god I don't know if I can do it without crying, but I will try."

"Let's get you in the car then you can do it." He put Jane in her seat and Moses packed

the wheelchair away in the boot getting in the back.

Jasper dialled James. "Hi Brother, everything okay"

"Perfect thanks James."

"Oh, does that mean it went to plan?"

Jane looked across at Jasper with shock on her face.

"You knew?" she squealed. "Yes we both knew love." Chicca laughed chipping in.

"Oh my god", she shouted hitting Jasper. "I can't believe you did that to me, I suppose everyone else

knows too?"

Chicca and James laughed as Jasper and Moses nodded. Jane buried her hands in her face fresh tears falling.

"I could kill you all, but I won't. I really thought I would never see her again. My heart was broken."

she laughed sniffing again.

"So tell them Belle"

"Oh yeah sorry, you two are now the proud parents of Harley, they need to stay with Lady for a

couple of weeks but you can come over as often as you like to see her." It was Chicca's turn to cheer. "We have to go shopping now James pleaseeeeee." she begged

"Everyone laughed. "We will see you there then James, we are heading to Pet Supplies." "Seems that way." He laughed Chicca was squealing in the background.

"See you shortly" They hung up and sat chatting on the way to the store. Jane was really excited. Jasper was so pleased he held back on her, he hadn't seen her this happy in a while.

They got to Pet Supplies, as they pulled up Chicca came flying into the space next to them. She jumped out of the car without turning the engine off and pulled open Jane's door squealing as she hugged her. The men stood back watching laughing. James turned the engine off grabbed Chicca's handbag and locked the car.

Moses lifted Jane out and they all went into the shop together. Chicca and Moses grabbed a trolley each and ran off down the shop. Jasper laughed and kissed Jane's head.

"I'm sorry Belle, I didn't mean to upset you."

She looked up at him and grabbed his cheeks. "It's a good job I love you Mr Mitchell, and I promise

to make it up to you later."

"I will hold you to that." he grinned running off down the isle with Jane, she was squealing as he stopped at the end meeting the others.

Chicca had loaded her trolley with beds, blankets, toys and jackets for Harley, Jane was going through it laughing at James who was pouting like a girl. Chicca grabbed his face squeezing his lips making a fishy face and kissed him.

"Stop sulking honey, she will look gorgeous in all this, and we have to keep her warm and dry." "She will look like a big girl all pink!, Why can't I have Davidson, I can make him look butch then, at least I won't look a dick walking down the road with Harley dressed in pink fluffy shit."

Everyone laughed, watching him sulking.

"Too late he has been taken by Ernie." Jasper laughed.

"I will swap them over, nobody will know if I wrap them in towels on the day."

Everyone burst into laughter, he had such a serious look on his face.

"Well you don't have to stay with me, you can always stay at home, me and Harley will be fine on

our own." Chicca teased.

"Come on get what you need and let's get out of here before I change my mind." he huffed "Someone has you wrapped around her little finger me thinks." Jasper teased ruffling his hair "Sod off, you can talk." He joked. Laughing

"Come on then boys, we have some catching up to do, and James, here knows which side his bread is
buttered as do you, so stop pouting and get on with it, we girls are not stupid."
Moses and Jasper clapped their hands laughing at James.
"Stumped by a girl." Moses teased.
James stuck his fingers up at them and walked away with the trolley, Chicca followed waving.
"See you guys later."
Jane went down every isle filling up the trolley with pink collars, big comfy beds and blankets. New bowls and toys.
"My Lady will never want for anything again, she will be spoilt and loved so much."
"Oh, your Lady?" Jasper questioned.
"Yes, my Lady, she grinned at him, she came to me remember."
"So, you will be paying for all this then will you he asked pointing into the trolley?"
"Yes, I will so there." she replied poking her tongue out at him.
"Got to beat me there first." he laughed running off with the trolley leaving Jane and Moses behind.
"That man is as much in love with Lady as you are Half-pint, you have no fear there."
"I know he is just trying to be firm and I get it, but she is so beautiful, I just felt a connection with
Her."
Moses laughed. "Half-pint you feel a connection with any dog or cat, you would have a kennels if you had your own way."
"No never, I couldn't bear to have any animal in a cage, but yes I would like lots of dogs and cats."

Moses shook his head and went in search of Jasper.
"Took your time, it's all paid for." He grinned packing the last of the bags, he put a bag on Jane's knees as it was light enough.
"We need to get you home before Alison arrives."
"Oh damn I forgot about her."
"Well you want your stitches out so we better get you home."

They dashed out of the shop loaded everything into the car and got home just as Alison pulled into the drive. Jasper carried Jane into the house as Alison followed, Moses and Jasper unloaded the car. "Wow looks like you have been busy, care to share?"

"We will leave you to Jane she will tell you" Jasper laughed.

"Can't wait" She smiled.

Alison went into the lounge with Jane. Moses and Jasper unpacked all of Lady's new things, they wondered around the kitchen trying to work out where to put her bowls and neither could decide. Alison was updated on Lady and removed Jane's stitches from her leg and stomach.

"Right then, just the plaster to go, it doesn't mean you are healed remember, but it should make it easier to move around. You need to start physio soon, but Mr Robinson will decided that next week once he has seen you, I have to say being home has done you the world of good, how are the panic attacks?"

"Thank you Alison, it feels good to have them out now. Roll on the plaster coming off I can really start to heal then. I had a panic attack yesterday while we were out, they were all playing around with the ball I was sat taking pictures of them and it just hit me. Tomorrow I will make some calls to friends in the UK who can help me. They all saw but didn't say a word which was nice. I couldn't get through this without them. But I am so tired."

"Jane you need to rest, I know you enjoy keeping up with everyone else but you can't, don't do anymore damage and end up back in hospital, you need to say no more often, you could do with getting away for a few days on your own with Jasper."

"Everyone except for Moses is going home tomorrow, so it will quieten down anyway."

"Oh, and everyone from the club, are they going too?" She laughed.

"Okay point taken."

"Hello ladies, how are things?"

"Hi Jasper, all sorted, Jane has her stitches out now, she does need to rest more, we were just talking about it, she needs to say no more often. I said you two could do with getting away for a few days on your own for some peace and quiet."

"Yeah sounds good, but we have Lady to think of now so we will have to wait." he smiled at Jane and winked at Alison, she could tell he was up to something. Jane hadn't seen the look on his face, she was too busy looking at her leg and the scar she had.

"Right then, I won't see you now until you come back next week, take care of her Jasper, say cheerio

to your friends for me, it was good to meet them all."

"We will thank you Alison." She bent and hugged Jane before she left. Jasper followed her out.

"I have booked 4 nights away for us, we leave in a few weeks. It's a place I went to before I met Jane, she will love it, the couple who own it will spoil her rotten, they will prepare all our meals too, it's a huge place, has a log fire beautiful grounds and a stream. I can't wait to take her there."

"I knew you were up to something, one of these days she will catch you out." she smiled at him.

"We will see." He smiled opening the door to let Alison out. He followed her to the car.

"Thank you for everything Alison we really do appreciate you coming her to see Jane."

You're very welcome. I look forward to seeing you both next week." She got into her car and Jasper

closed the door waving as she pulled away.

He went back into the house, Moses was with Jane, they were talking about Lady and what Alison had said.

"I was just saying to Half-pint she needs to listen to Alison, and take it easy, like sleeping during the

day. It will be easier once the gang go home you can get into a pattern."

"I agree, we will miss them all, but we do need to find a good pattern."

"Well I am here to help so let's get sorted."

"Thanks Moses, we really appreciate you being here, I will pop into site tomorrow and see how things are, pick up any post and come back, I need to get some calls made and go through my emails too."

"Listen just tell me what you need, I will do whatever I can, I'm not the best cook but I can do a

decent meal."

Jasper put his hand on his shoulder. "Thank you, I think between us we can make this work."

"Right Belle, I think we need to start now, you need some rest it has been a busy emotional morning I think you need some sleep?"

"Yes boss." she smiled saluting him.

"I think it should be in bed too, don't you Moses?"

"Yes, I do, best place to rest."

"Come on then love, I will take you up." Jasper bent and picked Jane up carrying her to the bedroom.

"Shout if you need anything Belle, I will leave the door open slightly for you."

"I will" she said pulling off her t-shirt and trying to pull her bottoms off. "Wanna see my scars?" She asked leaning back.

"Sure, let's have a look at you." Jasper bent down to look at her leg and kissed around the scar. "Now you can say you are a true biker chick, with the scar to prove it."

"Only a few of you could get away with saying that." She smiled, slapping him on the arm

"I know love, you know I don't mean it."

"Of course I do. It's okay honest."

"Let's see your tummy then." Jane laid down and showed her other scar, pushing her tummy up to him.

"You have to kiss that too you know." she smiled, Jasper bent and kissed round that one too and worked his way up her body past her breasts and up to her lips.

"Bra off my lady?"

"Yes please, I hate these things." she leant forward for Jasper to undo it for her and sighed as he removed it. She placed her hands at either side of her breasts and rubbed underneath pushing them up. "Kisses too please?" she smiled pushing them higher.

"You re insatiable Belle." He bent and kissed each nipple giving them a suck. "Now sleep young
lady please before I climb in there with you."
"Oh yes please." She cooed pulling back the covers for him.
Jasper laughed. "Such a bad girl Belle, I love you so much."
"I love you too honey, now go I need to rest." Jasper was lost for words and just laughed, blowing her
kisses as he walked out.

He went back down to Moses. "Not sure how long she will sleep but hopefully a while."
"Thanks for staying Moses, we really are grateful."
"Enough of being grateful, I wouldn't be here if I didn't want to be, you know how much I love Half- pint, but I am doing this for you too, you are a good guy Brother and I see how happy you make her, I don't know anyone else who could make her this happy and smile the way she does, she deserves everything good in her life."
Jasper nodded, feeling quite emotional, "funny how I wasn't impressed about someone coming here that I had to babysit, but to be fair I thought it was a guy, my boss got it very wrong and I can't tell you how happy I am about that."
"I have to agree, this is the right place for her."

"Right what do you fancy for dinner tonight, we have plenty in so we better go and check it out." "Whatever I will happily help out, just tell me what you want me to do."
How about a good roast dinner, not had one in a while and I know Belle likes them, we have a
Chicken."
"Sounds perfect to me."
"That's sorted, we will leave it while before we start it then, don't want her ladyship waking up and
wanting to interfere."
Moses laughed, "You know her so bloody well Brother."

"I was talking to Ernie about making an area for Lady to do her business so she doesn't spoil the garden, I don't mind her running around out here but not messing. I know it will take time to train her, but it will be worth it."

"I hear you, you don't want this beautiful garden spoilt, where were you thinking, shall we go and look?"

"Good idea. Let's go."

Jane slept for a couple of hours, they had managed to get dinner cooked and ready by the time Jasper went to get her, they sat together eating and chatting. Jane felt more relaxed, she didn't need to smile, she was with her two best friends, and knew she could be honest with them but in turn they were too. Jane had an early night Jasper went to bed with her, she was excited that Lady would be home but also sad she would be saying goodbye to her friends.

They got up early the following day, the gang were all going out for breakfast before they flew back to England. Jane was feeling anxious, she hated goodbyes and having everyone around her made her feel safe. They showered and dressed and headed to the diner. Everyone was waiting when they arrived they took over a huge part of the diner, all ordering a full breakfast to see them through the day. They sat for a couple of hours laughing and joking until the cars arrived to collect them for the airport, Jane was feeling tearful again as they followed behind. Jasper took her hand squeezing it gently.

They found a coffee shop and checked in waiting to be called, Jane felt like she was going to fall apart when they left. These people had saved her life, without them she wouldn't be alive. They had all bonded since she was taken, James and Chicca were talking about going to visit the UK. Jane sat with her head down while they all talked trying to get her emotions in check, they knew her as a strong person, who helped everyone, today she wasn't feeling that good.

Gwen was the first to come over to her. She got down on her knees in front of her and began to cry. "I'm really going to miss you Jane, this last couple of weeks have been emotional, and amazing, I am so glad you are okay and on the mend. Just wish we were all going together."

They hugged each other and cried.

"We will be back soon, I promise, I will skype every couple of days, so you will soon get bored of me."

"Girl that will never happen, just promise us you will get the support you need and come home soon?"

"I promise, I have you all to thank for saving me, I am not going to do anything to destroy that."

They hugged and wiped each other's tears. Before the others came over.

"Come on Gwen, move over let us in." Steve called across.

Jane started to cry again as everyone hugged her and said their goodbyes, she knew right at this moment how loved she really was. G was last to come across, everyone was saying goodbye to the others, he picked her up out of her chair so she was standing but he took her weight for her.

"I want a proper Doc hug, not one from that chair, because when I see you again you will be back on your feet just like now. Please take care, keep in touch and if you need anything at all even in the middle of the night, know I am there for you always. You are one special lady and I hope you know that now, we have been telling you for many years, but I hope this last few week's has proved that. I don't want to go but I am needed back home and I suppose you have the other two to look after you." he laughed.

"Thank you G, I do know and have always known how loved I am, you are really very important to me and always have been. I will never be able to thank you, any of you for what you have done for me and what you risked getting me out of there." She shuddered, G lifted her chin.

"Don't go back there, look to the future, you have the most amazing man who loves you, someone finally won your heart."

"You all have my heart especially you and Moses, you are part of me. I love you G. Now please go before I fall apart again." He kissed her head and nose and sat her back down in the chair.

"We love you too Half pint, see ya, beautiful." He blew her kisses as Jane sat wiping her eyes through the tears. Gwen and the girls came running back across and group hugged before they left sobbing again. Jasper came behind Jane and kissed her head.

"You okay Belle?" she nodded as Moses came back over, after talking to G. Chicca and James joined them.

"Right then, let's go and make that call see if our pups can come home." Chicca smiled.

They all walked out of the airport heading for their cars as Jasper called the vet. They were stood next to Jaspers car all holding their breath.

"Right yeah, okay I understand, no, no, it makes sense, okay, we will see you tomorrow then. Thank you again" He hung up and sighed. "It looks like they need to stay overnight, they want to make sure Lady has been to the toilet and has more fluid before she can come home, we can call again first
thing and if she has been we can go and get them straight away."

"Well it's for the best, at least they will spot anything while they are there. Call us tomorrow then once you know anything and we will come across, we will do all we can to help out before we can take Harley home."

They hugged and left each other as they got into their cars and drove home.

They spent the evening chatting, and Jane fell asleep laid against Jasper. Both men laughed, but knew it was important for her to rest. Jasper carried her to bed, undressed her and climbed in with her, pulling her into him. He loved the smell of her, he buried his nose into her hair, just to inhale the smell and running his fingers gently through it, he loved the length and feel of it. He told her often it was as soft as silk. He moved it off her shoulder, running his finger across her shoulder blade and up her neck then down her spine, he kissed her shoulder and up to her neck, tiny butterfly kisses, he didn't want to wake her just touch her. He nuzzled into her and closed his eyes.

They both woke early the following morning, Jasper went and made tea for them, he left Jane stretching and yawning making lots of noises that always made him smile, as he walked back into the bedroom Jane was sat up waiting. He put her tea down on the side table and bent down grabbing her bottom lip sucking it into his mouth, making her laugh, she loved him doing it. He let go and licked her across the lips slowly, smiling.
"Good Morning my love, how do you feel this morning?"
"Well after that kiss how do you expect me to feel?" she giggled, grabbing him and pulling him down onto her. "I feel good, it has made such a difference getting my stitches out, I know I'm not fully recovered but I feel better in myself."
"Oh good, well let's get you showered and we can ring the vet to see if the pups can come home
today, if her ladyship has been to the toilet." He smiled laying on his side with his head on his hand looking down at her.
"Yes boss, but please can I have my tea first, you know I don't like cold tea. I'm not like you drinking it cold."
"You're just fussy." he laughed rubbing noses with her and kissing it after. Jane scrunched her nose up giggling. He sat up on the edge of the bed passed her tea and sat opposite her rubbing her legs while she drank her tea.
Jane handed her cup to Jasper smiling after she had drank it all.
"Okay. I'm ready."
Jasper got up smiling, scooped her into his arms and went into the bathroom, they protected her and put her hair up before entering the shower. It was a quick wash before they came out wrapped in towels. They got dressed and headed to the kitchen. Moses was up already sat drinking coffee at the table in the garden. Jasper stood at the door with Jane in his arms, she nodded, he walked her outside and put her in the chair next to Moses.

"Morning you two, how did you sleep Half-pint?" Moses asked bending forward kissing her head.

"Okay I think, I don't remember dropping off just waking up to be honest."

"Well you did fall asleep on the sofa so I am not surprised," Moses laughed ruffling her hair, "just shows your body needs it."

"Yes, I know it does, I told Jasper I feel so much better today since my stitches came out, I can move
Better."

"That's good, just don't overdo it."

"I'm sure you pair enjoy lecturing me or think I am silly, I am a big girl and know when I can and can't do things."

"Less of the big Half-pint, that's called wishful thinking." Moses laughed and Jasper joined him, he got up and kissed her on the head.

"Belle if we didn't love you we wouldn't even be saying these things, don't take it the wrong way."

"I'm not honest." she moaned, looking up at Jasper stood behind her.

"Okay, so who wants breakfast?"

"I don't have an option so a piece of toast for me." Jane replied tutting.

"Stick a couple in for me too Brother."

"Coming right up." Jasper kissed Jane on the head and went back into the kitchen to make
toast and more tea.

They sat eating and drinking enjoying the sun on the patio.

"We better enjoy the quiet I think those pups are going to be a handful now they are better." Jasper
laughed.

"Oh my god I can't wait." Jane squealed. They both looked at her and laughed.

They finished up and Jasper grabbed his phone. They all sat quiet while Jasper rang the vet.

"Good Morning, it's Jasper Mitchell calling about Lady, Harley and Davidson." It went quiet Jasper looked at them and mouthed, "She has gone to check." They fell silent, Jane had her fingers crossed. "Hi, yes I'm here, okay great, we will see you soon, thank you." He hung up as Jane cheered loudly. They all started laughing, "Come on then, what we waiting for?" Jane was desperate to get out of the chair.

"Okay, okay, Miss impatient." Jasper laughed

"Go ahead and get you two sorted I will clear the dishes, see you in the car." Moses started

to clear the table.

"Thank you Moses, Jane squealed as Jasper picked her up.

"Anything for you Half-pint, and let's be honest if we don't get going, we won't hear the last of it." Jane turned and blew him a kiss.

They got their boots on and Jasper took Jane out to the car, Moses followed within seconds and locked the house up. They got to the vet and parked up, Moses got Jane out of the car and headed in, the dog cage was in ready. Jasper had called the others to let them know they would be collecting the pups and they were welcome over anytime. They rushed in the door as the receptionist looked up to see them coming towards her. Jasper apologised for them being so eager, she smiled and went off to get the Vet. He came out carrying the pups and the nurse followed with Lady, she went straight to Jane, her tail wagging looking happier than when they left her two days ago.

"Thank you Doc, we really appreciate your help, I have to say they all look so well." Jasper laughed as

the pups chewed on his fingers and his ear.

"Oh, you have your hands full with these little ones I can assure you. Give them another few weeks with mum then they can go to their new homes." He handed both to Moses and took the paperwork out of his pocket handing it to the receptionist.

Jasper paid the bill, they said their goodbyes until the next visit. They put Lady and the pups into the cage and got back into the car. They reached home and Chicca and James were waiting on the driveway. Chicca jumped out as excited as Jane was earlier.

Jasper looked in the mirror at Moses, "Two of them now Moses." He tutted laughing.

Jane looked around at him. "Meaning?"

"Nothing love." He laughed, ruffling her hair and leaning in to kiss her. "Let's get you in so we can

unload the pups.

They all got into the garden and the pups were put onto the grass, Lady laid next to Jane being fussed while the pups charged around with the men. Chicca came and sat next to Jane fussing lady. "Who are the big softies?"

"Yeah quite! and they said it was us." They both sat watching laughing at the men being chased.

Enjoying every minute.

The day went quickly, Jane was tired and went for a lay down, Jasper put his foot down not allowing Lady in the bedroom which made her pout at him, but he didn't budge on his decision. James and Chicca went home happy the pups were okay promising to visit most days and clean up after them.

Chapter 29

Time to relax

A few weeks passed, the pups were getting bigger, Lady had settled in with them and Jane was feeling better in herself, she had made contact with her friend who was a counsellor and had began talking about the event and her history with her ex, for the first time in a long time she was feeling really well. Her plaster had come off and now she had a couple of weeks left in the wheelchair before she started physio. Jasper had been back and forth to work, he and Moses had a great routine in place and it was working well. Whatever issue was between Jane and Moses about her knowing how he felt had gone, they had relaxed back to being the friends they were before she left the UK. The days Jasper worked they spent in the garden or going out for walks then he helped her prepare dinner for when he got back.

It was early afternoon Jane and Moses were sat in the lounge, it had been raining, the puppies were asleep on the floor with Lady, she had her legs up on the sofa stretched out just chilling with Moses. She was deep in thought, she felt something wasn't quite right, Jasper was coming home for lunch and they were going for a drive just the two of them, she began to worry about it a little bit.
"Half-pint are you listening to me?" Moses asked looking at Jane smiling, she had wondered off into
a little world of her own.
"Sorry….what did you say?" she looked over at Moses frowning.
"Oh, so you weren't listening then madam!" He teased
"Ummmm, probably not no, tell me again." She asked half smiling.
"It's okay love, it wasn't important, where did you drift off to anyway?" "Nowhere really, just mulling things over that's all."

"Do you want to talk about it?"

"It's nothing really, Jasper is keeping something from me and I am just a bit worried really." "How do you know he is keeping something from you?"

"Well he keeps grinning at me and muttering under his breath." Moses laughed. "You're worried because he is grinning at you and muttering under his breath,

where on earth does, he is up to something come out of that?" he continued laughing. "I do love you

Half-pint, you are a little blonde at times."

Jane threw the cushion at him that was beside her, Moses caught it laughing still.

"You don't understand what I mean, it's not like him." She huffed, folding her arms.

Laughing through his words Moses tried to compose himself. "You make it sound like he never smiles."

"Oh, forget it, you don't understand because you're a man." She huffed again slapping her hands onto her legs.

"Whatever you say Half-pint" He teased. "Right, I am going to get lunch ready, would her Ladyship like to supervise?"

Jane poked her tongue out at him as he got up out of his chair and walked towards her.

"Come on then." He put his arms out ready to lift her up.

Jane wrapped her arms around his neck as Moses lifted her, he kissed her cheek and laughed as he walked them into the kitchen putting Jane on the stool.

"You are so easy to wind up you know, I thought after all these years you would have seen that." "You just enjoy teasing me you always have."

"Well yes, that's true, but you know it's because you are so easy to tease and that I love you."

Jane screwed her face up at him and laughed. "Whatever, now get these bread rolls out so we can do

lunch Jasper will be back soon."

"Yes Ma'am." Moses saluted and walked towards the fridge grabbing everything he needed. Jane laughed at him as Jasper walked into the kitchen. Jane's face lit up as he walked towards her wrapping his arms around her and kissing her on the head. Lady and the pups came running into the kitchen to greet him. Jasper laughed seeing them all come running in.

"How's our girl doing today?" He smiled looking over at Moses. Jane bent her head back looking up at him, waiting for her kiss on the nose.

"I'm ok thank you, unless you were talking about Lady." she laughed.

"Of course, how could I not be asking about her?" he smiled, crouching down to greet the pups who were vying for his attention. Lady sat back like a proud Mum waiting for her turn. Jasper flicked his head calling her over, she dashed across to him her tail wagging and her lips curling like she was smiling, he grabbed her head with both hands talking to her in a silly voice.

"Have you been looking after your Mum and Moses today, have you, have you?" he repeated ruffling her head as her tail wagged even faster. "And I bet they have just been sat putting the world to rights haven't they, yes they have." he cooed at her as she stuck her tongue out and licked his face, leaving slobber behind.

"Ewwww, you can wash that off before you kiss me, I love her to bits, but you can keep the slobber."
Jane teased.

Jasper got up off the floor patting Lady and the pups darting towards Jane grabbing her for a kiss, she was arching away from him squealing.

"Oh my god Jasper, no!" she screamed.

"Spoilsport." He laughed, "I thought you might like a Jasper, Lady smooch?"

"Yuk, yuk, no thanks." Jane screwed her face up, Jasper laughed walking away heading to
the bathroom to wash it off.

Moses and Jane finished preparing lunch as Jasper came back in, Moses put the food on the table and Jasper picked Jane up moving her across.

"Are you ready for your drive out this afternoon Belle?" he smiled.

"Yes of course, where are we going."

"Let's see where the road takes us shall we?"

Jane shrugged, "okay, you know better than I do where to go so I will leave it up to you." They finished lunch Jasper and Moses cleared everything away. Jane was finishing her tea.

"Well no time like the present, I will grab our jackets and put them in the car and be back for you in a minute Belle, we may as well go now."

"Oh, already?" she span around in her seat glaring a Moses. He shrugged his shoulders at her. She huffed knowing something was going on but had no clue about what.

Jasper came back in clapping his hands together. "Right then Belle, are you ready, got your bag, phone?"

Moses walked in with her bag and handed it to her, she put it over her head and let it hang at her side.

"Well it appears so yes."

"Right then." he lifted her up in his arms. He turned to Moses winking, "We will see you later some time."

"I will be here. Enjoy your drive." He smiled back.

"See you later." Jane waved, she looked down to the pups, "Behave for Uncle Moses please?" She

smiled blowing them kisses. Lady looked up wagging her tail and the pups walked away.

Jasper put Jane into her seat kissing her lips softly. "Mmmmmm, you comfortable honey?" "Yes thank you." Jasper fastened her seatbelt, coming back to her face, kissing her again. Before getting in the car.

They drove out of town, Jasper knew exactly where he was going, it would be a good few hour's drive, but he was excited about it and knew he could chew the miles up without an issue.

He just needed to have excuses ready for how far out they were going. He was going to stop just after halfway for a piece of cake and a cup of tea at a nice café him and the boys stopped at previously. That was going to be one of his excuses. Jasper took Jane's hand and kissed her knuckles, taking a quick glance at her.

"You okay Belle?"

"Yes, thank you, it's actually nice to be out and not going to the hospital. Feels odd to be alone with
you too, I'm enjoying it."

He kissed her hand again and put them onto the centre console. He turned the music up, his playlist was on and Kane Brown crooned. "This is perfect, Come kiss me one more time, I couldn't dream
this up, even if I tried."..... Jasper began singing, Jane laughed as he tried to get as deep as Kane. "You and me in this moment, feels like magic only, I'm right where I wanna be." he looked at Jane grinning, she was laughing loving watching and listening. He continued with the song smiling.

"Everyone's talking like they just can't wait to go, saying how it's gonna be so good, so beautiful. Lying next to you in this bed with you, I aint convinced, cause I don't know how, I don't know how heaven, heaven could be better than this." He stopped singing, bringing her hand to his lips kissing her gently turning the music down.

"I know we are not in bed but just being in this car with you Belle is perfect." "Ohhh Jasper, you are so sweet, what did I do to deserve you?"

"Well where shall I start?" he laughed teasing her.

"Cheeky." she laughed slapping his hand.

He kissed her again and bit softly kissing it better.

"Fancy a cup of tea?" he smiled.

"Oh yes please." she almost begged.

"Great we are almost at a lovely little café, I thought you might like, it does some amazing cakes that
I thought we could try?"

"Now you are spoiling me, I hope you will still love me when I am as big as a house?"

"Well I didn't like to say anything," he cringed away smiling "but I noticed you are getting a little chubby" he laughed waiting for the impact.

"Oh my god! you cheeky sod, I have not got chubby at all, how dare you." she scolded him, swatting
at his arm.

Jasper couldn't help laughing. "I'm teasing Belle." "You better be." She pouted.

Jasper laughed pulling into the café, he stopped right outside, so he didn't need to get the chair out, they were going to sit outside so he could carry her to the seat.

He jumped out walked around to Jane's side of the car opening the door, she was just putting her bag over her head, he slid his hands underneath her and lifted her up pretending she was heavy as he lifted her.

"Ugh, sorry Belle, I forgot for a minute you're not as light as I thought you were." he laughed trying to keep a straight face but couldn't.

She swatted him again, "Oi cheeky, enough of that, or I go in my chair, I don't want to hurt you do I!? she scolded him, he kissed her hard to shut her up.

"I love you Belle."

Jane squeezed his cheeks making a fishy face. "Just remember how lucky you are Mr." she teased.

"Yes ma'am." He saluted picking her up.

Jane pushed the car door closed as they walked towards the cafe, there were a few other people sat outside, they all looked at Jasper carrying Jane but nobody said anything, he could see some women swooning as he sat her down and kissed her nose. He smiled.

"What would my lady like then?" he asked taking the menu out of the holder and passing it to her. "Lady huh, well that's a step up from Belle."

"No Belle, there will never be a step up from that, you will always be my Belle, Lady is because you are carried everywhere like the ladies in their sedan chairs of years gone by."

"You really are cheeky today, I will happily go into my wheelchair you know." she chided him.

"No Belle, not while I can carry you, I won't hear of it." he smiled blowing her a kiss.

The waitress came across smiling. "Good afternoon what can I get you both?" Jasper looked at Jane. "Belle, what do you fancy?"

"Umm, can I have Black forest cake please with tea?"

She nodded and scribbled it down on her pad. "Would you like cream with that?" Jane nodded "Yes please."

"And for you Sir?"

"Can I have German Chocolate cake please with cream and tea too?" "Certainly, I will be back soon with your drinks."

"Thank you." they replied in unison

The tea arrived, Jane's eyes gave it away that the cake was on its way as her eyes grew wide and her mouth almost hit the floor. He laughed watching her, she watched the waitress get coming closer.

"Oh my God Jasper, why didn't you tell me how big the portions were, you won't be able to pick me up after I eat that!" he laughed as they were put down on the table.

Jane sat staring at them both, she looked up at the waitress. "I only wanted one piece." the waitress
frowned not understanding her.

Jasper spoke up. "She's joking meaning the portion is huge." The waitress just smiled and walked away.

Jane poured their tea as Jasper poured the cream over the top of the cakes. "Would you like to try a bit of mine? I thought I better ask before I tuck in." "You trying to say I always eat your food?"

"No, I'm saying before you ask, I thought I would, because you know you will." He grinned. "Well okay then as you asked."

Jasper smiled digging the fork into his cake breaking off a good mouthful, he moved his fork towards Jane's mouth.

"Open wide." Jasper slowly pushed the fork into her mouth, there was too much on it, some fell off making a mess of Jane and the table, they both laughed.

"Oh yummy, that's lovely, would you like some of mine?" Jasper nodded as Jane loaded up her fork, hers had a cream topping, as she moved the fork towards his mouth she purposefully pushed the cream onto his nose and giggled.

"Oops sorrrrrry." She giggled.

She continued laughing as Jasper tried to eat the cake that had filled his mouth, he was trying to wipe the cream off his nose, Jane beckoned him to her with her finger biting her lip, he moved closer to her, she took his face with one hand and licked the cream from his nose and lips, she could see out of the corner of her eye that a woman slightly older than they were was watching her. She was dressed quite prim and proper, scowling at them.

"Mmmmm, maybe we should take some cream home with us, we could have lots of fun with it?" She said it slightly louder than she normally would, taking a quick glance towards the woman, who looked shocked, tutted, tapping her husband on the arm. Jane could tell she wasn't impressed with them. She wondered what kind of reception she would have got if they were in leathers and on the bikes. Jane laughed and looked back to Jasper.

"Someone has the devil in her today."

"Oh it's that snooty woman behind us she is looking down her nose at us, I was just thinking how she would react if we were on the bikes."

"Oh, so you don't really want to take cream home?"

"I didn't say that did I?" she grinned naughtily at him.

"That's my girl. We will have to find some then, I'm sure there is a shop not far up this road."

They both tucked into their cake sitting back patting their tummies when they finished.

"Wow I don't think I will need to eat tonight, I feel like I am going to burst." she laughed.

"Tell me about it, I will need to get back to the gym before long, I can feel I'm getting a food belly on
me" he grinned

"You and me both, they say sex is good for burning calories, maybe we should send Moses out for the night so we can have some fun."

Jane ran her finger across the plate covering it in cream and brought it to her mouth she rubbed it over her lips and beckoned Jasper to kiss her. He leant in licking the cream off moaning softly before taking her bottom lip between his teeth and sucking it before releasing it.

"Are you trying to make me hard Belle? because you are doing a damn good job of it and I need to
move out of this seat?"

Jane nodded, "Always, you should know that." She grinned

Jasper picked his cup up swallowed the last of his tea stood up and went into pay for the tea and cake, he was back within minutes before he scooped Jane up into his arms and almost ran back to the car with her. Jane was laughing at him.

"You're acting like you haven't had sex in weeks."

"No Belle, I'm just horny as hell around you all the time, carrying you like this doesn't help." He kissed her as he put her into the car. "You just drive me crazy."

She pulled his t-shirt bringing him back to her and whispered in his ear.

"Well my pussy is wet and aching for you right now so get me home stud!" she sucked his ear and bit
it gently.

Jasper ran around the car jumping in, knowing he only had an hour at most to drive. He looked at Jane with a huge silly smile.

"Your wish is my command Belle." He started the car and pulled out of the café. Turned the music on and relaxed back.

Jane took his hand bringing it to her lips, she ran her tongue down his index finger while looking at him. Kissing his palm and up his middle finger. Jasper looked at her.

"You are a naughty girl, doing that is going to get you into a whole heap of trouble." Jane grinned

licking his thumb, taking it into her mouth and sucking hard.

"Fuck woman you are killing me." Jane stopped and held his hand in hers, the car was too big to get his hand in her lap so she held it against her breast. Making sure he could feel her hard nipple as she brushed his hand upwards. He was grinning trying to keep his eyes on the road.

"Belle, do you want me to stop this car and rip your knickers off and bury my head in your pussy?" "Hell yes, I cannot wait 2 hours or more." Jane was nodding her head furiously.

Jasper couldn't stop laughing, "That's honesty I suppose. Okay I will find somewhere then."

They drove for a little while longer and Jasper heard gentle breathing noises from Jane, he knew she had fallen asleep, that helped him get to his destination. They were only 30 minutes at most away, Jane had freed his hand, he turned the music down a little an increased his speed just a bit to get there as quickly as possible. He looked over at her smiling, he loved seeing her asleep.

Jasper touched Jane on the arm to wake her gently. "Belle sweetheart wake up, I found us somewhere to stop. Jane stretched and looked out of the window as they drove into the driveway.

"Jasper this is private property, you can't just drive in here." She exclaimed looking around her. "You said you wanted me to eat your pussy out, this looked like the best place to stop." He was desperate not to laugh.

"Babe turn around please we can't come in here." She was patting his arm. As Jasper drove round

the bend and the house came into view.

"Oh my god look at that house it's beautiful, quick baby turn around before anyone sees us. Oh no! too late, we have been spotted someone is waving at us." Jane was annoyed they had been caught going into someone's drive. Jasper waved at the couple stood outside the huge house. Jane covered her face she was really embarrassed.

"Well how are you going to get us out of this then, say Hi there, this is my fiancée and she wanted her pussy licking, so I came in for some privacy!, oh my god I am so ashamed." Jane kept her head down as they got closer to the couple.

Jasper opened his window as the couple came towards the car.

"Hi Jasper." Henry greeted him patting his arm on the window.

"How are you, great to see you, this

must be Jane who we have heard so much about. Hi, this is my wife Lillian."

Jane looked at Jasper really confused. "Would you like to explain?" she scowled.

Lillian laughed. "Jasper I think you have some explaining to do." She smiled going around to Jane's

side of the car opening the door.

"Hi Jane, I'm Lillian but you can call me Lily, or anything else you wish. This is my husband Henry.

Jasper has told us all about you."

Jane relaxed a little. "Hi, lovely to meet you, I have heard a lot about you too, but had no idea we were coming here." she looked at Jasper and swatted him on the arm gritting her teeth. "I have no idea what is going on." she laughed nervously.

"Well let me fill you in Dear. Jasper here rang and asked us if he could bring you up once you were better, of course we said yes. You are staying for 5 days, or longer if we can persuade you too." She grinned. "Everything is sorted for you, Henry has a fire ready for this evening as it gets a little chilly out here now. Dinner is prepared for you and is ready to pop in the oven when you are hungry, I have stocked the fridge and will prepare your meals for you, I don't want either of you worrying about a thing, I will be in and out as quick as a flash, well as quick as these bones of mine can carry me, you won't even know I am here. We don't want to disturb your stay. So, Jasper come on and get your beautiful lady out of the car. Henry open the boot and help Jasper with the bags."

Jasper turned and looked at Jane grinning like the Cheshire cat, Jane scowled at him.

"Umm did you forget something I don't have any clothes?" she asked a little curt.

"Belle everything is sorted you don't need to worry." He got out of the car and opened the boot as Henry pulled the bags out. Jane watched her bags go into the house. Jasper came to her door scooping her into his arms carrying her up the steps of the house.

She whispered. "You are going to pay for this."

"He whispered back, oh I hope so." Laughing kissing her cheek.

As they walked into the house Jane's eyes opened wide and she began sniffing.

"Wow what's that smell?"

"Oh, that's your bread Jane, I popped it in 15 minutes ago, as Jasper texted letting us know you were an hour away."

Jane looked at Jasper, "You really are deceitful Mr." She raised an eyebrow at him.

"Not deceitful Dear just secretive, to make this surprise perfect for you."

"Oh my god what about Lady and the pups and Moses, we better call him and let him know." She

looked at Jasper. "…….He is in on this too isn't he?" everyone nodded.

"Belle I'm sorry, I wanted to surprise you, do something nice once you were out of plaster and

feeling better."

Jane grabbed his face and kissed him hard. "I love you so much Mr Mitchell." she laughed

"I love you too Belle."

"Put the poor girl down before you do yourself an injury Jasper." Henry said laughing.

Jasper walked to the sofa and put Jane down, Lillian was there as quick as a flash putting cushions behind her back.

"Jane anything the two of you need please call us, we are happy to help in any way we can, if you need a chat I am here too. I know you have been through a terrible time, so please if you need another girl to talk to let me know." She placed her hand on Jane's and squeezed it.

"Thank you Lily that's really thoughtful and kind, I am still a bit shocked about all this and in awe of your beautiful home."

Our home is over the fields, this is just rented out now, it's too big for us to be rattling around it, so

we decided to let others enjoy it. I will let Jasper tell you all about it, there is an album full of photo's

over there in the cupboard of when Henry was building it and of course the pictures on the wall. Right let me make some tea for you both and we will get out of your hair."

"I can do that Lil." Jasper called to her as she headed to the kitchen.

"Sit Son, it's okay, let me do it while you relax after your drive." She came back moments later with the teapot full and Henry following her with the tray full of fresh baked goodies.

"I have taken the bread out and it is cooling on the tray. Jasper tells me you love Lasagna so I made you one for tonight, it just needs 30 minutes in the oven, there is salad in the fridge ready too."

"Oh Lily, I feel like we have put you to a lot of trouble, please let us do something."

"I won't hear of it, you two need some down time and we will help to give you that, so relax and enjoy the peace and quiet."

"Thank you both, so very much." Jane put her hand on her heart. Feeling emotional. "Right you have the number for us Jasper call if you need anything."

"Before I forget Son, the quads are outside if you wanted to take Jane out, you can come across the field at a gentle speed and get down to the stream, you know they are hand controls anyway." Jane's face lit up she shot a look at Jasper willing him to agree.

"Thank you Henry, we may take you up on that, we will see how Jane sleeps tonight."

Jane nodded at Henry, "I know I will sleep very well thank you, I already feel like the weight has been lifted off my shoulders. This sofa is so soft I could sleep here." she grinned.

"Wait until you try the bed, you won't want to get up love." Jasper grinned "Henry made all of the

beds and the mattress is amazing, if you find it perfect I will order us one too."

"Okay we will be off now, I will be in tomorrow morning to cook breakfast and leave your lunch and dinner for tomorrow. How does 9am sound?"

Jasper looked at Jane, "We can go for a walk to the stream first thing love then come back for

breakfast?"

"Sounds perfect, thank you Lil. You are wonderful and I feel very spoilt but guilty."

"Jane please don't think about it. We will love every minute of doing it for you." Lil stood up Jasper did too and hugged Lil she bent down and kissed Jane on the cheek hugging her as best she could. "See you to tomorrow morning, enjoy the rest." Henry bent over the back of the sofa and kissed Jane on the head and shook Jaspers hand holding his arm.

They both waved as they went out the door, Jane relaxed back into the sofa, Jasper sat at the other end taking her legs and putting them into his lap.

"Is this really happening, because right now it feels like a dream?"

"Yes, Belle it is," he laughed "I'm not sorry I kept this from You."

"Oh really! Charming."

"No Belle, it was so lovely to see your face when I carried you in, the shock on your face when you realised it was all arranged was a picture." He moved her legs moving forward to pour the tea. "Biscuit, cake?" he asked laughing knowing full well they were both full.

"I don't think I have any room, had I known I wouldn't have had such a big piece back in the café." "We will save it for later then after dinner."

"Perfect, but if the size of the cake is anything to go by, I think we will have trouble eating the Lasagna." She laughed.

Jasper passed Jane her tea and sat back with her. "Would you like to explore the house after you've finished your tea?"

"Oh yes please."

"Great, we have a room down here making it easier for us."

"Thank you Jasper, this is so perfect. I love Moses very much, but I have been feeling a little restricted lately not having our time alone. I know he is here for us and I really do appreciate it and we couldn't have done it without him, but I just can't wait until it's us again alone. I will miss him like crazy though."

"I know love, I actually booked this when you were in hospital, I discussed it with Moses and he had already agreed to stay on and help. He knows we need this time away, especially for you to rest

properly."

"You have kept this secret all this time?" she looked shocked.

"Yes Belle, it has been hard to be honest, but I was determined." he laughed

They finished their tea and Jasper took Jane's cup and putting it on the table. He stood up and bent

down so she could climb into his arms.

"Lil has made up two beds so you can choose which room you want, the bags have been put in the room I had the last time but it's your decision. He walked them into the first room. Jane caught her breath when he pushed the door open.

"Oh my god Jasper, this is beautiful I could cry, it's so perfect."

He was grinning from ear to ear.

The bed had a pale blue handmade patchwork throw, with matching pillow toppers, the bed was huge, it had an even bigger headboard that went half way up the wall which was hand carved with a lace pattern, hanging from the back of the headboard were two cushions to make if comfortable to sit against. At the foot of the bed was a sofa, which had feet to match the bed, it was cream with matching blue cushions. In the corner stood a lace carved dressing screen painted white. There were lace drapes on the patio windows that pooled on the floor. Jane sat in Jaspers arms taking it all in her mouth still wide open. Jasper walked her to the window to show her the view, outside the doors was a swing with a huge cushion on it, which Henry had made for Lillian. Beyond that was the barn and the opening to the woods.

"Oh Jasper, can we stay forever please." Jane crooned

Jasper laughed, "Believe me Belle if they would sell it, I would snap it up. Wait until we go out tomorrow, you will love it even more. Come on let me show you the bathroom."

They walked into the bathroom Jane pushed the door open and gasped again. There was a huge bathroom certainly not an ensuite, it had a huge bath that stood in the middle with iron feet, the back of it was high so you could lay against it. Big enough for two people to lay in. Over in the corner was the sink that Henry had made on a beautiful ornate stand. Next to it was the shower which was a glass screen that ran across the whole wall, it had two shower heads close to each other. Jane knew she could stand long enough now, to quickly shower without over doing it, so she was looking forward to her shower. There was a window overlooking the field with a blind covering it for privacy if there were more than two people staying. Jane grabbed Jasper tightly hugging him hard and kissed him even harder.

"Oh my god, I am speechless, and don't say that makes a change."

Jasper laughed, "I wouldn't dare Belle, I am so glad you like it, I fell in love with it the first time I saw

it, when I met you I knew I wanted to bring you here." "What took you so long?" she laughed teasing him.

"Cheeky, I take it you like this room, would you like to see the other one looking over the front of the house?"

"No thank you, this is beyond perfect, let's unpack now and we can have a shower." "Yes ma'am" Jasper teased sitting her on the bed.

Jane swatted him on the arm laughing and grabbed a bag, unzipped it and started to put things in piles.

"How did I not notice these things missing, you sneaky sod!"

"Well it was easy because I got everything out for you every day, I brought extra washing things deodorant and perfume so you wouldn't realise." He grinned again knowing he had done well, he was feeling very proud of himself.

Jane just shook her head laughing unpacking more. Jasper put everything away and put the bags in the bottom of the wardrobe which stood like a guard on duty on the other side of the room.

Jane stripped off her clothes and put them at the bottom of the bed ready to go into the washing bag. Jasper walked out of the bathroom after putting their washing things in there.

"Someone's in a hurry to shower?" Jasper teased "Yes I am, have you seen that shower?"

Jasper picked her up and walked them into the bathroom, Jane didn't bother tying her hair up, the

shower heads came right out of the ceiling so there wouldn't be anywhere to go, she would worry

about sorting it out in the morning. Jasper turned the jets on and put Jane down helping her walk in gently. Jane was smiling happy to be on her own feet. But cautious with the wet floor, the tiles had tiny bumps on them to stop any slipping. The shower heads were powerful as Jane walked under the first one it took her breath away, she was soaked instantly, she began to giggle as Jasper stood under his.

He brushed the water out of his face and ran his fingers through his hair looking over at Jane, he smiled watching her bend back slightly letting the water fall from her hair. Jasper watched for a few seconds as the water touched every part of her body, it bounced off her breasts and cascaded like a waterfall down her body, her nipples were hard, ready for sucking, he felt his cock harden, he moved his hand down his body enjoying the view, rubbing across his chest pinching his nipple making himself hiss, his hand moved down to his stomach, he knew how good she tasted and he was enjoying teasing himself, he moved his hand down to the beginning of his cock and ran his flat hand to the end, teased the tip pinching it gently, groaning.

"Fuck." he groaned again.

He looked down at his cock he was rock hard, he twitched it watching it bounced around making him

smile, "Yes we are going in." he whispered to it.

He moved closer to Jane getting under her shower desperate to touch her. He moved right up behind her cupping her breasts from underneath, she leant back into him sighing, he moved his hands up to her nipples, rubbing them with his fingertips, flicking and pulling on them gently. Jane moaned loudly, he moved her hair away from her neck licking just below her ear as the water ran down. Her body was soft and glistened in the light. His hand moved down her tummy to her pussy, he pushed her legs apart from behind pushing his leg in the middle allowing the water to fall harder onto her pussy making her wetter, his hand moved up her legs, Jane was panting desperate to feel his fingers find her, she pushed her hips out to his hand, he smiled moving his hand away, his cock was pressing into her back the water hitting the head making him twitch more, he bent them both forward and grabbed Jane by her thighs opening her legs further, sliding his finger into her pussy.

"Oh god", Jane moaned loudly. "Yesss." she hissed

"Turn around Belle." He whispered. Sinking his teeth into her shoulder.

Jane did as he asked, he grabbed her face as she turned to him. His hands going into her wet hair, holding her face, his lips grazing across hers, his tongue following, gliding across them pushing into her mouth, dualling with hers, they were hungry for each other. He grabbed her thighs as gently as he could and lifted her up. Still kissing her, Jane held his face kissing him, desperate for him. He lifted her higher, moving his hands between her legs opening her pussy wider from behind, he slid her down his body slowly, Jane gasped as she felt his hard wet cock slip inside her, he lowered her all the way down filling her pussy. They both moaned as Jasper pulled out of her slowly lifting her almost off his cock, the head just teasing her at the opening to her pussy, Jane groaned in disappointment as he slowly impaled her again seconds later. Jane was gasping, as Jasper lifted her faster moving her to the wall. He pushed her against the wet cold wall, she squealed as her back hit the cold tiles. She wrapped her hands around his neck holding on tightly, waiting for his cock again, she felt it slide deeper into her pussy, she could feel his balls against her bottom, slapping each time he pushed deeper inside her, filling her.

"Oh fuck, yes baby, please don't stop." she moaned.

"God, I love the feel of your pussy wrapped around my cock, it's so perfect."

Jane squeezed her pussy muscles trapping him, laughing as he felt her squeeze and release over and over.

"Jesus Belle," his head fell back, "If you don't want me to explode inside you then you better stop." Jane grinned at him squeezing harder and releasing over and over, Jasper felt his balls tighten as he held her tighter.

"Fuck Belle, I'm cuming." he moaned loudly growling at her as his orgasm hit. His body shook as Jane released him, his cock twitching as he emptied himself inside her.

"You are so, so bad, fuck Belle I needed that." She grinned at him again kissing him hard.

"Good that was starters, I will let you recover for a while before we go again." Jasper laughed nervously seeing the old Jane back again, loving every second of it.

He put her down on her feet, checking she was okay, she nodded, he grabbed the shampoo and turned her around washing her hair, Jane put her hands behind her back stroking his cock, Jasper laughed pulling away, he was too sensitive still. Jane grinned knowing she would get her own way later. They finished washing up and Jasper grabbed the towels as he turned the shower off. He picked Jane up and carried her to the bed. Sitting her down and climbing on the bed with her.

He towel dried her hair and combed it through.

"What would you like to wear Belle, shorts and t-shirt, we can light the fire too if you like?"

"That sounds perfect." Jasper climbed off the bed and grabbed their clothes both dressing before Jasper carried Jane into the lounge.

He lit the fire and joined Jane on the sofa he sat up against the arm and Jane was laid between his legs, they sat quietly listening to music watching the flames in the fire.

"Are you warm enough Belle?" Jasper asked looking down at Jane putting his chin on her head. "Yes thank you, quite warm to be honest, if it gets any hotter I will be stripping off."

"Mmmmm Maybe I should stoke the fire even more then?"

Jane dug him in the ribs, "Is there anything else ever on your mind?" she turned looking at him smiling.

"Hmmm let me think, ummmmm with you around? Nope" He laughed grabbing her and squeezing her close to him.

"Right answer Mr Mitchell!"

"Oh really, and what about you Miss Kirkpatrick?"

"Hell No!, you know how much I love your body." They both laughed, Jane moved round so she could see Jasper and pulled her t-shirt off. She was grinning at him as she threw it onto the floor. Jasper moved and did the same not taking his eyes off her.

Jane bit her lip watching him, she put her hand onto his chest and moved her finger down from the V on his neck licking her lips, Jasper just watched feeling his cock getting hard inside his shorts. Jane let her finger glide down his chest onto his nipple, she circled and pinched it, Jasper hissed as she moved across to the other one.

"Fuck Belle, lick it please?" he begged. Jane shook her head grinning.

She continued tracing her finger down his body onto his stomach, she moved from side to side teasing him above his waistband. His cock was straining to get out of his shorts. Jane was smiling looking into his eyes, his breathing was increasing every time she moved her fingers. His cock twitching desperate to be touched. Jane moved her finger down, stroking across the head through his shorts, Jasper groaned. She ran her finger nail up and down his hardening cock..

"Jesus you are such a tease!" Jasper began hissing, his cock twitching.

Jane grinned continuing to run her finger up and down his throbbing cock. He couldn't take anymore, he lifted her up under her arms laying her down on the other end of the sofa, he jumped up and sat astride her, pinning her hands above her head. He held her with one hand. He ran his finger along her lips tickling her, she opened her mouth as he pushed his thumb inside, she closed her mouth looking at him and sucked his thumb in and out of her mouth. He hissed at her again pulling his thumb out rubbing it along her bottom lip. He bent down taking her bottom lip in his mouth biting gently, running his tongue across her swollen wet lips, he pushed his tongue inside. He moved his hand down squeezing her breast rolling her nipple between his thumb and finger. Jane moaned arching her back. He moved off her breast and onto her stomach tracing his finger up and down making patterns as he moved further down, he pushed his finger inside her shorts and moved it side to side. He touched her stomach pushing his finger in lower, Jane began whimpering, Jasper inhaled the air, he could smell her, the scent of lust, he knew she would be soaking wet. He moved his finger further down, he stopped kissing her just looking into her eyes. He moved to the very top of her pussy, touching the hood. He was right she was soaking wet. He slipped his finger into the top just dipping inside, his finger getting coated in her juices, Jane arched off the sofa.

"Please baby push it in?" she pouted whispering.

Jasper smiled, not taking his eyes off her. He pushed his finger back into the hood, his mouth was watering he wanted to dive in and eat her. He pulled his finger out and sucked it hard. "Mmmmmm you taste so good Belle." he smiled

Jane tried to move her arm, she was desperate to move, to suck him, she wriggled under him. Jasper smiled he was holding her tight, he wasn't letting her go just yet. Jane pouted making Jasper laugh. "Is my baby desperate to be sucked and licked?"

Jane nodded. Pouting. Jasper pushed his finger further into her pussy, making her moan loudly, moving his finger in and out he could smell her scent more. His cock was throbbing to get out of his shorts to slide into her pussy, to claim her again. He pushed his finger in deeper reaching her G-spot, Jane was lifting her bottom off the sofa to get more friction from his finger, he moved his thumb and rubbed her clit, Jane groaned louder.

"Fuck baby please don't stop". She begged him.

Jasper pushed harder, fucking her with his finger, bringing her closer to cuming. Slowly pulling his finger out. Jane groaned. He put his hand onto his cock through his shorts and began rubbing himself, Jane watched in awe. Jasper moaned not losing eye contact with Jane. He could quite easily cum but didn't want to, he wasn't ready yet. He stopped and moved down the sofa letting go of Jane's hand, she put her fingers into his hair. He pulled her shorts down as he moved further away from her, lifting her bottom up to take them off, he threw them onto the floor and opened her legs. He lifted them and put them over his shoulders and slid his finger from the bottom of her pussy to the top collecting her juices. Jane arched again up towards him, he caught her bottom and pulled her towards him, he sat on his feet and pulled her against his body, he dipped his head and licked the top of her hood catching a small taste of her. He licked his lips looking at her.

"Mmmmmm my Belle is ripe and ready for me."

Jane laughed at him waiting very impatiently for him to take her. He bent licking her again.

"You taste exquisite my Lady." He teased. Jane groaned again.

He opened her legs wide, opening her pussy wider with his fingers, he rubbed her clit making Jane mewl. He licked her wetness, moaning as he tasted her, he ran his tongue up and down taking more of her juices before pushing his tongue deep inside her. He lapped at her, she was soaked, he

couldn't get enough of her, he sucked harder, Jane could feel her orgasm building. Her body began to tingle. Jasper knew she was ready to cum, he licked harder and faster, his thumb rubbing her clit, Jane pushed into him for more friction from his beard. Jane's body was tingling all over, she felt herself floating, she trembled as it hit, her body going rigid as she came, she couldn't concentrate, she screamed.

"JASPER!!! Oh god! oh god.........! she panted as he licked catching more of her juices, she felt a second orgasm hit her, her body arching away from Jasper as it continued. He pulled her closer licking faster, Jane was pushing his head away without any luck, her body was so sensitive she

couldn't cope anymore. She felt Jasper smile as he continued licking and sucking at her juices. He let her legs go limp as she laid down properly on the sofa panting, Jaspers beard was full of her, he was sucking at the bits around his mouth making a meal out of it and making noises like he was eating the most incredible meal. Jane was laughing at him feeling exhausted, he came down to her kissing her, his wet beard smearing all over her chin, he moved from her lips and licked it off.

"I think you have been holding out on me Belle, you haven't cum so hard in a while." He grinned.

"Oh you think, I don't know how you think I could with that tongue of yours!?"

Jasper laughed, "Maybe you are just super horny for me today then?"

"Always my love."

Jasper moved her legs either side of him, pulling his shorts off, his cock springing out. He moved in close to her as she smiled watching him.

"Comfortable Belle?" has asked Jane nodded "Yes love."

"Good my cock is missing your pussy he wants his turn." Jane giggled.

He rubbed his cock up and down her pussy teasing her and pushed it in just so the head was buried inside her. Jane mewled. He pulled out of her grinning, before pushing a little more inside her. "You are such a tease, please baby fuck me?"

"Oh you want to be fucked do you?, and here was me wanting to make love to you...., in that case......" he lifted her bottom and spanked her pulling her closer, he pushed his cock in hard taking Jane's breath away.

"Is that what you want?" Jane nodded biting her bottom lip. He pulled out again, ramming in harder this time. Jane yelled.

"Oh Jesus Christ, yes, fuck me Jasper please?" Jasper grinned pulling her closer, spanking her again, and pushing harder into her.

"Are you my naughty little Belle, do I need to punish you?" "Yes please baby." she begged

Jasper felt a tingle through his body, he liked this side of her. He slapped her again making it sting this time then rubbed it better, Jane bucked into him, he fucked her harder feeling his balls tighten, he was ready to explode, he slowed down and pulled out so he didn't cum straight away, this new side of Jane was turning him on.

"Jesus Belle I'm going to cum if you keep talking like that." he groaned

"Cum for me Jasper, fill me with all your cum." She begged biting her bottom lip again.

That was the finish for him, his body was on fire, he felt his cock stiffen and he exploded into her, his body going rigid as he pushed against her.

"Oh fuck." he yelled, "Yessss." he hissed, pushing in and out of her faster, Jane squeezed her pussy around him again and again. His body was trembling.

Jane smiled watching his face, she loved the look when he came, he slumped onto her side, moving to lay next to her pulling her onto him.

"I love you Belle." He smiled kissing her nose. Panting trying to catch his breath. "But surely to god that was too quick, Jesus you will be the death of me but what a way to go." he smiled.

"I love you too Jasper, if you don't want me to talk dirty I won't!"

"I didn't say that, but it drives me nuts that's all." Jane grinned, knowing she had him where she

wanted him, round her little finger. He pulled her closer wrapping his arms around her.

"This is perfect, I could stay like this forever with you."

"Mmmm, yes, me too love, but I suppose we better put the dinner on before it gets too late?"

"Yes good idea, he kissed her nose and moved his arm sitting up. "Do you want your clothes back?

He laughed.

"No thank you, it seems like forever since we were naked together."

He picked up their clothes and folded them leaving them on the side, he went to their room and grabbed the wipes and a towel so they could freshen up. He left them with Jane and went into the kitchen to put the dinner in the oven returning to Jane on the sofa. He pulled her into his arms.

"Belle, I really don't know what I did to deserve you, you make loving you so easy and so real, you love me unconditionally. If anyone wants to know what true love is. I just have to show them your picture or point to you. You are the most precious heavenly gift. I promise to cherish you forever." He looked at Jane and watched as she wiped a tear from her eye.

"Hey, what's wrong?"

"You never fail to amaze me with your words, you spoil me that's all."

"it's all true Belle." He kissed her head holding his lips against her for a few seconds squeezing her tighter. He pulled a strand of her hair and twisted it around his finger, it was so soft, he pulled it towards his nose and lips kissing it and inhaling the smell.

The cooker alarm sounded letting them know it was dinner time. Jasper scooped Jane up and took her to the table while he got the dinner out of the oven. It was getting closer to dusk, they sat at the table overlooking the back of the house, Jane could see the woods and the fields. Beyond the huge shed outside.

"How do you feel about getting on the quad tomorrow and going for a ride, they are all hand controlled, the field is huge you can ride around it and then we could go down to the stream through the trees?"
"Oh wow, yes please that would be amazing, can we have the mud too so I can show you how to
ride properly?" Jane teased.
"In your dreams lady." he laughed
"Worth a try, but I will whoop your arse out there next time we come back."
Jasper laughed, he loved the feisty side of Jane. He kissed her hand smiling as they finished up dinner. He cleared the plates and carried her back to the sofa.

"I will be back in a few minutes, do you need anything from the bedroom Belle?" he asked picking up
the towel and the wipes.
"No thank you." Jane bent her head back over the arm of the sofa looking up at him.
Jasper went into the bedroom, he went to his bag in the bottom of the cupboard and picked the box out with the necklace in. He took the chain out and cupped it into his hands walking back into the lounge, Jane was laid on her back looking up to the ceiling singing to herself. He knelt down next to her, bent and kissed her nipple. Jane smiled without opening her eyes, he kissed her chin and onto her lips.

Music to my eyes Lady Gaga

"Belle?" he spoke softly.
"Hmmm?" she moaned still with her eyes closed.

"I love you so very much, there are not enough words to describe how I feel about you, how deeply I love you. I fell in love with the most amazing woman any man could desire. I ask myself regularly am I worthy of your love and I hope I can prove it to you for the rest of my life."

Jane sat up as he began talking, she saw a tear slide from his eye this time. She wiped it away cupping his face with her hand. She bent forward and kissed him.

"No baby I am the lucky one, you found me, you smiled at me that day."

I will forever be grateful to whoever it is up there looking after you." Jane smiled sadly.

Jasper lifted his hand and opened his palm. Jane looked down, putting her fingers on the edge of his hand, her other hand shot to her mouth.

"Oh my god Jasper!" She squealed, scared to touch the necklace. She was grinning. Not sure what to do.

"Belle I know your fingers are still swollen, and I wanted to give you this while you were in hospital but I decided to wait until we were here because you couldn't have worn it in there anyway."

He took it out of his hand and placed it in hers. Jane began to cry tracing her finger gently across the
two J's.

"Where did you find it? It's so delicate and beautiful?" she sniffed.

"I drew it and took it into the old jeweller in town, he added to it for me, making it what it is

Now." Jasper cupped her face and wiped her tears with his thumb. Kissing her nose.

Jane turned her head and kissed his cupped hand. Silently crying looking at the necklace, the tears running down her face. Jasper took it out of her hand gently and put it round her neck. Jane wrapped her hand around catching a sob in her throat. She looked up at Jasper her eyes full of more tears. She sniffed and roughly wiped her face.

"You make me feel so precious, like a delicate flower or a butterfly, it's incredible, I don't know what
to say to you though, thank you isn't enough, I am lost for words. I have never felt so loved and
cared for in a relationship as I do with you. It's like you are my final piece of the jigsaw." Her lip began trembling again, Jasper slipped his hand into either side of her head into her hair and brought her to him, kissing her hard, their lips crashed together, Jane's body tingled, Jasper forced her lips open with his tongue, his searching for hers, Jane grabbed his hands, pushing her tongue into his mouth, they duelled tasting each other. Jasper let go of Jane's face still kissing her, he slid his hands around her body, he sat on the sofa and pulled her onto his knee as he leant back into the sofa, Jane moved round and sat astride him. Jaspers cock was awake already, he wanted her again and again. He didn't want to hurt her they had made love a lot already, he shook his head and Jane pouted.

"No Belle, I want you all the time, but I am not leaving you in pain, I want to take you to bed and
wrap myself around you. Hold you in my arms until the morning."

Jane sat up letting go of him. "I could never imagine I could love you anymore than I do right now, any other man with a cock as hard as yours would have just taken me, but not you."

"Believe me Belle this is hard to say, but we have 5 days on our own why hurt you now just for the sake of having incredible sex over and over." He laughed.

Jane cocked her head to the side looking at him questioningly "That came out wrong Belle." he laughed again.

She put her hands on her hips and thrummed her fingers looking very unimpressed, she was teasing him, she knew exactly what he was trying to say. He grabbed her again pulling her into him.

"Grrrrrr I love you so much woman!" Jane couldn't be serious.

"I love you too stud, now take me to bed even if it is only to lay with me." She smiled.

Jasper spanked her bottom making Jane screech. "What was that for?" she pouted looking at him. "You are such a tease young lady." Jane grinned coyly. Jasper put his hands under her armpits and shimmied forward on the sofa standing with her. She wrapped her legs around his waist.

"Last chance stud." she giggled, wriggling around on him. He spanked her again making her bottom very red. Jane rubbed it mouthing *"ouch"* Jasper laughed turning the lights off over the fireplace and carried Jane into the bathroom.

They washed up and cleaned their teeth before Jasper picked Jane up and took her back into the bedroom. Jane laid on the bed and moved into the middle.

"oh my god I love this bed!" she said doing snow fairies, Jasper stood watching her laughing.

He knelt on the bed at her feet grabbing her when she closed her legs.

"Another reason that I love you Belle, you are such a child at times." he laughed.

Jane smiled at him and beckoned him to her with her finger biting her bottom lip. He crawled up to her on his knees Jane was laughing as he kissed up her body. He reached her tummy and blew a raspberry on her making her squeal with laughter. He continued to her nipples and kissed each one before moving up her neck.

"You are supposed to do that going in the other direction." she pouted.

Jasper laughed. "I told you enough for today, I will devour you again tomorrow."

Jane folded her arms sulking. "I might not want you tomorrow, you are so sure of yourself." Jasper moved quickly back to her tummy, blowing more raspberries on her, she started squealing again begging him to stop.

"Not until you admit you want me as much as I want you?" he teased her going back to her tummy.

"Okay, okay, yes ,yes I want you too, please stop!" she giggled trying to catch her breath.

Jasper stopped as Jane laid panting, he could see she was trying to think of something else to say, he laid down next to her pulling her into his arms, her bottom against his cock. He pushed it into her.

"This is what you do to me 24/7 Belle, regardless of what you are doing. I want you more than anything but like I said earlier I don't want to overwork your leg that muscle is still healing and you want to go out on the quad tomorrow so you have to rest."

"I know love, I just love teasing you, and I have gone long enough without your body I am making up for lost time." She grabbed his head with her hand bringing it down onto her shoulder and pushed her bottom into his hard cock. He sank his teeth into her shoulder nibbling at her and spanked her again.

"Such a bad girl Belle." Jane was grinning. "Now get under these covers it will get cold later in the night." They both moved their legs and got under the duvet and snuggled into each other. Jane suddenly sat up straight. Jasper jumped she moved so quick.

"Belle? What's wrong love?"

"My necklace, take it off please I don't want to break it in the night."

"Bloody hell woman are you trying to give me a heart attack?"

"Sorry but I don't want to damage it do I?"

"I know that, but you didn't need to scare the hell out of me in the process."

Jane giggle while Jasper unclipped it and handed it to her so she could put it on the nightstand. Jane laid back down and let out a huge sigh and snuggled back into Jasper.

They both woke up with the sun shining in through the window the following morning and to the smell of bacon cooking. Jane looked round at Jasper, he smiled at her kissing her nose.

"Good Morning baby. How did you sleep?"

"As well as you Belle I think."

"I don't think I want to get up either." she laughed

Jasper sat up stretching running his hands through his hair.

"Well I'm afraid to say my lady it is 9.15 and Lily is here cooking so we better get some clothes on and go and eat."

Jane stretched and moaned yawning. "No, no, no, don't make me get up pleaseeeeee." she begged. Jasper laughed at her getting out of bed and grabbing their pajamas, he sat on the bed next to Jane. "You either sit up now or I strip the bed and blow raspberries on your tummy, your choice?"

"You wouldn't dare, you know I will scream and do you want Lily to hear?"

"Oh Belle you should know better than to dare me." He pulled the bedding off her, she was grabbing at it trying to protect herself, He dived onto her blowing onto her tummy, Jane squealed loudly, Jasper stopped and laughed.

"So?"

"okay, okay. Spoil sport, I'm getting up." Jane pouted taking her pyjamas from Jasper and getting

dressed. He dressed himself and scooped her up into his arms and headed to the kitchen.

Chapter 30

Time for fun

They walked into the kitchen and Lily was busy cooking when they arrived, the table was laid with fresh juices, cereals and toast.

"Morning Lily they called in unison." She looked around and smiled at them both, moved the pan off the stove and walked up to them hugging them both.

"I hope you slept well?"

"Like a log thank you Lily, Jasper said neither of us moved in the night, and I haven't slept so well in a

very long time. I think I need to take your bed home."

"Well I am sure Henry would be more than happy to build you one."

"Oh no Lily, I wouldn't even think of asking him, the poor guy is enjoying his retirement of sorts."

Jasper replied shaking his head.

"Oh, he would love it, you boys are all the same Jasper, you love to tinker and do things, he is not happy unless he can get into the workshop. Anyway, sit, let me finish cooking, what eggs would you two lovebirds like?"

Jane blushed "Fried please Lily." "Same for me too."

"Coming right up. You know you to remind me of me and my Henry, we used to tease each other a lot too."

Jane looked over at Jasper with her mouth wide open mouthing "Oh my god, she heard!"

"Sorry Jane darling I didn't mean to embarrass you, these walls are thick, but somethings do come

Through." She turned and winked at Jane.

Jane buried her head in her hands and began laughing.

"Please don't be embarrassed, do you know how good it is to hear laughter and two people playing in this house. It's been a long time. My kids don't bother they are all too busy, having you two here is a breath of fresh air for us. Normally we get either men, like Jasper and his friends or families, then we are not really wanted or needed. I was so excited to hear from Jasper, when he told us all about you, I couldn't wait to meet you." She turned around with the two plates and placed them on the table in front of them wiping her hands on her pinny.

"Anyway, that is me done, please tuck in I will leave you two alone and drop your dinner in later. How does beef casserole sound with dumplings?"
They both nodded smiling.
"Perfect, I will leave it on the stove for when you are ready later. I will see you both in the morning. There is fresh bread and plenty of meat, cheese and spreads to choose from for lunch." She blew them a kiss and left.
Jane watched as Henry came walking across from the old barn, he kissed her taking her hand in his and walked her to their vehicle, he helped her in patting her bottom, walking round to his side climbing in before he drove across the field back home.
"I hope we are still like that when we are their age." She said tucking into her breakfast. Jasper put his hand out to take Jane's.
"Yes Belle we will." he lifted her hand and kissed her fingers.
"Oh you big smoothie talker."
"It's true Belle."
"I know but you are still a smooth talker, now eat while it's hot."
"Now you are sounding like Lily." They both laughed tucking into their breakfast.
They finished up eating and sat with a cup of tea chatting about the house. They talked about anything they would change to make it their perfect hideaway, Jane had fallen in love with the inside.
Jasper loaded the dishwasher and turned it on, he picked Jane up and carried her to the bathroom.

"Quick shower now Belle then we can get out on the quads, we can shower again later if you like?" "Oh my god yes!" Jasper laughed carrying her into the bathroom.

He stood Jane up and helped her undress pulling her top over her head and Jane pushed her bottoms down. He laughed watching her, she knotted her hair up as Jasper clipped it for her, they both walked into the shower watching each other as they quickly washed themselves down, Jane was struggling to keep her head out of the water, Jasper laughed watching her. They finished up, Jasper picked her up, wrapping her in a towel and walked them both into the bedroom, to get dressed.

"Ready Belle?"

"Hell yeah, Get me out there!" Jasper laughed, Jane was sat like a little girl waiting to go on a funfair

ride.

Jasper picked her up and walked out to the patio doors,

"If I leave you on the porch swing I will grab our jackets and boots, then we will go into the barn and get kitted up." Jane nodded, sniffing the air.

"Wow this is beautiful." She sat back on the swing rocking herself as Jasper came out and sat next to

her.

"Lovely isn't it Belle?"

"It's incredible and the smell of fresh air is amazing." Jasper handed her the boots and she put them on while he did his own, once they had their jackets on he picked her up and carried her down to the barn. Jane was clapping her hands in excitement when she spotted the quads.

"Put me down, put me down please." She squealed in excitement, Jasper couldn't help but laugh, he

loved seeing her like this.

He stood her up and Jane walked with him over to the quads holding onto his arm, she was squeezing him in excitement.

"Oh my god I am so excited, I want this one." she smiled pointing at the silver one.

"If your Ladyship pleases, but first you need to put your coveralls on and crash helmet." They walked back over to the cupboard and Jasper grabbed all they needed and helped Jane into her coveralls. They were too long for her Jasper laughed taking a quick picture of her stood with the crotch hanging down to her knees and the legs were gathered up to her knees. Jane swatted him with the long arms, he knelt down and tucked the legs up for her as she folded the arms up. He got up kissing her nose.

"Right, no being silly, no daredevil turns or silliness remember you are still healing, if you do then we won't come back out. Agreed?" Jane nodded frantically as Jasper held back a smile trying to be serious. He kissed her again slipping a disposable head cover on and then her crash helmet. He did it up for her before putting his own on and walked her to the quad. He picked her up and sat her on it passing her the gloves. Jane fired it up and revved the engine, Jasper shook his head not sure now he had done the right thing.

He climbed onto his quad and started the engine, Jane pulled away first, slowly. Jasper followed knowing that was hard for her to do. He was expecting her to go crazy on the field to let off some steam, he just hoped she was careful. He shook his head as they entered the gate onto the field Jane roared off, Jasper sat laughing watching her. He followed quickly. Jane looked behind at him grinning, waiting for him to catch up knowing she was going to be told off. Jasper caught up smiling at her. She sat revving the engine leaning forward making Jasper laugh, when she least expected it he shot off in front of her.

Jane laughed. Smacking her leg. "So it's like that is it Mr?"

She chased Jasper across the field, he stopped at the far end and turned waiting for her to catch up.

"Now who is playing games?" she asked pretending to be annoyed.

"Oh, did I do something wrong Belle?" he teased cocking his head to the side smiling at her.

"Of course not dear."

"Ouch! Someone isn't happy, you never call anyone Dear because you hate the word." He laughed Jane couldn't keep a straight face she burst into a fit of the giggles.

"Oh, I can't pretend to be annoyed with you no matter how hard I try."

"Glad to hear it." he pulled his quad up to Jane and pretended to kiss her through his helmet, Jane laughed at him.

She revved the engine, laid down against the handles and sped off in the other direction, Jasper was hot on her heels chasing after her. They played around for a while on the field, kicking up dust.

Jasper noticed Jane started slowing down, he pulled alongside her and motioned to go back towards the barn. Jane nodded as Jasper went in front of her directing her to the stream. They pulled into a quiet spot. Jasper got of his quad removing his crash helmet, and gloves getting off to help Jane. He helped her climb off then walked her the few steps to a bench and sat down, Jasper pulled her into him kissing her head.

"How are you feeling Belle?"

"Tired but great, I really enjoyed that." she smiled.

"Good, I kind of got the idea you were."

Jane turned, stretched her body up to him grabbing his face in her hands kissed him and caught his lip in her teeth. She sucked it into her mouth smiling, Jasper was laughing and dribbling as she continued to suck on it. He was making funny noises making Jane laugh. She let go of his lip and kissed him hard, Jasper grabbed her bottom with both hands pulling her up to him, Jane squealed as he spanked her. They both stopped suddenly their eyes boring into each other as they heard rustling behind them in the bushes. Jane gasped and turned quickly grabbing Jaspers hand.

"Oh my god, what is that noise?"

Jasper put his finger to her lips to quieten her, he had an idea, he got his phone out quietly and propped it on the back of the bench. They sat watching, Jane's heart was pounding. Jasper started to smile as he noticed a nose poking out of the bushes, then he saw the big black eyes, it stopped, Jasper was taking pictures waiting for it to show itself. Then its head appeared. Jane gasped and quickly put her hand over her mouth. The deer came out very slowly, Jane began to grin looking at Jasper desperate to squeal. The deer got a little closer. Jasper whispered to Jane.

"Don't move." she squeezed his leg, letting him know she understood.

The deer didn't take her eyes off them as she moved out of the bushes. They didn't move. The bushes rustled again, Jane's eyes grew larger they were like saucers. A smaller nose and head appeared, the mother stopped and looked back as her fawn followed her. He was more inquisitive and stopped, looking straight at Jane and Jasper, Jane was overcome with excitement. The fawn walked towards them. Jane thought she would pass out with excitement. He stood only feet away from them staring. They didn't move. The mother came towards them and took the fawn with her, as she walked towards the water out of their way, Jane gasped for air and shook her whole body

waving her arms about but not screaming. Jasper couldn't help but laugh. He grabbed her squeezing

her tight.

"Oh Belle, can you believe we just saw that!? My god that was incredible."

Jane was just nodding, "Oh my god, oh my god, did you see that, oh my god!" she repeated herself,

Jasper was laughing at her.

"Yes Belle, I did." he laughed. They slumped onto the bench, Jasper grabbed Jane into his arms.

"Let's see what we caught on camera." they huddled together as Jasper went through shot by shot,

they couldn't believe how good some of the shots were.

Jasper felt overcome with excitement, seeing Jane so excited and alive again he just knew she was going to be okay. He saw his girl coming back to him. He knew this is what they both needed.

"Come on let me show you the stream properly, if we sit on that rock there you will get a better
View."
Jane nodded and stood, Jasper took her weight but allowed her to walk to the rock. They sat down on it Jasper pulled Jane into him again.
The sun had caught the water perfectly is was shining like a mirror, there was a gentle sound of the rippling water as it cascaded over the stones, the wind was blowing gently through the leaves and the birds were chatting all around them.
Jane was looking up into the trees. "Do you ever get dizzy when you look up into tall trees Jasper?"
He smiled. Loving the odd comments she came out with.
"Can't say I ever look up Belle to be honest." he smiled.
"So, try please?" She looked at him questioningly. Jasper smiled and looked up.
"Sorry no Belle it doesn't, maybe it's because you are so short?" he cringed waiting for the slap and he didn't need to wait too long as Jane slapped him hard across the arm. He began to laugh and grabbed her covering her in kisses as she pushed at him to be let go.
"I'm sorry Belle." He laughed. "I was just teasing you."
"So, stop laughing then Mr, or you will be in the spare room tonight." Jane was trying to be serious but seeing Jasper desperately trying not to laugh she was fit to burst too.
"You wouldn't do that to me baby would you?" "Oh, don't tempt me."
"Belle I'm sorry baby." He begged still laughing.
"Of course you are, so why are you still laughing at me?" Jasper grabbed her again and kissed her
head and nose.
"You know I can't help but laugh Belle, you are so funny, you give me butterflies even though you
are here. I just love your silliness."

Jane pretended to be moody as Jasper held her tighter kissing her face and neck, he moved her hair from the back of her neck. Pushing her head slightly forward and began kissing her. Jane felt a tingle through her body, she leant her head further down as Jasper nipped at her following it with a lick. Jane trembled her body covered in goose bumps. He gently blew onto her neck as he kissed her further down, he moved her around and bent her head to the side, licking up to her ear, Jane moaned softly, she could feel herself getting wet. He knew this drove her nuts. She grabbed his thigh and squeezed.

"If you continue to do that, I won't be responsible for my actions." She grinned up at him whispering,

he grinned at her and sank his teeth into her neck. Pretending to bite her like Dracula.

Jane giggled as Jasper sat her up. "We don't want to shock the fawn and damage it for the rest of it's life now do we?" he laughed

"Very true, so what are you waiting for Mr Mitchell, get me home." she demanded.

Jasper scooped her up and carried her to the trike trying to growl and bite her like a tiger. Jane was giggling again as he sat her on the seat.

"We will come back tomorrow if you like and sit her a while?"

"That would be lovely." Jane grabbed her crash helmet and slipped it on, they were very close to the barn, but she wasn't taking any chances, Jasper did the same and they headed back in. When they arrived Henry was closing the gates. He waved as they pulled in.

Henry came over to them both as they parked up.

"Did you enjoy that?"

"It was fantastic thank you Henry." Jane grinned.

"You're both very welcome. Just leave your suits there I will get them cleaned off and ready for your next outing. Don't bother hosing down Son we are not expecting any rain its only dust they will do for another run out then I will wash them for you."

"I won't hear of it Henry, I will wash them down after the next run. You have both done more than
enough for us."

"Jasper we enjoy having you here, you and the boys were a lot of fun and it was nice for someone to actually be interested in the place and want to know about the build. We don't get many visitors like you up here. So please let us spoil you both."

Jasper nodded in defeat. "Nothing I can say to that really. Except if you ever reconsider my offer it
still stands, I will snap your hand off to buy this place from you."

"Now you are teasing me, come on you two let's get you in for some tea."

"I mean it Henry, I don't joke about money matters and this place stole my heart the day I arrived, it has since stolen Belles."

"Thank you both, you make me very proud, our kids don't bother as you know, so maybe Jasper one day I will accept your offer."

Jasper grinned in excitement just the thought of owning this place filled him with so much excitement, he could imagine many holidays here with Lady running around with them. He scooped Jane up and kissed her.

"Come on love, that's enough excitement for one day, I think you need a rest."

Jane nodded and laid against his shoulder. Henry went on ahead and opened the doors. They walked into the smell of cakes baking and fresh bread.

"Lily, you really are spoiling us!" Jane exclaimed

"Well it's nice to be able too, now sit, don't worry about the boots sit." "Sorry Lily, I will clean the dust up after for you."

Henry laughed behind them. "I would like to see you try."

"Would you please both join us?"

"Oh no we couldn't impose." Lily refused.

"We insist."

"As you said Henry, I don't refuse Jane either so please sit."

They both pulled a chair out and sat down. Lily played Mum serving everyone until Jane ordered her to sit and took over. They chatted easily talking about England. Jasper made them laugh with the story of how they met. Leaving out the naughty parts. Henry told them how he and Lily met and fell in love. Jasper watched them intently he could see after all these years how much they still loved each other, the small touches the glances between them both, Jasper smiled looking at Jane talking to Lily, the sun caught her hair giving her a glow like an angel, the different shades in her hair glinting like gold. He imagined that's how she was with her Mum, he felt so at peace here with them all.

"Jasper, penny for them?" Lily asked

"Sorry Lily, I was just looking around the table at you all feeling very relaxed and at home. After all that Jane has been through seeing her looking so relaxed with you both I realised how lucky I am. In such a short space of time you two have become very special people to me."

Lily got up and walked around the table with tears in her eyes, Jasper stood towering over her as she wrapped her arms around his waist. Hugging him hard.

"You are a very special man, we saw that the day you first arrived, we think a lot of you too and we are getting to know you more. Your calls mean so much to us, it's like having another Son and one that cares and always checks in with us. Having you here is very special for us both. Meeting Jane and seeing you so happy makes us happy too." Jasper kissed the top of Lily's head and squeezed her tight.

"Thank you Lily." She looked up at him, he could see the tears in her eyes, he wiped them away with his fingers smiling at her. Wondering how their own children could just forget about them, he didn't like to judge people but couldn't understand it.

Lily laughed, "Look at me silly old fool." She grabbed the bottom of her pinny, wiping her eyes again. Everyone laughed and stood coming together for a group hug.

"You will have us all in tears in a minute love if you keep on." Henry laughed wiping his own eyes patting Jasper on the back, they all sat down and continued chatting and laughing.

"Henry did you know you have a fawn around the stream, we saw it earlier?" Jane asked.
"Oh yes I took some pictures" Jasper replied grabbing his phone out of his pocket.
He showed them all, flicking through the various shots.
"Well we haven't had a fawn for some years, that is great news isn't it Lily?"
"Yes it is, how wonderful, they are so inquisitive too, just remember they don't understand the road,
we have lost so many out there.
"Hopefully they won't venture that way and will stay back here."
"We can only hope Son." Henry said patting Jaspers arm.
"Right then who has room for cream tea?"
Jane's eyes were out on stalks again and not for seeing the Deer. Lily took the cover off the scones,
they were huge, very misshapen and full of fruit.
"Wow Lily, I think I need some cooking lessons please!? These look amazing." Jane beamed at her.
"Oh, that would be a pleasure love, anytime." Jane clapped her hands.
"She will hold you to that Lily." Jasper laughed.
Lily got up and collected the Jam Clotted cream from the fridge.
"In the UK Lily when you go to Cornwall and Devon cream teas are very popular and they both have
their own ways of making them."
"Oh really, well it's pretty simple. Jam on then cream on top."
"Ah well that's the Cornish way. The Devonshire way is cream first then Jam on top, it causes many arguments like which way to hang the toilet paper."
"Oh my, how funny, so which way do you do yours Jasper. I am with you Lily, I love my Jam and you get more cream on if you do it last."

"Ahh well I have to be honest I think I must be Devon then, I prefer my cream on first." Henry laughed cutting into his scone and filling both sides with cream.

"Devonshire Henry." Lily laughed.

"So what is Devon like then Jane?"

"It's beautiful, very quaint, tiny cottages, next to the sea. It is called the Jurassic coast. It is stunning, that then goes into Cornwall which is a surfers paradise, if you look at the map of the UK it is the foot at the bottom left. It is also apparently the home of the mermaid. The legend says there were mermaids in and around St Ives and a singer in a church was swayed by the beauty of one and he disappeared into the sea never to be seen again. But fisherman believe they can hear him singing, and if you upset a mermaid it will bring bad luck."

"Sounds beautiful though, I do love a good love story." Lily replied.

"Yes, very romantic. The UK is full of beautiful stories of love. Just the men don't seem to be very romantic these days." Jane laughed. Jasper cleared his throat.

"Are you forgetting that I am British Belle? Am I not romantic enough for you?"

"Ah, but you have been in the US for more than 20 years so it's rubbed off on you."

They all laughed as Jasper pouted pushing his bottom lip out further.

"It's ok Son, I get told by Lily quite often I am not romantic enough when she watches one of her soppy sentimental films." He looked across at Lily winking at her.

"Well I hope we are like you when we have been married even half as many years as you two have."

Jane said looking at both Lily and Henry with so much affection.

"Oh, don't be fooled it hasn't been all plain sailing Jane love, we had our spats over the years, but we

never went to bed on a fight and always said I love you before we went to sleep."

"Oooh that's beautiful, I hope you are taking note Jasper?" Jane laughed

"Oh of course, you just remember that too lady." he teased.

"Henry, would you do it all again if you had your time over?" Jane asked

"Yes, I would without question, Lily is my best friend my soul mate, I knew the first time I set eyes on her, she came into the café I was in with my friends. I had just been called up, it was 1967 and the Vietnam war was in full swing, we were being shipped out within days and were saying goodbye to friends and family although most of us were going we didn't expect to be together.

She sat with her friend in a beautiful yellow dress, she had many underskirts on too, with a cardigan on her shoulders. She had her hair at her shoulders a picture of absolute beauty, and she has grown to be more beautiful today. I couldn't keep my eyes off her and decided I didn't have time to waste so went to offer to buy her a coffee, her smile lit up the café when she looked at me, I was mesmerized. We went for a walk after, her friend was very kind and left us to it. She had a boyfriend who was also being sent to Vietnam, we spent the next two days together living and

breathing in each other's pockets, she promised to write to me everyday and she did, we still have the letters. It was hell over there, but I knew my Lily was waiting for me to come home, she kept me alive every day, her smell on the letters brought me home every time I closed my eyes, we fell in love through our letters. When I got home she was waiting for me. I grew up very quickly but she kept me grounded." He looked over at Lily and winked at her.

"We were married within a few months of me getting back. August the 22nd 1968. Our oldest Son was born 9 months later. We have had just over 47 years together and I can say hand on heart I never regretted one. Lily is my life."

Jane wiped her eyes and laughed. "Sorry I think that is the most romantic thing I have ever heard." "Please excuse my lady she is very emotional at the best of times." They all laughed and Lily lent across hugging Jane.

"Right then let's get this table cleared and go home Henry, let's leave these two to relax."
"Leave it please Lily let us do it, we are more than capable." Jane nodded at her agreeing with Jasper.
She sighed. "Okay, okay." raising her hands in defeat, "You win." Henry laughed "Well that's a first, you gave in easily Lil."
"No, I knew I wouldn't win with these two." everyone laughed, Jasper hugged Lily. "As my Dad used to say, we are old enough and ugly enough to do it ourselves."
"Speak for yourself Belle." Jasper laughed. Jane threw her napkin at him across the table.

"Right that is our time to exit let these youngsters fight in peace Lily." He grabbed her hand and
walked her out of the house, they turned and waved, Lily was blowing kisses.
"See you two tomorrow, your dinner is in the fridge. All instructions are on the label."
Jasper and Jane blew kisses laughing as they walked out. Jasper came across to Jane and hugged her.
"Such beautiful people."
"Yes they are, certainly would be proud to have them as parents wouldn't you love?" Jane asked
looking up at Jasper.
"Christ yes, sure would. Right then let's clear this table. If I put you and your chair next to the dishwasher would you like to load it?"
Jane nodded. "Yes of course." Jasper picked her up and moved her to the dishwasher. "I didn't think
you would do that she squealed."
"Well I wasn't going to move you separately silly."
"Obviously." Jane laughed, she turned and began loading the dishwasher, Jasper added the last few bits and carried her back to the table with her chair then lifted her over to the sofa, he

turned and sat down holding her so she sat on his knee. She moved down so her head was in his lap and stretched out down the sofa. She stretched yawning.

"Do you want a sleep Belle? I can take you to the bedroom and let you sleep for a while, you look shattered?"

"Would you mind?"

"Of course not silly." Jane sat up, Jasper got up lifted her into his arms and carried her into the bedroom.

"Shout when you are awake and I will come and get you, I will be sat on the porch for a while."

He put her onto the bed, she pulled her clothes off and got under the duvet, Jasper lent across and kissed her head. He pulled the curtains, walked out and pulled the door closed slightly behind him, walking out onto the porch he pulled his phone out and sat on the swing. He was looking through the pictures he took of the deer and her fawn, he was quite pleased with himself.

He started to feel tired and his eyes were closing, he moved to the chair and sat back letting himself go to sleep.

He woke up sometime later feeling a chilly breeze, he rubbed his face to wake himself up and

stretched he looked at his watch it was almost 5.30pm he needed to wake Jane or she wouldn't sleep later, he stood and walked into the house and heard Jane calling him. He smiled as he walked into the bedroom.

"Sorry Belle have you been calling long, I fell asleep on the porch?"

"No love, I just woke up and didn't want to go into the bathroom without you just in case."

"Come on then." He said pulling the bedclothes back and scooping her up. Walking her into the bathroom.

"I would like a shower too please if you don't mind?"

"Of course, he sat her on the toilet and pulled his t-shirt off over his head, pushing his jeans down and pulling them off with his feet, he kicked them over towards the door with his t-shirt. Jane smiled up at him pulling him towards her from behind, she sank her teeth into his bottom and giggled. He span around his cock level with her mouth, Jane looked up at him and smiled. He was semi hard, she lifted it with her fingers whilst looking up at him teasing the tip making Jasper gasp, he watched her intently as she licked him up and down not taking her eyes off him. She covered the tip with her lips and sucked him gently

"Oh Belle, I will never tire of your lips on my cock, you drive me nuts."

Jane just smiled and continued sucking. Jasper grew harder, she moved her hand down his cock which was now standing on its own as she sucked him deeper, almost gagging as she tried to get him all in. Jasper hissed grabbing her head pulling her off and pushing her back on again.

"Fuck Belle."

Jane pulled him closer digging her fingers into his bottom, he clenched his cheeks and pushed into her mouth harder, Jane smiled. She cupped his bottom and sucked faster. She loved the control she had over him like this. She stopped suddenly pulling him out of her mouth wiping the saliva from her mouth and blew him a kiss. Jaspers mouth dropped open.

"Belle? What the hell are you doing to me?" he laughed amazed she just stopped.

She wiped herself and stood up flushing the toilet behind her. Like nothing had happened.

Jasper laughed, "Oh, it's like that is it you little tease? Two can play at that." He laughed supporting
her to the shower.

Jane just smiled. "I don't know what you mean?" She turned and switched the shower on and walked in smiling. Jasper joined her and smacked her hard on her bottom making her squeal. "Ow! What was that for?"

"Nothing Belle, my hand slipped." He grinned

He grabbed the shampoo and began washing Jane's hair, he bent down to her whispering.

"You will pay for that later Belle." he smiled carrying on washing her hair.

They both showered and Jasper scooped her up carrying her back to the bed. They dressed in shorts and t-shirt and Jane started drying her hair.

"Belle I'm going to get the dinner on. Give me a shout when you are ready." he bent and kissed her leaving the bedroom.

Marvin Gaye Lets get it on

Jane smiled to herself she had a cunning plan, she knew she could stand on her leg for a short time and she wanted to tease Jasper more. She dried her hair and got off the bed going to his wardrobe, she found what she wanted got changed and waited until she heard the music go on, she knew he would be sat down now, so she walked out of the room carefully.

Marvin Gaye Let's get it on started to play. "Perfect" she whispered to herself.

She saw Jasper sat on the sofa his head back with his eyes closed. She leant against the wall and cleared her throat. Jasper looked up, his mouth dropped open. She had her bad leg raised and bent up. Her good leg holding her up. She was dressed in one of his shirts which she buttoned up just below her cleavage she also found a tie and left it lose around her neck pulled on some stockings and suspenders, she would love to have put heels on but that wasn't a good idea. She had her red thong on, put her hair up and glasses on leaving them to slip down her nose. Jasper could see her stockings under his shirt, he grinned, feeling aroused already. He laughed nervously seeing her.

"Hang on let me put the song back on." He grinned.

He started the song again and got comfortable adjusting his already hardening cock and sat watching the show.

Jane started to move to the music running her leg up and down the wall swaying her bottom to the beat of the song. Jasper was grinning from ear to ear feeling his cock hardening. She pushed away from the wall pushing her bottom out, raising his shirt up over her thigh showing her stockings, looking at him smiling. She walked across the room to him as she undid his tie. She took it off and beckoned him with her finger whilst biting her bottom lip teasing him, she put it over his head, looking into his eyes licking her lips, pulling him towards her. He moved closer to kiss her, she smiled pulling away, kissed his nose and let go of his tie pushing him back. Jasper laughed in frustration and laid back against the sofa.

She backed away slowly swinging her hips to the beat undoing his shirt. Never losing eye contact. She left just a couple of buttons done up at the bottom and let it slip off her shoulder showing most of her bare breast. She moved closer again running her finger across his lips he opened his mouth and sucked it hard making it wet. She backed away and slid her finger down her cleavage circling her nipple, Jasper hissed. He lifted his bottom off the sofa to re-adjust his shorts, his cock was solid desperate to get out. He was moaning deeply biting his bottom lip watching her.

Jane turned away still moving her hips and bending in front of him opening her legs wide so he could see the wetness on her thong. As she stood she let the shirt slide down her back moving it from side to side looking over her shoulder at him. As she turned she undid the remaining buttons and let the shirt fall to her wrists showing her body. She twirled it around and threw it to him. He grabbed it screwed it up and inhaled the smell of her on it.

He was moaning desperate to grab her, he didn't take his eyes off her.
"Fuck Belle." He whispered. He couldn't take anymore he started to rub his cock through his shorts. It was straining to get out. He cupped his balls while smelling his shirt.
Jane slipped her fingers into the string of her thong and started to pull it down one side at a time still moving to the music. She turned, as she slipped it down over her bottom gasping as the cool air hit her naked wet pussy.

She let the thong drop to the floor and stepped out of it turning and kicking it towards Jasper. He grabbed it and held it to his nose, licking it tasting and smelling her juices on it. She unclipped her hair and let it fall down her back, took her glasses off and put them next to him. She pushed her fingers into her pussy letting her head fall back her hair touching her bottom. She moved closer to him as he replayed the song and put her fingers into his mouth so he could taste her. He sucked her juices off growling at her. She was stood close enough that he could touch her.

He opened his legs wide so she could stand between them. Her fingers moved up her body caressing herself. She squeezed her breasts together, pushing them out, she stopped and rubbed each one in turn, licking her finger rubbing it over her nipple then slowly pinching them licking her lips grinning at him. Her pussy was so close to his head he could smell her juices, he inhaled deeply.
"You're in big trouble Belle wait until I get my hands on you." he groaned, pulling his shorts down letting his cock spring out. It was rock hard and throbbing for her.

He slid his hand around his cock rubbing it slowly. Jane turned lowering her hips towards his cock teasing him as she moved her hips to the beat.
"Oh fuck." He hissed as Jane moved away.
She came back, put her foot onto his knee opening her legs wide so he could see her wet pussy.
Jasper leant forward to kiss her thigh as Jane stroked her fingers up her leg as she was about to undo her stockings. She pushed him back gently and waved her finger to say no.
He tried again and as she went to push him back he grabbed her hips growling at her. "You are such a tease I want you now!" he demanded.
Jane tried to pull back and put her leg onto the floor. She was going to make a dash for the bedroom but he had hold of her

too tight. He pulled her closer leaning into her breasts grabbing one with his lips sucking it hard and biting it making her yell out. He did the same to the other then licked up her

cleavage pulling her onto his lap. She straddled him on the edge. His cock between them throbbing and twitching to be touched. She wrapped her hand around it at the base and squeezed it as he kissed and bit her neck moving up to her ear. Her hand slid up his cock slowly as she reached the head she could feel his precum escape.

"I want to taste your cock."

He released his hold on her and she slide onto the floor between his legs. She pulled at his shorts, he lifted his bottom up so she could get them off. She left them on the floor pushing them away. She pulled his legs making him slide further down the sofa his legs wide open. She ran her fingers up his thigh and slid her nails gently over his balls. He hissed and inhaled deeply whispering.

"Fuck yes Belle, please!"

She held her hair back pushing his legs wider, she leant forward licking his balls from the bottom to the start of his cock, she looked at him as she licked the length of his cock to the head and across the tip tasting his precum before she slid him into her mouth. She moaned deeply loving the taste of him as she slid back up off his cock. She ran her tongue around the tip and over the top. His balls tightened as she squeezed them gently. He pushed his hips towards her.

"Ohhhh fuuuck yes, grrrrrrr don't stop!!" He growled, grabbing her hair and twisting it round his hand. Pushing her deeper onto his cock. She felt her nose barely touch his skin as she got closer to the base. Jasper was moaning loudly. As she came back up to the head, he pulled her head up grabbed her face and kissed her hard pushing his tongue into her mouth. He pulled her back up to her feet, pulling her bottom towards him. She sat astride him her pussy hovering above his cock. He slid his hand along her leg towards her pussy, he could see how wet she was.

"Jesus you're so wet Belle."

He slid his fingers into her open pussy teasing her pushing his fingers deep inside her. She was now aching for his cock wanting to be filled by him. Knowing she will come so quickly when he slid inside her. She loved her little show, it really turned her on. Jasper grabbed his cock, lifted her and lowered her onto him slowly.

"Oh, yessssss." she screamed as he filled her completely.

She wrapped her hands around his neck kissing him hungrily. He slid her up and down his cock she was biting his lip moaning loudly.

"Rub your clit Belle." He whispered.

She moved her hand down to her pussy parting her lips and rubbed her swollen clit.

"Oh god I want to cum." she moaned loudly as he moved his hips faster pushing her harder onto him.

Jane felt the heat rise in her body as his balls tightened and his cock stiffened.

"Fuck, fuck, fuck. Yes Belle." He groaned as he explodes inside her. Her pussy responded as she screamed out.

"I'm cuming baby, oh Jesus Christ!" Her body shuddered she lost focus as it hit her, she kept rubbing as another made her tremble. She came down from her orgasm as Jasper kissed her. She slid off his cock feeling the loss of him inside her as he pulled her into him. They lay for a few minutes together and Jasper suddenly jumped. "Shit, Belle the dinner!"

He jumped up dropping Jane onto the sofa and dashed to the oven, he pulled out the dinner laying onto the top of the cooker.

"Jesus thank god for that, it just started to burn on the edges. I would have eaten it burnt anyway

because that was worth it." He came back across the room to Jane kissing her nose.

"Come on let's quickly freshen up and we can eat." He bent and grabbed the clothes handing them

to Jane and lifted her into his arms.

"I think you have done enough on that leg today Belle, you might need to take something before bed to help you rest."

Jane nodded. "I know, I thought the same, it was worth it though." she grinned at him.

They went into the bathroom, Jasper grabbed the wash cloth and they both freshened up quickly. They put their pjs on and went back to the kitchen. Jasper brought the hot pot over and dished it up. They had some of Lily's bread with it. They sat chatting and laughing, Jasper could see how relaxed Jane had become. He knew her leg healing would help too. They finished up and Jasper loaded the dishwasher, they moved back over to the sofa and snuggled up together listening to the music.

Heaven by Kane Brown

Jasper got up and went into the bedroom, he pulled out her ring out of his drawer put it into his pocket and went back into the lounge. Jane was laid out on the sofa. Humming to the music, he knew this was the perfect moment to do this again. He smiled and knelt down on the floor in front of her, she opened her eyes. Moved over for him to get back onto the sofa patting it for him to join her. He shook his head. He moved onto one knee, Jane looked puzzled and sat up her legs cuddled into her chest.

"Belle, you are the most incredible person I have ever met, you make me smile every minute of the day, almost losing you still scares me, I have never loved anyone the way I love you. You're not just a special person you're more than you could ever imagine. With you I have found happiness, peace, joy and a reason to smile, my love for you doesn't have limitations. I crave to be every part of your

life, I want to be the air you breath, to be your sun and moon I don't want to miss another moment with you. I love you beyond words. I never thought anyone could love me the way you do, you brought new meaning to my life, you took my breath away the first time I set eyes on you at the

traffic lights. Belle, what I am trying to say is I don't want to wait any longer." He pulled the ring out

of his pocket holding it in his fingers out to Jane.

"Belle please marry me, make me the happiest man on this earth, I want to be your husband, you as my wife now, I don't want to wait, whatever you want, you can have, I don't care as long as you are happy and become my wife as soon as possible." He felt the tears creep out of the corner of his eye. He looked at Jane her eyes wet from tears, he moved closer cupping her face in his hand, wiping her tears with his thumb. Jane moved her lips to kiss his hand. She moved her legs and threw herself at him. Hugging him tightly, kissing his face like crazy, he fell backwards onto the floor as Jane sat on his chest.

"Say it again?"

"Belle?" Jasper laughed "Ask me again."

Jasper laughed. "Belle, please, please make me the happiest person in the world and say yes, marry

me become Mrs Jasper Mitchell soon?"

Jane jumped up and down on Jaspers chest like a child. "Yes, yes, yes." She bent over him kissing him again harder this time. Jasper wrapped his arms around her squeezing her tight, Jane laid on top of him. Jasper grabbed her face and moved her away so he could look at her again.

"Are you sure?" he laughed

Jane moved her head back and screamed at the top of her voice "YESSSSSSSS I WANT TO MARRY YOU."

Jasper started laughing and sat them both up, Jane sat with her legs wrapped around him.

"You are the funniest craziest woman I have ever met and god I love you." he kissed her hard holding her head with both hands. Jane put her hand out waiting for Jasper to put the ring on her finger. He looked around and couldn't find it.

"Shit, where did it go?" Jane started laughing.

"Don't you dare tell me after all this you have lost it in here?" Jane jumped off him they were both on their knees scrabbling around the furniture looking for it, Jane stood and went to the sofa pushing her hands down the back and sides of the cushions, Jasper went under the table, he spotted something glistening, he smiled grabbing it sitting up watching Jane pulling cushions up scrabbling around for it. She looked around at him to see why he had stopped as he sat holding it with a huge smile on his face. She joined him on the floor as he took her hand, he kissed the ring and her finger and slid it on, it went past the first knuckle, they both watched as it went on to the second and stopped. It was still a bit tight. Jane looked down.

"It's ok, won't be long now, by the time we get married and you decide on my wedding ring then it will fit."

"Oh. I'm deciding on your ring am I?" "Of course you are." Jane giggled.

Jasper grabbed her round the waist and began tickling her, she clenched her hand together so she didn't drop her ring, she was thrashing around as Jasper continued to tickle her. She could barely breath. She was begging through gasps for him to stop.

"Please , I can't breath." she panted begging him.

"Do you give in?" He laughed "Yes, yes." she giggled.

Jasper stopped, Jane was still giggling trying to catch her breath, Jasper pulled her up smiling and laughing.

"God I love you woman." He kissed her head smiling got up on his feet and lifted her off the floor and onto his lap. Jane opened her hand looking at her ring.

"You will never know how much that meant to me, now my proposal is really special, but did you

really think you needed to ask me again. I'm glad you did though."

"After what happened Belle, I didn't want you to have that as your memory in case it brought back bad dreams, when you pulled through I was determined to ask you again. Being here with you was the perfect time. But I mean it Belle, I don't want to wait, so you better make a decision, where do you want to get married. I don't care if I have to sell the car to fund it, you will have the wedding you want."

"You should know I am not materialistic, I just want our friends around us."

"Well why don't you talk to the girls and Moses and decide where is best logistically. I will go with whatever you decide. I just want it to be perfect for you, my guys will travel regardless."

"Well you know mine will too, we could always do it here and go back to the UK for a club party or
vise versa?"

"That's a great idea."

"However if you decide to do it here there is a place I would like to suggest for us, when we were buying the roses for the babies I told you about a Rose garden, I think it would be perfect, we could maybe have candles for them both and our parents, but you decide?"

"No darling it's our wedding, I want us to make all the decisions, it isn't about the bride you know."

Jasper smiled. "If that's what my Belle wants, then I am happy with that."

"Good that's settled, however you won't see my wedding dress until the day.

Jasper laughed, "I expected that. You could wear a sack and I would still think you look beautiful. Belle, do whatever you want"

She leant on his chest and kissed him softly on the lips. Would you pinch me please, I need to know
this isn't a dream."

Jasper laughed and started pinching her.

"Ouch ouch, I only meant once." She squealed.

"Oops. Sorry." He laughed teasing her.

"I think you should make a cup of tea and bring some of Lily's cake across so we can celebrate."

"Oh you think do you? I will be your husband not your slave lady."

"I would do it, but I have a poorly leg, I was shot remember and I am not allowed to walk around too
Much."

Jasper sat laughing holding his tummy, "I see where this is going to go, every time you are feeling lazy you are going to pull that one out of the bag."

"Yes of course I am. A lady has to use all the tools at her disposal." Jane got up off the sofa and went
to head for the kitchen.

Jasper grabbed her pulling her onto his knee. Laughing. "Don't you even think about getting up." Jane turned grinning at him. Sitting down on his lap. He kissed her from behind. Slapping her thigh.

"Move your bottom, let me make this tea for you." Jane moved off and sat down on the sofa, as Jasper went to make the tea and bring the cake back.

Jane grabbed Jaspers phone and went into the notes app and added a title *Our Wedding*

Jasper came back over. "What are you doing love?"

"I just added a new note for our wedding, is that okay?

"Yes love of course, good idea, what have you added so far?"

"ummmmm, she turned the screen around to show him. "Nothing there Belle." he laughed

"I know, it felt like a good idea at the time, but I didn't have anything to write."

"you are funny Belle, how about you start with a list of names, then it will give us an idea of where to get married, add a list for the UK and here."

"That's a good idea. Do you think Henry and Lily will come, I really would love it if they did. I really do
like them?"

"Well why don't you ask them tomorrow when they come down?"

Jane clapped her hands together in excitement, "brilliant idea. I will do that."

They sat together making lists of people they wanted at the wedding, and added a maybe list, Jasper joked his boss would be one of those, he may invite him out of respect to the evening more than anything, but he didn't know how he would react seeing all the bikers there, they both laughed talking about it.

Jane decided she would talk to the girls on Skype together, she wanted all the girls to be bridesmaids and Gwen her oldest friend would be her maid of honour. She didn't mind what style of dress after all they all had a better dress sense than she did and she would definitely be going back to the little lady in town who helped her with the dress for their black tie event.

"Oh god!! I just remembered you have a black-tie event coming up, can I get out of it please, I would
rather drive you there than have to go at the moment?"
"Thanks for reminding me I forgot about that too. Yes of course you can, it's just a bunch of old
engineers and councillors anyway love, it will be pretty boring."
"Well I could drive you there, then you get to have a drink."
"Or I could get a cab?"
"No, I need to get back in the saddle, so to speak so let me, it's a couple of weeks away anyway."
"We will see." He smiled knowing full well he would give in to her.

Jasper found the website of the Rose garden for Jane to look at she was completely lost in it, he knew she would love it. They had an amazing pagoda, they held the ceremonies in, and there was a beautiful little hotel near by to have the reception and stay overnight in. He was really excited at the thought of finally marrying her, knowing she wouldn't worry anymore about being found made it even better. Jasper grabbed Jane's phone and gave it to her, he wanted to start a list of music for the wedding, he had some ideas but wanted to build a playlist, he also wanted to start his speech, without her prying eyes. He smiled to himself knowing what she would do if she saw a folder about the wedding, her inquisitive mind would win and she would have to sneak a look. He thought he might even play with her a little. He created a file called *wedding stuff*. He was going to add some really cheesey things to it.
Jane looked over her glasses at him. "What' funny?"
"Oh nothing Belle, just making a list of wedding stuff." He lied.
"Oh, can I see?" she quizzed.
"No love sorry, its private, you will have to wait."

Her face was pure magic, he knew he had her hook line and sinker. He kept tapping on his phone and smiling, he could see Jane was watching out of the corner of her eye.

"Perfect." He whispered to himself.

They continued to make notes and try different music out jumping from one song to the next until they had built quite a good list. Jane had her heart set on the Rose garden too, they just needed to set a date and check its availability.

They talked about places for their honeymoon somewhere neither had been, it was a choice between the Elephant Safari Lodge Bali, or The Maldives. Jasper wanted to take Jane to both and thought it would be nice to surprise her. He wanted to spoil her completely, but he knew she wasn't bothered by gifts. It was more about people. But he wanted her to experience the Maldives and the Elephants, he loved them and wanted to see it too.

Chapter 31

Planning a new beginning

Jasper and Jane were sat on the decking with a cup of tea enjoying the early sunshine when Lily and Henry arrived.

"Good Morning you two, you're up and about early today?" Lily said coming up onto the porch to hug them both.

"We have news and somebody was a little excited and barely slept a wink, she was desperate to talk to you both."

"Oh?" Should we be worried, are you leaving earlier, I do hope not?"

"Please sit down both of you." Jane had prepared 2 cups for them both and poured the tea. They sat, taking the tea from Jane.

"Well last night Jasper decided it was the perfect time to propose again, so I had a better memory of

the event, even though the first was perfect and I can block out what happened at the end of the

night, anyway, he said he doesn't want to wait and wants us to marry as soon as possible."

Lily's hands shot to her mouth and they could see tears appearing already, Henry grabbed her hand and squeezed it.

"So we have decided on a place and just waiting to confirm a date later today, we wanted you both to know first, you are really important to Jasper and to me now too, we would love you to both be there with us. There will be a lot of bikers there which I hope that doesn't bother you, they are a

great bunch of people and my family."

Lily was openly crying using her pinny again to wipe the tears away. Henry cuddled up to her, he cleared his throat.

"It would be an honour, are you sure?"

"Couldn't be more certain, since I met you both all those months ago you have become very special to me, our weekly, sometimes daily chats are really special. I haven't had anyone check up on me in years, since Mum died I haven't had anyone in my life and then I met you both. There was something else too, Henry I wondered if you would be my witness. I have one of the boys doing the duty of Best Man, but to have you as a witness to our marriage would be really something else."

Lily sobbed openly "Oh Jasper, she got onto her feet and came to him hugging him, she pulled Jane in too they hugged together. Lily took Jane by the hand.

"I know you have a lot to do and decisions to make and a huge amount of friends but please think about it and I won't be offended if you say no, but I would be honoured if you would let me make your wedding cake?"

Jane began to cry. "Oh Lily, that would be incredible, I don't need to think about it, yes, yes, yes."

She hugged Lily the pair openly crying.

The men stood watching, Henry hugged Jasper.

"Thank you Son, it is indeed a surprise and a great honour to do that for you both. They hugged again and Henry wiped his eyes. He laughed at himself. "Christ I'm as bad as the girls, it must be my age."

"Thank you Henry, I can't tell you how happy that makes me, I don't mean about you crying." He laughed. "But that you will be my witness, neither of us have parents anymore and I have grown very fond of you both."

They both sat down again and the girls joined them.

"So what other plans have you made so far?" Lily asked.

"Well Jasper told me about a Rose garden that he has visited once before, I looked at the website and it looks perfect. I adore roses and we have brought some special roses in Jaspers garden, so it seems fitting."

"Jasper did tell us about your children, so very sad, I'm so sorry. We have been to the garden it is a beautiful place and very romantic, perfect for the two of you, they also do wedding receptions in the café, it's a lovely building with wooden beams they have it draped in beautiful fabrics."

"That sounds perfect." Jane exclaimed.

"June is perfect as they have events then to celebrate the roses in bloom, but they are still out for
much longer."
"We're hoping for August 15th. Neither of us have anything in July to celebrate it gives us enough
time to get everything prepared."
"Perfect Jane, I can't wait, you will need to let me know what colour you're having so I can make the cake match. Any ideas what shape you would like?"
"Nothing fancy, just something that matches our personality."
"Well that makes it easier then, I will surprise you both if that's okay?" "That would be lovely."
"Have you thought about a dress style yet, will you have a veil?"
"Well there is this Russian lady in town that used to make dresses, she helped me with a dress for an event I went to with Jasper when we first met, she said to me that day when you are ready for your wedding dress come and see me. I laughed at her that day and now look at me. So I think I will go back and see her. It was my friend Chicca that took me in there, it's the most incredible shop, she is from old Russian money, she is so lovely. I will ask if I can call the girls on video from the shop to show them the dresses she has. Gwen will be my Maid of Honour, the others my bridesmaids, I don't want to leave anyone out, they are all very special to me."
"Sounds perfect love, how exciting. Right now, all this chat about weddings you must be hungry let
me go and cook for you both, what would you like?"
"I'm happy with poached eggs on toast please if you don't mind? Jasper?" "Sounds good to me too please Lily if you don't mind, will you both join us?" "Poached eggs coming up, we have eaten already, but thank you."

"Are you going out on the quads today Son? If you do come across the field to the far corner, you
will see our place through the trees, come on over and have lunch with us."

Jane looked at Jasper her mouth wide open. "Are you sure, we don't want to put you to any

trouble?" Jane asked

"Of course we don't mind, I can bore your husband to be about my house that I built too."

"Well then we better say yes, thank you."

"Great, say 1pm then. I will go and get the quads ready for you, the suits are clean so I will hang

them up while Lil cooks your eggs, see you both later." "Look forward to it Henry, thank you."

They both waved and sat down at the table while Lily cooked for them, Jane grabbed Jaspers hand grinning.

"Eeek, I am so excited. I feel really honoured Lily to be coming to visit you."

Jasper smiled. "Yes it is very kind of you. We didn't expect that."

"Well let's just say it's a celebration lunch." She came over with their plates. "Be careful the plates are warm still."

"Thank you Lily." Jane smiled, Lily bent and hugged Jane kissing her on the cheek.

"You're very welcome, you both make me feel needed and it's a lovely feeling, you get to our age and people just pass you off as old and think you are incapable of doing anything, let me tell you I would give these youngsters a run for their money." She winked at them both and left waving as she walked out of the door.

"I think our Lily was a bit naughty in her younger days." Jasper smiled.

"Oh I think she may still be, they are both very young for their years."

"Okay enough I don't need to fill my head with thoughts of our friends doing that."

Jane laughed at him, "You are funny and sometimes very prudish."

"Cheeky mare I am not prudish at all. Or do I need to show you?"

"Anytime big boy." Jane teased.

She lifted her leg up slipping her slipper off and rubbed up his inner thigh. He slumped down in his chair so her foot would reach his crotch. Jane moved her foot to the middle and began pushing into his balls.

"Mmmmmm keep doing that and I will put you over my shoulder and take you back to bed!"

Jane pushed her foot in harder moving it up his cock, she could feel it getting harder.

"You better finish your breakfast you need all the energy for later when I whoop your arse on the field."

"Throwing the gauntlet down are we Miss K?" "Accepting the challenge then Mr M?"

"Of course."

Jane smiled finishing her breakfast and emptying her cup of tea. She pushed her chair back and stood up.

"Bring it on JDubz." she giggled.

Jasper stood up walked around the table, picked her up and threw her over his shoulder spanking her bottom. Jane squealed giggling as he spanked her for every step they took. He got into the bedroom dropped her on the bed, grabbed her shorts pulling them off her and dropping them on the floor.

Jane opened her mouth looking shocked as Jasper opened her legs and got down on his knees not saying a word, he went straight between her legs, he pulled her lips apart stroking her with his finger making Jane moan loudly. She was already wet he didn't need to make his finger wet, he dipped it inside her as he pulled it out it glistened with her juices he rubbed it on her clit making Jane buck towards him. He blew on her gently.

"Oh Jasper, lick me please?" she whimpered

Jasper smiled his finger still rubbing her clit, leaving it for a few seconds to tease her running it up and down the length of her pussy, he dipped back inside her covering his finger again with her juices and continued down to her bottom. Jane gasped as he circled her tiny hole. Jane groaned as he gently opened her pushing in gently, he looked up at her as he pushed in further, Jane could feel herself getting wetter, she began biting her lip, her fingers digging into the bedclothes screwing them up. Jasper slipped his finger in and out slowly, Jane moaned loudly lifting her bottom off the bed. Jasper moved his free hand from her thigh and began teasing her clit again, he pushed his finger into her pussy finger fucking her in both holes, Jane almost burst, her back almost off the bed, her head on the bed.

"Oh my fucking god!" She screamed, "Oh, Oh please, please don't stop baby." Jasper smiled.

He bent into her, opening her legs wider with his shoulders, he licked her clit. Just flicking his tongue over the top.

"Ohhhhhhhhhhh" Jane screamed she was twisting the bedding in her hands pulling it up the bed. Jasper smiled again breathing on her clit as he began licking faster, his fingers wet with her juices pouring out of her, she had never been so wet. He wanted to devour her, he licked more adding more pressure to her clit, his fingers still sliding in and out of her moving faster, he wanted to make her cum now, he pushed his finger into her pussy further curled it up hitting right where she needed it. Jane screamed. The room span and everything went white as her orgasm hit her. Her body quivering as she came hard, Jasper could feel it covering his fingers and his hand, she had never cum so hard. Jane's body was still shaking she was pushing up into his hand wanting more, he pushed harder for her giving her a second, as she came he removed his finger and pushed his tongue in fast he didn't want to waste any more of her nectar. He slurped and sucked at her making her moan more, his tongue finding every last drop of her. His finger slowed down in her bottom, he pulled it out as Jane trembled her body cooling down, Jasper continued to lick her, wanting more. Jane began to giggle feeling very sensitive pushing his head away, Jasper laughed and stood up his cock rock hard. He pushed his shorts down past his bottom shaking them off his cock swaying hitting his legs. Jane laughed watching him. He climbed onto the bed, lifting her legs up rubbing his cock against her opening.

Jane reached down and grabbed it pushing it inside herself, Jasper laughed.

"Is my juicy girl desperate for me?" "Hell yes I am. Take me Jasper?"

"My pleasure Belle." He smiled, lifting her legs higher pushing into her deeper. There was nothing gentle about this he wanted her, to show her he was in charge. He rammed himself in hard. Jane squealed. He retraced and did it again harder this time. Janes body moved up the bed, he grabbed her legs pulling her back again, he pushed in hard getting faster. His balls slapping against her bottom.

"This is my pussy, do you understand, and whenever I want it, I will take it." Jane nodded. "Ohh, I love it when you are so masterful." she smiled.

Jasper spanked her hard making her jump, he didn't smooth it this time, he grabbed her legs holding her into him and fucked her hard. They both moaned loudly as he picked up speed, he could feel his balls tightening and his orgasm building.

"I fucking love you Belle, you are mine." He gritted his teeth as he rammed into her, his voice deeper as he fucked her faster and harder. His cock was rubbing Jane so hard she could feel her body tingling ready to explode again.

"Oh fuck I'm cuming, Oh Jaaasppper." She screamed.

Jasper felt her juices wrap around his cock, he yelled loudly as he came, grunting as he filled her. "Fuuuuuck Belle." He growled "grrrrrrrrr." His body going rigid pushing into her. They were both panting as their orgasms calmed. Jasper pulled out of Jane and leant down onto the bed. He rubbed her nose and kissed her hard.

"Wow, that was intense." he laughed.

Jane nodded biting her bottom lip "mmmmmmm, yes it was. You can do that again any time you
Like."

"And you can push that foot of yours into my cock at the table any time you like too." He laughed
standing grabbing her foot and biting the heel making Jane squeal.

"Right, time to woop your arse." He put her leg down and spanked her bottom again. Jane put her hands up, Jasper pulled her up so she was sitting. He moved to the chair grabbing their jeans and passed Janes to hers so they could get dressed.

"Umm knickers please?"
"Nah you don't need those, knowing you are out there with none on will make me very happy." "Oh I think you mean horny?" Jane laughed.
"And that yes" he grinned.
"I need to wash first please?" Jane pushed herself to the end of the bed and Jasper helped her stand leading her to the bathroom. He helped her stand taking her weight while she freshened up. He then did the same. They dressed and Jasper picked Jane up taking her to the porch, they booted up and he took her down to the quads. Jane was grinning widely.

"Someone's excited?"
"Yes, I am, I'm going to show you how to ride." she giggled.
"Oh, in your dreams Belle, it's four wheels remember not 3."
Jane shrugged, "You better take me out on a track sometime then in your car, I will show you how to drive that too!"
Jasper started laughing his head falling backwards. "Oh, Belle you are funny, but if you insist I am sure we can find a suitable track." Jane put her hand out to shake his.
"Challenge accepted." She grinned. He took her hand shaking it.
"Get your pretty little arse on that quad lady and show me what you have."
Jane grinned knowing she hadn't shown him her best yet, she was excited to be able to race against him.
Jane climbed on the quad after suiting up Jasper kissed her before she put her liner and crash helmet on. Jane pulled out of the barn first, it was another warm day Henry had told Jasper the field was like a dust bowl and knew they would get very dusty. Jasper came out after Jane he tore past her roaring out onto the field, Jane grinned twisting the throttle of her machine and took off after him.
"I'm coming for you Mr Mitchell, let's show you how you ride shall we."

She cackled like an old witch and chased after him, Jasper slowed down, Jane bent over the bars and raced passed him, she got to the middle of the field and span round facing him revving the engine. Jasper sat laughing. "That's my girl, let's have some fun"

He took off heading for Jane as he approached her he bent down on the bars and roared passed her again as she had done, he knew she would chase after him, he didn't need to wait long, he heard her coming up behind him at speed, he looked over his shoulder and opened the throttle up, he wasn't letting her win this one, they had a good few miles out in front of them if they went left, Jasper headed off Jane was almost on his tail.

"Shit Belle, you are pushing it!" He accelerated more, his heart pounding loving the ride, Jane kept coming.

"I'm coming to get you Jasper!" Jane said in a creepy voice and cackled again. She felt alive, the

adrenaline pumping around her body, her heart racing.

She laid down and opened the engine up, she was getting closer to Jasper, she could see him

checking on her, he opened his engine and shot off again, Jane wasn't going to allow him to win, she opened the throttle up and within seconds was on his tail. Jasper jumped when he saw her behind him. Jane threw her head back and cackled as she shot past him. She didn't let up on the throttle just kept going, she could see the end of the field coming up quick, she knew she better slow down, she checked behind her Jasper had slowed down a bit.

"Oh dear does Jasper not like being beaten? diddum's." she laughed.

She slowed down to the end of the field as she reached the end she span the quad around and started back towards Jasper. As she reached him she blew him a kiss and tore past him. Jasper laughed and span around chasing after her, he could see Jane was slowing down thinking she had won, he opened up the throttle and raced past her blowing kisses as he did.

"Damn you!" she screamed after him, opening up the throttle chasing him to the other end of the field. They were now neck and neck as Jane caught up with him, he was laughing as she sat along side him. They both throttled off and Jasper put his hand out to Jane, she took it and they rode to the end of the field together. He came close as they stopped he pulled his helmet up and kissed her gloved hand.

"I will bow to my lady, that was a fair win, but I think you may have cheated." He laughed, teasing her.

Jane slapped him. "I don't need to cheat thank you, I told you I could handle it. I won that fair and square."

"How are you feeling love?" he laughed but being serious.

"Alive if I'm honest, I loved that thank you for not wrapping me up and over protecting me."

"I don't think that would be possible would it?

"Don't you believe it, Ask Moses, him and G have always done it but for good reason I suppose. "They love you Belle, so of course they would."

"Enough of that, what time is it?"

"12.45pm we better head towards Lily and Henry's place. I think if we head straight up the middle we should see it come into view."

Jane nodded, pulled her visor down and raced off. Jasper laughed knowing she would do it, he chased after her and rode alongside her, they both slowed down at the edge of the field, Jane pointed to it opening her visor.

"I thought you said they had a small place?" Jane sat with her mouth wide open.

"Well when you talk to them it sounds small." he exclaimed in shock.

They pulled across the lane as the cabin opened up in front of them, they both sat staring at it. Nestled in the trees and backing onto the lake was a single level cabin. It had a cross gabled roof. A huge stone chimney, going up the back of the cabin, it was elevated from the lake but had

level access from the front. It had trees surrounding it and a simple garden to the right. There was a wrap - around porch and floor to roof windows on every side. Henry and Lily came to the door to greet them. They climbed off the quads as Henry reached them.

"Hi, if I take you into the side of the house you can take your overalls off in the boot room then come into the house."

"Thanks Henry." they both replied

Henry lead them into a doorway which opened up into a 12 x 9ft room, it was very warm, it had racks of boots and jackets hanging up, there was a gun cupboard bolted to the wall and a washing machine and tumble dryer with a low stone sink. One wall was stone the others were wood. They took their overalls and boots off. Jane was just looking around the room in awe. Once they were sorted Henry led them through another door which had a connecting glass walkway to the main house, he opened the door which led into the back of the kitchen.

"Wow!" they said in unison

"Welcome to our home, 'Henlys'."

"Henry, when you said you had built a little place for you both I didn't expect anything so big and

grand." Jasper grinned in awe, he couldn't stop looking around the room.

"Lily just kept having other ideas like the boot room that was an addition as she didn't want dirty boots in the house. We only wanted a single level, so we don't have to worry about stairs as we got older and the garden is simple to look after. Lily has her vegetable patch and we have the house of our dreams."

"But I thought the other place was?"

"Yes, it was for our family, but I started to build this before I got too old as our retirement home, it

took about 5 years in total to finish the shell and Lily built up the inside over the years."

Jane looked around as Lily came out of the main living area to meet them, she had been setting the table.

"Oh Lily, I thought your other house was out of this world and it is, but this is just incredible, how

can you choose a favorite?"

"Well, like Henry just said this is our retirement home, the other will always have a special place in our hearts because we brought our family up there, but as they don't bother anymore this place is more special, it's just Henry and I as it was in the beginning and we love it. Come on let me show you through to the main room."

They walked through the kitchen door and Jane gasped. In front of them was a huge stone fireplace with a huge lump of wood through the middle as a shelf that looked like twisted wood, the lights were made of multiple sets of antlers. The windows overlooking the lake were three glass floor to ceiling windows so not to obscure the view. Either side of the fireplace were two huge leather sofas the same as were in the main house and two huge chairs in the middle, was a large handmade table that matched the house. On the same wall as the fireplace was a little nook, Lily grabbed Jane's hand and led her through the little door way into another tiny room, each wall was lined with book cases and the biggest chairs Jane had ever seen, they were well used and looked like giant marshmallows.

"Oh Lily, this is incredible." Jane felt tears prick at her eyes.

"Oh sweetheart you have just had the same reaction as I had the first time I saw it, Henry built it as a surprise for me, it only had two books on the shelf then, these I have collected over the years. It's my little piece of heaven. I come in here and read or listen to music if Henry is watching one of his programmes or football. Jane turned to see an additional small fireplace that connected to the chimney.

"I don't think I could ever leave this room Lily." Jane held her hand against her chest, overcome by
the beautiful feeling of the room.

"I don't sometimes. When I need to get away from life, I come in here and Henry just leaves me to it, he brings me a drink and chocolate but never stays. Sit Jane, we have plenty of time."

Jane sat down into one of the big chairs, "Oh my, it's like sitting into a cloud."

"Yes it is." Lily laughed sitting back.

"Tell me about you Jane, I have heard a lot from Jasper, we did spend a lot of time on the phone
with him when you were in hospital. But I want to hear about you."

"Jane took a deep breath and began telling Lily about losing her parents and how she married her husband after he played on her emotions when she was at her lowest. She didn't go into detail about the abuse just skimmed over the top, but she knew Lily knew more about it. She didn't mind that she knew, she still hadn't spoken to Jasper about how he felt about it all. She knew it still affected him, he and Moses had done so much for her.
"You know if you ever need to talk I am here. I will give you my numbers so you can call at any time." "Thank you Lily, that is so kind." Jane reached for her hand and squeezed it.

"We felt we knew you before you arrived as Jasper talks of nothing else but you. He reminds me of Henry and the way he has been with me all these years. I hope you both have as many happy years as we have." She squeezed Jane's hand.
Jane wiped her eyes as the men wandered in.
"I thought you might get stuck in that chair, lovely isn't it Jane?"
Jane looked up at the men smiling
nodding at Henry.
"Well I was hoping I could strap it to Jaspers car so we can take it home."
 "I think she is serious Henry." Jasper laughed.
"Well you are lucky to be in here, I never stay, this is Lil's little peace of heaven. I get the look from her if I come in."
"Oh, you get that look too do you? I think it's a woman thing." Both men laughed.
Lily stood up "Right then let's get lunch sorted, the table is ready I will just go and get the meat and bread, take a seat please."

They walked out of the nook and headed towards the windows overlooking the lake. The table was laid, it was big enough to sit

12 people the chairs were huge wood and fabric, handmade by Henry. They sat down at one end of the table, Lily had put the tablecloth on and there was an array of accompaniments from salad to dressings. Lily came out carrying homemade bread and carved meats.

"Lily you really know how to spoil people, I am sure I will be putting on weight this week." "Well it won't hurt you love." she smiled.

"Lily I have said the same, but she won't believe me."

Jane put her hands up. "Okay, okay I get it." she laughed.

Lily passed the bread round as they sat chatting. They all had a full plate and tucked in. Jane sat back in her chair once she finished rubbing her stomach.

"Oh my god Lily, that was incredible. I don't think I can eat again tonight." She puffed out.

"Well you have a soup for later and it's a light one in case you get hungry." She laughed Jane took her hand.

"You really are amazing, I think I need some lessons for sure."

"Well if you ladies want to spend a day in the kitchen when Jane is back on her feet I can take Jasper fishing in the lake."

"Well that's a good plan." Lily said excitedly "You won't hear me argue Henry."

"Me either I am already planning our return, I just need to check your diary of bookings Henry." Henry clapped his hands together and winked at Lily. "That's sorted then. You let me know when and I will check it out for you Son." They shook hands, everyone was excited.

"First things first, get this wedding arranged and then you can come back and relax before the big day."

"You're right Lily, a lot to prepare. Jasper called the venue and they said they are free when we want it, so tonight we will call Moses, I want him to give me away then we can skype the gang in England and let them know. Jasper is going to call Graham and James. I will then get Graham to bring his daughters over and ask if they want to be flower girls when we get back."

"Oh perfect, so you are going traditional then, something old something new?"

"Yes we are, we talked about it and we both want it."

"Sounds perfect!"

"What was your wedding like?" Jane asked looking at both Lily and Henry.

"The biggest memory for me was seeing Lily walk down the aisle, she took my breath away.

Lily teared up listening to Henry.

"She wore this beautiful dress it was lace at the top and like sheer fabric at the bottom." He was

moving his hands around trying to describe it. Lily started laughing.

"What he means is the neck was stood up which dropped into a V long sleeves which was all lace.

It had a bodice underneath it. Then the skirt was full and sheer. I wore a simple tiara and a long

train."

"I don't mind admitting I was a bag of nerves and really emotional when I saw her." He smiled

remembering the day.

"What did you wear Henry?" Jane asked

"Oh well, I was very trendy, I had a white suit with flared bottoms which had a gold trim. With a

black bow tie and a pink hankie to match the bridesmaids." He sat looking very proud

"The bridesmaids had those floppy hats and pink dresses, they were quite plain as they were all different ages and sizes. We had a traditional church wedding and a 3-tier cake, which was very fancy with lots of icing again to match the bridesmaids. Looking back, it was a bit garish, don't worry yours won't be."

Jane laughed listening.

They talked for hours about the wedding, Jasper and Jane were loving listening to them both, Lily went and got the wedding album out, as she opened the album a tune began to play, it reminded Jane of her parents album. They laughed through the pictures. Henry had platform shoes on which he had forgotten about. They laughed a lot about the clothes others wore too. By the time they had finished it had gone 5pm. They had moved to the sofas and relaxed with each other. Jasper sat up looking at his watch.

"Wow have you seen the time?" He said shocked. "It's just gone 5pm, we better make a move Belle." "I will take you back across in the car and put the trikes on the trailer tomorrow to save you getting kitted up again."

"Are you sure Henry, we don't want to put you to any trouble?"

"It's no trouble at all. Come on let's get your shoes on and we can get you back."

They all stood up, Jane was a bit stiff, she turned and hugged Lily.

"Thank you so much for a wonderful day, I really have had a lovely time." "You're very welcome."

Jasper bent and hugged Lily too. "Thank you, for spoiling us."

"Anytime, you know that."

They headed out to the boot room to put their boots on, Henry wiped them over with a cloth to get

rid of the dust. Jasper bent and did Janes up before sweeping her into his arms.

"I can walk to the car, I'm okay."

"No Belle, it won't be long before you are dashing around again so let me do it, besides, you have been busy on your feet today."

"Oh, Jane you have a good one there." Jane grinned. Nodding. Lily kissed them both before they went out to the car. Within minutes they were back at the house. Jasper carried Jane up the stairs and into the house. He laid her on the sofa and grabbed her phone off the side.

"Right, if I make a drink you can call Moses."

Jane saluted. "Yes boss."

"Cheeky." He smiled walking away to make a drink.

Jane dialled Moses and put him on speaker phone. "Hello love, how are you, how are the pups?"

"Hello Half-pint, all good here, how are you both doing?"

"We're good thank you." Jasper returned with their tea. "We wanted to ask you something, can you

turn your camera on please?" "Sure hang on, okay."

Jane waved frantically as he came on camera. "Hi, that's better I can see you now, are you okay, you're looking tired?"

"I'm okay love, just back ache that's all, so what did you want to ask me?"

Jasper joined on the camera.

"Hey Brother, how are you?"

"Great thank you relaxing plenty and enjoying the fresh air. I have to agree with Belle, you are

looking a bit rough, you sure you're okay?"

"That's good to hear, yes just back ache, not sure why, it came on a few weeks ago never thought anything of it, probably because I'm being a lazy arse." They all laughed. Moses knew he was lying but he wasn't spoiling their time away.

"Anyway, the reason we called I wanted to ask you something."

"okay love."

"You know you are my best friend, you mean the absolute world to me, without you by my side the last 10 years my life would have been very different." Moses nodded feeling tearful, he rubbed his eye.

"Well we have set a date for the wedding, I wanted to ask if you would give me away?" Jane was

grinning at him.

Moses chocked back the tears. "Well it's about time." He teased. He was struggling. "I would be honoured Half-pint, thank you."

Jane clapped and cheered tears springing to her eyes.

Jasper grabbed her hugging her. "I never thought I would ever ask that question." "Well you just did, I couldn't be happier for you, have you spoke to the gang yet? "No of course not, you come first." Jane frowned. "Why would I?"

"Just checking love that's all."

"Okay, anyway we have set it for August, I want to get married here then we will go home and have a party with the club, is that okay with you?"

"Of course it is silly, it's your wedding, wherever you are you know I will always be there."

"I want to ask the girls to be my bridesmaids and Gwen to be my maid of honour."

"Oh she will love that, gives her an excuse to come back sooner too. Especially as I will be back there to sort the gang out."

"Of course, I forget you are not living here." Jane felt her heart drop, she wasn't sure why, but
something felt off.

"Thank you both, that really has made my day, now bugger off and go and have more sex or whatever it is you are getting up to, I will see you in a couple of days." He blew kisses, Jane returned them.

"See ya. Love you."

Love you too Half-pint. Take care."

"Always Moses."

Jane hung up and sighed heavily. "I will miss him when he goes home."

"Me too, but he will be back before you know it for the wedding." Jane turned and kissed Jasper.

"Did I tell you today how much I love you?"

"Actually, no you didn't." He grinned teasing her.

"I love you more than words, you are my life, my love, my other best friend and my soul mate."

Jasper laughed. "I like that best, your other best friend."

"Sorry but nobody can take his place."

"Belle, that pleases me too, because you can never replace him. I wouldn't want to."

Jane grabbed his face sitting on her knees and kissed him again.

"Right call the gang and I will call the others."

Jane sat back down nodded and dialled home. Gwen answered

"Hey gorgeous girl" she squealed

Jane waved at her. "Are you working love?"

"Where else would I be?"

"Can you gather everyone for me please?"

"Sure chick hang on, cover your ears." Gwen bellowed out to the others who soon came rushing in, she connected to the TV so everyone could see her.

Jane waved again. "Hi, how you doing?" "We're all good, why the call this late?"

"Sorry didn't mean to worry you, we have some news, and I wanted to talk to you all together, we

have booked our wedding and we want you all to be here, but it's in August?"

The girls began to squeal Gwen was the loudest.

Jane began laughing, Jasper got up and walked into the bedroom knowing he couldn't make a call

with that noise. He laughed blowing kisses to Jane.

Jane laughed and tried to quieten everyone. "Listen please. Ladies I would like you all to be my

bridesmaids, I don't care what dresses you wear, as long as they are a colour that suits you all, you will need to speak to Chicca too, Jasper is on the phone to her and James now. Gwen, I wanted to ask if you would be my Maid of Honour?"

The girls erupted jumping up and down screaming. G and Steve stood shaking their heads.

"Oh my god, Oh my god, that means I have to come back out way before the wedding?" Jane nodded laughing at her. "Yes please."

"What about your dress, who is going to do it?"

"Don't worry got that sorted already, Chicca took me to an amazing shop when I went out with Jasper to a black tie event remember, and the lady told me to come back when I wanted my wedding dress, so I am going to see her, she was amazing. Chicca will look after me, it will be like a dual role for you both, she will be my chief bridesmaid."

"Great idea, love it, okay. Well let's catch up when you are back home and we can talk over the finer details. Oh my god I can't wait." Everyone waved behind Gwen. Jane blew kisses and hung up.

She sat drinking her tea waiting for Jasper to come back in as her phone rang it was Chicca. "Oh my fucking god, arghhhhhhhhhhhh." Jane laughed. She loved how dramatic Chicca was. "Deats please?"

"August in the Rose garden, not far from the house, they have a pergoda and there is a café they have that they use for weddings, it has open beams and everything, I will send you the link. I spoke to Gwen and the gang, I have asked the girls to be bridesmaids and Gwen to be my Maid of honour and I would love you to be chief bridesmaid to keep us all in check?"

Chicca screamed. Jane held the phone away from her ear and let her stop running around the house screaming.

"Are you done now?"

"Yes sorry." She said panting

"Good, I want to go back to the Russian lady in the shop, remember she said come back for your wedding dress, well I couldn't think of a better place to go."

"Oh my god yes, that's a perfect idea!"

"I told Gwen and the girls to talk to you, I don't care what style of dresses as long as you are all happy, and choose a colour that suits you all and we will work round it."

"Hang on love, this has to be about you and JDubz not us."

"It is but there is nothing worse than being in a dress that you don't like with a colour that looks hideous, so I want my girls to be happy."

"I love you woman, and yes I would be honoured, now bugger off and jump that sexy man's bones

while you are alone"

Jane laughed "You're as bad as Moses, he said the same thing of sorts."

"Well we can't both be wrong, can we? anyway I have a lovely body here I need to abuse so please go away."

"Enough information thank you. I will call you when we get home." "See ya sweets."

They hung up, Jane was so happy everyone was pleased for them, she could tell it would come together easily. Jasper came back into the room.

"How did it go, I heard all the screaming?" He laughed knowing it went well.

"Very funny, how did yours go?"

"Yeah good, Graham said the girls will be ecstatic."

"That's good, we will see them when we get back and sort it out."

Jane scooted forward on the sofa to let Jasper in behind her. She laid back into him, looking up into his face.

"I could stay like this forever."

"Me too Belle." he bent and kissed her head.

The next couple of days they relaxed and looked at ideas for wedding favours and ideas for the

reception, it wasn't going to be a huge wedding, the reception in the UK would be bigger, and the party at the dealership they wanted to hold for them. Jane had spoken to Shadow, the club agreed they would hold a separate party after for them. They didn't want to overrun the venue with bikes, so only those that knew them well would be going. Afterall they were a noisy bunch. Shadow contacted Bullet and let them know, they promised to be back for the reception at the club too.

Chapter 32

The kindness of new friends

It was time to go home, Jane was doing really well on her leg, she had walked about in doors a bit more and across to the stream with Jasper, she was ready for Physio and to get back to work. Lily and Henry came across to say cheerio. Henry asked Jasper if he could have a quiet word with him and took him outside while Lily caught up with Jane, she brought her some things over in a box.

"This is for you love, please don't open it until you go for your first dress visit, then give it to the lady
you told me about, you can say no then if you like."
"Oh Lily", Jane hugged her hard. She was fighting the tears.
"Every bride should have the traditional items, and in here are a few, you don't have to use them, but if you do it would be lovely, but not if they don't match your dress, that's why I want you to give them to your dressmaker."
Jane was wiping the tears from her face, Lily hugged her, I don't have a daughter to spoil and when my Sons got married, we didn't have any input into the weddings. So, to give this to you just seems perfect" Jane hugged Lily tightly.
"I don't know what to say Lily, you really have surprised me. Thank you so, so much. I will let you know how I get on. Actually, does your phone have video calling?"
"Apparently yes, not that I have ever done it. Hang on let me get it out of my bag." Lily went back to
the kitchen and grabbed her phone bringing it to Jane.
"Here you go, pop your number in too, saves me getting frustrated trying to add it, then you can tell me how I call you."

Jane turned the phone on and entered her number, found the app she needed and downloaded it. "Right then, let's try it now, if I video call you this will come up." she pointed to the app, Lily nodded. "All you need to do is press this like you are answering a call and you will see me."

"Oh that's fantastic."

"Right, stay there and I will pop outside so we can try it, remember press the green button."

Jane went outside and called Lily. She answered within a few rings.

"Hi can you see me Lil?"

"Well yes but I don't think I can watch you if I have to keep talking into the microphone and
listening."

Jane laughed. "Lil look down at the bottom, there is a button like a speaker press it." "Oh, my you are loud now, that's wonderful, and we can do this all the time?"

"Whenever you like. I will hang up and come back in." Jane walked back into the cottage.

 "Oh that was wonderful, thank you love."

"Right when I go to the shop to find my dress, I will call you and you can be part of it with Chicca and me."

"Oh, Jane that would be wonderful, is it allowed though?"

Yes of course, it will be absolutely fine, once I have set a date with Chicca I will call you, just to make
sure you are free, if you have guests though and can't make it just let me know."

"You don't need to worry about that."

"Great, I can't wait now." Jane hugged Lily again.

"Right let's find out what's happened to these men." As they went towards the door Jasper and Henry walked in.

"Well where have you two boys been, cooking up trouble no doubt?" Lily laughed.

"No just a man to man chat is all." Henry grinned. "Right then let's grab these bags and get you both on your way." Henry and Jasper took the bags outside as the girls walked onto the porch.

"Lily I cannot thank you both enough for spoiling us, I never thought it would be so hard leaving a place or two people, you and Henry are very special and this house is just perfect. I can't wait to come back and see you both, but before then I will call you anyway and we can catch up."

"It has been an absolute pleasure, it is good to see you on your feet too, just be careful. This place

will be here when you are ready to come back."

They hugged each other again as Jasper came up the steps.

"My turn Belle." He laughed turning to Lily hugging her. "Thank you so much for everything, you will

never know how happy you have made us." He winked at Lily as he let her go.

She held her finger to her lips as Jane turned to speak to Henry. Jasper smiled and turned to Henry.

"Thank you doesn't seem enough, you both are something else." He shook his hand and Henry hugged him, "I think we are past those formalities Son." He laughed squeezing him hard.

Henry turned to Jane. "Look after yourself, we want to see you running around next time you are here." He pulled her into a hug and kissed her head.

"Definitely! thank you Henry. She stood on tiptoes and kissed his cheek."

"Right then, come on Belle, let's hit the road." He turned to Jane and scooped her into his arms carrying her down to the car. He put her into her seat and walked to his door. Henry and Lily were stood on the steps waving.

Jane blew kisses out of the window as Jasper started the car. They were all waving like crazy. Jane wiped her tears as they rounded the bend at the end of the drive, Jasper grabbed her free hand and squeezed it.

"You ok Belle?"

She sighed heavily. "I have never felt so relaxed in a place, your house is perfect don't get me wrong but this place, I don't know, it's like it has magic powers as you walk in the door you automatically

relax."

Jasper smiled. "I couldn't agree more Belle, I feel like we have been gone weeks."

"So do I." she grinned lifting his hand kissing it. "Thank you for everything. The surprise break away, my beautiful necklace and my second proposal. It has just been an incredible 5 days." She sat stroking her necklace round her neck.

"Thank you Belle too, you made it perfect for me, when I first came here I knew one day I would
bring a special someone here that would make it perfect and this week I did."
"You really know how to make me melt don't you, such an old romantic aren't you?" Jasper laughed. "Sadly, yes and I don't intend on changing." He kissed her knuckles again and let her hand go as they pulled out onto the main road heading home. Jane fell asleep in no time, Jasper looked over smiling. Within a few hours they were home, he decided not to stop as Jane was asleep, he pulled into the driveway just after 4pm. He touched Jane's arm gently to wake her up.
"Belle love, we're home."
Jane stretched yawning. "mmmmm, okay" she scrubbed her eyes with her fists as the front door opened and Lady came bounding out with Moses. She opened her door, as Moses came to help her out. "Just help me down please I can walk to the house okay now."
He looked into the car at Jasper, he nodded. He held out his hands as Jane slid out of the car. Not waiting for Jasper to lower the suspension. She got down on her knees as Lady came running into her arms, she was licking her face. "I think someone missed you." Moses laughed.
"Oh and you didn't then?" she laughed getting up brushing her knees down.
"Of course not, me and the pups have had a great time chilling out." Jane punched him in the arm
playfully.
"Cheeky sod." He grabbed her hugging her tightly.
"I will always miss you Half-pint you should know that." She kissed him on the cheek and pulled away
as the sleepy pups came running out of the house.

"Oh my god what have you been feeding them they are huge!" she laughed covering her face in
shock.

"I did as I was told no more than that."

Jasper walked around the car, "Wow I see what you mean." He laughed getting onto his knees, the pups ran at him. Lady walked over her tail wagging but allowing her pups to fuss him first. Jasper got up after talking to Lady and her pups, opened the boot grabbing the bags with Moses, they took them straight to the bedroom as Jane made them a drink. They sat in the lounge catching up, Jane told Moses about the necklace, he smiled and nodded.

"lovely."

"You knew?"

"Of course, I did." He laughed

"Did you know about the proposal again too?"

"No, he kept that to himself this time, I have to say it was a beautiful thing to do Brother." "Thanks Moses, it just felt right to be honest. I didn't want Belle having a bad memory of it."

"But I told him I wouldn't, the proposal was perfect it was after that."

"Well count yourself lucky you had two then. "True. Not forgetting my necklace aswell."

"Ummmm, I have booked my flight home now you are back."

Jane looked shocked. "What?"

"I need to get back love, you are back on your feet and if we are coming back for the wedding I need to get some things sorted and you know Gwen will be out sooner rather than later. Maybe you could take her to work with you."

"I'm sorry that sounded very selfish of me, I know you have to get home, how is your back now?" "Oh it's ok love, I must have slept funny." Jane raised her eyebrows not believing him.

"When do you leave?" Jane asked suddenly feeling sick.

"In two days, love."

Jane felt tears pricking the back of her eyes, she looked down, saying nothing.

"Right dinner is on me, fancy a take-away as you have been spoilt with all that home cooking?" "I don't mind I will go with the majority." Jane replied.

"Chinese it is then." Moses laughed

He grabbed the menu they ticked off their choices and Moses rang it through. Jane went to get changed, Jasper followed her minutes later.

"Close the door please love." she whispered

"You want me already?" Jane threw her top at him.

"Sex mad you are, no I wanted to ask you about Moses. Did you notice he was struggling to get up?

He looks quite grey too. I am a little worried." Jane wrapped her arms around herself.

Jasper walked over to her wrapping his arms around her. He kissed her head.

"Belle I am sure he is fine and there is nothing to worry about." he pulled her closer.

"Hmmmm, I'm not so sure, he's also going earlier than planned too." She frowned looking up at

Jasper.

"Yes he said because of the wedding and you are back on your feet. Don't read too much into love." He rubbed her back kissing her head again, he looked at the wall and pulled a face, he didn't believe it either.

They went back down once they were showered and changed and the bags were unpacked, just in time for the food delivery. They sat at the dining table together chatting, Moses was joking about going home and having an American accent, they both laughed with him, but watching every move he made to see how in pain he was.

It was still early after they finished eating and Jane wanted to have a walk down the garden, she was telling Moses about the house and stream and the Deer and fawn they had seen. Moses smiled, he loved seeing her happy. They got to the rose bed they were all in full bloom, Jane gasped when she saw them.

"Oh my god they look amazing." she felt tears prick her eyes again, she wiped them away laughing.

Jasper looked down at her. "You ok Belle?"

"Yes, just emotional, you know me." he pulled her in kissing her.

"Yes I do." He laughed.

They walked over to the swing and the lovers seat and sat down.

"I will miss this garden, it has been nice having peace and quiet while I have been here, certainly not

like that at home."

Jane laughed, "Definitely not, maybe you should move and have a garden of your own." "Good idea but can you really see me gardening?"

"Actually yes, I can, you are not getting any younger, you need to slow down, what the perfect way to relax. Jasper enjoys it, don't you love?"

"I'm not as old as he is!" Jasper exclaimed.

Moses laughed "I didn't mean that silly."

"Phew" Jasper laughed wiping his brow, for a minute there I thought you wanted a sugar Daddy

putting all those years on me!" He teased.

Moses laughed. "Careful Brother I'm not that much older." They all laughed. Sitting back on the love seat. They chatted for a couple of hours watching the sun go down over the garden, the pups were sleeping at their feet with Lady.

"Right I am going to hit the sack, I need to go over to the club tomorrow I have some things to sort with Shadow, before I leave. I will be gone most of the day, that ok with you both?"

"Yes of course, do what you need to do."

"Do you have any washing that needs doing before you leave, I can put it in with ours?"

"It's ok love, I am all up to date with that. Did it all today. I am all but packed, you know me." Jane nodded. "Okay sure." She bent towards him and kissed him goodnight, he hugged Jasper and walked away, both Jane and Jasper watched him before he went round the corner.

"He looked okay Belle, don't you think?"

"Still not convinced, something isn't right, but I will just keep bugging him once he is home and ask

Gwen to keep an eye on him."

"Good idea, shall we go to bed too, you have had a lot of time on that leg of yours and I wouldn't mind getting them up for you." he smirked.

"Well if you insist." Jane pretended not to be bothered.

Jasper scooped her up making her squeal, the pups barked dashing away in front of them heading into the house. They locked up the house, Jasper took Jane to the bedroom and went back down to get their water before bedding the pups down for the night.

All to myself Dan and Shay

He got back to the bedroom, Jane was laid out on the bed naked her kindle in one hand, her other hand under her head, one leg up the other spread out across the bed. Jasper stood at the door laughing just looking at her. He licked his lips at her.

"You can stop that, you told me I needed an early night." she whispered opening her legs wider "Yeah well that was before I saw you laid like that, but if you would rather read that smut then I will just go to sleep." He pulled his t-shirt over his head and threw it onto the wash basket, his shorts sitting low on his hips, he swayed from side to side, Jane got on her knees and crawled across the bed at him like a tiger going for her prey. She crooked her finger at him beckoning him to her, Jasper pushed his shorts down and stepped out of them, he climbed onto the bed with Jane, he crawled to the middle meeting her, kissing her.

"On your back Mr."

"What for?"

"Do as you're told." she demanded.

"Oh, I like it when you are masterful." He laughed

Jane pushed him down onto the bed spreading him out like a starfish. She grabbed her scarves out of the drawer and tied his arms to the bed. Then up to his head with another and blindfolded him. She kissed his lips as she moved down. She moved to the cupboard where she had all of the goodies the girls had brought her, she pulled out the nipple clips.

"Darling, are you happy for me to try anything?" "Within reason yes."

"Okay, remember the bag of goodies the girls made you buy? well there are a few things in there we may like to use, if you don't like what I am about to do then please say *Harley* that way I know you want me to stop."

Jasper laughed nervously. "Ok Belle, if you say so."

She moved down the bed and licked his nipple biting it gently, Jasper moaned, she took the first clip and put it to the back of the nipple. Jasper winced.

"Are you okay?"

He nodded, Jane adjusted the tension so it wasn't too tight and went across to the other, doing the

same, Jasper winced again. Jane licked around the clamp, Jasper bucked off the bed groaning.

"Jesus Belle." He hissed.

Jane grinned, knowing he was enjoying it.

She went back to the drawer and grabbed her new toy, it wasn't large, but it was long, it was black with nobbles up the length, that you would feel as it slid inside you, she slid it in her mouth and made it wet. Jasper was trying to listen to what she was doing. She climbed back on the bed and pressed the head of the toy against his nipple. She turned it on to a gentle vibrate. Jasper hissed again, the clips had stopped the blood flow, it was a pleasure pain feeling, the vibration was going straight down to his cock. He opened his legs wider, pushing his body up desperate to be touched. Jane moved the toy to the tip of his nipple.

"Oh my fucking god!" He whispered through gritted teeth.

Jane moved away and across to the other side doing the same thing, as she moved away down his chest she continued with the toy moving down the centre of his body, she sucked the toy to keep it wet as she moved down to the start of his cock, she switched the vibrate up higher this time, moving it backwards and forwards across his body.

"You little tease." He moaned.

Jane got down between his legs, moving the wet toy down into the crease of his leg, it was touching his cock and balls as she moved it further down, Jasper shuddered. Jane moved it down to his thigh, away from his cock and balls, Jasper tried to close his leg to feel the vibration again, Jane knew what he was doing and turned it off. She went back to his nipples, she didn't want them to hurt him so decided to remove them early, she licked the toy and placed it on his nipple turning it on higher vibrate as she released the clip, as the blood flow went back to his nipple Jasper groaned loudly the sensation with the vibrator was a great turn on, Jane followed across to the other and did the same. Jasper hissed at her, his cock standing to attention. He pushed his body up to her again. Jane smiled and moved down the bed. She sucked the toy again and started on his cock head, it vibrated across the tip, she pushed it against his hole circling it. She moved down to the edge of the head and went around the outside. Jasper was going out of his mind, Jane licked his cock and the vibrator making it wetter, she continued to tease just the head with it, she got down onto her tummy pushed his legs as wide as they could go and flicked her tongue on his balls, the vibrator still on his cock head.

"Holy fuck, where did you learn to do that?" Jasper groaned. Jane laughed and didn't speak.

"Fuck Belle, please take my cock, suck it baby please?" Jane didn't reply.

She flicked her tongue at the base of his cock and continued circling his head with the toy, she moved it down the length slowly, her tongue meeting it half way, she sucked it again making it wet and licked down to his balls the toy following.

"Ooooooohhhhh Jesus Christ......." He yelled.

Jane reached his balls and sucked one into her mouth, she placed the toy onto the other, Jasper bucked again, she knew he would explode when she let him. He was pulling on the scalves desperate to touch himself and her. Jane continued sucking, moving across to the other one, and moving the toy. She moved it to the middle of them and pushed it in, reaching the base of his cock, His cock was solid, it was twitching wanting to be touched, Jane wrapped her free hand around it and slowly rubbed it from top to bottom. Jane remembered the friction gel, she moved so she could reach the drawer and grabbed it, she squeezed a good amount onto her hand and the vibrator, she wrapped her hand around it and spread it up the length of it. She grabbed his cock and rubbed him fast for a few seconds, Jasper was ready to cum, he was panting hard.

"Baby please, Belle please?" He begged.

Jane moved the toy down to his balls and worked her way underneath, she found his soft spot and teased him, Jasper lifted his bottom, Jane moved the toy and circled his bottom, he puckered at the sensation.

"Mmmmmm you like that don't you?" Jasper nodded. "Yesss." he whispered

Jane moved the toy over his hole and held it there. Jaspers bottom came off the bed completely, she gently pushed it in.

He groaned loudly "Fuck you, Belle."

Jane pushed a little further in, Jasper pushed against it now, wanting more. Jane began licking his cock again, moving her head to the tip, she licked the head, pushing her tongue in as she tasted his precum.

"Oh baby is that for me?"

Jasper nodded. "Suck it baby I need to cum for you."

Jane pushed the toy in further and began to fuck him with it. Jasper got louder.

"Yesssss, fuck me Belle, oh baby don't stop." He hissed, Jane covered his cock with her lips and took him as deep as she could, matching the movements of the toy. She knew Jasper was about to explode so stopped. He groaned as she pulled him out of her mouth.

She moved herself and pushed her bottom up to his face, she squatted leaving her pussy over his face, his tongue came out immediately lapping at her juices, she was desperate to be touched she was aching for his cock, but wanted to tease him a little more. She rubbed her pussy against his face, he was pushing his lips and tongue into her, Jane pushed against him, as he caught her clit and bit it gently. She laid across his body and took his cock back in her mouth and slid the toy back inside him. She knew it was going to be quick but hers was too. She rubbed herself on Jaspers beard harder, his tongue and nose hitting in the right place, the faster she moved her bottom the harder and faster she sucked him and fucked him with the toy. Jasper was moaning, she felt his balls go solid and his cock, he pushed into her hard as his orgasm hit, she didn't stop sucking and continued to fuck him his cum hit her in the back of the throat, she choked slightly, swallowing hard as more arrived, he kept cuming, she swallowed it all panting as her orgasm hit her, she picked up speed on his face, she screamed onto his cock as she slowly pulled the toy out of him, Jasper was shaking as he swallowed her cum, she felt him gulping, she continued rubbing herself, his soft beard teasing her. She flopped onto him as it stopped. Moving her bottom to the side. They were exhausted, both laughing their bodies on fire. Jane got up and moved, laying next to him, she undid his hands first then removed the blindfold. Jasper grabbed her kissing her hard.

"Fuck Belle, were you trying to kill me, that was fucking amazing?" Jane laid in his arms grinning at

him. He kissed her again. "God I love you woman. I really don't know where you get these ideas from but fuck, I promise I am not complaining."

They snuggled for a while, until Jasper decided he needed to clean up. Jane laughed watching him go into the bathroom. She followed and cleaned up with him. Teasing him tickling his bottom. Jasper spanked her all the way back to bed.

Chapter 33

My best friend

The day Jane had dreaded had arrived, the previous day Moses spent at the club, he said he needed to sort things out with Shadow so she hadn't seen much of him, he was on an early flight home so
they didn't stay up too late. Jane didn't know what could have taken all day, but she knew some of it had to do with her. She knew regardless of everything being over he was still going to protect her from afar.

They got up early and showered. Jane had that sicky feeling in her stomach, Jasper left her to do what she needed, he knew she was dreading the day, they went downstairs together and made tea. Moses came into the kitchen, he could tell she was anxious, he walked over to her and hugged her. "It's only for a couple of months love, then I will be back."
Jane shook her head fighting the tears. She handed him his drink and toast joining them both at the table.

"We will need to leave in about 30 minutes Moses." Jasper said looking at Jane.
Moses nodded. "Sure thing."
Jane pushed her toast away and drank her tea, she got up and went to the bathroom. As she shut the door the tears started. She walked to the mirror. Angrily wiping her tears away, she looked at herself then up to the ceiling.
"God, I know you are up to something, I know there is something wrong with Moses, I will beg you
every day not to do this to him, I really can't take anymore, he is my best friend, please don't do this." She fell onto her knees, her body wracked with tears.

She wrapped her arms around herself, as the tears fell, she was feeling sick and crawled to the toilet. She began to vomit, she was reaching, there was nothing but bile and tea. She crumpled onto the floor sobbing. She heard a knock on the door.

"Belle, you okay love, we need to get ready to go?"

Jane tried to hold back the sobs, Jasper heard her and forced the lock, he opened the door to see her wrapped around the toilet bowl. He bent down and picked her up, she wrapped herself around his neck and cried. He took her to their bathroom and sat her on his knee, he took her face in his hands. "Talk to me love, what's going on, this isn't just because Moses is going home is it?" Jane shook her head.

"I don't know how I know, I but I do, you have to believe me, something is wrong with Moses. I'm scared Jasper." She broke down again sobbing into Jaspers chest, his shirt was soaked with tears. "I believe you Belle, but we need to let him go home, if he feels poorly he will see a Doctor, he maybe stubborn but he's not stupid and if you think he is putting things in place then he will do something about it." Jane nodded. Jasper grabbed a clean washcloth out of the drawer and filled the sink up. He put Jane onto the stool and wet the cloth. He slowly washed her face off and dried her, she gargled some mouthwash clearing the taste of bile away. Jasper led her to the bedroom and pulled her t-shirt off with his, he dressed her in a clean one and himself. He took her face in his hands again.

"Listen to me love, we have to let him go, you have to be really strong now, once he goes through

the gate you can cry as much as you need to okay?" Jane nodded.

He took her by the hand and led her to the lounge. Moses was waiting for them with his bags by the door.

"Half-pint? You okay love?" He took her in his arms.

She was fighting the tears and nodded, "I was just sick, but I'm ok now."